ZERO SUM

ALEXI SOKOLSKY: HOUND OF EDEN

BOOK 3

JAMES OSIRIS BALDWIN

A GIFT HORSE PRODUCTIONS BOOK

A huge thanks to Stacy Schonhardt for her excellent
copyediting and tragic puns.

Artwork, layout and design by James Osiris Baldwin.

ISBN: 1976162912

ISBN-13: 978-1976162916

Books in the Hound of Eden Series

Prequel: Burn Artist

http://jamesosiris.com/alexi-sokolsky-starter-library/

Book 1: Blood Hound

http://hyperurl.co/bloodhoundnovel

Book 2: Stained Glass

http://hyperurl.co/stainedglassnovel

Book 3: Zero Sum

http://hyperurl.co/zerosumnovel

Other Titles

Fix Your Damn Book! A Self-Editing Guide for Authors

Find all my books, bonus chapters and more at http://www.jamesosiris.com

FREE BOOK OFFER!

WHEN SHIT GETS TOO WEIRD FOR THE MOB TO HANDLE, HITMAGE ALEXI SOKOLSKY IS THE GUY THEY CALL TO FIX IT.

Set 5 years before Blood Hound, Burn Artist is a prequel to the series which reveals more about Alexi's past. What were the events that shaped him? Why did he murder his own father? And what are his true feelings for his best friend?

Get your free copy of Burn Artist when you sign up for my author newsletter. You can unsubscribe at any time.

Visit: <u>HTTP://JAMESOSIRIS.COM/ALEXI-SOKOLSKY-STARTER-LIBRARY/</u>

CONTENTS

Chapter 1 9

Chapter 2 24

Chapter 3 32

Chapter 4 49

Chapter 5 63

Chapter 6 75

Chapter 7 92

Chapter 8 103

Chapter 9 113

Chapter 10 126

Chapter 11 141

Chapter 12 149

Chapter 13 156

Chapter 14 162

Chapter 15 171

Chapter 16 186

Chapter 17 203

Chapter 18 217

Chapter 19 229

Chapter 20 245

Chapter 21 251

Chapter 22 261

Chapter 23 277

Chapter 24 283

Chapter 25 292

Chapter 26...306

Chapter 27...319

Chapter 28...327

Chapter 29...333

Chapter 30...347

Chapter 31...364

Chapter 32...374

Chapter 33...387

Chapter 34...409

Chapter 35...420

Chapter 36...432

Chapter 37...447

Chapter 38...456

Chapter 39...463

Chapter 40...472

Chapter 41...492

Chapter 42...506

Chapter 43...524

Chapter 44...533

Chapter 45...541

Chapter 46...550

Get your Free Copy of Burn artist............................563

More Books by James Osiris Baldwin 564

Other Titles...564

Afterword & Acknowledgments 565

"There are a couple of watersheds in human evolution. Most people are comfortable thinking about tool use and language use as watersheds. But the ability to play non-zero-sum games was another watershed."

– JONATHAN HAIDT

CHAPTER 1

Revenge is a filthy addiction, a drive as banal and compelling as the craving for sugar, or nicotine. I knew vengeance was bad for me, that it was unsatisfying, but every time I sat by Vassily's ruined grave trying to think of an alternative, I always arrived at the same grim conclusion: that a bloody zero-zero draw was better than letting the motherfuckers sweep my chips off the table and walk away.

Part of it was that I knew now I'd never have the man I loved, even if there had never been a chance to begin with, and I wanted them to suffer as my family and I had suffered. Part of it was that no matter how far I ran from the Mafiya, it lived on in me. The ecstatic wisdom of a mage is always tempered by the selfish impulses of a wiseguy: the knowledge that I could squeeze a trigger, pull a blade, cast a spell, and find at least a fragmentary relief in the act of destruction.

This selfishness drove me to Wall Street on the morning of October the 25th, 1991. The dreary gunmetal sky was gravid with rain, looming over the four of us - myself, my cat, Jenner and Angkor – as we pulled up in a one-way alley not too far from the New York Stock Exchange. I clambered out onto the narrow sidewalk into a bitter wind that slapped at the vent of my suit jacket. The suit was slightly too large, loose over the padding I'd taped around my midriff. Angkor, seated in the back, held my agitated familiar away from the door and passed me a carry-on suitcase, then a black leather briefcase. I took them with a wan smile.

"All set, soldier?" Jenner had cleaned up a bit to better fit in with the Manhattan crowd, which meant she'd given herself a razorgirl haircut with a bowie knife, worn her best eyepatch, and shrugged on a denim jacket over her 'Satan Loves Pussy' t-shirt. She'd tried.

I set the carry-on on the ground and pulled out the telescoping handle, then nodded. "Give me an hour, including walking time. If I'm not at the Charging Bull by twelve thirty, cruise back to this alley and scope the entry to the building."

Angkor checked his watch and set the timer, idly pushing Binah back from the window as my Siamese suppository tried to follow me onto the street. "It's 11:35 now. I'm coming up to look for you if you're not back within seventy minutes."

"I'm sure I'll handle it." I leaned in and rubbed Binah's sail-like ears, waggling them from side to side. She glowered at me. She did not like being left behind.

"I'm sure you will." Angkor flicked his dark gray eyes up to meet mine, mouth sly. "Take care up there, and good hunting."

Something about the look he gave me briefly drove all thoughts of revenge from my mind. Angkor was beautiful enough to stop traffic. I cleared my throat, and offered a quick, stiff smile. "Thank you. I mean it, both of you."

"No worries. Go kick some pedo ass." Jenner winked and clicked her tongue. With a final lingering look, Angkor wound the window, and the pair of them cruised off to rejoin the main road.

Stage one complete. Time to find my mark.

Yegor Gavrilyuk, CPA, worked out of a private suite at 44 Wall Street. In a neatly pressed suit and tie and a good-quality wig of fashionably blond, slicked-back hair, I looked like any other yuppie bustling between his office and the New York Stock Exchange, one of many nameless faces pushing through the canopy of black umbrellas bristling in expectation of rain. No one gave me or my carry-on bag so much as a second glance as I entered the atrium of Yegor's building, stepped into the elevator, and pressed the button for the 28th floor.

Camouflaged in the forest of suits and several inches taller than usual, I read the front page of the Wall Street Journal and listened to the awkward throat clearing, clicking rustle of too many people crammed into a too-small metal box. My stomach gnawed at me, and I was queasy from the press of bodies around me by the time I reached my floor. When the doors opened, I gratefully pushed through and clacked my way across the checkered marble floor to the glass-fronted reception of Weiss & Co. Financial Services.

The lady at the desk - financial executive receptionists were always women, weren't they? - was a pencil-thin redhead with dark eyebrows and brown eyes. She wore an artfully fitted gray dress that was probably worth more than both my suits: the one in the carry-on, and the one I was wearing.

"Good morning, sir," she chirped. "How can I help you?"

I didn't bother smiling, and dialed up my Slavic accent from a three to a nine. "I am here for appointment with Mr. Gavrilyuk."

The woman's brow creased slightly. "Sir, I'm sorry, but… Mr. Gavrilyuk doesn't have any appointments until twelve."

"Yegor forwards his calendar to my boss in case we need to speak with him urgently," I replied. "Please call his extension, and tell him that Mr. Chiernenko would like to discuss the AEROMOR accounts."

The receptionist blinked at me, deer-like and indignant, but she slowly picked up the receiver and began to dial.

While she hung on the line, I nosed around the office, marking the fire escape, the location of cameras, and the orderly geometric patterns of magical energy in the room. Practically every building in the Financial District had wards - good wards, wards that I, a single mage working alone, could not hope to overcome in an emergency.

"It is just as well we will not need to." An inner voice like the whispering of leaves over dry ground broke through my reverie. *"They were not made with our kind of work in mind."*

Kutkha did not speak aloud. My soul's voice was an intrusion into my thoughts – a welcome intrusion.

"*Mm. They're fire alarms, I think.*" I thought back. The wards laid into the building were beautiful in the orderly way that cathedrals were beautiful, and playing my senses out along the elegantly formed web of magic woven through the stone and metal was a good way to stay relaxed before the job. By their persistence, pitch, color, and geometry, I knew these were enchantments laid down by the Adepts of the Inner School – one of the older occult fraternities who'd come to the East Coast with the Puritans. Back in the day, before mages had reason to fear the Vigiles Magicarum and the concept of 'illegal arcana', the Orders who were contracted to protect these buildings signed them with special patterns of magical energy, like maker's marks. I now knew that this energy was called Phi, but those men - mostly men, back then - probably did not.

I tuned back into the material reality of the room when I heard the receptionist talking behind us. "Hello, Mr. Gavrilyuk? Yes, this is Lisa… I have a Mr. Chiernenko here who would like to see you regarding one of his accounts, if you have time? He says it's urgent. No, he's alone. Alright, thank you. I'll let him know."

I turned as she hung up, and she smiled with double rows of laser-white teeth. "Someone will be out to see you in in just a moment, Mr. Chiernenko. Please, take a seat."

"Thank you, but I would rather stand."

She smiled again, a little woodenly this time, and then turned back to her monitor and keyboard.

Five minutes passed before another woman strode around the corner from the same direction I'd first arrived and pushed through the glass door separating the reception from the lobby. She was also well-dressed and startlingly beautiful, her blonde hair pulled into a tight bun. When she saw me, her eyes narrowed slightly.

"Mister… Chiernenko?" She asked.

"Yes?" I turned, hands jammed in my pockets, shoulders hunched. It was how Nicolai usually stood.

"Oh… I'm sorry. Excuse me for saying so, but I remember someone who was… less well-built." She spoke Russian. There was an uncertain lilt in her voice, green-yellow.

"I am Anatoly Chiernenko. Nicolai is my cousin. He is thin and tall, and I am fat and short." I replied in the same language, forcing a small smile and trying to make the most of my temporarily blue eyes. "Like those video game characters, eh? Mario and Luigi."

Her face suffused with hidden laughter. She gestured with hand and head toward the door. "Yes, well, please come this way, Mister Chiernenko."

The P.A. - I assumed she was the P.A. - led me back to the elevators. Yegor Gavrilyuk was one of the silent engines of the Yaroshenko *Organizatsiya,* New York's largest 'Russian' Mafia. He was a man few could name, but many relied on. As Sergei's American stockbroker and financial manager, he couldn't be expected to work in the boiler room with lesser brokers and market analysts. No, he had his own private suite: a well-insulated suite, in a building as old and solid as this one. Twenty years of near-anonymous success within and outside of the *Organizatsiya* had made him king of the castle. He was well-liked, and he had become complacent.

I was led to a solid oaken door in a gold-and-cream corridor. The P.A. swiped her card, knocked, and then opened it a crack, but before she got too far, I gently touched her wrist with one gloved hand.

"Excuse us, please," I said in Russian, meeting her eyes. "This is a sensitive matter."

"Oh… of course." The lady blinked and withdrew from the momentary contact, smiling nervously as she glanced at my hand. I didn't have any of the distinctive Vory hand tattoos: but I was in the business of letting people think I did.

After she was a good way down the hall, I opened the door myself and then closed it behind me with a sharp click. Yegor looked up from his ledger, then stood in alarm. The blood drained from his face.

"YOU! What are YOU doing here?" He pushed back from the edge of the desk, putting distance between us. "I'll call security, I'll-!"

"*Kaph.*" I spoke the single-letter word calmly, forcefully, and made a sign with my fingers.

Magic thrilled through my body and out into the room. The lights blew; the door behind me made a grinding sound as the lock short-circuited. Every other electronic device in the room simply died. We were left in the confines of a strange, humming silence.

Yegor stared at me in desperate shock. He was a soft, paunchy man with a fleshy face, small eyes, and a fluff of brown hair. He'd turned the same color as his yellow linen shirt.

"Please, Yegor Vladimirovich. It does not become an Authority of the Organization to stand. Take a seat." I motioned to his chair. "And put your hands on the desk where I can see them, or I will speak another word of power and boil your brains in your skull."

"You can't." Shaking, sweating, Yegor dropped back into his chair. He thumped both his hands down on his desk pad, almost petulantly. "You don't know how. You're not that good."

"Are you sure?"

"You're just a thug with a couple of magic tricks."

"And I'm well on the way to filling my new spellbook with the names of the dead." I arched an eyebrow. "Grigori. Kir. Lev. Demyon. All gone. Are you feeling froggy, Yegor?"

His nostrils trembled. He did not reply.

"Let me tell you a story," I said, setting the briefcase down on the edge of the desk. "After years spent knowing that you piece-of-shit muzhiki called me and Vassily faggots behind our backs, it turns out that all of you were fucking children together."

His eyes narrowed. "Don't be disgusting. I have no idea what you're talking about."

I opened the case, staring at him. Inside was an ordinary ball peen hammer.

"Of course you do. You're a smart man, aren't you? Vanya's *Advokat*." I took the hammer out and set the briefcase aside. "His direct adviser and confidant."

Yegor's eyes widened, fixated on the weapon in my hand. "All I do is the money for him, Molotchik. Just the money."

I blinked slowly, and glanced at the far wall of his office. Photos of Yegor, trimmer and with slightly longer hair, standing with a fair woman and two small children, both boys. "You do, in fact, handle the money. And it occurred to me, while I was recovering in hospital, that Vassily was your direct competition."

He glowered petulantly, like a child. "I didn't have anything to do with that business. I liked Vassily, and his family."

"Perhaps. But you had everything to gain by putting him out of the picture," I said. "So I admit that I'm not sure what disgusts me more: that you accepted whatever Nicolai offered you to support his bid for power at Vassily's expense, or that you're a man who fucks little boys on camera while doting on his own sons at home."

My proclamation was met with resounding silence.

"I have two issues. Firstly, Vanya arranged for someone to rape Vassily in prison," I continued, walking a serpentine trail away from and around the desk. "Someone who got him sick. Then Vanya and Nicolai got him hooked on drugs. Drugs are expensive, Yegor. Smuggling them in takes money. And what do you do?"

He swallowed. "I didn't-"

"You handle the money," I said. "Now. Vanya and Nicolai arranged to kidnap twenty-one kids from a group home last month. Boys and girls, eight to fourteen years old. He and his men fucked them, filmed themselves doing it, sold the videos and photos, then cut up some of them for their organs on the black market. And that's the other reason I'm here. We only managed to rescue twelve of them. Where are the others?"

"How the fuck am I supposed to know?" Yegor's face flushed dark. "What is this? Alexi Sokolsky to the fucking rescue? What, you think you're fucking Superman, now?"

"I'm more of a Rorschach, actually," I replied.

"Like you have clean hands." He was sweating profusely now. I'd brought zipties with me in case I had to bind him, but he was paralyzed in his fury and fear. "Don't pretend to be some kind of saint, Alexi. You were part of this."

"It wasn't my flabby ass pumping away in a few of the photos of those kids," I kept my voice low and steady. "Why do you think I came to you, Yegor? Of all the good old boys in the Organization?"

He sneered. "You didn't see any photos."

"We pulled them off Moris Falkovich's computer."

Yegor blanched.

I smiled. Pleasantly. "You never were a brave man, Yegor. So now, you're going to answer my questions, or I'm going to break all of your joints, sit on you, and choke you on my fist. Who was buying the tapes?"

"I-I don't know," Yegor stammered, but I caught the flicker of desperation in his voice. Reading faces was hit or miss, but sounds had a color and texture that were hard to conceal. His voice had shifted to orange, sharp and tangy. He had what I wanted, but he wasn't quite ready to give it up.

"You do the money, Yegor. Everything Vanya buys and sells goes through you. Who. Was. Buying?" I grasped the hammer around its rubber haft and leaned across the desk until there was only a foot of space between our noses.

Yegor was breathing quickly. I saw his leg jerk as he hit a panic button with his knee, but it was as dead as everything else in the room.

"They'll kill me, Molotchik." His face went from yellow to green. I could smell him now, the acrid pungency of terror in his sweat.

I fixed him with a reptile's glare. "I'll kill you, right here in front of GOD and everyone. Answer my question. Who was buying the skin flicks and organs?"

"MinTex Oil and Gas," he blurted. "Or I mean, that was the shell company. V-Vanya knows more than I do. They-they nearly all used shells, b-but there were some individual clients from Israel for the organs. It was handled by a couple of rabbis. All the money for the porn came from offshore. Now, please just-"

"Do you have a list of names?"

"Ps-pseudonyms." He pointed at his filing cabinet. "That's it. Now let me-"

"No. That was the first question" I could see the artificial blue reflection of my eyes in his glasses. "I want to know where Vanya keeps his cash. Physical cash. I don't care about the Organization's accounts."

His jaw trembled, then tensed as he gathered his willpower and his resolve to refuse. I slammed the hammer down on his desktop with a sharp bang, and he jumped in his own skin.

His eyes welled up with tears. "Alexi, please-"

This time, I slammed the hammer down onto the back of his hand. The wet crunch I felt through the handle was drowned out by his piercing cry of agony. Yegor clutched his shattered hand and pushed himself up to stumble away, but he knocked his chair so hard that it tumbled over and spilled him to the floor instead. I stalked around the desk, put my hard-soled shoe down on his broken hand, and twisted.

He squealed, voice raw with pain. "Help me! Anya! Security!"

I glanced back at the door, then down to Yegor. The door was probably armored, thick enough that I didn't have to worry just yet. "Where is the stash, Yegor?"

"Won't tell you anything! Fucking suka!" He spat at me, and then squealed as I hauled up on his hair, my foot still pushing down on his hand. "Grrr-AAARGH-I'll tell Sergei about this-"

I backhanded him with the flat side of the hammer and let go of his hair. He went to the floor, shielding his face as I beat him over the arms and head, but he couldn't hold his guard up forever. When his arms faltered, I grabbed him by the front of his shirt and pulled him back up to his knees.

"You don't get it. I *want* Sergei to know I was here." I pressed the ball of the hammer against his temple. "So let us reason together, Yegor. Do you really want to die like this?"

His nostrils flared as sweat from his nose and blood from his ears dripped from his face to the floor. He sagged in my hands.

"Where does Vanya keep his cash?" I repeated, calmly.

Yegor squeezed his eyes closed, pushing out a wave of fresh tears. I saw and felt him break, watched the armor shrink and fold away as he went limp.

"We don't keep cash any more. Not since Rodion died. There's… there's guns, drugs. That's it," he said, his voice thick with mucus and pain. "I swear, Alexi."

I wrinkled my nose, disappointed. He seemed to recognize the sign of my displeasure, because he kept babbling.

"It's all at Kozlowski and Sons, you know, the scrapyard. T-There's a locked yard where they keep all these old school buses. Vanya u-used it as a switch point. He stores things in the buses… in the floors of the buses."

"And what kind of security do they keep around these buses?" I knew K&S well enough. Biggest scrapyard in New York. We took our stolen cars there.

"I don't know! B-barbed wire. Dogs. V-Vanya might have men there, I don't know. Let me go, Molotchik, I didn't have anything to do with Vassily—"

Before he could continue - before I had time to get angry - I smashed the ball of the hammer into the side of his head several times, hard and fast. When I felt the steel catch, I tugged it free of his skull, pushed him away and stepped back, letting him fall like jelly to the floor. For several long minutes, Yegor gasped and convulsed his way through death, a process not nearly as sudden and final as movies were wont to portray. Eventually, he fell still.

When word got back to Sergei that Yegor was dead, he'd know exactly who had taken his piece off the board. My klichka, the nickname I earned in the *Organizatsiya*, was Molotchik, 'The Hammer'. I'd earned that name – half-honorific, half-stigma – after I put down my father like a rabid dog with his own prison sledge, continuing a tradition of patricide that had begun when my grandfather killed his father for joining the Bolsheviks in Ukraine. Sergei was good to be reminded how Sokolsky men dealt with their patriarchs.

I went back around to the suitcase, set it on the desk, and opened it up. It held a roll of thick paper bags, a grooming kit, a small squirt bottle of bleach and one of isopropyl, and a complete change of clothes. Black leather gloves, shoes, socks, an identical blue tie, trousers, shirt, and a jacket, all neatly rolled. The suit was of a different material than the linen I'd worn into the office, a heavier wool suit in a similar, but not identical color.

The aftermath of a hit was a ritual performed in very specific steps. From smallest to largest; from dirtiest to cleanest. I wrapped up the messiest things, the hammer, my jacket, and tie, and then stepped around to squirt Yegor's exposed skin with the bleach. Face, hands, neck. The odor of chlorine burned my nostrils, a clinging, lurid pink smell.

After that, I stripped and packed the dirty clothes into the suitcase along with everything else. I checked myself for blood, dabbing at my face - carefully, so I didn't take off all the makeup I'd used to subtly change my features - then swabbed my hands and forearms with dilute bleach. Alcohol-soaked cotton got rid of the chlorine smell, and then I was able to investigate the filing cabinet.

Yegor was right. A saint would know better than to think revenge was going to fill in the void Vassily had left behind. But it wasn't just for me: it was for Jenner, who had lost her partner and friends; for Angkor, who was still trying to heal the brain damage done to him by the Deacon and his men. It was for Josie, the little girl I'd pulled out of a mad surgeon's dungeon. That kid was going to need therapy for the rest of her life. Some of the others were still missing, being used to breed monsters. Others were dead, or locked in their own minds. Forever.

"May your sons grow up to be better men than you and I, Yegor." I set the carry-on down on the soft carpet, the best that money could buy, and locked the door on my way out into the relative cleanness of the city.

CHAPTER 2

Back outside, I merged into a thick crowd of suits, teased hair, blue jeans, and pork pie hats. A storm was coming. It was almost dark out, the sky swirling with hurricane clouds. As I passed by the bronze Charging Bull on Broadway, I heard a thick wet splat to my left, and turned to see a long, thin, dark stain - like gull shit - splattered across the bull's head. A deep, bruised, rotten purple smell stung my nose, clinging all the way to Morris Street.

Jenner and Angkor were waiting for me near the intersection, parked semi-legally by the side of the road. Jenner turned the engine while I got into the back with Angkor and my cat, pulled the wig off my head, and sighed with relief.

"Jesus, Rex. I thought you said you worked clean," Jenner said, the disgust in her voice palpable. "You smell like fucking roadkill."

"I do." After what I'd just done, I didn't feel much like chit-chat. Silent, I held my hands out to Binah. She left Angkor's lap, stretching out like a ribbon of cream and lilac fur, but she hung back with uncharacteristic

24

aloofness. Instead of throwing herself at me, she sniffed daintily over my fingers and the cuff of my suit jacket, her ears flat to her skull. When she relented in her inspection and oozed onto my lap, I brought my wrist to my nose. It wasn't the smell of the office that I'd brought back: it was a faint shadow of the reek I'd breathed in while walking past the statue.

"How did it go?" Angkor asked. If he noticed anything unpleasant, he was too polite to say so.

"I got a name and some paperwork," I replied, smoothing Binah's ruffled coat under my palm. She crouched warily on my knees "MinTex, a shell company. According to Yegor, Vanya was using it to launder the proceeds of his operation, and as a cover to communicate with his clients. The kids' organs were being handled by rabbis affiliated with the *Organizatsiya*."

"Crooked rabbis, huh?" Jenner wrinkled her nose. "What about that doctor-guy who was holding the kids in his basement? The house of horrors?"

"Moris Falkovich. He was a middleman, did some of the implants stateside."

"Mmm. Well, it's not much, but it's a start," Angkor slouched back into his seat, and I caught a glimpse of the long knife he carried concealed under his coat. "What about the money?"

"The *Organizatsiya* no longer keeps physical cash," I said, reluctantly. The pair of them had agreed to come out with me for this job and split the profits between us and the kids' rehab. "He did, however, give me the location of a dead drop. We can go there and see what we find."

Jenner made a sound of agreement. "What do you think we'll scrounge up?"

"Guns, probably," I replied. "Maybe drugs. Maybe jewelry."

"Well, hey, guns are good. I like guns." Jenner perked up a little, but then sneezed and wiped her nose on the back of her arm. "But fucking hell, Rex, whatever you brought back in that suitcase of yours, it fucking stinks."

I looked over to Angkor. He shrugged, so I returned to Jenner. "Is your sense of smell as good as a tiger's in HuMan form? Because I did clean up and change clothes."

"Not as good, but still better than yours. I dunno – maybe I'm getting a migraine."

"Perhaps. Anyway, I have a contact who can find the organ brokers, the rabbis. I think that if you want to know where the rest of the children are, we're going to have to get to the bottom of that and crack MinTex."

Rain began to pelt the windshield, blurring out the surrounding street as we crept through the bumper-to-bumper lower Manhattan traffic.

"Ayashe can tap the right shoulders and follow that up in the Bureau. I'll set Talya on it, as well. Girl's some kind of computer genius." Jenner's voice was glutinous. She sniffled loudly, and both I and Angkor twitched. I was about to offer her a tissue when I noticed the edge of a rotten-meat stench cycling into the cabin.

The ambient light outside dropped, sharply, as a sonorous moan tore the air and rumbled through the car. An awful ripple of energy washed over me in a crawling wave, and a heavy thump struck the roof of the car. Binah flew off my lap, spitting and slashing when I tried to catch her, and the water sluiced away by the windshield wipers turned pink... then crimson. Our view of the road disappeared under a greasy layer of blood and shredded flesh.

"Jesus fucking doggystyle Christ!" Jenner switched the windshield wipers to their fastest setting, clearing a streaky window into the street just as a young yuppie in a business suit fell face-first to the ground in front of us, brained by a hunk of frozen meat and fat the size of a pot roast. Screams of horror rang out from all directions, and traffic froze as mobs of panicked, blood-soaked pedestrians surged between the cars, running into each other, slipping and falling on the suddenly treacherous ground. An older woman in a blue pantsuit was bowled over and fell to her hands and knees, screaming as she was drenched in the same rich, gruesome scarlet that was now pounding down in sheets over everyone and everything. Through it all, the sky continued to moan: a deep howl that made my teeth buzz.

Angkor reached out and gripped me by the arm, nostrils trembling. "Alexi. Do you know the Story of the First War?"

I jumped, surprised. "The First War?"

"The First War was not a war. It was a rout. It came with the First Star to ever light the Mirror of the Sky. It came when that Star fell, screaming-"

"-to the White ground," I finished, pulling the words from the memory of a fever dream. Or rather, I'd thought

27

it had been a dream. "Never forget that when The Morphorde appears... the skies scream."

Angkor nodded, face tense with controlled fear.

In spite of the hellish downpour, traffic was moving again. Sort of. We were boxed in from the sides and unable to move forward while Yuppie Guy clawed his way up over the hood of our car with the help of a woman who'd been crossing the road with him. She was doing her best to get him on his feet, her fine white blouse plastered to her skin with blood, chunks of flesh nesting in her immaculate coiffure. Once he was up, she started trying to talk to him while he swayed against our car.

"Get the fuck out of the way!" Eyes watering, Jenner laid on the horn and struck the wheel with her other hand. Horns were blaring up and down the road, mostly at us since we were the ones blocking traffic. White Blouse managed to pull Business Suit off the road far enough that we could pass around them and catch up to the cars in front.

I was struck dumb by the noise, the smell, and the glimpses of the street I saw through the blinding flash-bang bursts of sound. To either side of us, blood-sheathed cars loomed out of the foggy steaming mess like skinned steers. On the sidelines, dozens of people had slipped and fallen as they ran and crawled to any shelter they could find. They crammed into doorways and alcoves to escape the falling chunks of meat and gristle. Umbrellas were smashed and abandoned; a disheveled man with a stringy beard, rail-thin and glassy-eyed, held his arms up as if in greeting, laughing at the groaning sky.

My belly clenched with a sharp pang. *Never forget that when the Morphorde appears, the skies scream...*

The old guy had been carrying a sign. It floated face-down in the gutter, which was backing up from the meat that was now falling more heavily than the blood. Chunks of it were striking the ground with such force that we heard them explode, frozen missiles shattering windows, puncturing awnings. A woman tried to protect her screaming children, bent over a terrified toddler strapped into a double stroller with her infant clutched to her chest and weathering the blows with her back. We all jumped at a second loud thump on our roof, then a bang, and then our view of the street vanished a second time as something round - the size of a human head - smashed into the windshield like a cannonball and smashed the glass. It bounced away in a tumble of dark hair.

"Fuck fuck FUCK FUCK FUCK!" Jenner braked hard and swerved as cars piled up ahead, but the wheels slid on the layer of hamburger pounded into the surface of the road. We hit the corner of the fender in front of us and jolted to a stop.

Sirens had started up from every direction. I winced, jamming my fingers in my ears and folding over as the sound bored into my back teeth and up behind my eyes. My senses were getting overwhelmed by the cold, the stench, the wailing, the feeling of clothes clinging to my skin in the humid, frigid air.

"Look. Up there." Angkor pointed around the smashed-in part of the windshield. "There's the edge of the storm. We're almost clear."

With difficulty, I did, and he was right. The meat fall and the near-darkness was being pushed back by an advancing line of sweeping rain. I nodded, unable to speak, and instinctively clutched at his arm as my body just gave up under the agony of fifty different types of fucking sirens as police, fire, and ambulance all burst onto the road ahead and behind. Angkor was warm, a physical anchor I held onto as my vision simply shut off, leaving me blinded behind a wall of sound. At a loss, I reached back for Kutkha, for my magic. My Neshamah was there, and with the brief synaptic connection between us came a revelation.

Harbinger. I tried to say the word aloud, but only managed a kind of spastic moan. My tongue and throat just wouldn't work together. I shook my head and hands, pulling away from Angkor. He was saying something, his voice green flashes against the white. I couldn't understand any of it.

A roar built outside of my body, the meshed sounds of sirens, engines, people shrieking, feet on pavement, wheels on the road, while my Soul whispered the litany of the First War into my ears, over and over, like a skipped record. The rain was a harbinger, and as I ground the heels of my palms against my eyes, I returned to a vision of Eden.

Mirrored sky. Glass land, White trees like coral, their leaves touching, their trunks surrounded by creatures of living spun glass. Their daughters, the Gift Horses, crouching on their branches... watching in innocence as the gentle wind whipped up into a tempest, and the moaning sky above their heads cracked and opened up the Void. The first color they saw was Red.

"*Red is the color of Wrath,*" Kutkha said gravely. "*The color of Hate, and the Force that inspires War. It is the color of the Siege, and the Fire that comes with it. Red is the color of the Sword, Alexi. And I fear that is what is coming.*"

CHAPTER 3

There came a point where my body just gave up under the sensory assault and quit. I looked and sounded like a guy who'd had a stroke, complete with slurred speech, painful contorting tics, and the uncontrollable need to shake my hands and head. It was like retching without actually vomiting, dry-heaving through the muscles of the face, hands, and chest instead of out my gullet. It made me look like some kind of retard in front of Angkor. Being pissed about how ridiculous the tics were made them worse, and so I was in full Rain Man mode by the time we pulled into Strange Kitty and came to a clanking, smoking stop.

"Rex? Are you dying?" Jenner's harsh voice cut through the air like sword strokes. I jerked as each word landed against my skin, red and sharp. "Speak to me, man."

I was fully conscious inside of the opaque bubble of stimulation, but incapable of actually speaking beyond one word. Unfortunately, when I said it once, my mouth kept repeating it. At volume. "No. NO! NO!"

"Don't worry, Jenner. He's fine. Just having a, uh, neuron tangle." Angkor's voice felt like the rippling of milk, a sensation so strong that I could taste it. He slowed down his words when he spoke to me. "Come on, Alexi. Grab my sleeve."

Fuck. He thought I was a retard, didn't he? Red-faced, I fumbled out and clenched his wrist through his clothes, letting him lead me blindly out into the rain. I still couldn't see: the world was a flashing field of phosphine white, and I was a passenger riding along in a short-circuiting tank.

I could smell that we were in the bikers' clubhouse. First there was the smoky, boozy garage hangout, then the cleaner, dusty, old-house smell of the interior rooms. Angkor led me to a bed and helped me to lay down in the dim, cold room we shared, the bunkhouse informally known as the Barracks.

"Sleep." He only said the one word, and left me to lie alone.

He didn't have to tell me twice. I shuddered my way into sleep, restless with the memories of the blood rain, the evidence still burning a hole in Jenner's car, and the haunting not-memories of Eden.

When I woke a couple hours later, I hurt all over. Binah was balled in the crook of my arm, her little body pressed to mine. I stroked her, and she began to purr as she uncurled and rolled onto her back so that I could reach her belly. The soothing, sky-blue sound felt like smooth fur, flowing over me in reassuring waves. After a few minutes, my sight faded back in. My familiar had her eyes closed. She was kneading the air with her paws.

"Good girl." I mumbled. It still came out without much in the way of vowels, but at least I could shape words again.

Twenty minutes of feline-aided meditation later, I was able to get up and limp to the bathroom. A cold shower helped, as did a fresh shave. After that, I went back outside to get my things and change them over to my car. Someone called out to me, but I didn't understand what they were saying. Consumed by tunnel vision, I mechanically acted out each required step. Dirty murder kit in the front seat under another bag. Keys, stick, gas, indicator. I drove us to a burger joint, got a combo meal and an extra cheeseburger, and gave the patty to Binah so we'd have something to eat during our scenic three-hour tour of New York City's dirtiest waterways and wetlands. Everything I'd used to pull the hit on Yegor had to go. The suit, contacts, and eventually the suitcase all went, flung out into long grass or trash cans or piles of junk. The gloves I'd worn were burned, to make sure no one could read my fingerprints—or my psychic imprint—from the impressionable leather.

Once everything was disposed of, I should have gone back to Strange Kitty. Instead, I found myself going west, drawn to Green-Wood Cemetery by a deep, powerful need for... something. I wasn't sure. It drove me, even though I knew that Vassily's grave was a stupid, isolated, predictable place that Sergei almost certainly had under watch. If there was one thing the last three months had taught me, it was that there were things more powerful than my common sense.

Every member of the Lovenko family was buried or memorialized in the same family plot, a small fenced-off yard shaded by a large plum tree. Sergei's men had knocked the tree when they cracked open Vassily's grave and exhumed him, shaking overripe plums everywhere. Fruit had tumbled into the empty pit and onto the broken granite and turned earth to either side of it.

Hail struck my bare head like pins as I exited the car and climbed the hillock with the Wardbreaker close at hand. I sat down heavily on the edge of Mariya's tomb, staring at the rotten fruit stewing in the muddy water at the bottom of the hole and shuddering with tremors that had nothing to do with the cold. My face was stony, the skin stiff over a mask of muscle and bone.

My whole life, I'd taken pride in how much I knew about life. Magic, philosophy, the Occult, my work. I'd treated knowledge like a currency, and sanctimoniously encouraged everyone around me to explore themselves, learn more about themselves, study the Mysteries, pursue wisdom... as if a sheltered Mafiya brat like me could ever know what 'wisdom' actually was. I knew that now, but I'd believed my own bullshit for nearly thirty years. When I looked back on Yegor's death, there was little pleasure. There wasn't anything except a vague sense of guilt, both for the death itself and for the fact I'd fed right back into the *Organizatsiya's* feudal cycle of blood for blood, gold for gold. As ridiculous as it seemed, the blood and meat rain felt like a personal omen.

I lifted my eyes to Vassily's headstone. Slavic graves normally have a picture of the deceased: A photo, a statue, or an etched image. For the Mafiya, laser-etched portraits are the norm for those who can afford it. When we were in our twenties and planning our future funerals, Vassily had been able to afford it. He had a proper rectangular slab headstone as tall as he'd been in life. He was a sharp-featured man, lean and hawkishly handsome. He'd been etched in his favorite trench coat, leaning on the hood of his car, and surrounded by images of other prized possessions. At my urging, the artist had included a couple of esoteric symbols in the design. Apples and wheat, for Osiris. The ankh pendant I'd given him for his 23rd birthday hung out of his collar on a chain. There was a notebook with the symbol of Saturn on the cover, the planet ruling his astrological chart. The artist had done an excellent job. Vassily's portrait smiled at me with mouth and eyes, but I couldn't smile back.

Yegor had been right to remind me that I'd been a part of the trade in children. Just because I hadn't known didn't free me up. That was where the guilt was coming from— the reflective knowledge that, however unwittingly, I'd enabled these men with my own sweat and sinew, killing for them, protecting them while they kept kids in little cages, fucked them, cut them up. Taking hits on wiseguys, roughing up troublemakers around Brighton Beach, and policing our drug and financial rackets were one thing. What Sergei and the Deacon were doing was something else entirely.

There was no way to know how long the *Organizatsiya* had been receiving children for the Templum Voctus Sol. It had to have started during Lev's reign as Avtoritet, because Jana had been in the picture, and it had to have been approved by Sergei. I'd figured out that's why he'd wanted me to go to Thailand with him. It was a Mecca for pedophiles, and the *Organizatsiya* could pick desperate kids off those beaches like gulls hunting baby turtles. My guess was that it had been in the works for at least five, six years... and that Vassily had been taken out of the game because the men who were involved knew Vassily would have done everything in his power to stop it.

I frowned. In one way or the other, the *Organizatsiya* had taken all of them. I was the last man standing out of both my families, the family of my blood and the family who'd adopted me. How I'd survived was a mystery. I was plain, dull, and not particularly lucky, while Vassily had been none of those things. Maybe it was as Yuri had told me—we were machine parts, some more bare and essential than others, and I'd simply been a cog instead of a whistle.

"Alexi...?"

Whatever feelings had been pushing to come out vanished in the heartbeat it took me to leap to my feet, pistol in hand. It was Angkor. The sight of him here was like a slap of cold water to the face. I snapped around, heart thundering in my ears.

Angkor was dressed more nicely than I'd ever seen him. A long black wool coat, gloves, suit and shirt, no tie. He was carrying a large black umbrella. I couldn't read his expression.

"Sneaking up on men like me is an excellent way to get shot, Angkor." I scowled, slowly easing down. I holstered the gun, doing my best to mask shaking fingers, and fought the urge to turn around.

He shrugged. "Sorry. I noticed you were gone from the Barracks. I was worried, so I thought I'd… you know."

"It's fine." It wasn't, but some part of me was… flattered? that he'd decided to come and find me. Flattered, and paranoid. I dropped back onto the edge of Mariya's sarcophagus, waiting as Angkor swept as much water as he could off the stone and perched alongside me.

"They really made a mess of this place, didn't they?" he asked, with a sigh.

I resumed my cold contemplation of the grave. "Shortly before he died, Vassily accused me of hating people. He was joking around, as usual. I denied it, but he was right." I gestured to the hole. "I really do hate people, because they do things like this."

"You're not that bad. Everyone hates assholes." Angkor reached into his coat and pulled out a battered cigarette case. "You're a better person than you think, you know."

I snorted. "Really? What tells you that? My sparkling sense of humor, or maybe the philanthropic way I just used a hammer to beat a father of two to death in his own office?"

"The way you treat Binah, actually." Angkor tucked the umbrella between neck and shoulder while he lit up, cupping his hand around the end of the cigarette. He was the sort of man I'd expect to smoke with his wrist cocked back. He didn't. He pinched the cigarette between thumb and fingers, smoking with the efficient intensity of a soldier or an ex-con. "Binah, Talya, Jenner, me. You care about your friends. I think you'd do anything for them."

"Perhaps. But I still prefer animals all around. They're honest by default."

"I think most people try to be honest if they can be." Angkor shrugged. "HuMen are a mix of good and bad. Some are DOG-bit. If you grew up in a mafia, a lot of the people you knew were more Morphorde than HuMan."

Fair enough. I flexed my fingers against the sharp granite ledge of the tomb.

"You know, I used to have a horse," I said, haltingly. "Back in high school, I rode every day. Polo, dressage, show jumping. Her name was Katerina – she was an absolutely stunning Andalusian-Arab mare. We were the 1978 champions at my school, and then we won two years running in college. I used to joke she was my *dukh*, my spirit. She was my pride and joy."

Angkor nodded, listening.

"My father killed her because I wouldn't loan him money to pay for his drug habit," I continued. "I got a late-night callout to the barn from the owner. Katerina woke him up with her screams. My father went into her stall with sugar cubes and cyanide and poisoned her."

"GOD." Angkor made a sound of disgust in the back of his throat. "What a piece of shit."

A deep leaden weight settled in my chest. I shook my head. "It changed me, because until then, I couldn't imagine anyone capable of looking this beautiful, guileless creature in the eye and murdering her, not even my father. That was the beginning of the end for my career in the *Organizatsiya*, looking back. All the men I knew said that my father was a 'great guy', that he was a good soldier.

They laughed off his murdering a horse, and I realized that... that there was something wrong with them. Looking back, maybe I was sensing the Morphorde in them. Yegor, Nicolai, my father. All of them."

"Sounds like it." Angkor scowled, drawing deeply on his cigarette. I breathed in the greenish smoky smell of the tobacco, and oddly, my mouth started watering.

I grimaced, and turned my head away from it to try to banish the odd craving. "Anyway, now that I've set up the rest of the day's depression, I have to ask – how did you know I'd be here?"

"You just went and took care of someone in revenge for Vassily. You don't drink, so you weren't going to be at a bar. There's really only one other place you'd go."

"Am I that predictable?"

"Everyone's predictable once you're old enough," Angkor replied.

Frowning, I glanced across at him. Angkor was just as fascinating in profile as he was from the front. The long sweep of his neck, the strong jaw, the faint freckles just a couple shades darker than his olive skin. He was Korean, but he reminded me a little of the famous bust of Nefertiti from the side. The same grace.

"Exactly how old are you?"

"You wouldn't believe me if I told you."

"You're a Biomancer. And you've already told me you're older than you look."

Angkor's lips twitched. "Fifty."

"Oh. Is that all?" I sniffed. "Well… you made it sound like it was going to be something outrageous."

"Sorry to disappoint you." His mouth drew up on one corner, but then he averted his eyes. The humor faded quickly as he looked over at Vassily's headstone. "Is that him? Your friend?"

The moment of levity passed. I nodded.

"He looks like he was a lot of fun to have around. The kind of man who could light up a room."

The tremors returned, the sensation of the world quaking under and around me. My memory, faithfully photographic as always, pressed me down under the weight of the many thousands of moments I'd shared with Vassily over more than half my lifetime. Laughter as we wrestled as children… the smell of him inside a stuffy car while we watched movies at the drive-in as teenagers. Watching him get his hands tattooed. The way light sometimes played over his throat and face when we were driving at night. I remembered him watching me and Katerina take the championship in our last year of high school, whooping and yelling from the stands while the rest of the WASP crowd awkwardly leaned away. We shared meals, homework, games of chess. Vassily lit up parts of me that were normally buried from sight, and starting from the day he'd gone to prison, life had become gray. Gray and dry. I withdrew into the desert of contract killing and *Ars Magica*, atrophying in place. And to a large extent, I was still there.

"He was." I croaked out, unable to lift my voice. "But he changed after prison. He went in for… for bloodless white-collar bullshit, before everything with Zarya."

"Who?"

"The Gift Horse," I replied. "Vassily never killed a man in his life, you know. He was clever. Inventive. He would have been better off staying at college or going into banking or something... he was too gentle for the life. He had amazing ideas, and I used to listen to him and try to encourage him..."

I trailed off, not even sure where I was going.

"And you loved him," Angkor said softly.

It struck like a slap. I flinched before I could stop it, and was about to snap something and get to my feet when he shuffled in closer, leaning against my side. He tipped the umbrella to better cover us both.

"My brother died when I was ten," Angkor said, his head now very close to mine. "His name was Jae-Gung. Jae was a standout... good student, good grades, went in for his military service and did really well. I loved him because he was my *oppa*, my older brother, but I was jealous, because my parents once told me they wished they'd never tried for a second child. I was a disgrace to them."

"Why?" The sudden contact left me momentarily breathless. My skin crawled under my wet shirt for a moment, but relaxed against the warmth that radiated through his coat.

"Lots of reasons," Angkor said, his voice turning a dark burnt orange with bitterness. "Jae-Gung was always kind to me. He came to visit me in the hospital when he was on leave that summer. I was in the middle of chemotherapy, and Mom asked him to go to a department store to get a new humidifier for the room, because the air was dry and it was making me cough. He went to the Sampoon Department Store the day the building collapsed."

"An earthquake?"

"No." He snorted. "A fuckup. The building was held together with spit and happy thoughts, and literally just fell down one day. Five hundred people were killed. My brother was one of them."

I frowned, not sure what to say.

Angkor sighed heavily. "The point is, I guess, that it can be harder to be the one left behind. That, and it's okay to still love someone when they're gone, but you have to be careful that it doesn't eat you alive. I blamed myself for years, even though there was nothing I could have done and it wasn't my fault. You're going to have to make the same decision I did at some point."

"And what decision is that?"

Angkor smiled. "To become your own individual person. I used Jae-Gung as an excuse for my failures for a long time. I didn't have to succeed or become my own person because the shadow of my brother always stretched so far. But one day, I realized it was exactly that: a shadow. I had to become someone. A real person, not just 'the one our parents didn't want'."

I eased down inside my skin. He had a point, because I knew that when I thought about anything, it was filtered through the *Organizatsiya*'s lens. Reductionist, paranoid, ruthless, medieval. The Russian Mafiya saw itself as a kingdom; the *muzhiki* were princes, warlords, and bandits in opposition to a repressive society of weaklings. We played pretend with semi-automatics and real blood, but it was all an artifice to justify the avoidance of reality... so why did I still defer to it? To those ways of being?

"Mm." My brow furrowed. "You know, I can think back to all the people I knew – other than Vassily and a couple others – and there's a word I can use to refer to them all. Vacuous. If you asked any guy 'what are you?', the answer effectively added up to 'my dick, this gold Rolex, football, and Adidas'. The women weren't any better."

"Vacuous is a good word to describe Morphorde." He grunted with amusement, and leaned his head in the crook of my neck. Strangely, I didn't mind that, either.

A good ten minutes passed that way, his hair soft against my skin, our breath steaming the air. As time crawled by, I could feel it pulling me out of the heavy pall of grief, warring with an entirely different set of feelings. Angkor's increasingly familiar perfume, masculine spice blended with the aromatic sweetness of the Phi bound into his flesh by years of hunting Gift Horses. It stirred hungers I felt in my jaw, in my fingers, the pulse in my crotch. Glancing at Vassily's headstone, I couldn't help but wonder if he would have been disgusted with me.

I shuddered, skin prickling, and pulled back. "Alright... enough of this. Time to go."

"Sure. And... I'm sorry if I, I mean I was trying to tell you I relate, but it probably sounded like I was making it all about me." Angkor forced out a short, unhappy laugh and was suddenly off the ledge and on his feet, patting around for his cigarette case again.

"No, I understand. But we need to get back to Strange Kitty." I hopped the short distance to the ground, jerking my shoulders back under my wet coat. "Jenner is going to want to debrief, and she'll already be making noises about those guns. How did you get here?"

"I walked," he said. "It's only a few miles."

"You can drive back with me, if you want."

"I'd love to. And I admit... I had an agenda when I went looking for you." He handed me the umbrella. "I'm not an expert on this world. Have you ever read about any other blood-and-meat rains like this one? I figured you'd be the person who would know."

This world? I nodded. "There was the Kentucky Meat shower in 1876. Meat fell in a 100-by-50-yard radius on Allen Crouch's property near Rankin. No piece exceeded 3.9 inches." I rattled it off like pulling files from a drawer. "The Black Plague in 1348 was supposedly presaged by a rain of blood over Hanover, Germany. So was World War One: Massive blood rain over the village of Whitby. That was determined to be caused by a water twister that sucked up a herd of sheep on the English coast, but it was eerily prophetic, nonetheless. Arguably, the blood rain actually foretold the Influenza Epidemic of 1918, which killed over a hundred million people."

"Hmm. The fall today was human remains. I'm positive." Angkor fell into step with me as we headed down the hillock, careful not to slip on the wet grass. "And

45

that weird moan we heard… that sound is a harbinger of the Morphorde"

I nodded. "My thoughts exactly. First a Gift Horse Mare turns up, now this. I don't know what's happening, but it's not good."

"No," he said. "It's not."

"Any thoughts?"

Angkor shook his head. "No. I feel like there's something I should have known before today. Something I have to do, that might be related to all of this stuff. It's so frustrating that I can't remember."

"The Deacon must have really knocked you around."

"Yeah. He did." The sourness was back, but with it, something oddly vulnerable. It was in the way he suddenly carried himself. Without thinking, I held his door for him when we reached the car. He accepted with a smile, dipping his eyes and sliding onto his seat without a word of protest. The graceful ritual made my pulse jump. I wasn't sure what I was supposed to do about how I felt, but I knew I had to do something.

I cleared my throat and composed my words while the engine roared to life and he lit up again, leaning out the window. "Angkor, I was going to… well, I wanted to ask…" I tripped on the words a little, despite taking the time to think them over. "Would you like to go to dinner with me sometime? To discuss things beyond death and mayhem, I mean?"

Angkor looked back over at me in surprise, eyebrows arched.

"I know we got off to an awkward start, but you saved my life last month." My heart was hammering now, voice uncontrollably terse. "I've… enjoyed your company these last few weeks, and I've sensed we probably have a lot to talk about, but Strange Kitty isn't very, well…"

"Private," he finished.

I could feel myself flushing. "Precisely."

His smile spread into a grin as he glanced down again, then back up to my face. "You saved my life first. And you know… I'd love to."

Yes. He'd said yes? My palms were sweating. Asking that one question had given me a kick of adrenaline almost equal to what I'd gotten from taking out Yegor. "Well, great. Alright. What do you like to eat?"

Angkor playfully pinched his tongue between his teeth. "Gift Horse. But I'll settle for good French food if you know where to find it."

I scoffed, forcing myself to keep my eyes on the road. "Of course I do. I'm *blatnoi.*[1] I'd be ashamed of myself if I didn't know every ostentatious restaurant in the city. But not tonight: I'm going to pick up Binah and go on a short road trip to cool my heels. Even with the blood rain taking up the headlines, Yegor's death will make the news. What do you say to seven p.m. tomorrow night?"

---

[1] BLAT' IS THE RUSSIAN TERM FOR 'FACE' OR 'HONOR': A VERY IMPORTANT CONCEPT IN MOST EASTERN EUROPEAN AND ASIAN COUNTRIES. BLATNOI ARE PEOPLE WHO HAVE 'FACE' – WHO ARE SOCIALLY IMPORTANT AND ABLE TO LEVERAGE FAVORS.

"Sounds wonderful," he replied. "I'll be working on my memory all night tonight, so the timing should be perfect. Do you know where we're going?"

"I'll call the restaurant at home and write the address down for you. Or I can just pick you up." That was what you did for dates, wasn't it? Pick them up?

"I'd rather meet you there." Angkor smiled, as mysteriously remote as the Mona Lisa. "No telling what we'll be up to tomorrow."

CHAPTER 4

The Twin Tigers M.C. compound was the closest thing I now had to a home. It was comprised of two large buildings on a big dirt lot in Williamsburg. Their business, Strange Kitty, was a two-story red brick butcher's slab, a dive bar and lounge fronting Marcy Avenue that hosted a loud crowd of punks and down-and-out spooks. A sea of gravel, cigarette butts, and motorcycles divided the club from the derelict clapboard house behind it. The front was boarded up and heavily graffitied, shielded from the road by a chain link fence topped with barbed wire.

The yard was currently bustling, despite the rain. People chattered and smoked under faded blue umbrellas, where Jenner was holding court. We parked and got out, collecting coats and slamming doors. I almost didn't see Zane until he peeled off from the wall. He was the kind of man that usually only existed in Calvin Klein ads and women's wet dreams: dark, quiet, handsome, hard-cut, with startling pale green eyes. He also turned into a cougar the size of a small pony, and was as gay as a Boy Scout jamboree – not that I was in any position to judge, given that I'd just asked another man on a date.

"Hey, Rex." Like the other bikers, he still used the nickname I'd given to the shapeshifters the first time I'd met them. "How's tricks?"

"Tricks?" I was still a little slow from the sensory shit-fit from earlier in the day. "Oh… nothing much. What's happening?"

"Jenner wants to raid this depot of yours," he replied. On his feet, Zane was close to seven feet tall. His voice was a deep rumble, a few shades deeper than Binah's purr. "She's worried after what happened on Wall Street. Think you're up to it today?"

"I need to change clothes and get ready for tonight, and then we can be on our way." In truth, I wasn't really up to a – but it was better to get it done now, while the *Organizatsiya* was off-balance. "You heard about the storm, I assume?"

"Yeah. I don't know what it means, but it doesn't mean anything good." He jerked his head toward the car in the middle of the yard. "Tally and me are going to be working on that all week."

Jenner's beautiful white 1969 Impala, formerly pristine, was trashed. It was smeared with rusty dried blood. The roof and hood were dented, the fender scraped, and the windshield bowed in by a concentric web of cracks where the frozen head had struck it.

Angkor winced. "Jeez… I hadn't even really looked at it. What a mess."

Zane grunted his assent. "Well, go tell Jenner what you're planning. I think we all just want to get it over with."

Jenner was once more dressed the part of a rivethead biker queen: a spiked leather jacket plated over the shoulders and down the arms, black jeans, and boots that looked too heavy for her petite frame. She was an anomaly in the male-dominated world of America's biker gangs, but her men listened to her and respected her—and no wonder. Jenner was a shapeshifter tigress and the *Malek-Kah*, the Elder shapeshifter of New York. She had something to the tune of five hundred years of collected memory as her *Ka-Bah*, her animal self, reincarnated over and over through the centuries. In this lifetime, she had found her niche in the motorcycle world, and at the age where most Asian women were perming their hair and breeding canaries, Jennifer Tran ran guns and drugs from Mexico to the Canadian border through a diverse network of truckers, bikers, and Vietnamese Triads. She was kind but tough, ruthless, and refreshingly straightforward. I held her in high regard, and for whatever reason, she seemed to like me in return.

Her eyes lit up as we pushed our way into the ring of people that encircled her. "Hoi, Rex. Angbutt. How are we doing?"

"I have to get ready, then we can go," I said. "Better to raid before Nicolai knows what hit him."

"Sounds good to me." Jenner took a swig off her beer, and leaned against the little patio table that held the umbrella. "What can we expect to find?"

"The depot is at K&S, a scrapyard out in Babylon. They own four yards. The main one is where all the activity is: the crusher, metal sorting, baling, that sort of thing. The other three store intact vehicles. We're headed for one of those yards. Tall fences, not too much protection, probably dogs and a couple of contractors. We usually hired Chechens for jobs like these. Most of them are veterans who've seen front line action, but there won't be many of them."

"Right. Let's plan for six, which means we need to take around fifteen people. Overwhelm them with numbers, get them to back down, and loot the place bare." Jenner crossed her arms, sucking on a tooth. "Six of us in the back of the truck, a couple of cars, five bikes for escort. Think you're good enough to ride your bike out that far, Rex?"

I nodded. I'd inherited a handsome red and black Softail custom from the former Road Captain of the gang, Duke. Zane had been teaching me to ride. With the exception of one unfortunate incident involving the throttle and the chain link fence surrounding the compound, I'd taken to it readily.

"Good. Go get your pants on, and then we'll be off on our treasure hunt, gentlemen." Jenner flashed a wolfish, sharp-toothed grin to my left. "And hey, Angkor: if you're gonna go suck Alexi's dick before we troop off, you better get to work."

I flushed. "Jenner-"

Angkor's eyes widened, and he lay a hand over his chest. "Me? How dare you. Jenner, come on. You know I'm saving myself until marriage."

She threw her head back and laughed. "Angkor, you are literally the biggest whore who ever whored in Whoretown, okay?"

"Your mom is a bigger whore than me," Angkor said.

"My mom paid your mom to-"

"Okay. That's enough of that. I have reached my limit of terrible mom jokes for today." I said.

Jenner wrinkled her nose. "Your mom's a... mom... joke?"

Exasperated, I turned and stalked off. The pack of men – mixed Blanks[2] and Weeders, shapeshifters – broke into chuckles and snorts behind me. God, what if Angkor told them I'd asked him out? I'd never hear the end of it. I hadn't even considered that.

The only way into the clubhouse was through the garage out back, which had been converted into a biker's paradise: a private bar garnished with war memorabilia, flags and banners, medals donated by the veterans in the club. There was a pool table, a jukebox dedicated to rock music, and approximately two ashtrays for every one person. Binah was pacing on the pool table, yowling as only a Siamese could. "Miiiau! Miiiau!"

"I know. I abandoned you. I was gone forever." I went to her and let her jump up onto my shoulder, giving her a couple of seconds of chin-scratch time before heading into the house. While Binah continued to kvetch beside my ear, I made a beeline for the barracks-style dorm Angkor and I had been sharing for the better part of a month. It was blessedly quiet for now, the air still, the light muted. My magical tools were laid out on the dresser beside my bed, a makeshift altar that was a miniature replica of the one I used to have in my apartment. A tarot

---

[2] A SLANG TERM FOR NON-MAGICAL PEOPLE.

card took center place beside a small obsidian knife and the space where the Wardbreaker typically sat. This week's card was The Chariot, the only card I hadn't colored during my stint on the streets. Of all the Major Arcana, this card was best left in black and white.

I showered, shaved, and called Club 21, a French-American bistro downtown. When I put the phone down, heart hammering, I paused for a moment to make sure I wasn't having a stroke and let out a terse, tense breath. Christ. What the hell was I doing? I'd asked a man on a date, an attractive man who had once offered to… do things. Yes, *things*. Things he probably still wanted to do, assuming he hadn't just said yes out of pity or… or something.

Shaking my head, I wrote down the address and left it on a card beside Angkor's neatly made bed, then packed my motorcycle panniers for an overnight stay out of town. I zipped Binah into the front of my riding jacket and headed back out with the panniers slung over the other shoulder.

Jenner was giving a pep talk to the men she'd picked for the job. They had formed a ragged rank beside a large panel van now parked beside my car. Jenner's Road Captain, Big Ron, lounged on the driver's side with the door open and a cigar in his fingers, gut hanging over his jeans. The youngest member of the Big Cat Crew was in the cab beside him, watching everything with the eagerness of a Spaniel puppy. When I'd first met her, Talya Karzan had looked like a Native Siberian Girl Friday: prim, pretty in an insecure, girlish way, just this side of chubby. She was now slightly less plush, and she'd swapped the brown tweed and Oxfords for jeans, halter tops, and piercings. Now that she didn't have to worry so much about White sensibilities in the office, she'd gotten tattoos in the Aleutian tradition: parallel lines that ran from her bottom lip to the edge of her chin. She'd become more confident and less nervous since leaving the Four Fires and joining the Twin Tigers, but she was still green enough that you could have poured dressing on her and called her a salad.

I sidled into the raid group just as Jenner pointed at Zane. "You. Go get your gear on and grab a couple of AR-15s. You'll ride in the back with Johnny, Cliff, me, and Band-Aid. Rex, Angkor, you two join the escort."

"Aye aye, chief." Angkor flashed her a flippant salute.

The whole operation—and the Tigers' enthusiasm—set me on edge. I had no idea if we'd even find anything at the depot, and even if we did, there was no way to know the value of the goods. "Sure thing."

The ride out to K&S gave me time to think, to get back into my own head. Assuming the Meat Storm didn't herald the imminent demise of our world, I knew Yegor's death would destabilize the *Organizatsiya* in ways both profound and unforeseen. Yegor hadn't been the most visible member of the *Bratva*, but he was the lynchpin between the intake of money and the outflow of payments to grease palms at the Port Authority Customs. Now that he was out of the picture, they would be scrambling to manage AEROMOR, the shipping business that handled the majority of our imports and exports.

My prediction was that Nicolai would make a bid to manage AEROMOR himself, leaving the security side of things to his second in command, Petro. In the process, he would rapidly overextend himself and—central to my plans—would become suddenly and dramatically wealthy. Nicolai's weakness was his greed, and there was nothing in this world that killed off gangsters faster than a sudden windfall. I could name dozens of my contemporaries in the Mafia, the *Organizatsiya* and the Triads who'd had successful careers up until the moment they struck it rich. Money would spin Nicolai's head, make him overconfident and sloppy, and when he screwed up, I would be there. Waiting.

It was drizzling by the time we reached Kozlowski and Sons. K&S was the largest scrapyard in the state, a field of lots surrounded by poorly maintained roads, a skeletal railway, and old, moth-eaten factories. I gestured to Ron, and rode ahead of the pack to lead them to the correct yard: the one used to store decommissioned heavy vehicles, some of which I knew hadn't been moved in nearly fifteen years. When we cruised by on the first pass, it looked like the yard full of hulks was abandoned—but on the return, I saw movement. Two men dressed in generic blue security uniforms, but with the hard, nut-brown leather look of old soldiers. They watched us with slow eyes on our way back up the road.

I pulled up around the corner and parked the bike by the side of the road where the convoy had stopped. While Angkor got his helmet off and his rifle ready, I went over to the truck. Ron called back to Jenner, then rolled the window down. "How'zit lookin' down there?"

"Two sentries," I said, watching behind Ron as Jenner stuck her head through the curtain dividing the cabin from the cargo hold. "I think we should go with shock and awe. Let me go ahead, then follow up. I can hold their fire."

"Suits me. Saddle up!" Jenner disappeared back into the hold.

While they assembled, I withdrew and centered, breathing deeply.

All acts of magic begin with a spark of Phi, the energy exchanged between a magician and their Neshamah, energy that was condensed with a Breath, capital B. It was *pneuma* in Greek or *ruach* in Hebrew, and it meant something deeper than drawing air into your lungs. It was the act of chambering Phi with the intent to fire.

Witnesses weren't a concern in this part of Babylon, and the spectacle of fifteen heavily armed people and a truck heading for one of the rotting scrap yards went unobserved by everyone except the two guards, who had come to the fence line. Now that I had a decent view, I recognized one of them.

"Constantin Dadayev!" I called out to them in Russian, opening my arms as I walked toward the gate. "What a surprise to see you here! You're looking very alive, for now."

Dadayev's eyes narrowed, first in confusion, then recognition. He was holding an AK-47 in his hands, but not aiming. "Alexi? What are you…?"

His friend tugged on his sleeve, pointing past my head, and the words froze on his chapped lips.

"I'm here to collect on damages," I said. "So, if you'd like to leave here on two legs instead of being carried out under a sheet, I suggest you throw those guns down and lace your hands behind your head."

"You traitorous bitch!" Dadayev snarled, aiming and firing in one smooth motion. The hail of bullets drowned out my voice as I barked a word of power and threw up a hand. Magic surged, and the spray hit a thin kinetic shield spun from Phi and the dust in the air. The first bullets zinged off it, deflecting, but then it began to absorb the energy... and when the smoke cleared, I stood with fingers outstretched, the rounds smashed into and trapped in a field of charged Phitonic energy. I twisted it a little, and the lead liquified and spread out like a curtain.

The pair of men blanched. Dadayev dropped his gun and put his hands up, his skin the color of milk. His companion shortly followed. Breathing hard, I held the field until the Tigers advanced past me, then dropped it. The sheet of molten metal hit the ground in a line, sending up a wall of steam and smoke that swirled and parted as the bikers charged in past me, shouting, yelling at the men to get on the ground. That was when the rush hit me. GOD, it felt good to have my magic back.

There were ten or so buses like the ones Yegor had described. When we pried up the floors, we found a dragon's hoard: Uzis and AK-47s, the workhorses of every armed non-military organization in the world. They were neatly cased in hardened plastic and foam crates, eight to a box, and they radiated hot magic.

"Wait," I said, motioning them back. "Can you feel that?"

"I feel a tingle in my lady bits," Jenner replied. "What is it, Lassie? Is there wizardry afoot?"

"Hilarious." I passed a hand over them, feeling for wards or other protections. The energy was diffuse, though, not the orderly cycle of Phi I'd expect from a security measure. "Well, they should be safe to handle. We'll see."

"If I explode, tell Ron I always loved him." Jenner passed her pry bar to Zane and pulled one of the rifles out with eager hands. It came out glowing. The barrels were engraved with lines of sigils that burned with blood-red light, just like the Wardbreaker. My eyes widened. If Dadayev had been using one of these instead of his Plain-Jane AK-47, I and several bikers would be dead.

Jenner whistled. "Well, hellooo baby."

"What do these do, Rex?" Zane had to crouch to avoid hitting his head on the sagging ceiling. "Do you know?"

"If they're anything like my own weapon, they're made to pierce magical defenses," I replied. "Shields, wards, and the like. They're made to hurt things like us."

"They must be planning a witch hunt then, huh? This is a really nice haul." Jenner held the rifle up, appraising it with an expert eye. "And look: no serial numbers. These are ghost guns. We can raffle these off for five thousand a pop, easy. If the other cases've got the same amount of kit, we could be looking at a hell of a lot of money."

Zane banged the tall iron bar on the floor and ducked outside. "Okay, we're good. Bring the van up! Let's haul out!"

All up, there were twenty cases of eight guns each—and at five thousand dollars per gun, we were looking at close to a million dollars of hardware. It boggled me to think they'd only put two guards on it. The other unspoken question, of course, was 'What the hell was the *Organizatsiya* doing moving eight hundred thousand dollars' worth of witch-hunting equipment?' In all my years of working for them, I'd never seen anything like it.

I caught up with Jenner as she and Talya carried one of the cumbersome crates to the back of the panel van. Angkor was holding the door for them, a cigarette hanging from the corner of his mouth.

"Jenner, I'm going to head out from here on." I looked between them, arms crossed. "I'll meet you back at the clubhouse late tomorrow. Yegor was high-profile: I need to go to ground for a night."

"No worries." She grunted as she swung the case up to Ron, who hauled it into the depths of the van. "We got this. We'll figure out something to do with the Russian boys over there. Any suggestions?"

"Lock them in an empty gun crate together," I said. "Naked. The only reason this much hardware would have so such low-profile protection is because it's not here for very long. I suspect it was moved in as recently as yesterday and could be scheduled for pickup tonight."

Jenner nodded. "Right. That settles that then. By the by, next meeting is on Sunday night."

And I had a date tomorrow. "I'll be there."

"You better."

I nodded, and crooked my fingers to Angkor before I left, motioning him to follow me. He arched his eyebrows inquiringly as I walked off and put a bit of space between us and the others. When we had relative privacy, I turned back.

"Club 21," I said. "The address is on your nightstand."

Somehow, Angkor had ended up close to me, close enough that I could see the lines of pewter and cornflower blue shot through his eyes. Angkor had very dark violet-gray eyes, an unusual color in an Asian face. From a distance, they looked black. It was only when he was here, like this, that I could discern their true color. "I guess I'll be seeing you there, then. You know... That was a really hot piece of Phitometry you did back there. I'm envious."

This close, the synesthetic feedback of his voice rippled through the skin of my scalp like a caress. I glanced past him to the others. They were oblivious to our intimacy, and the thundering of my pulse lifted enough that it nearly drowned out the sound of their chatter. "It was just Inotropy. I... uhh..."

"'Just' Inotropy, he says." Angkor rolled his bottom lip under his top teeth in a way I found very distracting. "So, Club 21, nineteen hundred hours. I'll meet you there. Be careful... I know Jenner's excited about these weapons, but they make me nervous."

"Me too. And I will." The urge to kiss him was more powerful than I'd expected. His eyes hooded to dark crescents, and he lingered, maybe waiting to see if I'd take it further. But how could I?

We parted without saying anything else. I watched him retreat into his cheerful mask, laughing and teasing Talya as they got ready to pack up. Binah was waiting for me on the motorcycle, and she purred and arched against my hand as I took the saddle and opened my jacket for her. "GOD help me, Kutkha. What the hell am I thinking? What the hell am I doing?"

"Learning to live a little, finally," Kutkha sounded distinctly amused.

"I mean that this is… ugh." I shook my head, annoyed. "Forget I said anything."

"As you say, my Ruach."

CHAPTER 5

It was a hundred and fifty miles to Albany, a journey made fresh by the concentration needed to ride instead of drive. I pulled into a motel I'd never stayed at before, the romantically named 'Budget Motel'. It was a U-shaped clutter of clapboard buildings with peeling paint and a grimy office window entirely obscured by creeping kudzu—on the inside of the window. They offered cheap beds, thin walls, an old T.V., and a don't-ask-don't-tell policy of conduct. I paid cash for a twenty-five-dollar room, ordered some Mexican food at the payphone in the office, took a shower, and ate tacos with only Binah and silence for company.

Budget Motel wasn't exactly a luxury resort, but I hadn't gone here with luxury in mind. To the contrary. The first hour after a public job – the kind where you left the body out intending for it to be found – was the hot zone, the time you were most likely to screw something up and incriminate yourself. The next twelve to twenty-four were hotter than hot. By this time, the body's been found, cops are crawling over it like maggots, reporters are busting through the yellow tape, and a very tired detective and their lab team are doing their very best to find you. Meanwhile, the earnest wetworker is also tired and strung out, and if they got money for the job, very likely to spend their ill-gotten gains in an attempt to relax. I needed the ritual self-abnegation to remind myself that I wasn't rich, that I wasn't shit hot, and I was in fact one of the bottom-feeders, a 'thug with a couple of magic tricks', as Yegor put it. The reason I'd never been arrested was because I'd never put myself in a position to get caught.

I turned the T.V. on to catch the news while I brushed my teeth and got ready for an early night, listening from the bathroom sink.

"Five people were killed and thirty-two injured, seven critically, when a rain of human body parts fell over the Financial District today." The news anchor—a woman with big blonde hair and a pink power suit, her voice laden with dry disbelief—sat beside a cutout reel showing the scenes of carnage as the red rain swept across Wall Street. People running for shelter at the Exchange; crowds huddling in the mouth of an underground car park. "Our sources can confirm that this bizarre event occurred almost entirely in and around Wall Street. Viewers, if any of you were caught in the rain today, the CDC is urging you to please report to the nearest hospital to be tested for blood borne diseases. At least two people have already tested positive for the Hepatitis B virus. Citizens are to be advised that HBV can survive in dried blood for over seven days. and while clean-up crews have been dispatched, HBV transmission remains a major concern for employees such as custodians, laundry personnel and anyone else who may come in contact with the blood or any other potentially infectious materials."

Looking at the images, there was no denying where the meat had come from. Some shots of the street were almost completely blurred out to conceal smashed human heads, limbs, other recognizable body parts. The cameras had caught videos of people in HAZMAT gear helping screaming, hysterical men and women into chemical showers, as well as firefighters in gas masks sluicing the streets with high pressure hoses. The triangular zone between Broadway, Wall Street, William Street and Beaver Street was closed off by the National Guard.

"*Bozye moy*[3]." What a mess. I shook my head, turned to the sink and spat.

"...Some people are even suggesting that this event has religious significance. The CDC has refused to make a statement on the nature or consequences of the Wall Street Meat Storm, saying only that they are currently looking into the matter. Let's go live to our special guests for tonight. We have Professor Phillip Lawson, Head of Atmospheric and Meteorological Sciences at Oswego University, and Pastor Zachariah Goswin, the founder and lead minister of the Church of the Voice of the Lord."

I frowned, looking back out to watch as the two talking heads came up on screen. They were filming the pastor in Chicago, judging by his photo backdrop. Zachariah Goswin was a stocky, plum-faced man with an Ivy League haircut and a look of studied concern. He was in a black shirt with a purple stole, and I unconsciously

---

[3] 'MY GOD'.

searched his features to see if they matched The Deacon while they worked through the introductions.

"What do you have to say about this, Professor?" I tuned back in as the newscaster spoke.

"There have been numerous instances in history when meat and-or blood has fallen out of the sky as part of a weather event." The professor, a gaunt, clean-shaven man with neat hair the color of slate, regarded the camera steadily. "Firstly, there's a phenomenon called 'red rain' or 'blood rain' that results from dried algae being picked up by the wind. When it mixes with water, it forms meat-like clumps of jelly that are easily mistaken for beef or human fl... human biomatter."

"This event clearly involved human parts, Professor. We've got footage of legs, hands, heads-"

"Well, it's quite possible that a number of very unfortunate people were swept up from the ocean, or possibly an air transportation accident. I think as we get news from around the world, the mystery will begin to resolve itself. And, oh, as the lady said—if you were in contact with any of this bio-waste, please self-report to your local hospital or even just your doctor as soon as you can."

The news anchor nodded. "I'm sure the religious perspective is quite different, Pastor Goswin."

"Yes. I really think this event is a very serious wake-up call." Goswin's voice was strong and resonant, a little raspy at the edges, but he exuded patrician confidence. His eyes were very blue, but he didn't sound or hold himself like The Deacon, the strange Temporalist who had nearly killed me the month before. "I think we have experienced a remarkable event, truly remarkable in that the epicenter of the storm was the Financial District and specifically the Wall Street Stock Exchange. There is a strong religious ground to take that as a sign being given to us all. It's a very bad sign."

He sounded very reasonable, but my eyes narrowed all the same. Admittedly, I was biased. The ringleaders of the child-trafficking racket we had busted up in September were both Voicers, adherents to his megachurch. The Church of the Voice of the Lord was half Calvinist church, half self-improvement program. They believed that people had to work for the right to be considered 'real' Christians, and it wasn't enough to simply declare Jesus your savior and repent on your deathbed. An interesting sentiment, in theory... in practice, it boiled down to: 'if you're not rich or successful, God doesn't love you and you're going to hell'. For this reason, it had become a bit of a thing among religiously inclined celebrities... and apparently, shapeshifting child molesters.

"What kind of sign do you believe this represents?" the woman asked.

"I don't care to speculate. That's up to the Lord," Goswin replied. "But I think that we should be alert, and I think we should be afraid."

"Well, that's a very interesting perspective from two very different people. We'll be right back with further updates…"

After the ads, Yegor's death only got a passing mention from an anxious news reporter in a white filter mask—not even a Crimestoppers composite. They moved on quickly. "In other news: Professor Lee Harrison, the famous anthropologist, explorer and diver who filmed the award-winning documentary 'The Blue Holes of the May: Gateways to The Underworld' has been reported missing shortly after her arrival in New York. Anyone with information on her whereabouts is encouraged to contact the New York Police Department. We now head back to Wall Street for the latest."

I sighed. My luck. A famous missing person and The Wall Street Meat Storm had provided an incredible layer of obfuscation I hadn't counted on. Not a bad thing, but I'd been hoping for a headline. With nothing left to do, I turned the T.V. and lights off, got into bed, and stared at the map of light and shadow on the grimy ceiling for the half-hour or so it took me to pass out.

When I woke up, it was snowing over Albany. Stripped to the waist, I watched the silent white blanket lay itself over the highway while Binah wound around my legs, butting at me for attention. My nose was stuffy, and my jaws ached from grinding my teeth all night. The quiet drabness of the motel that had been so comfortable the night before now made the back of my neck crawl.

I moved restlessly to the little bar fridge and opened it to look inside. Besides my leftovers, there was an overpriced can of Coke and two bottles of Corona. Without thinking, I reached for a beer and cracked the lid, stopping only when the yeasty, yellowish smell of it hit my sinuses and made my stomach lurch.

What the hell? I hate that shit. I recoiled from the odor and put the bottle back in, jamming the cap back down. Maybe it was a carbohydrates thing. Beer was high in carbs, and I'd had a physically intense day without much food. Shuddering, I got the bag with the rest of my takeout and slammed the door.

After a cold breakfast of leftover tacos, Binah and I were back on the road. It was icy, the air swirling with snow. The conditions necessitated a leisurely pace that gave me ample time to become increasingly restless... and fixated. I'd already lost the glow of satisfaction from dealing with Yegor, and now I had my sights on Celso Manelli and the Manelli's pet spook, Carmine. The plan was to make it appear to be a hit by the *Organizatsiya*, drawing the full weight of the city's largest Italian Mafia family down on Nicolai's head. I could hardly wait.

"My Ruach," Kutkha said, his voice stirring up out of the blue. *"Do you recall what Angkor said about the nature of Yen?"*

"Vaguely." While riding, I didn't care about replying to Kutkha's telepathic voice aloud. The only one to hear me talk to myself was the cat, and she was too busy watching the world go by from her nest inside my jacket.

"Do you remember that the Yen infection causes compulsions, harmful behaviors?"

"Yes."

"Like blood-thirst, perhaps?" He suggested, delicately.

"Then this Yen can help me hunt these motherfuckers down," I replied. "I've been wanting to do this since before I got Yenned."

"Yes, but you are burning the candle at both ends again, to borrow your own preferred expression. You should consider at least giving yourself a month to cool down."

The ghostly odor of the open beer stirred in the back of my mouth. I ground my teeth until the crowns locked. "We don't have a month."

"Look at yourself in the mirror."

Haltingly, I obeyed. He had a point, because to put it frankly, I looked like shit. Even behind a visor, my eyes were sunken, my face sharp and hungry. I needed a shave. My scalp and face were thick with dark blond stubble that stood out on my blueish-white skin.

The last time I hadn't listened to Kutkha when he'd advised restraint, I'd ended up homeless, pumped full of toxic vampire blood, and stripped of my magic. While I had many faults, the inability to learn from my mistakes was not one of them. I'd eaten one too many dead raccoons to willfully ignore my Neshamah's advice ever again.

"Fine," I said. "I'll give a rest for a while. But we can pick up the file from Doctor Leventhal today and fix a plan. Do you have any objection?"

"I have no objection at this stage. The time for escape is now long passed, and the Morphorde in our locale remain a threat," Kutkha replied. *"In theory, we had a brief window of opportunity for freedom which rushed by and has now receded into the past. But as you learn, my Ruach, so do I."*

"Oh?" I glanced at my mirrors, instinctively checking for tails. "About what?"

"The decision you made to stay here." In my mind's eye, I could see him. Kutkha used the diminutive form of a name possessed by a very ancient Siberian god, and in the spirit of that god, he assumed the visual form of a raven

made of black, filamentary smoke. His eyes were solid, blazing white, spitting and burning like tiny stars. *"It may not have been a decision at all."*

"What's that supposed to mean?"

"Free will is illusory," he replied. *"Not in the sense of augury or fate, my Ruach, but in the purely mechanical sense. You are one mote of mitochondria in a body so large as to beggar comprehension. Do you think that mitochondria has free will?"*

"No. Of course not. Genes control it. It acts according to a pattern."

"As do we," Kutkha said. I could feel him smiling—a sensation that creeped and prickled across my skin, like goosebumps. *"And I now wonder if you merely acted in accordance with the code, which I assure you is far more complex than any mere Neshamah could ever know."*

"So ending up destitute and on the street was my destiny, then?" I snorted.

"I don't know what your destiny is, my Ruach. But you have made our bed. Now, we will lie in it."

***

I drove us back into the city on good time, stopped for coffee to try and get rid of the weird beer craving, and regretted it from the first sip onward. It tasted like the water in the bottom of a dumpster smelled. I drank it anyway, with an urgency I rarely felt. I needed the caffeine, or I wasn't going to be sharp enough to make the most of my next stopover: The Doctor's office.

Doctor Yusef Levental lived in a white brick rowhouse in Crown Heights, which was slowly returning to its old, sedate, upper-middle class neighborhood feel after the Crown Riots in August. Because of that, I was surprised to see three police cars parked outside the gate and down the street. The NYPD had put more force on the ground here to head off violence between the Chassidic Jews and Caribbean Blacks who coexisted uneasily in this part of the city, but the way they were all lined up in the gutter made my gut twinge with warning.

I looked for signs of the blood rain here, but if it had fallen anywhere outside of Manhattan, the sweeping rain had washed away the evidence. There was no blood or shredded tissue clinging to the short, sharp spikes of his fence, or on the tiny juniper seedlings that flanked the concrete pillars beside the front door. I buzzed the doorbell, withdrawing under the shallow balcony to stay out of the rain, and waited.

After a few seconds, the intercom hummed to life. "'Allo?"

The voice was young and male. One of the doctor's sons, no doubt. "Levi? It's Alexi Sokolsky. I'm here to see your father."

The intercom dropped out, but the door didn't buzz and open. Frowning, I waited with my hands jammed in the pockets of my coat. I was about to hit the doorbell again when the door creaked open. It was Levi, Doctor Levental's oldest son, a shy and darkly handsome Chassidic man only five years my junior. He was in his usual black suit and yarmulke, but he looked like he'd been gutshot.

"Alexi. *Aleichem Shalom.* I'm sorry, but… we cannot admit guests." His Russian was stuffy and thick. "The police are here."

"Has something happened?" I frowned.

He nodded. "Father went missing yesterday morning. He went to buy bread before work started, and he never came home."

"And no one saw anything? In this neighborhood?" My gut twisted nastily with an eerie intuitive feeling of wrongness.

"I heard he walked off with a man in blue and a woman who didn't cover her hair, but that was just old Rebekah down the street talking scandal, like she usually does. Mother is with the police upstairs." He clutched the edge of the doorway, his fingernails digging into the wood. "Why? What do you want?"

I sighed. "Levi, I'm very sorry to ask, but I was due to pick up a packet of documents from here. I brought your father's commission with me."

He grimaced, as if in irritation, but he took the bagged bundle of cash and retreated into the house, closing the door in my face. I waited ten minutes or so, and was beginning to wonder if I was going to have to buzz again when Levi's shadowy image appeared behind the frosted glass. The deadbolt rolled back and the door opened just a few inches.

The younger Levental regarded me with solemn, hard eyes as he passed me the envelope. "It's not my place to tell my father what his business is… but I know what you do and who you associate with. Everything was fine until you asked him to help you. Don't come back."

He slammed the door before I could reply. At a loss, I tucked it under my arm and headed back out to the street with an unsettling sense of pressure on the back of my neck.

A man in blue and a woman? There were any number of people who had reason to vanish the doctor, but only one came to my mind with any immediacy.

Sergei Yaroshenko.

CHAPTER 6

My head rang all the way back to Strange Kitty. I knew, intellectually, that there was no possible reason for Sergei to target Levental. I hadn't even gone to him for information specifically about the *Organizatsiya*, and I wasn't the only person who found him useful. Levental was part of our network of Sixers, and he was like Switzerland: agreed neutral territory. My common sense also told me that nothing was guaranteed in regards to people holding men like the Doctor sacrosanct, but... no. It could have been the Manellis. He'd been digging around on Celso, after all, but I trusted the Doctor's discretion and methods. No one had pulled him up in fifty years of providing services to the underworld.

I was getting paranoid and vain, trying to loop every uncommon event back to myself. Common sense told me it probably wasn't anything to do with me. If – and it was a huge 'if' – Levental had been given a ticket by the *Organizatsiya* or the Manellis, it was far more likely it had something to do with the change in leadership. Mafia restructuring is very similar to corporate restructuring, in that it's mostly pointless, ego-driven bullshit that enriches and empowers the very few at the expense of those lower on the food chain. Mafia instability tends to result in just as many lost jobs as a corporate takeover, but a lot more work for the city's morgues. Nicolai *was* currently in an awkward position as Avtoritet. Sergei was breathing down the back of his neck and Vanya was in custody, probably squealing about everything he knew. If he'd decided to take out the Doctor, that was the most likely reason. Remove possible weak links: it was one of the first lessons you learned operating in the *Organizatsiya*.

That's what common sense said. My intuition didn't agree. It told me that they'd somehow learned that he had helped break up the child trafficking gig, and that I needed to leave New York City for everyone's sakes - and soon.

When I turned into the dirt parking lot that divided the bikers' clubhouse from the back of Strange Kitty, I saw an unfamiliar car already parked outside the garage entry. Dark charcoal gray, sleek, tinted windows, interchangeable government fleet license plate... it stuck out like a sore thumb among the motorcycles and stacks of tires and parts. I frowned as I got out and brushed down my clothing with absent hands on my way to the door. When I passed by the strange car, it hummed with magic that beat against my skin as I passed by... a ripple of warning heat.

My suspicion was confirmed when I entered the garage common room and saw it emptied of the usual crowd of bikers - human and not - and Club associates. Instead, on the ratty sofa sat the woman who matched the vehicle outside. Special Agent Ayashe Richardson had the build of a triathlete and the sanctimonious air of royalty.

She was in a pantsuit today, the creases sharp enough to shave with, her long falls pulled back into a high ponytail. She was a rhinoceros shifter, an Elder like Jenner. Unlike Jenner, she was a pain in my ass, *musora* bought and paid for by the government.

"Welcome to the party, Rex." Jenner was standing behind the bar with a bottle of Jack Daniels by her elbow and a full glass in her hand. "As you can see, we're having a blast here. You know a drink won't kill you, Ayashe."

"And you know that I don't want to go back to the field office stinking of booze," Ayashe replied. "Because I literally just told you."

Jenner rolled her eye, singular.

"What's the occasion?" Acting cool around the police was an artform, and one I'd had a whole lifetime to perfect. I went to the bar and took a stool, putting myself between the two of them, and immediately noticed the smell of old ...and new... booze. My mouth went dry, and I frowned.

"You," Ayashe said. "I've been told to speak with you."

"Told?" I tried not to look over at the rows of bottles. Instead, I arched an eyebrow, sitting side-on to her with one elbow on the counter, the other loose by the open lapel of my jacket. "You don't sound pleased about it."

"I'm not, but that's not really relevant to the situation at hand."

"By whom?"

Ayashe's lips quirked unhappily. "My boss. That's all I'm saying."

Curious. I glanced at Jenner, who shrugged. "Well, I'm here. Go on."

Ayashe sighed. "First up: this talk is off the books. Period. If anyone asks you anything about this, neither of us were here. In fact, anything that deals with you or Jenner is stuff that never happened, alright? The Agency is really unhappy with last month's body count."

"I'm not thrilled about it either, Sparky," Jenner said, her tone suddenly very dark and stiff. "So maybe the Agency should stop cocking up before they make judgments on shit they have no business being upset about?"

"Jenner." Ayashe's voice also dropped. "This isn't helping. We need some privacy. Come on, Rex, let's go out back."

"No," I said.

Ayashe hadn't been expecting the flat refusal. She'd already moved to rise.

"I'm not going off in private with you anywhere," I replied. "Not after you tried to arrest me over nothing in the Smithsonian. No."

"Kapow. Right on the money." Jenner clicked her tongue and pointed at her with thumb and forefinger, like a pistol. "You're gonna have to live with discretion, girl. I'm the Malek-Kab of this state, and Rex is one of my people. Damned if I'm letting the Feds speak to him without a referee." Jenner waved the bottle of Jack in my direction. "You want a drink, Rex?"

My mouth itched with the same bizarre craving I'd felt in the hotel, but stronger. Much stronger. I swallowed against the nasty sour taste in the back of my throat. "Maybe… one shot of something citrusy, in seltzer water?"

Jenner was slightly taken aback. "Jeez, I wasn't expecting you to take me up. Marnier and water, coming right up."

"Don't make it too strong," I said.

Ayashe didn't look happy to have Jenner push her way into the meeting, but then, she rarely looked happy about anything. "Then you're liable as well, Jenner. This is sensitive information."

Jenner slid me my drink when it was done, then took a swig off the bottle of Jack. She thumped her chest and burped. "Just as well I'm a sensitive lady, right?"

"Jesus." Ayashe sighed again, and fixed her eyes on me. "Fine. A Vigiles Agent was murdered night before last. The murderer…" she paused, trailing off as she gathered her words. "The body shows signs of torture."

I shifted on the stool as adrenaline jolted from heart to hands. An FBI Agent had been murdered, and they'd come to me? I began running through my mental catalog of words of power. I could probably get a spell off faster than she could clap a pair of cuffs on me. "I'm very sorry to hear it."

"They left a calling card," Ayashe said. "'Soldier 557'. Remember him?"

The growing tension in my chest ebbed a little, and I frowned. "The Templum Voctus Sol's hitman."

"We never caught him, but not for lack of trying."
Ayashe crossed her ankle over her other knee, wagging her
foot in agitation. "The guy's a goddamn ghost, and now
he's hit one of our people. We don't know why, we don't
know how. He dismantled her physical and magical
security, got in and out of her house, and no one heard a
goddamned thing."

"Fuck," Jenner said. "I'm sorry, Ayashe."

"You figured out this psycho's coded bullshit the last
time. The regular consultants available to the agency just
aren't turning up anything we can use," Ayashe said to me.
"I put in a good word for your skills."

This was some kind of setup. It had to be. Only fairly
recently, she'd tried to spontaneously arrest me under
RICO and failed to intimidate me enough to pull it off.
Ayashe had been polite ever since I'd laid down my life to
help rescue most of the surviving kids, but her crossed
arms, crossed legs, her woodenness... I wasn't convinced.
She wanted to get me alone so she could separate me from
the protection offered by Jenner's people. Besides that, I
had ethical issues working with the police on anything...
though the mystery of Soldier 557 had been nagging at me.
That, I couldn't deny.

I made a show of bringing the drink to my lips while
I weighed up how much she knew of me. I'd intended to
just wet my lip, but before I really thought about what I
was doing, I pulled a mouthful and swallow. It was... hot.
Red/violet, and oddly refreshing. I grimaced, shaking my
head, and pushed the rest of the glass away. "I'll consider
it, but I don't work for free. I also want a written contract,

signed and dated. We each get a copy and burn it at the end of-”

“Nuh-uh.” Ayashe interrupted me. “No way. There’s no way that’ll fly.”

Who the fuck does this musor’ think she is? A thrill of anger lifted my pulse. I felt my eyes harden as I leaned toward her, hands laced between my knees. “Then go find a *putz* willing to work without a safety net. You’re the one looking for the contractor, so you either hire me on my terms, or you take a hike.”

“I’m not in a position to make this official,” she said through gritted teeth. “I’m the middle-man, okay? You should be grateful that it’s off the books and the Agency isn’t digging up dirt on you.”

I scoffed, and turned back to get my drink. “You, or your Agency, don’t know a damn thing about me. What are they going to dig up? My parking tickets? The only reason you’re treating me this way is because you know I’m a magus.”

“You admitted to working for the Russian Mafia, asshole. To a federal investigator.”

“No. I told you that I knew people in there and could get you some information. Everyone who grows up in Brighton Beach knows someone involved with the *Bratva*. Are you in a gang just because you grew up in The Bron

Rolling her eyes, she threw up her hands in exasperation. “The heads of the Agency don’t give a damn about the difference, and you know it. If they really want to press you, they’ll press you. So maybe consider compromising a little?”

"Of course, forgive me: who wouldn't leap at the chance to work for someone issuing threats on behalf of her faceless organization, without even a basic level of assured security?" I warred with myself for a moment, and threw back another mouthful of soda and liquor. That was it, though - I pushed it away again.

"Rex is right. You want a freelancer, you hire them on their terms, on contract," Jenner said. "And if you don't want to disclose the name of the contact, then they pay up front. Trust for trust. Mister Nobody doesn't get to hire someone on spec."

Ayashe's eyes narrowed. "Fine. It's the Special Agent in Charge of the NY-OSP. Happy?"

I shrugged. "What's the OSP?"

"Office of Supernatural Phenomena," Ayashe replied. "The Vigiles are the investigative and operations branch of the OSP. And they know who you are, Alexi."

Using my name to scare me now. Cute. "I never told you my name, so how, exactly, does the Special Agent in Charge know it?" I tapped my fingers along my thigh in a wave, listening to the modulation of her voice. I could read it better than her expression.

She snorted. "What, you figured blowing up your apartment wasn't going to attract an investigation? You hid a bunch of evidence and revealed a lot more, is what I'm guessing. Don't blame me – I wasn't assigned to that case."

Ayashe was lying: she'd ratted on us, or I'd eat my own fist. Jenner had gone still and cold behind the bar, listening.

"I'm sure you filed a report on everything," I said.

"Sure I did. I have a job to do. But believe me, I left a LOT out. Too much. The only reason I did it was because of the kids."

So, what, she expected me to trust her because she'd only ratted out on me a little bit, and it was 'for the children'? It was comically amatuer. Typical police bullshit. "Look – you're the one breaking all these vaunted laws by trying to bring me in and omitting things from reports, alright? You don't get to hand off all the liability of this 'off the books' consulting business to me. Because what you're really saying is that your boss wants me to kill Soldier 557 for you all, aren't you?"

Ayashe's grim silence told me everything I needed to know.

I stared her down. "No. I know what happens to spooks who work for the Government on the Government's terms - they do their job, and then they get ghosted."

"We're not the bad guys, Rex." Ayashe got to her feet, hands fisted. "This motherfucker raped and murdered a woman in cold blood. Kristen was a good person and a damn good cop, and people like her work around the goddamn clock while sanctimonious assholes like YOU make life miserable for everyone in this goddamn city!"

The grinning predator in me had a good laugh at that. I jerked my chin up, and turned my head back to the bar. "Go tell that to the Wolf Grove kids. We're done here."

"We sure as hell are. I'll go find someone with a conscience." Ayashe's voice curdled red with barely suppressed fury.

"Sure thing," Jenner chirped. "You just walk into the nearest Masonic lodge, and be like: Hey there wizard friends, who wants to go take out a murderous rapist psycho? Nothing in it for you, of course, and no guarantee of support because you're warlock scum, but hey, want to take a crack at it?"

I snorted. "Ayashe, there isn't a spook on the street that will touch this job. Rutherford made it crystal-clear that the 'law' doesn't serve people like you and me." I got to my feet. Ayashe was a foot taller than me in high heels, but I wasn't going to back down – not if she was going to try and drag other spooks into this. "We don't have any damned rights, as far as your Super Special Agent is concerned. This is a pump and dump and you know it."

"And I'll say it again. We are *not* the bad guys here, Alexi."

I fixed her with a level glare. "Listen. Your 'Agency' puts people like me on the same tier as hepatitis and rabid dogs. And you think I'd hunt for them? Advise them? Kill for them? So like Jenner says, go right ahead and turn up at the local mage haunt and flash your badge around. Try the sob story about the dead cop when their friends were disappeared by your people the year before. I dare you."

Ayashe snarled. It was the only warning I got before she was on me, too fast for the HuMan eye to follow, even as my own naked instinct made me throw my guard up, bracing for the impact, but Jenner had already vaulted the bar to the ground in front of me. She took the blow that would have snapped my neck or broken any other bone Ayashe pleased. As frail as she looked, she didn't even stagger. A shivering wave of energy crawled over my skin as Jenner shoved Ayashe back with equal supernatural strength, putting distance between us, and stepped forward.

"If Alexi wants to pick a fight with me, let him deal with the consequences." Ayashe's voice was guttural, an inhuman throaty rumble that she seemed to pull up from her feet. "You're pushing it, Jenner."

"No, whelp – YOU'RE pushing it." Jenner's voice had thickened and deepened as well. "You want to mount a challenge for the state against me? Go right ahead. I'll remind you why I'm the Malek-Kab, and you're not."

Ayashe's eyes had gone completely black, the white sclera retreating to the edge of her eyes. She lowered her head and snorted, shoulders mantling. "And you'd best remember that you're a fucking criminal!"

Now that I had my magic back, I could feel what I'd only dimly sensed before. They both radiated incredible vital force that whipped through the room like a silent thunderstorm around us. Ayashe's was earthy, Jenner's fiery. The hair on my arms stood on end.

Jenner sneered like a cat, licking her teeth. "You don't get to pick and choose your allegiances, Ayashe. You don't get to quote the right of challenge, then turn around and insult your Queen. You've worn out my patience and your welcome."

Neither of them had shifted, but the difference between them was becoming starker by the second. Jenner's age, her Phitonic Mass, perhaps, was far greater than Ayashe's. The weight of centuries pressed down around us, and it threatened to suck my knees to the ground; resisting the urge to kneel made the ends of my femurs ache.

"You can give yourself any stupid title you want. Spotted-Elk proved the Ib-Int is worthless, and so is your attempt to lord over me." Ayashe sounded petulant, her dark face flushed a deep coral red. "I'm-"

"You're one smartass comment away from being declared Outcaste," Jenner's voice was deep, and very old. "It's bad enough that you're working for the Order. Leave. And come back when you remember what you are."

Ayashe's face rippled with rage, but she was slowly being overwhelmed by the weight of Jenner's power. She took a step back, tossing her head and shoulders before she fled, never quite breaking eye contact with the tigress. Jenner stared her down all the way as only a big cat could. The garage door slammed shut, leaving the pair of us in a weird, eerie silence.

"Fuck!" Jenner finally snarled, and slammed the edge of the pool table with her open hand. Her nails caught the worn green felt and tore it, a casual slap that left quarter-inch gouges in the hardwood. I watched her warily as she spun back toward me and stalked back to the bar. "I don't fucking need this right now!"

I swallowed, composing myself, and retook my seat. Binah was nowhere to be seen. Sensible creature. "Are you alright?"

"Fucking fantastic." Her eyes were blazing and bright – orange that transmuted to a vivid gold-green. She had pinpoint pupils that abruptly dilated back to regular size as she thumped bottles back onto their shelves.

"Well, now that the smell of bacon is subsiding, I have bad news." I eyed the half-empty glass, and swallowed against the dryness in my mouth.

"Me too. Let's take it outside. I need a break." Jenner skittered her hand along the countertop, like a cockroach, and pointed at the ceiling before rounding the counter and heading for the door.

Good idea. I needed to get away from the bar before I made myself sick. This happened sometimes… I'd get stuck on eating or drinking one particular thing, fixate on it for a while. One month in college, I ate nothing but BLTs for three meals a day, every day, until Vassily was about ready to strangle me with my uncooked bacon. But it had never happened with alcohol before. I hated booze and always had. The couple of swallows I'd had of the orange-flavor seltzer was churning in my stomach.

While Jenner got her jacket on, I searched for Binah. She'd hidden herself inside the back of the jukebox, and showed little inclination to come out and join us in the cold. The snow in Albany had given way to icy rain in New York, and the yard was shrouded in greasy fog. We trudged over the slushy gravel toward the rearmost rank of motorcycles, the row of bikes recovered from carnage last month. Foremost among them was Mason's old

Bobber. It had been badly damaged in a tumble down a hill the night he disappeared. Jenner had been working on it by herself for the last few weeks. Along with the uptick in her drinking, it was the only visible sign of her grief.

"You think the place is bugged?" I said, once we were away from the building.

"I'm not willing to take the risk. Ayashe can mouth off in there, but I've been careful that we don't talk about anything too sensitive inside for a while now, just in case." Agitated, Jenner pulled the bright blue tarp off Mason's bike, palming the fuel tank with a callused hand. "You go first. What's the situation?"

"My contact has gone missing, the one who helped me find the children. Someone's vanished him. I don't think we'll find the rabbis who were working for Sergei, not unless we capture someone and grill them, which is unlikely. My old tovarischi are going to be on high alert after Yegor."

"Fuck. So this 'MinTex' thing is all we've got left." Jenner made a sound of disgust. "I have some shitty news, too. Ayashe didn't want to touch MinTex, so I'm handing it over to Talya in the hope that she can work some kind of nerd-magic and dig up some intel. Also, while you were out camping, I got a call from one of the Grand High Assholes of Chicago. Guy named Otto Roth. He's what we call a *Khayty*, an outcast, someone who doesn't follow the *Ib-Int*. He also runs an M.C., the Nightbrothers. They're a mixed crew... mages, Weeders, and a few Feeders in the gang. They just rolled into town after they somehow learned that the Tigers are 'only' being managed by a woman. He wants to take over as Malek of the Tri-State Area. He's already the Elder of Chicago."

"Did he threaten you?"

"He wasn't asking me to a fucking line dance. Of course he threatened me." Jenner snorted. "He wants us to clear out and hand over our assets. Claims the club is 'leaderless'. If he pushes me, I'm going to make sure he pisses sitting down for the rest of his life."

"What flavor of Weeder?" I asked.

"No idea," she said. "I'm waiting on contacts of my own to get back to me about him and his forces. The good news is that I found a buyer for the guns."

I arched my eyebrows. "Already?"

"Yeah. A Triad down in Miami wants the lot. Doesn't surprise me: Mexicans are trying to move in on the heroin business down there. The Cartels pack a lot of magical defense." Jenner shrugged her thin shoulders.

"Mm." I loathed the drug business almost as much as trafficking. It was petty, bloody, unnecessarily messy, and it was always the worst sort of people who got into the trade. Even so, it was better to let rival outfits shoot themselves up than to have one or the other side pull ahead and unbalance the ecosystem. "Speaking of dangerous men of East Asian descent, have you seen Angkor?"

"He went out pretty soon after we got back," Jenner said. "Said he was going to stay in a hotel and be back later tonight. Why? Got something to do?"

The first flutters of a totally different sort of anxiety ruffled my gut. If I could tell anyone about asking him to dinner, it would be Jenner, but I couldn't bring myself to say it. "Nothing of concern. I was just wondering."

"No idea where he went." Jenner sighed, gaze roaming over the old motorcycle. "I'm taking the Big Cat Crew to our changing ground tonight. Now that Roth is waving his weenie around, it's time the gang went hunting and spent a bit of cat time together. We haven't been out since before we lost Mason. Think you can hold the fort?"

They were going out? My spirits lifted a little. The timing couldn't be better. Angkor and I had often mourned the lack of privacy we had in the clubhouse... to talk about magic, of course. "I'm going out this evening, but shouldn't be gone for too long. Angkor will be back, too."

She glanced at me, eyes sly. They'd bled back to their usual dark brown. "Meeting up with him, are you? A rendezvous, one might say?"

I cleared my throat. "Something like that."

"You be careful around that boy. Something's not right with him." She turned back to the bike. "It's been a month, and no one knows anything more about him than we did the day we rescued him."

I bristled a little. "He's opened up to me a bit about his past. I understand his need for secrecy... as Ayashe just demonstrated, mages have every reason to be private."

Jenner grunted. "Call it a hunch. There's more to him than meets the eye."

"You haven't talked to him?"

"I've tried," she says. "But it's like trying to catch a wet bar of soap. You ask him a question, and twenty minutes later, you realize you've been talking about yourself the whole time."

"Hmm. Well. I'll take it under advisement." Disquieted, I looked back toward the house. "Alright, well, I have to go and get ready. Is there anything you need?"

"No. Go have fun." Jenner waved me off with a little shoo-shoo motion.

I turned, preparing to leave, then stopped in my tracks and looked back over my shoulder. "Thank you, by the way. For intervening. Ayashe has it out for me."

"No skin off my back. You've hauled ass for the club ever since you got here." Jenner lifted her chin. "You don't need an excuse, Rex. Ayashe's an Elder. She should fucking know better than to attack one of my boys. She thinks the Order have her back, and it's making her cocky."

"Which 'Order' are we talking about, exactly?"

"I knew them as the *Venator Dei*, but that was a long time ago. They're the *Deutsche Ordern*, the Teutonic Knights. Crusaders, basically," Jenner said. "But that's a story for another time. Now, off you go. Wouldn't want you to be late for your date."

And there it was: the dreaded D-word. I doubted she knew she'd hit it on the mark, but I flushed anyway, turning fast enough that she probably didn't notice. Probably.

CHAPTER 7

"What do I do, Kutkha?" I spoke to him as I trudged back to the house, leaving Jenner to brood over her lost partner's bike. "I shouldn't be this wound up about having dinner with someone."

"What do you think you should do, my Ruach?"

I rolled my eyes, slipping back into the house and pushing my way through the door to the back. It was darker and quieter here; the house hadn't seemed to ever leave the 70s. It smelled like leather and motor oil, clean laundry, pasta sauce and coffee. The shag carpet had that musty pleasant smell old houses have. "For once, could you just give me a straightforward answer? My one and only attempt at dating was a disaster. I just asked a man out to dinner. Was it a good decision? I'm trying to be... I'm pushing myself, Kutkha."

"Indeed. Do you find him attractive?"

The flush crept back into my face, heat I felt, even if I couldn't see it. "Of course. I... what does it mean, though?"

"That he's attractive to you," Kutkha replied breezily.

"It won't… cause any problems with you? With magic?" Even after I'd asked the question, I wasn't sure why that had occurred to me.

Kutkha guffawed by way of reply.

"I'm glad *you're* amused." Annoyed, I stomped my way to the bedroom. "I don't know why I'm doing this. Maybe he was right, and I was in love with Vassily. But I never… I don't think I could have ever told him. Doesn't this mean I'm gay? If I find other men attractive?"

"Perhaps. What do you think?"

I ground my teeth as I got my shower kit from the locker, and slammed the bent metal door closed. "I think you're my GOD-damned soul, not a fucking therapist, and you need to give me some insight instead of this psychoanalysis bullshit."

"Am I your immortal soul, or a performing seal?"

"I'll cram a fish right in your fucking beak, your piece of shit." Scowling, I stomped off to the bathroom.

Dating. I didn't date, and for good reason. My one attempt at dating had been a genuine nightmare. I'd met a girl while I was in college, the wealthy daughter of a Chinese businessman and his Anglo-WASP trophy wife. Tina Cheung had been smart, quiet, a little conservative in a repressed, pent-up kind of way. My ritualized courtesy and cold chivalry was appreciated by her parents, and for three or four months, it was good enough for her, too. She and Vassily loathed one another – he and I were sharing a dorm and fought every other week over her – and so the question of her coming to my place was never something I had to worry about. I made the mistake of agreeing to go on a skiing holiday with her one Christmas, though, where I learned three things: firstly, I was far too blue-collar for the chalet life. Secondly, I had no sexual attraction to women, and thirdly, I had an uncontrollably violent response to anyone who tried to grab my dick when I wasn't expecting it. I ran away and never looked back.

It was stupid to be this wound up about something as banal as sharing a meal with someone I'd been sharing a room with for weeks. Angkor wasn't going to twist my arm to do anything beyond eating dinner, but that wasn't the point. The point was that I wasn't attracted to the people I was supposed to be attracted to. Staring at my reflection in the mirror, I heard echoes of my father's taunts, of the slights and slurs of my old 'friends'. 'Faggot' was the least of them. There were *muzhiki* who went gay-bashing on a lark—or more specifically, the bashing of transvestites or transsexuals, because they were the only people they could reliably identify as 'gay'. They believed it was a moral duty, like picking up trash or going to church. Even Mariya had thought queers were the lowest of the low. And maybe I was one of them.

The combination of knowing what those same *muzhiki* had been doing to kids, plus knowing Zane and Angkor—both perfectly masculine men who were not in any way like the stereotypes I'd been raised on—had brought me to this point. The slurs of my youth couldn't stick to the grim, hard-eyed, fit man I saw in the mirror. Even if I turned out gay, it was just another thing that my father was wrong about.

I let out a deep breath, jogged my shoulders a little and stood up straight, then reached for the foam and razor. "Alright, Alexi. Everything will be just fine."

Kutkha had no further input, other than a sense of distant, dark amusement as I went through my suits and shirts, second-guessing myself on what looked best until I realized that no matter what I wore, I still looked like a short, shark-faced bouncer at a high-end strip club. With two hours to kill, I got myself some coffee and took it to the den with the envelope Levi had given me, the dossier on Celso. Nothing to take the edge off a man's pre-date anxiety than planning a hit. I lay a thin blanket over my lap for Binah, and did my best to push thoughts of Angkor and Ayashe from my mind as I broke the seal on the packet.

The Doctor had included a couple of manila folders and a bunch of photos clipped together. The notes were in Cyrillic longhand, and as I laid it out, I realized just how much work had been put into it. It was a full dossier, the kind you had to hire a P.I. to acquire. Addresses, vehicles, hangouts, observable routines—even photos, each one neatly annotated on the back. I pulled one out and turned it over. Celso owned a stake in a gay bar? That was a new one to me.

At the back of the pile of papers was a letter intended for me. It was short, the writing larger and more fluid than the other documents. Frowning, I unfolded it, and read it aloud under my breath.

"I heard you saved a number of children from a terrible fate— bless G-D, who in His wisdom instilled man with courage and good heart. The ways in which you used His gifts are inspiring. I hope you

continue to choose in the spirit of service. Everything we could learn about Manelli is contained in this packet. Take this with my gratitude and blessing and continue to make use of your gifts, for Vassily and Mariya as well as yourself. Please take care, and when you have the time, come and see me. You are welcome to join us in reading Parashat Vayishlach on the 23rd. Y.L."

I set the letter down and sat back, a hand resting on Binah's back. The Doctor's words sucked the wind out of me. He'd been... inspired? Grateful? He'd put real work into this, into helping me – more work than what I'd paid for. What if I had led someone to him? The tenuous certainty I'd built up crumbled as I thought back on what Levi had told me. He'd last been seen with a man in blue and a woman, he'd said. We only had one woman in the *Organizatsiya* – Vera. But no one I could think of wore enough blue for it to be notable.

"You know what... it doesn't matter." I looked down at my cat, brow furrowed. "I have a duty to find him, Binah. Or avenge him, if someone's taken him out. There's not enough people in the world like him. You know what I'm talking about, right?"

Binah squinted her white-blue eyes and rolled onto her back, paws curled in the air. I shook my head, and began reading.

The jitters set in about half an hour before I was meant to leave, and stayed with me through the final preparations and the drive to Manhattan. I took Binah, but the cat had to stay in the car while I was at the restaurant, so I locked her in with a fleece rug, some water and kibble from the corner store, and a puppy pad in her spare litter box – just in case.

I arrived at Club 21 ten minutes early. There were still more waiters than customers at this time of night on a Sunday, so I didn't feel too odd being shown to our table by myself. Watching the staff bustling around, I had to wonder—would they know? I had no idea if men actually dated each other the way I'd dated Tina. Dinner, little gifts, that kind of thing. And if they did, who was supposed to do the rituals? Pulling out chairs, opening doors, picking up an extra copy of the newspaper or flowers were all things drummed into me by Mariya. Most of the women I'd known knew the counterpoint to that social dance: Crina, for example. That was just how things were supposed to happen. I didn't think I could stand to be catered to that way by another man. If Angkor tried, would it offend him if I refused? Would I offend him if I tried?

I passed a hand back over my head, checking over for patches of stubble I might have missed. When the waiter came around, mild and inquiring, I shook my head. "I'm waiting for someone."

"Ahh." He smiled knowingly. "Would you like anything to drink? An aperitif?"

I did, kind of, but I pressed down on the baseless craving and shook my head. "Just water."

After he left, I sat back and checked my watch—it was exactly seven o'clock. New York traffic being what it was, I didn't expect Angkor to be right on time.

The waiter brought a pitcher of water, two glasses, a little basket of bread. I ate a piece to take the edge off the dry-mouthed urge to order a glass of wine. Ten past. Eleven.

When the door to the restaurant opened and a lean, broad-shouldered silhouette shadowed the wall, I perked up, only to frown when a thin man in a cheap suit and open blazer stepped inside, closely followed by a woman in a cocktail dress. I wasn't the sort of person to be easily bored, but I found myself fighting the urge to fiddle with napkins as people began to filter in and the clock crept toward seven thirty. My thoughts turned to my cat after a while. Binah had water and food out there, but my imagination conjured up images of opportunistic thieves poaching her out of the car. Idle anxiety, really.

Every now and then, the waiter passed by like a cruising shark, eyeing the empty seat and clearly restraining himself from speaking to me. As the minutes ticked by, tables were filling up with couples and groups of friends.

All of a sudden, I felt like everyone in the restaurant was looking at me: the lack of food, even a drink, and the guilty empty seat with the untouched glass. The pressure of the crowd of strangers weighed on the back of my neck, which was itching under the edge of the fresh white collar. On the next pass, I flagged the waiter down.

"Yes?" He pulled up hopefully.

"Wine," I said. "What do you recommend?"

"What are you planning to eat?"

I looked over at the empty place. "Probably nothing. What do you have that's sweet?"

"We… uh… well, we have a very nice house Riesling."

"Sure." I had no idea what a Riesling tasted like, but it had been Vassily's go-to dinner wine. The server brought me a big bubble glass. It had a weird fruit-juice aftertaste, but it was stronger than beer or the mixed drink Jenner had given me. Before I knew it, it was a couple minutes past eight, the glass was empty, and I was swaying in my chair. I waited with faint hope that Angkor would stride in through the door, flush-faced and embarrassed, but hope didn't have a fighting chance against the humiliating reality. The fucking asshole had stood me up.

When I motioned for the waiter, he came to the table with his notepad in both hands, like a shield.

"Bad roads, I guess." I ground the words out through a vise, taking out my wallet and pulling a ten and a five from it. "I'm sorry for taking up the table for so long."

"Not a problem." The waiter now looked as embarrassed as I felt. "Are you sure you don't-"

"No." I slapped the money down, pushed back from the table, and wove through the tables of laughing people with the weight of their eyes on my back.

I stumped down the wet sidewalk, realized I'd forgotten the umbrella, didn't care. I was dizzy, sick, and my head was buzzing with bad noise, like a T.V flicking between channels. On one channel, we had Alexi Sokolsky—short, bullish, beaten around the face—now the hot gossip among the staff at Club 21. Maybe they felt sorry for me. Maybe they thought the 'girl' I was waiting on dodged a bullet by skipping the date. Either way, I wasn't ever going to be able to go back to that place again.

The next channel was fear that something had happened to Angkor, that he wasn't just on one of his typical jaunts out into the hills. He wasn't stupid, and he wasn't absent-minded. He was, however, not invulnerable. The Deacon had gotten him once before. Fuck.

I cut down an alley on the zigzag route back to my car. About halfway down, a shadow peeled away from the wall behind me, trembling ahead on the dim pavement. I headed past some windows and used them to look back for my tail: nothing but a lone mugger. Blue-white skin, thin build, black hoodie. He walked with the skulking manner of a coyote, and as soon as I slowed, he called out to me. "Hey! Sir! Sir? You got a light on you?"

A mugger? They usually took one look at me and... oh, right. I was all dressed up. New suit, nice shoes... I probably looked like an easy meal from the back.

The prospect of violence turned the heat down on the churning boil of self-loathing, humiliation, and murderous fantasy I'd been stewing. I stopped and turned to face the guy, sizing him up. A bit taller than me, decent reach, the kind of bottom feeder who relied on being too scary to refuse. He moved like a scavenger, not a predator. "Sure. Come here and I'll fix you up."

He was already reaching inside his coat, grin broad and cocky. His tool of choice turned out to be a plain old carving knife. It had been sharpened to a thin crescent.

The kid held it out level with my face, arm at full extension, elbow locked. "Get your wallet out and hand it over, man, and no one has to-"

I stalked forward, grabbed his wrist, and pushed it up high as I pulled him into my knee. He was so shocked that I got two good blows to the groin and a headbutt in before he had time to react, and by then, it was too late. He flailed, yelping in alarm as I charged him back into the nearest wall and slammed him back against it. I prized the knife out of his soft fingers and jammed the point of the blade up under the soft of his jaw, like the knife in the dream.

His eyes were white and wild. Like a frightened... Horse. "Hey... hey man, please... I was just trying... I mean..."

I was breathing hard. Not from exertion. The world had narrowed down to the smell of terror, the rapid jump of his pulse against the blade. Even with gloves on, the sensation of his living heart carried through the metal to my fingertips. When he reached up to pluck at my arm, I ground the tip of the knife in just enough to draw a thin trickle of blood. His expression, the way his body shifted into abject submission, wasn't only satisfying. It was exciting. My craving for booze vanished, replaced by bloodlust.

The Yen. It was the Yen making me do this shit. But just because I knew what it was didn't mean I could stop it. Or that I didn't like it.

"Let me tell you something, you little punk," I hissed a cloud of wine-scented breath into his face. "Tonight I went out on a limb for someone and was stood up, and you know what I want? Right now?"

"No!" He squeaked.

I pulled him down until we were nose-to-nose. "I want nothing more than to take your little pig-sticker right there, slowly insert it into your chest, cut a circle around, pull out your fucking heart like an apple core, and throw it at the nearest fucking wall."

"Okay, man! I get it! You're fuckin' crazy!"

In the frozen moment before I pulled him away from the wall, shoved him, told him to get lost, I heard a sharp *pafph!* of sound. Something hit me in the ass. That was the last thing I felt before my knees wobbled and gave out, and I crumpled unconscious to the wet ground.

CHAPTER 8

When waking up inside of a walk-in freezer is the highlight of your day, you know you screwed up somewhere between getting out of bed and getting nailed by a tranq dart by government stormtroopers. I was betting my screw-up was about five-foot eleven, dark skinned, had long braids, transformed into a belligerent herbivore, and had now officially written herself onto my hit list.

The freezer wall hummed against my back. They'd partially stripped me, leaving my underwear, undershirt and socks on, barely enough to stop me from passing out with hypothermia. I was groggy, heavy-limbed, and had to struggle out of a weak narcotic haze to get my bearings, such as they were. I was blind, deaf, and dumb. There was a heavy gag in my mouth that depressed my tongue; I had a blindfold on, and earmuffs over what felt like foam earplugs. The only reasons I knew I was in a freezer were because of the sharp biting cold, the vague stale food smell, and the buzzing I felt through my jaw. I'd thrown enough bound men into freezers that I could put two and two together and get four. There was only one reason you chilled guys like this, too. They were softening me up for something, and given the illegal nature of the arrest, I doubted it was a free call to my lawyer.

The rumble of boots on a metal floor telegraphed through my cold flesh, breaking my reverie. Skin jumping, I turned my head towards the source of the vibrations. I was not surprised when two pairs of hands reached down, scooped me up by the elbows, and set me on feet made painful from the chill. I didn't get to stay on them for long: the Vigiles dragged me out of the freezer like a carcass headed for the saw room. I didn't help them any. Instead, I hung like a dead weight as I sharpened my teeth, gathered my wits, and prepared to duel.

I had no idea where I was, and no idea where I was going. As far as I could tell, twelve hours had passed since my arrest, maybe fifteen. Wherever we were, it was wet and cold. The air had the damp, chilly, almost-but-not-quite moldy smell of an ice skating rink. I didn't mind New York winters, but I generally wore clothes, not my boxers and ten pounds of cold iron around hands and ankles. After what felt like half an hour of pushing and pulling, we passed a threshold with a ward so powerful that the hairs on my skin lifted as we passed. Dizziness washed over me in a leaden wave, and for a moment, I was sure that the magic laid on this place had cut my link with Kutkha. A spike of fear shot through my gut as I groped for him, vanishing when he reached back to me and cool clarity returned.

After a few stops and starts, the enforcers pushed me down into a chair with straps on the armrests and legs, holding me down with unnecessary force. They left the mitts on even once my arms were bound. The tension was just beginning to ebb from my chest when my nose stung with the smell of alcohol, just before latex-gloved fingers swabbed the inside of my elbow and then inserted a needle and catheter. A few seconds later, a cold sensation spread through the vein and up my arm.

My whole body armored with base animal fear, ears ringing, mouth and eyes drying up. No one I'd heard of who'd been arrested and sent to Silverbay had ever returned. There was a possibility that it was because they put down spooks with lethal injection by default. But then why the beating and the cool down? I swallowed around the gag and focused back on my breathing as they taped over the IV and left.

Someone pulled the earmuffs off, then pulled out the plugs. The blindfold was next. I squinted at the flood of white light that replaced the warm darkness, unable to see anything for several eye-watering moments. The gag was loosened and then worked out past my teeth. It was the ratchet kind, with a short tongue depressor some Inquisitor had designed to keep us warlocks from mumbling hocus-pocus when we were supposed to be quiet. Blinking away involuntary tears, I turned and squinted down at my elbow to see what they'd done. The IV was attached to a tube that wound up and away behind me. As far as I could tell, it was plain old saline.

There were only three other things in the room besides me. A mirror on wheels, directly in front of me, and two identically dressed, but very different-looking men. The one on the left was a pinch-faced egghead: tall, slender, young but balding, he looked like the human incarnation of constipation. He wore a pair of frameless glasses on his beaky nose. The other man was Hispanic, dark-complexioned and handsome in a heavy, sullen way offset by how dim he looked. The guy might as well have been a wax figurine. He stared vacantly at a spot just below my nose. The lights were on, but no one was home.

"Alexi Sokolsky. What a pleasure to finally meet you." Egghead had a stiff, formal Gold Coast lockjaw accent. He was so WASP-ish that I was pretty sure he built nests out of chewed-up tax returns and old copies of the Wall Street Journal. "I am Agent Keen, and this is Adeptus Black. I'm sure you have at least some idea of why you might be here?"

"You're really into macrobiotics, aren't you?" I squinted at him. "Bowel health."

Agent Keen's brows contracted slightly, like he'd smelled something unpleasant. "You assaulted an FBI agent today, Mister Sokolsky, which is more than enough for me to rule you unfit for release today. I suggest you listen and comply."

The KGB used this exact tactic to erase political prisoners under Stalin: accusing them of things the government had actually done. If you'd been beaten and robbed by a cop, you were the one who'd committed an 'assault'. Fuck that. "You illegally detained me."

"Human beings are 'illegally detained'," Keen replied, cocking his head at an angle. "You are an unregistered warlock, and by using your magic to assist with murders, kidnappings, torture, and other lovely adventures, you put yourself into the special extrajudicial process also reserved for other kinds of terrorists."

I rolled my eyes. "I don't even have a parking ticket to my name."

Agent Keen looked down his nose at me. "But you have been identified as the practitioner who killed Yegor Gavrilyuk, and are a suspect in at least twelve other murders on behalf of the so-called 'Brighton Beach Mafia', Mister Sokolsky."

Only years of experience in The Game kept me from freezing up.

"We have first-hand testimony of your role from multiple sources, after the arrests made in September in connection with the Wolf Grove kidnapping," Keen continued. "And not only testimony. Several members of your old Organization were able to give us quite detailed descriptions of your magical and non-magical activities and provide artifacts you'd made for them."

My only reply was stony silence. He took an honest-to-god silk monogrammed handkerchief from his pocket and unfolded it, revealing a pendant engraved with old Slavonic runes.

"Recognize this?" He arched a thin eyebrow.

"It's a protective talisman," I said. "And?"

"The nature of the talisman isn't the reason it interests me." Keen motioned to Black with an ivory cold-fish hand. Black hadn't moved for the duration of our conversation. "Adeptus Black here is a very specialized type of magus, Mister Sokolsky. Tell him what you do, Tomas."

"Arcane Forensics." Tomas' voice sounded like a recorded message.

"Tomas can 'match' the residual resonance of magical workings to the person that cast them. Every warlock has a kind of fingerprint to their magic, you see. We call it a matrix. A warlock's matrix is unique to him or her, and can be matched over a series of scenes until we find the practitioner." Keen wasn't even trying to conceal how smug he was about this. "You've been leaving your fingerprints all over the place for years, and we have a record of every one of them. How many people, Sokolsky? Fifteen? More?"

I didn't feel like anyone was trying to get inside my head, so I had a think about it. I'd killed my first man at sixteen – in self-defense – and taken my first hit at nineteen. I'd averaged four hits a year for ten years, plus collateral when times were crazy. The crack boom in the mid-80s was the worst for that, so my headcount was really closer to forty. "That's the biggest load of horseshit I've ever heard. Some mages work with specific formulas and magical patterns with endurance in mind, but the energy itself doesn't hang around indefinitely waiting for your pet automaton to come along and match it up. I'm a practitioner, I won't deny that – and I'm a good enough practitioner to know you're talking out of your ass."

Joshua smiled indulgently. "I'm very sorry to burst your bubble of incredulity, but individual Phitonic matrices are a very well-established form of evidence. For example, the tangled mess you left behind at the murder site of Eric Kovacs."

Well, shit. I *had* killed Eric Kovacs back in 1986, and there was only one person still alive who knew that I had

– Nicolai Chiernenko, my old Kommandant[4]. "So why are we here, then? Summary execution?"

"If you are sent to our facility, execution is a possibility," Keen replied. "But we understand that magical ability of your level is rare, and we prefer rehabilitation when possible. Your cooperation could earn you a more lenient sentence. Tomas used to be a warlock for the *La Familia Michoacana*, actually. Now he's one of us."

I glanced at Adeptus Black. "Tomas looks like he had a bad back-alley lobotomy."

He frowned. Maybe there was someone home after all.

"Fine. Keep on with this infantile behavior, Mister Sokolsky. See where it gets you. We have a cult to disband and a cop killer to catch, and I would be more than happy to send you off to meet your maker, write up the incident report, and then get back to work." Keen's self-congratulatory manner faded into sobriety. He stood, hands folded behind his back. "There is a pump ready to administer a very large, one might even say 'lethal' dose of cyanide and tetrodoxin behind you, in the event you were to try and perform magic. I could claim your hands twitched the wrong way, and my superior would give me a slap on the wrist and have me interviewed before I was sent along my merry way. But the fact of it is, you have real experience with the Templum Voctus Sol, and I'd

---

[4] A CELL COMMANDER OR THE LEADER OF A BRIGADA, WHO ANSWERS TO AN AVTORITET. THEY ARE GENERALLY HANDS-ON STREET COMMANDERS WHO LEAD SMALL TEAMS AND DIRECTLY SUPERVISE CRIMINAL OPERATIONS.

prefer to reach a deal rather than claim self-defense. Work for us, and you get to assist Agent Richardson with her case. You may even get conditional freedom as a valued asset on the street. Wouldn't you prefer that, too?"

I ground my jaws together. No matter how much I hated The Deacon, Nicolai, and Sergei, I wasn't a snitch. I was preparing a retort when Kutkha's eyes flashed into my inner eye, along with his voice. *Submit.*

Keen's bland, murky blue eyes glinted with the cold patience of a killer. He'd probably taken out spooks who'd done half the shit I'd done, and felt good about his role in cleaning up the streets. His conviction in my inherent lack of humanity was clearly absolute.

"What do you want, then?" I ground the words through my teeth.

Keen smiled. He almost looked relieved... or disappointed. "Compliance with Ayashe Richardson, to the letter. We need someone who can take out this 'Soldier 557' person without needing to jump through a million hoops. There are operatives capable of it, but they don't have the required leeway on US soil."

"You want me to kill him," I said.

"A flock of little birds told me that you're very good at it," Keen said. "And like you, Soldier 557 has forfeited his rights under conventional law. Unlike you, he's murdered one Federal Agent and kidnapped another, and there is no chance of a deal. He will be put down like a dog at the first opportunity. We know the Templum well enough to believe that a chance of interrogation is slim to none. We can infer a lot of information from his body."

"You're sure it's a 'him'?"

"Our first victim was raped," Keen replied. "The sex of the perpetrator was very obvious."

Well, I guess that cleared that mystery. "I'm not convinced Soldier 557 is human."

"It doesn't matter, as long as they're taken down. Treat this seriously, Mister Sokolsky. Your life is conditional on this investigation, and you have three days to make a report. We will reassess your role at that time."

"Three days isn't long enough to do anything." The moment of inner reconciliation evaporated then. "You don't even know where he is, let alone if he even was-"

"We know it was this 'Soldier 557', and the Templum Voctus Sol. That is not in doubt." Agent Keen inclined his head to the side and glanced past me with a small nod. I tensed, searching the mirror reflection, but only saw a shadow stir at the edge of the glass. A human silhouette, tall and broad-shouldered, but lean. "But first, something to remember this by."

"What-?" I couldn't move in the chair they'd bound me to, not even to twist around. I was searching for a way to move when my face and scalp began to itch. Cheeks, chin, upper lip, my bare brows... they crawled like a carpet of insects. My hands twisted painfully inside the metal gauntlets as I squirmed. There was rippling, creeping pain as hairs twisted out the pores of my skin, growing with unnatural speed. The sensation of itching built to a fiery extreme as my hair erupted, lengthened, and curled. I shook and twisted, cursed, sobbed, broke my nails against the inside of the gauntlets. If I'd been able to reach my face, I would have torn it off. Agent Keen watched on in amusement while Adeptus Black stared with flat black eyes.

The prickling creep slowed, then came to a rustling stop. I opened watering eyes to see an unfamiliar face. My hair fell down to my upper arms, floss-like and fine. My beard was down to my collarbones, unkempt and patchy. I'd never grown facial hair before, ever. Keen made a small gesture with his hand, and I felt magic throb through the room.

The color drained out of my formerly mousy-blond hair, turning it all the color of steel. I was staring at it, aghast, as Keen came up behind me. He took a pocket knife from his jacket, wound a lock of hair around one lily-white finger, and nicked it off.

"Three days until we touch base, Alexi. Do not try to flee; do not attempt to bargain, and do obey Ayashe's every word when it comes to this case," he said, his voice a fluted yellow-green buzz this close to my ear. "We have your photographs, fingerprints, blood and hair, and we *will* find you."

CHAPTER 9

I was kicked out of the back of a van near the parking lot where I'd left my car. They'd tied a soft cloth hood over my head and around my neck with a bow. I tore at the hood while the doors rolled shut and the van roared away, and gained my vision just as they rounded the corner. Furious, I stumbled up after it, only to discover the slipknot cuffs around my ankles. Face, meet road.

It was past dawn, light enough to see by. They'd tossed out a bag with my clothes, keys, and knife. Irritated, I rolled to sit and freed myself, then picked it up and stumbled off to the car. Binah had her paws up on the window, meowing frantically as I limped across the lot and unlocked the door with shaking hands.

What a perfect end to this complete shit-wreck of a day. When I tried to curse, the beard tickled my mouth and I began to spit and sputter. Twitching uncontrollably, I found something to tie my hair back and used the knife to frantically saw at my face. After a couple of months of voluntary baldness, the prickling creep of hair against my skin was agonizing. I was coming out in hives, and all the hair was gray – all of it. Head, arms, body, crotch.

There was nothing to do after that but try to get comfortable and sleep off the tranquilizer fog. Several hours later, I woke up overheated and dry-mouthed. It took me several seconds to realize that I was still in my car, that the windows were foggy, and that everything smelled like cat shit. Someone was pounding angrily on my window. The attendant, or a security guard. Grimacing, I started the car and backed out, scattering him away from the door. When I was sure he wasn't going to leap in front of the grille to stop me, I pulled the steering wheel around and turned the car with a screech, then accelerated off before he had the sense to take my license plate down.

God help me. I needed a haircut. And no matter how much I told myself I didn't want it, I needed a drink.

When I was able to park again, I opened the windows and dumped the contents of Binah's litterbox into a trashcan. Reeking, I stumbled into the nearest barbershop. I probably looked like a drunk hobo. We were third in line, and I struggled to stay anchored on my familiar instead of scratching frantically at my face.

When I got into the chair, the barber looked at me inquisitively. "So… what can I do for you today?"

"Off," I grunted, trying not to look at my reflection. "The beard, off. Then talk."

He gave me a watery smile and picked up a pair of shears.

I only regained my ability to properly human once the beard was down to half an inch or so, but I still couldn't meet my own eyes. Once I could speak without pain, I had the barber give me my old hairstyle: hair cut short and slicked back down to a point at the nape of my neck. Combed and oiled, it looked like polished pewter.

"Hafta say I never had a man as young as you with hair like this," the barber said once we started settling up at the register. "Let it get away from you, did you?"

"Something like that." I still couldn't bear to look at myself in any of the mirrors. I'd gotten used to going bald, and the gray hair made me look like a stranger to myself.

He groaned knowingly. "Jeez. I know how it is – last time I didn't have a job, I gained, like, twenty pounds, yanno? You clean up good, though. Good luck, buddy."

Oh, I had a job. I had to find an elusive, invisible Morphordian killer that had eluded the best efforts of the Vigiles and the city's shapeshifters for three months, and bring him down within three days or face execution by the *musora*. Alternatively, I could pull a trigger in Ayashe's face for getting me into this mess and skip town for as long as I could. The only thing - the *only* thing - that was keeping Ayashe alive right now was the fact that she had two young daughters.

I retraced my steps back over the Williamsburg Bridge, but slowed down in front of Strange Kitty as my eyes snagged on something out of place. The metal double doors that opened up into the bar were slashed with red spray paint, the image was of a crudely rendered horned skull. All the fluorescent tubes that advertised the different beers the dive served up had been smashed. Zane and three other men were standing outside, smoking and talking with lowered heads and folded arms. They all turned when they heard the crackle of my tires over the gravel, and when I stumbled out, Zane broke from the pack at a quick walk.

"Jesus, Rex... are you...? Is that a wig?" He stopped a few feet away, staring.

I let Binah out, then reached up and ran my hand back over my head. "No, it's real hair. The short version is that I was kidnapped by the Vigiles last night and they wanted to make sure I had something to remember them by. What's going on?"

Zane frowned. "The Nightbrothers gatecrashed Strange Kitty sometime last night. Broke the lights and upstairs windows, tagged the door, threw gas grenades in through the holes they made. Jenner's about to go nuclear."

"I can't blame her." I jerked my shoulders. "When are we going?"

"Huh?" Zane tilted his head.

"To trash them," I said. "We aren't going to let them fuck up the place and walk, are we?"

"Oh, right... well sure, if we knew where to find them, we'd be over there stomping the shit out of them." Zane hung by my side as I wove toward the entry to Strange Kitty. "Problem is, we don't know where they are. We're working on it."

"*Kurva blyat.*" I stomped up to the graffitied doors. "Has Angkor come back?"

Zane shook his head grimly. "No. You might not want to mention his name around Jenner, either."

At least half the club was present and accounted for inside the empty bar: all of the Big Cat Crew, the inner core of shapeshifters, plus the plain old human tough guys. The air was hazy with smoke, the atmosphere oddly oppressive. By night, the bar was lively. During the day, without patrons or music, it looked like a cramped, dirty, brownstone hovel. The bar, central pillars, and walls were chewed up with bullet holes from when the TVS had raided the place. In the spirit of the establishment, the Tigers had filled the holes in with clear putty and varnished over them so they could still be seen.

"Well, look who just walked in out of the gutter." Jenner planted her hands on her hips as I trudged in, her scarred face twisted in a scowl. "What the fuck is going on, Rex? We were about to launch a fucking search party for you and that Korean piece-of-shit thief."

"Thief? What?" My stomach clenched unhappily. I was so hungry that I felt sick.

"The little fuck took money out of the strongbox," Jenner said. "Picked the lock or something. We didn't notice it was gone until today."

"Couple of grand in cash right out of the gawldamn safe," Ron said. "You know anythin' about it, Rex?"

I shook my head in disbelief. "You're sure it was him?"

"You were wherever the fuck you went," Jenner replied. "Angkor was the only one who spent enough time after we picked up the guns to get away with a job like that. AND he took a bunch of ammo, smokes, and all his shit out of the Barracks."

Now I definitely felt sick. My mouth was dry, pulse throbbing under my tongue, and I found my gaze drawn to the bar against my will. "I went to meet him for dinner last night and got stood up. Ayashe went tattling to her boss about me refusing to work for her, so the Vigiles rolled me as soon as I left the restaurant. Shot me in the ass with a tranq, put me on ice, and threatened to kill me if I didn't do what they want. They didn't ask anything about the club, and I didn't tell them."

Abruptly, the room seemed to swell with the sort of energy that heralded a storm as the gang members exchanged glances, and then as one, to Jenner. Her expression was grave. "You're sure?"

"Yes. The Agent in charge mentioned her by name a couple times," I replied. "Said I'd 'assaulted an FBI agent'. Could only have been Ayashe."

"That fucking bitch." Jenner's eyes narrowed. "I'm calling a meeting with the Pathfinders tomorrow. Fuck her. What did the Vigiles want?"

"The same thing she did. For me to hit Soldier 557 and take the fall." I sighed.

"You need to leave," Ron said. "T'aint safe having you stay here anymore, Rex."

"You shut your goddamned mouth, Ron." Jenner snapped. "People don't throw people to the fucking Templars."

"Agreed," Zane said. "Don't want to hear that kind of talk from anyone, about anyone."

Ron sniffed, glaring at me. "I don't like it."

"And you think I do?" The compulsion to drink something came over me, a sudden stab of impulse. Before I knew what I was doing, I'd stalked behind the bar and found myself sloshing gin into a glass. When I looked up, everyone was staring at me.

"What?" I narrowed my eyes.

"Rex, are you…?" Talya squinted back. "Are you okay?"

"As good as anyone who was shot in the ass and spent all night chained to a chair could be. Why?" The gin smelled like Pine Sol, and my hand shook for a moment before I resolutely threw the drink back. It hit my empty stomach like fire, and for a moment, I thought I was going to be sick... until the heat spread through my gut and up, all the way to my hands.

"You just…" she glanced at Jenner.

Jenner was staring at me in naked confusion as I poured a smaller second glass. She shook her head, as if clearing mental fog, and blinked a couple times. "Okay. Before we go any further, I want to acknowledge something. Everyone's riled up. The Nightbrothers and the Vigiles both know we're low on manpower. Don't let these fucks divide and conquer us, alright? We fucking know better than to let ourselves be sliced and diced by the enemy."

Big Ron grunted, looking at Talya. She hissed, like a cat, and he grimaced and turned away.

"Angkor's another story," Jenner continued. "He's betrayed the trust of the club."

The second shot of gin went down easier than the first. Waves of relief spread through me, so powerful that I thought I was going to lose my feet. I held onto the edge of the counter and leaned forward. The effect it had was... humiliating, mostly.

"Yeah. Something's up with that guy," Zane said. "You hung out with Angkor the most, Rex. What do you think?"

I gathered myself, pushing through the fog of liquor. My mouth tasted awful. "I thought I could trust him, until last night. He made contact with the club about a week after the children were abducted from Wolf Grove, correct?"

"Yeah." Jenner frowned. "He said he was in New York to look into a human trafficking ring."

Talya cleared her throat with a prim little 'hem-hem'. "He told 'John Spotted-Elk' that he was searching for a missing person. They talked in private after that... I don't know what was said."

Frowning, I rinsed the glass under the tap, and belatedly realized that my gloves were still on. "Did he ever tell you what his affiliation was?"

Jenner shook her head, her expression darkening to a scowl. "No. He talked the talk, though... knew everything there was to know about our laws, terms, customs. Spotted-Elk vouched for him. So did Michael."

"And that counts for fuck-all," Big Ron added. "One wuz a liar, the other's dead."

"He convinced John to tell him where to find Lily and Dru's changing ground," Talya added. She sounded nervous speaking up, but the others were listening. "Then he went there, and disappeared."

"That was when The Deacon must have captured him, tipped off by John," I said. "Assuming that's what even happened. Because I don't know any more. You're right, Jenner. He's been avoiding questions."

"It doesn't make any sense to me." Zane rocked back on his heels. "He pulled his weight right to the end. Healed people up, fought alongside us. Hell, he passed out when he was trying to keep Rex here alive."

"Sure. But he still could have been spying for someone that whole time," Jenner said.

Legions of small things - things I'd noticed in passing, but never connected - were coming together in an unpleasantly satisfying way. I didn't even bother to conceal my growing bitterness. "Well, if you think about it... what better cover for a spy or a saboteur than a devoted healer?"

My words seemed to shut off the sound in the room. Glances were exchanged, arms crossed.

"His erratic behavior started with the blood rain," I said, after a pregnant pause. "He's talked to me in the past about having sustained frontal lobe damage from the torture the TVS inflicted on him, but he has been working magic to slowly heal that damage... so I doubt he had a physical problem that caused him to compulsively steal money and run."

"Yeah. Fucked if I know what it is." Jenner made a motion with her fingers, thumb and little finger extended, and gestured toward herself. Talya nodded, and went around me pour her a drink. "You ever get that feeling like someone or something is arranging pieces on a board? It looks like a puzzle from your side, but it's a strategy on theirs."

"It's beyond a feeling. It's a reality. I have three days to find a lead on Soldier 557." The lapse of tension was beginning to fade into an even more powerful sensation of nausea.

"So what? You gonna work for the cops?" Ron snarled. "You a fuckin' snitch, now?"

I didn't give a shit if he shapeshifted into a lion. I was going to tear him a new asshole. Furious, I pushed back from the bar and nearly kept going, stumbling as my head reeled. "Now you listen to me, you fat-!"

Before it got any further than that, Zane materialized by my elbow and took my arm. The sudden shock of contact made me lose my train of thought, the old skin-crawling discomfort of unsolicited touch.

"You heard Jenner, Rex," he said. "Ron, you need to cool the hell down."

"Zane, go take Rex and put him to bed," Jenner said. She sounded tired. "And Ron, you and me are gonna have a talk. Upstairs. Band-Aid, Cliff, I want a plan for the Nightbrothers by tomorrow night. Get a warband worked out and track those assholes down."

"You got it, boss." Band-Aid, one of the humans in the Tigers, saluted two fingers to his faded red mohawk.

Zane steered me to the hallway leading out to the back yard. As the smell of the toilets roiled over me, my stomach lurched. When we emerged from the darkness of Strange Kitty into the light outside, I stumbled blindly to the nearest wall and violently retched into the grass.

Zane shadowed me anxiously. "You know... Talya had a point in there. None of us have ever seen you drink, and you just chugged a whole lot of neat Bombay."

"Revolting st-stuff," I gasped. My head was pounding, spastic tension gathering in my hands and face. Fuck, not this again. "I have-HAVE-to s-s-sleep."

"We need to get you inside." Zane seemed to recognize the need to speak slowly and clearly. I gave him the 'okay' gesture with thumb and forefinger, swayed to my feet, and tried not to look at his face on the way into the clubhouse.

The Barracks was blessedly quiet, the air still, the light muted. I sat down heavily on the edge of my bed, flinching at the sound of the curtains being drawn. The raspy sound and the change in light set off a fresh round of twitching. "You... said he cleared... out? Did you... check the tr-tr-trash?"

"Huh. Good idea." Zane stood, and I shuddered as the springs in the bed creaked under his bulk, the sound like an electric shock. "Let's see... nothing here, really. Note with an address on it, a couple of menus... you know what's at 21 W 52nd St?"

Club 21. My cheeks burned with a fresh wave of humiliation and anger. That piece of shit hadn't even intended to meet me. He'd chucked the address. I was so pissed off that I forgot how to speak English. "*Vin khuyzbyrav kompromat!*"

"Huh?" Zane turned back to me.

I drew a deep breath, getting back into the right stream. "Compro...mizing... information. Angkor... gathered compromising information. Took notes. Won trust. Left."

Zane didn't say anything for a couple minutes – maybe he was frowning. I couldn't tell. "You think he's gone for good?"

I nodded, throat thick. That fucking asshole.

"You need sleep," Zane said. "Rest up. Don't worry about Ron either, alright? We'll sort him out."

Zane's shadow fell across me, wavered, and then withdrew. I lifted my legs and heaved myself onto the bed properly, a hand over my eyes. Tiny thrills of spasming motion jerked through my limbs until the door closed and the room fell still.

Angkor had gotten himself mixed up in something bad - that was the only reason people acted this way. A small, dark voice told me the events of the night before had been awfully coincidental. Somehow, the Vigiles knew where I'd be, and were in a perfectly timed position to be able to take me out. The mugging had surely been staged, meaning they probably also had a good psychological profile they'd been building for a while. But where had the input for the profile come from? And how had they known I'd been the one who killed Yegor, when I'd taken such pains to clean up after myself?

I wasn't buying the 'Phitonic matrix' thing. Wards and other static enchantments had matrices, but once an act of magic was done, the energy left behind was diffuse and blobby. Places where certain kinds of magic was performed over and over again - churches, temples, oratories - or where particular kinds of acts took place accrued a magical thumbprint of sorts, but that egregore was also diffuse and fragile enough that it generally dissolved when neglected. Keen's assertion that a mage could be profiled by the magic they left behind just didn't hold up. The only time I could see it being true would be if they were profiling an enchanter, drawing patterns from permanent magical effects. That meant the Wardbreaker was a potential liability, but I hadn't used the Wardbreaker to kill Yegor. The *Organizatsiya* had ratted me out to the cops, and the 'magical evidence' was a contrivance to get me to find and kill Soldier 557.

Soldier 557 had torn apart two Elder shapeshifters before they'd had time to react to his presence. He was possibly a Weeder, possibly a Feeder, maybe an evil summoned entity, like a DOG, maybe something else. All I knew is that he seemed to know something about me, that he had a flamboyant, proud streak and a flair for the theatrical, and that he didn't recognize the value of technology. A HuMan couldn't have taken Lily and Dru Ross out the way he had, and magic couldn't directly affect Weeders - so that ruled out the Deacon's time magic trick. He had to be someone very good, and very specialized.

And now, I had three days to find him. Just wonderful.

CHAPTER 10

I roused in the early evening, head pounding, mouth dry. The urge for alcohol was back, irritably dismissed in preference for food, even though my stomach felt punched full of holes. I didn't have a whole lot left to go off: some kasha, bagels, some Russian-style chicken salad. There was leftover pizza in the fridge, as always. Weeders loved pizza. I don't know if it was something all shapeshifters were into, but even Ayashe seemed to be uncommonly partial to it. Shifting burned a lot of calories, and there were few foods as palatable, convenient, and calorie-heavy as pizza.

Before anything, I had to clear my head, and the best thing for that was exercise. A punching bag and some basic free weights were set up in the yard behind the house, so I lay into the bag for a while, did some upper body work, and then turned to magic. I'd been working on variations of the *Aysh* spell, magic crafted and used in desperation while on the verge of death. The fundamental basis of the spell was to pull together the normally invisible aerosol particles of dirt, metal, and water in the air into a temporary solid, a way to exploit the kinetic potential of New York's omnipresent pollution. *Aysh* used that field of matter like a match on sandpaper, striking flame from the air. The main variation I was interested in was a spell I had bound to *Tzain*, the Sword: a punch augmented by a spike of compressed matter and force that shattered and diffused after impact.

The first couple of tries, there was a flash of light and a projection the length of a small nail. By attempt number twenty-two, I could reliably put my enhanced fist through a wooden plank and half-snap, half-explode it.

The sound drew Talya after a couple of tries. She hung back while she watched me turn another old piece of scrap wood into kindling. I moved to look at her properly, and found her picking at one of her fingernails and frowning.

"Ayashe's here," she said in Russian. "She, uh, says that she was sent to pick you up."

"Pick me up?" I kicked the broken fencing out of the way and shook my hand out.

"She's down in front of Strange Kitty, waiting. Jenner won't let her on the property," she replied. "Listen, when you've got some time, I need to talk to you. About MinTex. But not here."

"Mm. Found much?"

She nodded enthusiastically, chewing on her lip.

I rubbed my eyes, tired and woozy. Why was I so dizzy? Oh, right. Gin, followed by cold pepperoni pizza and two hours of exercise. "Go tell her I have to get dressed. I'll be out shortly."

Leaving Ayashe to stew, I went to get sorted, but no matter how I tried, I couldn't seem to get the crisp look I preferred. It was the grief, plus the embarrassment of having dared open up to someone only to be promptly betrayed. Grief was making me sloppy, sentimental, and weak. It was also making me do stupid things like let my guard down at night on the street and buying into Angkor's honeypot tactics, letting him gain *kompromat* on me in the process. '*Kompromat*' was one of those Soviet words that didn't have an easy translation to English, even if the word sounded similar to 'compromising'. *Kompromat* was information that not only compromised you socially, but that actively devalued your worth as a person, dehumanizing you to some extent—and it was valuable, a form of definite currency which was wielded as a weapon and used to exterminate a person's *blat*, their reputation and ability to get help from other people. My knowledge that Nicolai and Sergei were tolerating, even encouraging, pedophilia in their ranks was *kompromat* if I ever had the opportunity to share the proof with another *Organizatsiya*, but they also held *kompromat* on me: I had turned traitor, and being a *suka* in the underworld was a crime in the same tier as child molestation and homosexuality. In the prison camp, it would get you forcibly branded with tattoos proclaiming your outcast status.

I trudged out to the front of the gate, where Ayashe waited in a trench coat and boots: black tac-boots, like the kind SWAT wore. She looked about as pleased to see me as I was her. Neither of us bothered to offer a handshake.

"About frigging time," she said, by way of introduction. "Let's get this over with."

"Why? Is it time for my next drugged beating already?" I cocked my head.

She squinted at me, her lip curling on one side, and only then seemed to notice my hair. "What? No, I was told to pick you up and take you to Kristen's house. The agent who was murdered."

"I'm sure your good friend Agent Keen was delighted to bring you the news that I'm now helping you," I said, brittlely.

"Who?" She frowned.

"Agent Keen and Adeptus Tomas Black?"

Ayashe mulled on that for a few moments, then shook her head. "No idea who you're talking about. The S.A.C got in touch with me and said he'd contacted you directly and hashed things out."

"That's one way of putting it." I ran my hand back over my hair, pressing it flat. "So why, exactly, am I being taken to a cold crime scene? Other than to waste your time and mine?"

Her momentary confusion turned to a scowl. "Because the S.A.C said so. We're meeting two officers from Central Office there, so let's get moving."

"I've already ridden the Vigiles Express one time too many," I replied. "Give me the address. I'm riding my bike."

"Suit yourself. You can follow the car." Ayashe tossed her head and stalked off down the driveway, her falls swishing behind her.

And follow her I did: all the way to a tidy rowhouse in Flushing, Queens, a brownstone set on one of those iconic, pretty leafy streets where no one needed fences or window bars to keep out men like me. The tiny yard had been staked and marked with yellow tape. Small white evidence flags were planted like weeds in the soft grass, and there were police cars up and down the street. A pair of tired-looking NYPD beat cops were talking to each other by the front door, but they stopped and stared as I glided to the curb and cut the throttle, leaning the bike to stand while Ayashe collected her things.

"Okay. Here's how we do this." She marched over to stand in front of me, holding out a lanyard. "You wear this around your neck. Don't go anywhere you aren't told to go. Don't touch anything. And wear these gloves."

I had brought my own damn latex gloves—thicker black ones, to compensate for my over-sensitive hands. I let Binah out of my jacket onto my shoulder, and once she was out of the way, dropped the lanyard over my head. "How about you don't treat me like I'm stupid? Because I might just forget all my expertise when I'm put on the spot, you know?"

"She was raped and murdered, you piece of shit." Ayashe looked like she was about to spit for a moment, but instead pivoted on her heel and led the way to the stairs.

The boys in blue watched us like wary dogs as we hustled from the car to the doorstep, but when Ayashe got close, one of them offered her a hand. "How you doin', Agent? Can't stay away from us, can you?"

"Lured here by our manly charms," the other one chuckled.

"Only charms you got are the kind that comes in a box with cereal, Mitch." Ayashe took the offered hand and shook, fixing a veneer of professionalism over her rage. "This here is Rex. He's a consultant for D.C. Are they in?"

"Yeah." The other cop—Kitchener—looked me up and down.

"The fuck's with the cat?" Mitch asked. "You can't go taking a cat in there."

Binah was riding on my shoulder in her harness, her slender tail wrapped around the back of my skull. "She's a necessary part of the job."

"Bullshit. It's a fucking cat."

"Cool it, man," Kitchener said. "But yeah, if the detective finds out we let a cat into a murder scene-"

"Then you tell him that the Government's Magic Roadshow came through and the cat was part of our box of tricks," Ayashe said. "This guy helped solve a similar case with me way back when. With the cat."

The cops looked at me, then each other, and Kitchener shrugged. "Right, whatever. Just don't let it shit on the carpet."

"And if Waterhouse comes though, you're the one that gets to explain the cat," the other cop said.

When Ayashe opened the door, the cheap perfume and rust smell of decaying blood billowed out into the air. Kitchener coughed as we passed by him into the hallway. It was plain, save for the usual flotsam: coats on hooks, framed pictures of Michael Jackson and baseball players on the walls. Every light in the house was on.

"Don't touch anything." Ayashe walked ahead of me. "*Anything.*"

I followed without deigning to reply this time, looking around with growing interest. This was a first. I'd never been at the scene of a crime after the police had been through it. "So. There been any other killings like this, or is it a lone incident?"

"Not off the top of my head." Ayashe pulled a pair of latex gloves from her pants pocket, snapping them on. "Though there was another weird B&E Agency death back in July. One of our confidential informants was gunned down in his apartment. Someone smashed the ward on his door somehow, got in and murdered him and his wife. He told us he was worried about someone sending a spook after him."

Oh, I knew who that was: Semyon Vochin. He'd been my last official hit on behalf of the *Organizatsiya*, and his cat was currently purring against the side of my face. "Oh? Did he name any spook in particular? I might know them."

"Nope." Ayashe opened a door and held it for us, waving me through into a scene straight out of *Hellraiser.*

It was the living room, not the bedroom as I thought it might have been, a modern den that clearly belonged to a music lover. The room was dominated by a T.V and a sound system—both of them cracked open like oyster shells—shelves that had held records and cassette tapes which were now scattered over the floor, posters of various pop stars torn and hanging like shredded skin off the walls. The furniture had been shredded, like it had been stabbed over and over with something large, round, and sharp. There were gouges in the carpet, and blood over everything. Lots of blood, dried and stiff as hair gel. There was a long smear, like the lick of a giant paintbrush, that led into the adjacent room. Voices drifted through the open doorway, getting closer. We waited until they joined us: a tall, strapping black agent with close-shaved hair and three days of stubble, and a comfortably overweight, mustachioed Indian man with buggy eyes and an incongruously neat side part.

"Richardson," the taller guy called out in a rich blue baritone. "This our man?"

"Sure is. Can you take it from here?" Ayashe said behind me. Her voice was heavy with fatigue.

"Sure can." He flicked dark eyes to me. "I'm Agent Robert Mattson, this is Adeptus R.C. Varma. He'll be taking you back into the crime scene as we found it so you can look around and see where things were."

"I see," I replied. "Were you sent by Agent Keen, or...?"

"Who?" Mattson got the same look of confusion that Ayashe had, and so did Varma.

"Never mind," I said. "So, what do I have to do?"

"Come with me. I will be able to take you back into the scene." Varma waved me forward. He had a thick accent, cultured and vaguely British. "That is your familiar, yes?"

"Yes." The kitchen had a dark pall over it. I felt the psychic depression immediately, the gaping cold wound of a place that had been the site of some kind of NO-presence, dark magic that had killed and terrified.

"She will share in the vision I will show you." He stopped in front of a counter, where he had an array of gold and brass tools laid out on a small ceremonial cloth, a bright altar of warded silk that served the same purpose as a ceremonial circle. While he got ready, I looked around at what the police had left for us to see. The Occult part of things had been painted on the wall across from the stove. 'Soldier 557', his signature, written a bit over six feet off the floor. Beneath it was a seal inscribed within a circle that contained the letters: 'AVLORI CET'. Underneath that, almost as an afterthought, he had written 'Ground Zero'.

"Part of a symbol by Paracelsus," Mattson said from behind me, gliding toward the island counter. His shoes were quiet on the tiles. "German magician from the late 1400s. The rest of it, we're not sure about."

"I know who he is. This is part of Paracelsus's Seal of Cancer," I finished. "He was foremost a magician, but is credited as the founding father of toxicology and the first to acknowledge the existence of mental illness as a pathology."

Mattson grunted. "Not bad. And funny you say that. First report we got back from the labs was that Kristen had been poisoned."

"Poisoned? With what?" I petted Binah to give my hands something to do.

"Analysis hasn't come back yet. First impression's apparently that it's some kind of animal venom. Neurotoxin, the kind you find in spiders and some kinds of sea creatures."

Now that he mentioned it, there was an odd smell in the kitchen: it reminded me of the smell of millipedes, the kind of musky smell you got when you lifted up a brick from damp soil and found creepy-crawlies and snail shit.

Varma turned to me, and waved me forward. "Come here, and close your eyes."

I approached him. He reached out and sketched something over my brow, murmuring under his breath. His magic was a cool, effervescent thing, a rippling wave of gold-tinged orange I felt course over me. He didn't feel like a Phitometrist, a mage in direct contact with his Neshamah. Mages like that had a gravity around them this man lacked, but his magic was effective all the same, because when I opened my eyes, the reality of the past was laid over the present like a shimmering veil. I blinked, looking around and through the flickering shadows that whispered around me in the room, a crowd of ghosts that moved around the murdered woman on the ground like a bubbling river around a large stone.

Kristen Cross had been raped—that much was immediately obvious. Her clothes had been cut down the middle, pulled off in rags, legs spread, everything below her waist torn and bruised. Her face and chest were swollen beyond human limits: her eyes and mouth almost obliterated by the distension of the surrounding tissue, which had erupted in places from the internal pressure. The ulcers, split like four-pointed stars, bled brackish brown fluid down her neck, face, and chest to the floor. A horrific way to die.

My eyes flicked from one detail to the next. Injuries on her forearms, mangled hands with deep puncture wounds, like stigmata. They were neat, deep, and not discolored. A revolver had skittered over the white ceramic tiles and hit the skirt of a kitchen cabinet, where it was being tagged and photographed by a spectral tech.

"Interesting ability you have," I said, walking around the empty space where the memory of the body lay. "What can you tell me about this woman?"

"She was part of a taskforce that looked into paranormally active cults and societies. She specialized in ritual abuse and murder." Ayashe answered me, speaking from the doorway. "She spent about a third of her time here, the rest travelling or at our headquarters in Virginia. A lot of her work overlapped with the Organized Crime Taskforce."

I let Binah down to the floor, shaking my head as I looked over the assembled pieces of the puzzle. "Alright. Can you remove this effect?"

The Adept grunted, and made a slashing gesture with a small sickle. The illusion cut, leaving me in a mostly empty room with the trio of Agents.

Cautiously, I closed my eyes and let my senses drift, focusing on the color-texture synesthesia that was carried by the smells and sounds of the house. Both sound and smell have colors and textures I felt in my mouth, usually at the back of my tongue. When I utilize it in conjunction with magic, looking at the world Phitonically, the color associations suddenly make perfect sense.

I opened my eyes into a different, liquid world, a world of particles suspended in a superfine fluid reality one step above our own. Phi flowed and pulsed in time with a heart so distant it could not be heard, but so powerful that it could be felt Everywhere. I wasn't sure about an individual Phitonic matrix, but the room itself carried echoes of the magic that had been used to it. The overriding sensation wasn't Pravamancy, NO-magic. It was Illusion—Varma's magic, orange and fresh on my palate—and Biomancy. The Green residue hung like a haze over the room.

"No," I shook my head to clear the Sight, and moved to the wall. I crouched slightly, reaching up toward the writing. "No, no, no."

"No? No what?" Mattson said behind me.

"It's not correct." I ignored the pair of men, pushed past Ayashe back into the den, and looked over the gutted electronics. "You've got it wrong, unless... Was there a chair near the wall where the signature was written?"

Ayashe frowned at me, clearly remembering my comment back on the street. "Uhh... not that I know of. I can ask."

"Then no," I murmured again, looking back into the kitchen. "Soldier 557 didn't do this. This isn't his crime."

Ayashe stared at me in what could only be silent, infuriated disbelief.

"He's short," I said. "Almost child-sized. He had to stand on the beds to write on the walls before. He doesn't know anything about electronics, doesn't know what computers are. He's too proud to rape or use poison. He has always tried to communicate something meaningful, something that justifies what he's doing. This message doesn't mean anything significant: if he was trying to evoke Cancer, then the body should have been laid West to East. It's a bad frame job."

"That's ridiculous," she said. "We have evidence from multiple scenes where this guy has killed. Lily and Dru's, most notably."

"There was Life magic used here," I said.

"None of our Adepts picked up anything resembling 'life magic'," Mattson said. "And Kristen wasn't a mage."

It didn't make any sense to me. I could see it around us. Had she tried defending herself with a magical item against some kind of NO-thing, or a demon or demonurge? I searched for Binah, and found her sitting at the entrance to the hallway and stairwell, waiting patiently for me. "Whoever was here, they were looking for something. I think there was more than one person. I need to look in the other rooms, alone, to try and pick out whose magic is whose."

Ayashe's voice soured. "Alexi-"

"Let him go. There's nothing up there." Mattson joined us, and lay a comradely hand on Ayashe's shoulder. "You said he's worked on things like this before, right?"

I tuned her reply out, following my familiar up the narrow staircase to the second floor. The house had an odd, unlived-in feel to it. The den was obviously the place where Agent Cross spent the most time, because her bedroom was less personal than the average hotel room. White sheets, no pillowcase on the pillows, a double bed with no evidence of a sleeping companion, a full-length mirrored wardrobe with sliding doors and hardly any clothes inside. What little there was here had been ransacked, up to and including the mattress. It had been cut open in places, the stuffing pulled free.

I set Binah on the floor and went into the bathroom one door down. It was also fairly sparse. A suitcase had been set down near the cabinet, the tags still on the handle. She'd only just gotten back from Washington?

Binah's resonant meow echoed from the bedroom, the deep urgent squalling that I'd come to associate with her distress or warning. Frowning, I went back to the bedroom and found her pacing back and forth in one of the corners of the room, pausing to claw at the edge of the carpet.

"Hmm? What is it?" Curiosity piqued, I joined her and crouched down. The carpet had some bare staples where she was pawing at it, like they'd been added as an afterthought.

"Mrrr! Mraaw-aoo!" They were the noises she made when she was bringing her toy to me for me to throw for her. She liked to play fetch.

I used my pocketknife to jimmy the staples out and peel the carpet back. Tucked between the underlay and the floorboards was a small white paper packet with a single word, all capitals, written on the outside in ball-point pen. 'ZEALOT'.

"Zealot...?" I opened it and looked inside. Down in the bottom of the packet, jammed down along the seam... were seeds. They were large, almost squarish in shape, and black.

"Huh." I held the packet out to Binah. "What do you think, girl?"

The cat sniffed it over, then arched her head and flank against the packet and my hand. I snorted and almost smiled. "Hmm. Important, I guess."

There was the dull thump of feet in the staircase outside. I stood quickly, pocketing the packet, and was just hoisting Binah up to her perch when Ayashe threw open the door. "Rex, what the hell do you think you're playing at?"

"I'm not playing," I said. "I told you what I observed, and followed the magic I sensed to this room."

"She wasn't a mage. This is, what, the third time I've told you that?" She scowled. "So did you find anything?"

"No, unfortunately." I breezed out the door, turning my shoulder to avoid hitting her on the way out, and headed for the stairwell. "Not a damn thing."

CHAPTER 11

We returned to an empty house. I turned the garage lights on, then cooked dinner in the cold, leaden silence while Binah played with her favorite bumblebee toy on the floor around my feet. I used to think I'd go nuts if I ever had to share my space with anyone else other than Vassily, but I'd gotten used to the routine of Strange Kitty and the presence of the human Tigers and the Big Cat Crew. I'd found a quiet pleasure in sharing my table with Angkor and Zane and Jenner, when she wasn't out managing the club's business in parts unknown. Talya would often be at her desk in the living room, tapping away on a keyboard, or outside with Zane as she learned the ins and outs of the Harleys. There were small annoyances—messy stacks of books, toilet paper put on the roller the wrong way, dishes not stacked correctly, the odd discarded needle and syringe—but I'd found something here I hadn't known I'd missed. The absence of other people hung over the house like a shroud.

It was that pall that led me to avoid the bedroom. Instead, I set up in the den, a room which looked and smelled like it had been decorated by college students who'd gone around with a truck and collected furniture off the sidewalk. It was surprisingly comfortable all the same, and I'd spent more than one evening here whiling away the small hours in conversation with Jenner. It was also the best place to get some room to perform a ceremony. The bunk room was too large and impersonal for me to concentrate, especially when the risk of interruption was so high, but the den was rarely accessed at night during the week.

To me, Agent Cross was just a dead cop: one less crusading arcanophobe. I could pity her for having died the way she had, but if Soldier 557 wasn't involved, it wasn't my circus. I don't know who hit Kristen Cross, but it sure as hell wasn't Soldier—even if she *was* investigating the Templum Voctus Sol. It was possible she'd been killed by some sort of DOG, but I'd never smelled that ammonia-acid reek around DOGs before. They had a very recognizable stench, like candied rotten meat. It left you feeling sick, too, in the sense of being unwell—like the early stages of the flu. There was none of that at Agent Cross's house: just diffuse Green energy and a packet of ordinary seeds stashed in an unorthodox place. They would live in my locker for the time being. Maybe 'Zealot' was the name of the flower that grew from them. Some kind of fancy petunia.

My first business was finding what had happened to Doctor Levental. He was one of my people, and he'd done me a solid the month before. His information eventually led to us recovering the majority of the missing shapeshifter kids, and if the *Organizatsiya* had somehow found this out, then I had a duty to help him—or avenge him.

The first step was to focus. I arranged beanbags in a makeshift circle on the bare wooden floor, then got my chalk and string and set about creating a circle, immersing into the ritual geometry as inspiration kindled into determination. I was going to try dowsing.

As I understood it, the basic formula for map dowsing was to take a map, rule it into quadrants, and then use a pendulum to determine the direction of the desired person or thing. Then you ruled that part of the map into four, and so on and so forth until you had an approximate location. Then you went there in person and dug around. The map was easy enough: The Tigers' clubhouse had plenty of maps, all of which were well-worn and marked with rest stops and symbols representing coded information I didn't have the key for. I only had one pendant to use as a pendulum: Vassily's old ankh necklace. It was a good tool for this work, given how much energy had gone into the thing over the years.

Once everything was ruled up and ready, the circle cast, I hummed a simple rhythmic rising and falling tune under my breath and focused in on the pendulum. The tune made me think only of what I was doing, giving my brain something to gnaw instead of imagining where Leventhal might be in New York. The actual invocation was said only in my mind, each word thought in time with the cadence of the tune. It gave Kutkha a clear path to release the energy required for the pendulum to swing in the accurate direction.

I set up a little cross-stand out of books and a coat hanger, and hung the pendulum over the center of the map. It dangled from its chain, trembling a little as I focused power into the metal… and at the conclusion of the chant, I held my hands up over it and waited.

The pendant jerked, once, and then fell still. The charge peaked and died too fast for it to gain traction.

I sighed. "Well, then."

During the second attempt, I tried holding the chain in my fingers over the map. This was something I'd have preferred to avoid, mostly because of the way my hands ticced and twitched, but once I zoned in on the magic, the pendant began to wobble and then, slowly, swing back and forth. The feed of Phi was a small, low flame, like the pilot light of a gas stove.

"There we go…" I tried to keep my eyes on the middle of the map as the ankh began to circle aimlessly around. Then I felt it—a distinct tugging sensation, as if something was pulling the end of the ankh toward the southwest.

My heart sank as I reluctantly refocused in the center of the quarter that encompassed the oceanside parts of Brooklyn, and once the pendulum began to swing, I had to check myself from fixating on its likely target: Red Hook. This was a problem I'd heard about with dowsing. The hand was naturally unsteady, and, guided by the mind and imagination, more likely to be motivated by the subconscious than the objective truth.

A cool shiver of magic passed through my fingertips, as delicate as a bursting bubble. I shuddered, that someone-walking-over-your-grave feeling, and the pendulum began to wander… just before it jerked so hard that the chain slid from between my fingers and the ankh clattered to the map over Red Hook.

A wave of weird dizziness flushed through me, transforming into an intense, burning cold sensation in my hands and feet... which was followed by the acrid smell and taste of burned wax crayons. I startled up to my feet from the floor, breathing hard as the reek grew in intensity. A second chill passed through me, stronger this time.

There was a flicker of motion out of the corner of my eye. I spun, arming a word of power, but there was nothing. Another flash from the opposite direct made me twist on my feet, flickers of color and a gathering whisper that seemed to come from the walls. The lines on the wallpaper started to wiggle and crawl up and down, skittering like kaleidoscopic lizards.

"Not this again." I backed up a step, glancing around so as not to cross the edge of the chalk circle inscribed on the floorboards. The magical design was spinning slowly, the lines morphing and jumping under my feet. The acrid wax smell was burning my sinuses and in my mouth, and as I shook my head, I accidentally glanced down at my arm. Black. The veins visible on the underside of my forearm were black, undulating like worms. "No!"

The room breathed around me, the walls exhaling Sergei's voice. *Two more infusions of blood from me, and you'll do anything I say.*

He'd said that to me after the first taste of his blood, when he'd been mining me for information on the Gift Horse. One dose had been enough to force me to talk. He'd shot a second into the crook of my arm, but that was over a month ago.

The blood doesn't just disappear, my boy. I heard him speaking from every surface, his jovial, booming voice hissing through a mouthful of needle-sharp iron teeth. *You're mine.*

"No! Leave!" My heart sloshed in my chest. Every time I blinked, I saw Sergei's gaze boring into me, staring at me with the heartless, murky eyes of a deep-sea predator. "I am a Magus, and my Will is the-"

A billowing, translucent shade lunged across the circle toward me. I caught a glimpse of a screaming, fang-filled mouth and stumbled away from it. My shins hit a chair I didn't know was there. I tripped and fell on my chest, arms and head outside the circle.

You're mine. I raised you, taught you, led you, and now you will return to me. It's time to come home, Alexi.

Shaking my head, I pushed up to hands and knees before I knew what I was doing. I fought against the urge to get up to my feet, breathless. The wax smell was making my mouth water now, and as I shook through waves of icy chills, visions of Sergei offering me his bloody hand shot through my mind's eye.

I invested in you, Alexi. He loomed above like a mountain, his face receding into the sucking darkness of the ceiling. His blood was a dark russet orange, trembling, almost floating from his skin with bittersweet Phi. *I don't want you to do as I say. I want you to WANT to do as I say. And you do WANT to, don't you?*

Oh GOD. The compulsion to walk out of the room, get in my car, and drive myself to Red Hook was getting stronger with every passing moment. Fear surged, and as it peaked, I lost the battle. My feet finally got under themselves and I lurched like a drunk toward the living room door, desperately catching on to anything I could grab on the way past. My fingers clutched at the doorframe, then slipped off as the next wave of compulsion and irrational, powerful hunger pulsed through my body.

Fuck this. Fuck this to Hell. He was going to turn me into a slave. I couldn't stop it. I had to stop it. What had I done to let him in, and how the fuck did I get him out again?

A shape darted in front of me, ramming into my legs. Awkwardly shambling, twisted up in a battle against my own body, I tripped without any ability to break my fall. It knocked the wind from me in the split second before the ground mashed my nose and broke it.

"Fucking SHIT piece of crap... motherfucker!" I rolled onto my back with my hands over my face, blind with agony. I pinched the bridge of my nose and tipped my head back before I bled any more over the Tigers' Clubhouse floor. Fear took a sideline to pain, and I realized that I had control of my limbs again. For now.

In the dim light coming from the kitchen, the blood pouring from my nose was black, gleaming and iridescent like oil. My chest spiked through with a wave of fresh anxiety, and as it did, I felt the control of my limbs become more tenuous.

Fear, I realized. *He feeds off fear.*

But fear didn't turn off like a switch. My hands spasmed, forced away from my face as my body rose, swaying. I tried to think of something, anything besides the terrifying loss of control as I lurched off down the hallway. Binah leapt on me this time, digging into my back with her claws and raking my skin with her back feet, and the pain once again served as a distraction—but it wasn't enough to stop the inevitability of my staggering out into the sleeting rain toward my car.

CHAPTER 12

It was fear that made my hands unlock the car door and haul it open. Binah leapt in ahead, meowing like an air-raid siren, but focusing on her didn't stop me from lurching into the driver's side and jamming the keys into the ignition. I tried to think of my friends: training with Zane, the thrill of my first motorcycle ride, the brotherly affection I'd come to feel for Talya. My hand shook on the keys, rattling them against the dash, but slowly, haltingly, it turned them and started the ignition.

Panic swelled again. It was no good: I was afraid of what they made me feel. Memories of Vassily didn't help, either, given what Sergei had done to his body. I had to search back further to find the antidote to terror.

The car thrummed to life. My feet and hands operated smoothly now, robotically, and I couldn't even shut my eyes as I lit on the painful, bittersweet memories of my horse. I could still remember the dark gentleness of her eyes as she followed me like a dog from her stall to the round pen, no halter required, and the smell of her sweat as I leaned into her flank, sweet and green. It made my heart ache with a pain I'd done my best to bury. But it banished the fear.

I drove out onto the street, and my body fought to turn the wheel right, toward Brighton Beach. I grit my teeth, mouth watering helplessly for the poison in Sergei's veins, and forced the wheel left onto 5th to merge into the light traffic heading for the Williamsburg Bridge.

Pain lanced through my skin, an electric shock that nearly startled my hands off the wheel. My hands were wet with sweat, or at least I thought it was sweat until I looked down and nearly ran myself off the road at the sight of blood: a lot of blood. It was squeezing out of my pores in dark droplets from the DOG-scars on my left arm, running down to drip on my already-fucked-up slacks. When I glanced in the mirror, more of it was forcing its way through the pores of my cheeks, the corners of my eyes. My nose had bled all the way down to my chest.

I had some notion of what I was doing by heading north—but if I was wrong, I was going to bleed out and run myself into the side of the bridge tunnel. This was punishment. I was defying Sergei's orders, and he was trying to kill me from a distance now. If I'd been given the third dose of his blood, he surely could have. My only hope of breaking the hold: getting across the flowing water of New York City Bay.

I hurtled across the Williamsburg Bridge, twenty miles over the speed limit for the first part of it, blinking blood out of my eyes as I tried to think of everything I knew about upir. Vassily's grandmother had told us monster stories growing up, stories traditionally told by wise old women in Ukraine. The vampire can walk in the sun with impunity, dressed and smiling like any other man, she said. You knew an *upir* by his red hair and face. During the day, vampires hid their iron fangs. They ate raw fish and human flesh, preferably the flesh of children, who they devoured in front of their parents. A vampire could be kept from entering a village by plowing an egg into a freshly-turned field. Vampires didn't like garlic or salt, or hallowed ground. They could enter graveyards but not churches, and they couldn't cross running water unaided.

Once I was past the halfway point on the bridge, the dark cloud of needling, furious magic wobbled, then snapped like a broken rubber band so suddenly that I nearly swerved into the side of the bridge tunnel. When I glanced in the rear-view mirror, I saw a pale, panting ghost of a man with a broken nose, a face mottled in bruises and covered in fine tracks of blood. Thicker trails leaked from the corners of my eyes. I looked like I'd been slugged in the face.

"How the hell did that happen, Kutkha?" I barked aloud, keeping my eyes on the road. "Why couldn't we stop him, and how do I stop this from happening again?"

"You ingested his blood, my Ruach. It cannot be undone." Kutkha said. *"You could not see my work, but I fought to seal the gate... He was trying to make your brain bleed. I forced it to the skin instead."*

"Fuck." He could have killed me from a distance, just like that. "How do we stop it? I don't know any of the metaphysics at work here. The spell wasn't even related to him... unless..."

151

"Unless he has your doctor and has ensorcelled him as part of a trap, counting on your loyalty and your reliance on remote methods of seeking him," Kutkha finished.

"Suka blyad!" I struck the wheel with both hands. "That motherfucker!"

"My knowledge of Feeders is limited," Kutkha said. *"None of your Ruachim have great experience with them... but they do have experience with the Animus at the heart of every Feeder— Wrath'ree, and by extension, the Hive."*

"Wrath'ree. That was the thing that was used to bind my magic away from me," I said. "I have no damn idea what a Wrath'ree actually is. And what do you mean by animus?"

"Wrath'ree are GOD's inflammatory immune system response," Kutkha replied, his voice gaining clarity as we came off the bridge and into Manhattan. *"Macrophages. They are the children of the Suffering GOD, the I after it was violated by the Morphorde. They function now as white blood cells do in HuMans."*

"They attack Morphorde? Or HuMans?"

"Morphorde. Usually. They are creatures of battle, driven by rage, hunger, and the impetus to engulf and destroy any Morphorde they encounter. They are rapacious consumers of dirty Phi."

My skin was sticking to my shirt, my clothes to the car seat. I pulled the car to the side of the road when I found a clear spot, just to catch my breath and assess the damage.

Blood. A lot of it. The bleeding from my head wasn't really as bad as it looked, but I looked like a poster child for hemorrhagic fever. 'Alexi Sokolsky, the face of Ebola.'

The greatest saturation was on my arm and stomach, the DOG claw scars and the scar from Sergei's seal on my connection to Kutkha. I could make out traces of the sigil he'd used on the front of my shirt.

"So Wrath'ree are intelligent?" I reached up, felt around my nose, and pushed it back into place. The pain was breathtaking. I tried to keep it to a manly grunt.

"Extremely, but they are all quite alike. This is because they are part of The Hive, the collective consciousness of all the Wrath'ree in all of GOD. The Hive is focused around the infected part of the Theosphere, the site where the Morphorde continues to burrow ever deeper into GOD's tissues. This site is called The Drill."

The Drill. I shuddered, and turned the engine off. "What relation do they have to vampires? Feeders?"

"The Hive relies on numbers, so it is constantly innovating ways in which to multiply. They drift around HuMans like ghosts, as they are usually incorporeal, moving through GOD's interstitial fluids like stinging jellyfish. Now and then, a HuMan becomes subject to the right conditions where they die in a way which parts the soul from the body very suddenly or... destroys the soul. An opportunistic Wrath'ree bonds itself to the HuMan in a flash of transference, effectively becoming that HuMan's new soul. This is how a Feeder is created. A vampire is a HuMan corpse which has retained its mind, but which is animated by the energy and hunger of a Wrath'ree."

"And the Wrath'ree has the impetus to breed, so it's driven to create more Feeders," I finished, nodding. Exhausted and bloody, I was still interested enough to be connecting the dots. "Then why is Sergei as twisted as he is?"

"He is Morphorde," Kutkha said mournfully. *"Even Wrath'ree may be infected."*

Mind swirling, I turned down a narrow one-way alley off Times Square and felt my heart sink a little. The Voicers' church was contained inside a refitted hotel, a stately old Gotham building with a glass frontage and rotating door, which was currently unmoving and sealed off from the street. The building was dark.

The rules of magical zoning could be quite technical. I didn't have to be under the roof, surely—I could potentially squat on the roof or just inside the doorway to get the benefit of coverage. It wouldn't protect me if Sergei figured out I was here and sent a brigada after me, but it was better than nothing.

I parked the car in the half-empty underground garage across from the building, hiding my car between two of the black SUVs owned by the church. I cleaned up as best I could and slunk out with Binah riding on my shoulder. The cat fussily washed the blood from the side of my face as we mounted the ramp, and I was about to put my foot out on the sidewalk when something flickered in my vision and stopped me cold. I waited, and then it happened again: the swirl of dark-on-dark from inside the building.

Security? I should have figured. But something about the place felt off. I couldn't see the person roaming the reception area clearly from across the road: not by myself, anyway.

"Alright, girl. Time to do some work for once." I reached up and scruffed Binah in between licks, setting her on the ground at my feet. "Go take a look inside."

I really had no idea if she understood me or not most of the time. I knew she could sense magical energy, and would reliably respond to it. Sometimes she acted with what seemed like frightening intelligence, or did naturally animalistic things at just the right time, such as tripping me up in the hallway to prevent me from dancing straight into Sergei's arms. Other times, she acted like how she did now. As soon as I let her go, she swarmed up my pants leg and stomach—with claws—and struggled her way back to my shoulder.

"Fucking hell—did you really have to climb?" I hissed.

Seemingly content to hang her head and front legs over one side of my shoulder and her ass off the other, Binah whapped her tail across my broken nose in irritation.

After several minutes of creative—but quiet—cursing, I looked up through watering eyes to see the shadow inside the building moving toward the front door. On reflex, I ducked around the edge of the parking garage door into the shadows and dropped to a knee, instinctively reaching toward my armpit for the gun that wasn't there. Grimacing, I risked a peek around the edge of the doorway, then recoiled and had to look a second time. My blood turned to ice.

The man inside The Voice of the Lord church was carrying a full-sized military assault rifle with a long suppressor. And he was not human.

CHAPTER 13

Researching and collecting information on paranormal phenomena was part of my job as a spook. A lot of it was nothing more than modern mythology, but I'd been squaring away stories, rumors, sightings, magical events, UFO encounters and abductions from newspapers and 'zines since I was a teenager. My memory was exceptionally good at retaining written information, and I had a massive catalog of reference points for most of the common supernatural happenings in the USA.

Without a shadow of a doubt, I was looking at a Silencer. One of the Men in Black.

From what I could see of him, he was tall—very tall—with milk-white skin dappled gray by the shadows inside the building. He wore the classic black suit, black overcoat, white shirt, black tie, and was absolutely hairless. When he turned, the light off the street hit the back of his head. It shone like the moon through the glass.

Now that I was paying attention, I spotted a hole cut into one of the windows that faced the street. It was big enough to get a man's arm through, a darker patch against a sea of duller shades and colors. Someone had used professional tools to be able to pull that job off. The window with the hole was near the revolving door. Whoever was in there now had probably opened the doors or disarmed an alarm, or both.

I knelt back and rubbed my eyes, wondering if I was hallucinating from the ghost of the Feeder blood in my veins. Whoever had broken into the church, they didn't belong there. But who the hell wanted in, and why? The only thing I could think of was the church's involvement with the Vigiles' supernatural pastoral care program. I didn't know the details of the program, but I knew that the manager of this church, Pastor Christopher Kincade, was aware of Aaron's work.

Intuition and excitement—or fear—tugged at me with icy fingers. Soldier 557 was an excellent name for a Man in Black. Maybe we'd been wrong all this time. What if he wasn't a single murderer? What if 'Soldier 557' was a team? And in that case... what was the Deacon's link to them?

The only warning I had that something was wrong was Binah. She hissed and bolted from my shoulder, too fast to follow. I stood, mouth open to call her, and turned to find two Silencers with Uzis pointed straight at my face.

Under light, the Men in Black were even more uncanny. Bald, tall and pale, their eyes a heartless milky blue. The submachine guns aimed at my head radiated hot magic, their barrels crawling with arcane energy that glowed like embers in the engraved, flowing line of sigils writ into the metal. They looked exactly like compact versions of the guns we'd found in Vanya's junkyard cache.

"Sir, we're going to have to ask you to come with us," one of them said. "Immediately."

"Who the hell are you to be ordering me around? This is a public parking lot." I put my hands up anyway.

"This is a matter of national security," the Man said. "It's in your best interest to comply."

The other Man had split to the side, circling me. I breathed through the sudden buzzing rush, the shuddering in my chest and belly. "Hey, no need to point that thing at me. I'll leave. My car's over there."

I gestured with my head toward the vehicle, which was parked deeper in the parking lot—the direction they must have snuck up on me.

"We just need to ask you some questions downstairs, then we'll escort you to your vehicle and ensure your safe departure." The other one had the exact same voice as the first: cadence, tone, texture, everything.

I wasn't stupid. What he'd said was code for 'we're going to take you somewhere no one will hear us when we shoot you in the head'. I was not in a good position. Call it an educated guess, but the magic written into those weapons was almost certainly something akin to the Wardbreaker. I wasn't willing to bet my life on a magical barrier against them if they opened up.

I stepped away from the wall, hands still up. "You don't look like the cops, sorry to say. Who the hell am I dealing with?"

"That is of no importance." The one behind me jammed the muzzle of his Uzi into my back. "Move."

Call me proud if you will, but I really don't like being forced to do anything at gunpoint. More importantly, these two had no intention of letting me go. They'd get me to the car, shoot me in the head, and let the police deal with me as a 'gang killing'—assuming they didn't simply dump my body somewhere.

I nodded, and stumbled forward enough to get some space. Whatever pain I was in, I couldn't feel it anymore. Space was all I needed.

We were fully in the open when I spun back, smashed the Man's arm to the side with one arm and grabbed the barrel of the Uzi with the other, wresting it out of his hand, all in the blink of an eye. The next blink had us entangled—me with the gun, him groping for my collar so he could headbutt me. He was insanely strong. I pressed the muzzle to his sternum and squeezed the trigger.

The bullets made hardly any noise. Their bizarre, muffled rattle did nothing to stop them from turning the Man into a jerking mess of blood and limbs. His blood was white, not red: it sprayed back and forward as the other Man opened up his gun. I expected to die, to have the bullets punch through the dead man in my arms, but they didn't. I swung the gun up under the armpit of my inhuman shield and let off a burst, forcing the other Man in Black to scramble. He hit the ground, rolled, flipped to his feet and spun around about to aim when Binah shot out like a thunderbolt of fur and threw herself into the one leg that was on the ground. He stumbled, tripped, and that was it for him—my rounds took him in the skull, and his head exploded in a spray of white liquid, like powdered milk that had been mixed too thick to drink.

Barely fifteen seconds had passed, but my heart was hammering like I'd just run a mile at a sprint. I dropped the body in my arms, and he tumbled to the ground like a doll—a doll that was rapidly turning into an amorphous mass of white goo that rapidly oxidized to a dark gunmetal gray. I kicked him over, and saw that the Uzi spray had definitely hit him. His suit jacket had some kind of armor in it. "Fucking hell."

I went to investigate the second body. This Man was also decaying into slime, but his jacket was intact. I pulled it from the body and shrugged it on. It was comically large for me—the vents hung just behind my knees—but that wasn't actually a bad thing. It was heavy: the back, front, and sleeves had a firm, gel-like layer under the silk lining. I searched the pockets, but the Man hadn't been carrying anything except a couple of spare magazines.

Binah limped over to me, her fur on end. I scooped her up under one arm, the Uzi braced against my other hip, and let her scramble up to my shoulder. Now that we were across the water, Sergei's control over my body had lapsed, but I could still feel him pulling at my blood, at my mind. "Kutkha, does Sergei know where we are?"

"I don't know," my Neshamah replied. *"Perhaps. It will take him time if it is possible... A Wrath'ree in its pure form does not have the same limitations as the HuMan Feeder shell. If he were to send one after you..."*

"Then better to assume yes." I had no idea if the 'vampires hate churches thing' was even real, but it couldn't hurt. There were arguably better churches than this one, but I was here now. "So we get in, take out the Men in Black, and then camp out?"

"That is the best option. The connection between you and Sergei will weaken with the dawn. If you cut it now and wait, we will have time to prepare a talisman against possession tomorrow. And you must take the cat—she is part of me, your I. If she remains outside, she may fall prey to the same blood geas by proxy."

That wasn't great, but damned if I was going to end up a slave. I replaced the almost-empty clip on the Uzi and glanced over the sigils on the side. They resembled the symbols I'd engraved on the Wardbreaker, though this job was a lot more professional than my hand-engraved Commander—almost as if they'd been machined this way. "Right. Well, no running away. Come on, girl. Let's go clean house."

CHAPTER 14

I found a way into the building from the back. There was a mechanical parking lift that took up the lot right beside the church, so I scaled the side of it up to the bottom of the fire escape on the back of the building. Binah jumped off my shoulder to land elegantly on the platform. I was far less graceful, crashing into the side of it. I pulled myself up over the railing, and limped along the wall to the window. It was locked but not alarmed—those had been shut off. I cocked an ear, listening until Binah hopped up onto the ledge and began pawing at the glass the way she did when she couldn't get into a room she wanted in. The coast was clear.

I broke the window with the stock of the Uzi, bashing in the glass until I could climb in without slicing myself up like a ham. The headquarters of the Church of the Voice of the Lord was once one of the ritziest hotels in Times Square, one of those old Art Deco places where flappers hung off the arms of guys in top hats and bow ties and everyone got screwed up on absinthe. It had been renovated with offices and classrooms, a couple of chapels, counseling rooms, a library, a bookstore, even a little cafe on the mezzanine level. The gaudiness had been obliterated under robin's egg blue and beige paint, subdued carpet, and the clean, functional lines of glass and steel.

The carpet muffled my footsteps as I headed for the internal stairwell. I opened the heavy door and crept down, listening intently. The magically-silenced Uzis were quiet enough that I wasn't going to hear any fire unless I was a couple rooms over, but the stairwell carried voices well—and when I passed the entry to the second floor, I heard shouting from somewhere inside the building. Fearful shouting.

"Shit." I checked over the gun and kept my finger off the trigger, going to the door and cracking it open. Once the air could get in, I heard the guns. The submachine guns and the assault rifles themselves were quiet, but the bullets tore up wood and plaster as noisily as much as any other round. There was someone else in the building. I hadn't just walked into a robbery—I'd waltzed into a small-scale raid.

I busted out into the hall, looking around and up, and followed Binah as she broke into a loping slow run down the corridor and stopped at the far corner. She turned back to look at me. We were in sync, somehow. It wasn't verbal communication, but Kutkha was a part of her as much as he was a part of me, working with her brain and lungs.

There was a male scream from somewhere back in the building, then the sound of clothes rustling from around the bend. I rounded the corner low to the ground and fast, and opened up a burst on the Man in Black before he even had time to turn. He went down in a spray of milky blood. This one was different than the tall Men I'd met in the parking lot. He was smaller, lean and athletic, his skin tawny. He looked vaguely Asian, but his mouth was too small, his eyes too large. Creepy as hell. He had been guarding a pair of modest double doors, which I kicked into an auditorium.

The Church of the Voice of the Lord was a megachurch. Their public services were held at the Manhattan Center Studios because there were usually too many worshippers to fit into their church. This chapel was for the 'Confirmed' members, the ones who had passed whatever standards were required for entry, and it was still big: there was room for about two hundred people. I counted five Silencers plunging down the narrow aisles between the rows of seats, chasing a dark haired, long-limbed man who threw himself from cover to cover, scrambling in and out of sight around the huge curtains that hung behind and around the stage-like pulpit. "Go away! Help! Security! Help me!"

Christopher? I sighted down, eyes narrowed, and opened fire on the agents without a second thought.

Two of them went down before the rest of them caught on. The three Men turned, rifles raised, and I took another one down before I dropped down to my belly under a hail of fire. They had bigger guns, with rounds that tore up the seats over my head as I pulled myself forward by my arms and rolled out onto the stairs. This was the great part about being short—I was hard to spot over the furniture, and so when one of the MiB surged up over the chairs, searching for me, I nailed him under the chin and set him crashing backwards, the rifle falling from limp hands. The next one was right behind him, and he knew where I was. I threw the nearly empty gun at him, forcing him to dodge or take eight pounds of metal to the face, and lunged forward to take him down and half-roll, half-slide down the stairs toward the pulpit.

The Man got out from under me and flipped up to his feet. I wasn't fast enough to stop him from hauling me up by the collar. He headbutted me in my already-broken nose. The pain was blinding, and he managed to knee me in the gut twice before I got my bearings. I blocked his next punch, turned it into a lock and flexed the limb back against the joint. Usually, it broke with a satisfying crunch. This guy's elbow popped and then flexed in the opposite direction. The moment of surprise was all he needed to drive his knuckles into my face.

"*Chet*!" There was a brief blue glow, and the Man's fist hit an invisible barrier at full strength instead of soft flesh. The force of the blow rippled through me like a wave, and his knuckles broke with an audible wet crunch, but he didn't make a sound. Over his shoulder, I saw his partner aim and steady a rifle that shimmered with heat haze. He couldn't get a steady bead on my core while the two of us struggled our way up and out onto the stage.

I kneed the Man in the groin twice, fast and hard, peeled his fingers off me and shoved him away. Then I ran—first for the lectern, which I kicked off behind me to slow them down—and then for the edge of the pulpit. Bullets tore a line through the floor; I leapt and rolled just as the heavy wooden lectern flew over my head, flung by someone with inhuman strength—and speed. I'd barely turned from my roll when the now-disarmed Man in Black pounced me. We wrestled on the floor, but he got control of my left wrist. I couldn't stop myself from yelling as he twisted my hand and got on top of me, his fist descending toward my face.

"*Tzai-!*" I only got half the word out before the blow snapped my face to the side, but the charge was there. I drove my knuckles up into the Man's chest from underneath with my remaining strength. The spike of condensed matter pierced him just under the sternum and up into his chest. He coughed a gout of white liquid onto my face and neck as I fumbled inside his suit jacket, hoping and praying for a side-arm. GOD was not here tonight, apparently: I couldn't find a pistol, and the last of the MiB was advancing, silent and focused as he sighted along the barrel at my face.

"RRRRARRGH!" Pastor Christopher, his shirt torn, his handsome face wild and red—came up from the other side of the stage with a vase. He swung with everything he had as the Man jumped, breaking it over his arm as he blocked it to the side. I wriggled out from under the bubbling corpse and lunged out, grabbing two stake-sized pieces of broken wood. The first I threw, giving Christopher the chance to tackle the guy from behind while he fought to get his bearings. The second I hung onto as I charged up into the pulpit. I knocked the gun aside and stabbed him in the side of his throat, both hands wrapped around the spike of wood.

The Man's pupils flooded black. He clawed at the stake and pulled it free in a pressurized spray of chalky blood. His finger twitched on the trigger of his rifle just before his eyes rolled and he swooned to the ground, limbs jerking.

"Oh good God." Christopher was pale and sweaty, his skin the color of milk. He stumbled away from the body, unsure what to do with his hands. "Oh Jesus. Oh my God, he's dead."

"Looks like it." I put a shoe down on the back of the Man's neck and stomped just to make sure. The flesh was too soft to be HuMan. It felt like stepping on a piece of tilapia.

The pastor watched me with flat, haunted eyes. "Rex? That's your name, right? You're… You were here about the children."

I turned to face him, and for the first time since the fight started, I saw him. It was like a punch to the gut. Christopher was sharp-featured, an angular, mobile face made for broad, dimpled smiles. Narrow straight nose, deep-set eyes… no matter how much I told myself he didn't look like Vassily, I saw his reflection in the priest's drowning blue eyes. "Yes. That's the one."

He looked like he was about to cry. "I… thank you. You saved my life."

"Maybe. That depends on whether or not they called for backup." I crouched down and turned my back so that I didn't stare, pulling the assault rifle from the evaporating pool of sludge. "Can you use a gun?"

He shook his head rapidly. "No… No, I-I can't, I mean I-"

"It's alright." I pushed the safety switch from 'Semi' to 'Safe' and slung the gun over my shoulder, ransacking the MiB's empty suit for ammo. "Find a place to hide. I'll scope the building. Do you have security?"

"Y-Yes, of course. I don't know what happened to them. They should have been… oh God, no. What if they killed them?"

Then they killed them. I came up with a spare clip and shook it clean. The blood and goo didn't seem to stick to anything: it rolled off like mercury, beading before evaporating with a strange metallic odor. Christopher watched me, hands wringing the edge of his shirt.

"Go, now. Hide. I'll keep you safe." The cartridge slid home with a satisfying snap.

"Okay… okay, thank you." He nodded jerkily, backing away at a jog across the stage.

Me, my cat, and my new assault rifle marched off up the stairs and outside. At the end of the hallway leading down to the first floor, I found the first security guard crumpled against the wall, blood fanning from the back of his skull up to the ceiling. The closer I got to reception, the more bodies I found. I breathed through my mouth, as quietly as I could, and tried to block out the smell as I slid through the door that led into the mezzanine.

The lobby of the Church had been converted into a one-stop shop for the religiously challenged. The majority of the mezzanine was taken up with an open-plan bookstore, while off to one side was a room with a big screen TV playing reels of Pastor Zachariah Goswin, the Church's founder, being interviewed on Oprah and preaching at stadiums. A glass railing looked out over the lobby, which was joined to the mezzanine by two sweeping flights of stairs at either end.

The foyer was dark, the air vibrating with tension so thick I could have cut it. I crept out from the door, hiding behind shelves of books and racks of pamphlets with the only sound being my own harsh, bated breaths. I looked out into the room with the Sight, tuning into the stillness and straining to sense any disturbance. There was one dead guard on the left-hand stairwell. Two more had been laid out for transport and disposal behind the reception desk.

As I waited for movement, Binah hung close to me to the point where it became obvious that no one else was there. After several tense minutes, she chirruped and arched her body against my shins with a long, lazy yawn.

"Mmph." I dropped the muzzle of the rifle, waiting for the jump-scare. The mezzanine and the ground floor were totally still. Outside, several of the cars had gone: the black town cars I'd noticed while crossing the street. There were security camera monitors at reception. All four screens were blank. "Looks like they decided whatever they were here for wasn't worth it. What a waste of life."

"Mrraow," Binah replied helpfully.

I picked my way back to the chapel hall, and called from the back of the room. "Okay, pastor. It's over."

For a few minutes, nothing stirred. Eventually, the curtains at the back of the pulpit stage shifted, and I saw him there, crouched with a clip of bullets in one shaking hand. "Rex?"

I thumped down the stairs, wincing on every step. The combat high was starting to wear off, and with it came pain and bone-deep, profound exhaustion.

"My god. You're covered in blood." Christopher was still pale, his face sweaty, hands trembling as I drew up and sat down, leaning on the rifle. "You're injured. We-we have to get you to the hospital."

"Huh?" Everything was hurting so bad it took me a moment to work out what he was talking about. "No, no hospital."

"You're bleeding." He came to me and took my wrist with careful, nervous hands, gently pulling my arm out from my side. I hadn't realized I'd been guarding it.

"I lost a lot of blood on the way here," I said. "Long story. I can't go to the hospital. Is there somewhere I can get a shower?"

"Y-Yes, of course. One in the First Aid Room, one in the staff locker room." He was still shaking, but crouched down to help me up. My joints were stiffening up with pain. "Come on. Slowly now."

He looped an arm around my waist and one under my shoulders, and helped me get to my feet. He knew the place better than me, and took me out past the back of the stage, through a hall cluttered with production equipment under plastic and lighting on wheel-in rails, and into an elevator. I kept the assault rifle braced in against my side, just in case, but there was no one left to disturb us en route to the first aid room. The only sounds were us, and Binah's anxious meowing following us down the hall.

CHAPTER 15

We stumbled into a clean white room. It was well-appointed: hospital trolley bed, shelves of medical supplies, a bathroom with sink, shower, and wheelchair. I broke away from him, looking over the cabinet. The world was spinning slowly and persistently to the right. "Need sugar. Go get me a can of Coke. Something sweet."

Christopher ran a hand back through his sweaty hair, squeezing it back along his skull. "Okay, alright. S-Stay here, we have Coke. You aren't going to bleed to death, are you?"

"Not if I can help it." There was a slur in my voice, but I was able to find what I needed. Dressings, alcohol, saline, antibiotic ointment, bandages, tweezers.

"Thank God." Christopher practically bolted from the room.

I was thinking GOD didn't have a whole lot to do with any of this. While he was gone, I had a quick shower and put my pants back on, then returned to the bed. I had to focus on my hands to stop them shuddering as I uncapped the bottle of isopropyl. The clean, harsh smell stung my nose—and made my stomach growl. I had the passing urge to swig it as I splashed alcohol into the little plastic tray. "Goddammit, Yen, not now. You have to be fucking kidding me."

It wasn't. I tried to reach back to Kutkha, searching for connection to something other than overwhelming need, but it was like groping at a distant shadow through a field of white noise. The dizzying urge to drink the hospital-grade alcohol only grew stronger as I set up the swabs and gauze, and the agitated, panicky sensation I'd felt when Sergei had hijacked me returned—only this time, it was the Yen, not my old *Pakhun*.[5]

I startled as Christopher returned with an arm full of cans and bottles. He'd brought three sodas... and half a bottle of brandy. "Here, I have-"

I snatched a can from him, cracked it, and threw back half with three long swallows. It seared my mouth and jerked me back to wakefulness. I held it back out. "Brandy."

His eyes widened. "Coke and brandy isn't a very good-"

"Please." Even saying the word made me feel sick.

Christopher flashed a watery smile as he obeyed, topping up the can with acrid spirits. He took a heavy seat at the other end of the bed and drank straight from the bottle.

---

[5] THE ULTIMATE AUTHORITY OF AN *ORGANIZATSIYA*. THE PAKHUN (LITERALLY 'PRINCE') IS GENERALLY A THIEF-IN-LAW WITH GREAT SENIORITY.

The agitation only grew as I sipped at the can and shuddered with distaste. If self-loathing had a flavor, it was cheap brandy and coke, but the first mouthful went down with the same intense, frantic relief I'd felt at Strange Kitty. "So what happened? Start from the beginning."

He glanced at me as I began to clean the nastiest of the cuts, the bullet graze, swallowed, and looked away. "I... Okay, well. It's Sunday, biggest day of the week. I was just closing up after finishing all my paperwork for Father Zach, turning the lights out, and... I guess they broke in through the front, somehow. I heard shooting only when they were close, because those guns hardly make any noise. I ran back to my office—I keep a small pistol in there, just in case—but they took the elevator and I barely made it back down to the chapel."

"They were targeting you, specifically?"

"I... I don't know," he replied. "Why would they be trying to kill me?"

"My hunch is that it's something to do with the kidnapping last month," I said, taking a swig off the can. The sugary-sour stuff did, at least, shut the Yen right up. The dangerous urge to drink the isopropyl vanished, subsumed by the need for more caffeine, more sugar, and definitely more brandy. "Is there anything here they'd want?"

Christopher got a strange look on his face: eyes distant, mouth slightly open. Then he shook his head, rubbed his face with a shaking hand, and took another pull off the bottle. "Oh, the kidnapping. Of course. Lord be praised you were here, Rex, or I'd be dead. But... why were you here?"

"Good old-fashioned sanctuary," I said, patting the freshly bleeding wound. Drinking and self-surgery really weren't a good combination, but I had little choice. "I was being pursued by something bad. Had to get across the river, and given that the old story about vampires seemed to be true, I wondered if the story about the undead hating hallowed ground would also bear out."

"Vampires?" Christopher blanched.

"Don't worry. Babushka's story seems to be holding up so far." I fumbled a piece of cotton wool, and had to sit back and close my eyes for a few seconds as the room spun.

"Here. Let me do that." Christopher leaned forward, the bed squeaking under his weight.

It occurred to me that I was shirtless when I felt him touch my skin. I flinched away on the first contact, but he persisted, taking up the gauze with soft, cool hands and getting to work. The alcohol took the edge off my skin sensitivity, so I had another swig off the can while he dabbed away, and tried to ease down.

"If you don't mind me asking, were you a soldier?" He asked tentatively.

"Of a sort."

"You certainly act like one."

"I had a good amount of training. Unofficial, but thorough."

"I wish I'd had the chance to learn how to fight when I was younger," he said, wistfully. "Would have saved me a lot of trouble growing up."

I shrugged. "Maybe. Maybe not. Sometimes knowing a little of something as a kid makes the adults in your life beat you harder."

Christopher smiled, but it wasn't a happy expression. "Sounds like someone speaking from experience."

"Long experience." I closed my eyes again, swaying a little. My nose was throbbing, but the pain was receding under the influence of liquor. "Returning to the immediate situation. Seen any UFOs lately? That's the usual reason the Men in Black show up."

"Men in Black? No, no. Nothing like that."

"Any involvement with the Government at all?" I handed Christopher the tube of wound cream and the bandage.

"No, not really. The supernatural outreach program is in review... but since we learned what happened to the Wolf Grove children, it's been quite subdued." He began to dabble cream on my arm, lips pursed. "But... there is one thing. You're a... well... a warlock, aren't you?"

"Warlocks are what the Vigiles call us," The sensation of his fingers made me shudder. "I prefer 'magus'."

"Well, there has been one thing happening to me that's strange," he said. "Recently I've been... I don't know how to describe it, other than I've been losing time."

Losing time was a common side effect of contact with the Men in Black. Curiosity piqued, I lifted my head, better to hear him. "Go on. When? How?"

"At night, usually." Christopher sounded nervous again, fingers trembling. "I didn't think anything of it because of my history. I told you about that, didn't I?"

He had, in a candid way that made me think he still had some serious boundary issues. Abused as a child, taken into sexual slavery by a trafficker who forcibly addicted him to heroin, used and abused until his teens, until he ran away. Then something about having worked as a street hustler, before being picked up by Pastor Zach. Christopher still had a hole right through him that he thought he'd filled with the Bible, like most addicts who'd found relief through religion. "Yes. You did."

"Do you know what dissociation is?"

"It's when your emotions retreat back behind a wall of nothing," I said.

He made a soft sound of agreement. "When I was young, I deliberately built that wall. I called it 'going to my room'. It was a way to detach, something I did to survive, and it took years and years of therapy to unlearn. I still do it, but not as badly. Until a couple of months ago. It was after I came back from the mother church meeting in Chicago. The night of the 17th of August."

"Specific date," I replied. The brandy had settled over me like a heavy blanket, my skin humming pleasantly under Christopher's gentle hands as he bandaged my arm.

"Yes. I remember it because it was the last date I recalled before I blacked out," he said. "I woke up in an alley, sprawled out in a heap of trash bags. Trash was everywhere. It smelled awful. I thought I'd been mugged, so I gathered my luggage and went to hospital. Nothing was wrong. I found my wallet, everything. But it was the 19th. I'd lost two whole days."

I grunted. That fit the stories I'd heard about Men in Black and the abductions they were associated with. "Go on."

"It's been happening ever since." Christopher slid off the bed, moving around me to get a look at my other injuries. "Once or twice a week, I'll wake up somewhere I don't remember going. Sometimes I'm... dressed strangely."

I cracked an eye open to look at him. "Strangely how?"

To my surprise, he flushed. "Sometimes nothing at all. Sometimes in... well... in other people's clothing. It doesn't seem to matter what gender. I'll have a mix of things on, like someone who had no idea how to dress a person had dressed me while I was asleep. Shorts, raincoats, dressing gowns, underwear I don't recognize. I woke up with one high heel on once. Just one. I haven't known what to say or who to go to, but you seem to know a lot about strange things and... I'm afraid. After tonight, I'm, I don't know what to think. And... there was something else."

"Go on."

"My eyes," he said, looking at me. "They didn't use to be this color. They changed while I was blacked out. If you look at my old photos, they weren't this color at all."

The back of my neck prickled with some half-formed instinct. I regarded him with what I hoped was an authoritative, serious look. "It's possible that you were abducted. In the paranormal investigations sense of 'abduction'."

He recoiled a little, a weird half-smile playing over his mouth. "Abducted? What, by aliens?"

"More likely it was by whoever fields the goons who were trying to kill you tonight." I scrutinized him, and momentarily, found myself wishing that Angkor had been here. I had enjoyed working with him, watching him fight, watching him perform magic. He could have scanned Christopher for implants or something, helped me figure shit out. We'd worked together like oiled parts in the same machine the few times we'd faced shit like this, but now...

Christopher rubbed his face, shoulders hunched. He looked terribly young. "I'm worried. And I... I haven't known what to say. I thought about telling Father Zach, but I'm afraid he'll say I'm possessed."

"That's also a possibility," I said. "Unfortunately."

"God, no. Please, not again." He leaned against the edge of the bed, and covered his eyes.

"Again?" I sat forward, resting my forearms on my knees.

He didn't reply, and it took me a few seconds to realize why. He was crying, stifling the sobs against his palm.

"I can't. Something's wrong, and I've tried, I've tried keeping my journal, and I've been doing all my therapist's exercises, and praying and praying, but I just can't stop it." He was trying to hold it together, and failing. "I lose all this time and it's been, it's scaring the shit out of me, but I can't stop it!"

The number of times I'd seen a man cry in my lifetime were few and far between, and of those instances, the general response around me had been other men telling them to man up. I froze up as Christopher broke down further, crushed under terror and weeks of built up stress layered over a lifetime of trauma. What the hell did I do now? What would… Talya do? Or Mariya?

"Hey, kid," I said, haltingly. "Hang in there. It'll be alright, okay? I can take a look at this for you in a couple days, once I've had some rest. If I'm still around, I'll follow it up."

The priest looked up at me, his pacific blue eyes even more vivid now that they were ringed with red. "I'll p-pay you to, to do whatever it is you do. Just please, if someone's doing something to me, I-"

Maybe it was the brandy, or maybe it was the cocktail of his eagerness and vulnerability, but I found myself doing something I'd never believed myself capable of. I reached out and put my hands on his arms.

"Seriously," I said, meeting his gaze with my own. "We'll sort it out. I helped stop a guy that liked burning people to death with curses, once. Don't worry, alright?"

"This is… you, thank you, for helping me. I'm sorry, I'm not usually like this." He sniffled, and before I knew what had happened, he had his arms wrapped around me, head buried against my shoulder. He was standing now, and I was sitting on the edge of the bed. It put him at just the right height that he didn't have to bend over.

Uncertainly, I patted his back and waited, glancing down at my sleeping familiar before turning back and getting a lungful of male scent from Christopher's shirt. Good cologne, nothing too strong, and the warm, woody-savory scent of his sweat. My pulse leaped as Christopher pulled back, his hips grazing the front of my pants. Before I quite knew what was happening, his mouth was close enough to kiss. His lips smelled sweet, his breath heavy with alcohol. The Yen liked it. It liked it a lot, and Christopher sensed it as only an experienced victim could.

"Are you okay?" The priest whispered against my mouth. He still had tears in his eyelashes.

I knew if I spoke, it would break the spell. I knew I didn't want to break it, and I knew why even though it sickened me. He looked like Vassily, and with the Yen pumping venom into my psyche, it was enough.

I grasped him by the back of his head and pulled him toward me, but not toward my mouth. Instead, I pushed his head over my shoulder and went for his neck, pushing his collar away to bite down and suck. He cried out in surprise and pain, fingers clutching at my arms. There was a moment of resistance, of fear, and then he relaxed into my jaws and hands with a shudder.

"Please." He got his hands between his body and mine, almost but not quite pushing back. "Rex, please-!"

I let go slowly, tasting salt, and licked it off my lips. Christopher was breathing quickly, eyes black and feverish as he stared at my mouth. He was rock-hard despite being drunk, a fact that became obvious as he swayed against me.

"I think that's enough," I said hoarsely.

"You know, it's been a long time since a man looked that way at me." The old Jersey accent crept out from under the Manhattan affectation as he fingered the bloody tatters of my shirt.

"Looked at how?" My heart stuttered in my chest. "I... what?"

"Like someone who can control me," he breathed.

My pulse leapt, and I froze, bewildered, as Christopher pressed his hands flat against my shoulders and his mouth against my jaw. He was still shaking from the combat high, but he knew how to touch. No light, sticky fingers, no hesitancy. Firm, confident, as he exhaled hotly and let one hand slide down the front of my body. I caught his wrist before he got further than a feather-light touch over my fly. "No. You're drunk."

"I'm a big boy." He laughed, and slid down to his knees. "And you're hard."

And getting harder. Christopher was gazing up at me from the floor, and everything about it—his position, the fact we were in a GOD-damned church, the way he unselfconsciously yearned toward my body—brought on a hunger so real that I was stunned into stillness by it. I didn't know him. I wasn't ready. His eyes were the wrong shade of blue, and my cock was beginning to hurt with the familiar tearing pain even as it swelled with need.

"You're drunk." I squeezed his wrist until it creaked, and then let go.

"Please." He leaned in against my knee. "Please... Sir?"

The word hit me down low, a thrill almost as intense as the excitement I'd felt being held at gunpoint in the parking lot.

"Open up your shirt," I was suspended in the disbelief of what I was doing. "Slowly."

Christopher blinked back at me, but after a breathless moment, he obeyed. His fingers fumbled on the buttons as he undid them, baring the lean, hard lines of his body. He had a decent amount of hair on him, but the old abuses of his past were written into the stretch marks and scars on his taut stomach. Half-seen words and symbols, layers of fine razor lines, probably self-inflicted. He waited on my word, vulnerable and uncertain.

"Pull your cock out," I said.

For a moment, I thought he'd refuse: fight me, say no, but then he reached down with trembling hands and unsnapped his belt, eyes dark with need, his mouth flushed with anticipation. He looked so much like a younger Vassily that my heart twisted.

"That's it." My mouth was very dry, hands papery hot.

Christopher pushed his open fly down, reached in and freed his erection, searching my expression for approval. He was circumcised, neither impressive nor disappointing, but the sight of his naked body was like another shot of liquor. My breathing was quick as I looked him up and down, and he squirmed like it was a real touch, like my hands were on his skin.

I licked my lip. "Stroke it."

He looked almost as shocked as I felt. Slowly, haltingly, he obeyed, running his soft hand up and down the length of it. I reached across for my drink and took a long pull off it, watching him the entire time.

"Good." I set the can aside, and leaned forward to grasp a handful of his hair, twisting it to bring his head up as he tried to bend down around his fuck and focus in on it. Carefully, I drew him forward until his mouth was pushed against the outside of my fly. He huffed against it, the heat a shocking pleasurable jolt I felt all the way back into my gut.

"Please." His begging was muffled against the fabric of my slacks, voice syrupy with desperation. "Rex, Sir, please!"

Sir. It nearly undid my self-control. Christopher felt the kick, the way the word made my cock jerk and strain. Sensing weakness, he opened his mouth and pressed his tongue against the layers of cloth. I let him, but I didn't let him expose me, and as he worked himself into a froth over what he couldn't have, I heard and smelled and felt his excitement grow. He was fucking his own hand in earnest now, moaning softly in his throat, and I was drunk on it: every whimper, every breath of scent he gasped; the weak, submissive pluck of his fingers as he tugged needily at my pantsleg.

"Good." I ran my gloved hand through his hair and rubbed against his lips, and he shuddered, flushing darkly with humiliation. "That's a good boy."

His breath hitched, and that was the only warning I had before he climaxed, gasping, wrapping his arm around my thighs and leaning in against my legs. He made a thin sound of anguish, panting open-mouthed as he looked up at me. The priest was an intoxicated mess, his brilliant eyes vacant with sullen ecstasy. He held his wet, cum-slick hand like he didn't know what to do with it, his erection still jerking spasmodically as it slowly softened.

Power. It had never occurred to me that there was power in sex. I was in a kind of trance, my usual prudish terror overridden by pure excitement. I'd had this kind of power, and never used it? My lips parted as I stared down, watching him squirm. "Now suck your fingers clean."

For a moment, I thought I'd pushed it too far. But then Christopher brought his hand up and began to lick and suck, face burning. The room was small, and my ears were full of the soft, wet sounds of his tongue and lips. My fingers twitched in time with them, thrills running through the nerves as the leather that covered them buckled and rubbed.

"Yes. Good." I struggled to keep my breathing regular as he twisted with lust and humiliation on the floor in front of me, hair damp with sweat. When he was done, I reach forward again, and stroked his hair and his ears and cheeks with gloved hands. Christopher was hot to touch, nearly feverish, and he shook like a bird against my palms. "Very good."

"Oh no," he whispered. "Oh no. I shouldn't have done that."

"No, no, no, it's fine," I said, trying to blink away the fog. "You didn't do anything wrong."

"No." He shook his head, breathing deeply and quickly, and fumbled with his clothes in awkward haste. "No, I-I… I'm sorry. Rex, please. You need to go."

The bubble had burst, and with it, the illusion of power. I was a relative stranger in someone else's church. Numb and still a little drunk, I watched him move to the counter and throw back the remaining brandy, gulping thirstily. While he drank, I eased up onto my feet. "Christopher-"

"Look, I just lapsed, okay?!" He raised his voice, a staccato bark that hit my ears like a whip crack. "Please, just go before I fuck up worse. I'm sorry."

My skin crawled. Vampire or no vampire, I wasn't any safer in this place than I was outside of it.

"Thursday," I slurred. "I'll look at this, this curse of yours Thursday. Try not get shot. Remember to call the police – there's bodies downstairs."

Christopher waved me away, shaking his head, and when I closed the door, I heard him sob, and then the shattering of glass as he threw the empty bottle across the room.

CHAPTER 16

I left the church in a state of deep confusion, delirious with fatigue. When I got back home, I went straight for the shower, turned it up as hot as I could stand, and endured the pain of it running over the cuts and bruises I'd taken in the fight with the Men in Black. I needed to sort out my head, and wash Christopher's smell off my skin.

As the booze wore off, I found myself feeling used, burned out, and angry. Fear of Sergei and what he'd tried to do to me was a manic current underneath my thoughts as I ran over the chain of events, back and forth, trying to make sense of what had happened. Sergei was trying to enslave me. The Men in Black were real, and they were trying to kill Christopher. We'd gotten drunk, and… yes. At first, I thought I'd taken advantage of him—but when I picked it apart, that didn't hold up. I'd just done what he'd wanted, hadn't I? And what did that make me? A pushover? Gay? Not gay? Because it wasn't like I touched him. After the rest of this ridiculous excuse of a week, it didn't even feel real.

Once I was scrubbed clean, I sat on the edge of my bed with a street surgery kit and took stock of the night's toll on my body. I had a number of deep impact bruises that were getting stiff. The bullet had skipped through the outer edge of my triceps and had torn a long track of skin, but I'd avoided penetration. I rubbed lidocaine into the long cut, hissing at the initial sting, then cleaned it out and stitched it up. After that, I got some painkillers and precautionary antibiotics into me, brushed my teeth, and stared at Angkor's empty bed for a while before I lay down and passed the hell out.

I slipped into another world, flowing through the cracks of reality like sand: a technicolor, hyper-realistic vision that was too real to pull away from, but not real enough to convince the lucid mind that it was anything other than a dream.

It was Eden. I ran barefoot across the soft ivory loam, chasing a plume of shining white hair through a thick field of fleshy, shivering trees. It was Zarya, the Gift Horse. She was laughing joyously ahead of me, a sound that made my heart pound with raw, primal need. The hunger was erotic, a need so bad that I thought my stomach was going to turn me inside out. I needed to sink my teeth in her throat and bear her to ground, pin her as she struggled, her body arching against mine, and eat. She was fruit, THE Fruit, and I knew her heart ached for the knife as much as I ached to pierce it.

We plunged through a thicket of underbrush, and I cut around the path of the chase on instinct, a wolf heading off a deer. My blood was pumping, jaws aching with anticipation as the gap between us closed. I skidded down a hill and into a gully, knife in hand. It was little more than a long shard of fine, razor-sharp glass bound to a piece of carved antler.

Zarya flashed by, a ghost of pearly dappled skin and white hair, and I bounded from cover to catch her around her slender waist. She threw herself around with a cry of mingled surprise and delight, and we tripped and tumbled painlessly, dizzily down the hill into a soft bed of mother-of-pearl ferns. She was stunning, a face of all races and none, aristocratic and unearthly. Her skin was like nacre, rippling with subtle colors. Her eyes were Blue, the color of Earth seen from space.

I had the knife up under the edge of her jaw, the edge pushed against her pulse. She laughed, fearless, and pushed up against it to kiss me. Her mouth was shockingly sweet, an electric honeysuckle punch that coursed from my lips to the rest of my nerves in a wave of pleasure. I leaned into it, shifting from the hard tension of a hunter into the flowing closeness of a lover, but it was no longer Zarya who lay beneath me. It was Angkor.

His eyes were hooded with sensual languor, lips and cheeks flushed. My breath caught and my cock stiffened painfully as the nature of the hunger abruptly shifted from food to sex. I was between his legs, vaguely aware that I couldn't see any part of my own body. Before I could think to move away, he reached up, grasped my wrist, and pulled the glass knife into his own throat.

Silver. He bled silver. At the core of Angkor's dark violet-gray eyes was a halo of intense, brilliant green light, and as the silver Gift Horse blood crept up along the glass and over my bare skin, his lips framed a single word, a question.

Zealot?

I fell to the bed from a great height, eyes flying open as my body jolted and then fell still. I was face down and clutching my pillow, and I was in a lot of pain.

"Ow, oww... akh!" My foreskin was stretched so tight it felt like it was going to tear. Breathing through my teeth, I shoved a hand down and freed the trapped flesh, exhaling only when the agony began to subside. "Good GOD."

The light from the window was hazy, the kind of uniform snow-sky gray that obliterated any sense of time without a clock. Once I had my bearings, I found that I felt... awful, really. Beaten up, seedy, heavy and stuffy, like my immune system was working overtime to clear itself of disease. I could hope that the MiB's bullet hadn't contained some kind of biological or radioactive payload. It was possible. Many paranormal researchers and UFOlogists had become ill after contact with the Silencers.

I wasn't surprised to find it was close to 8pm when I got to the kitchen. Binah followed me in, meowing with the kind of tragic desperation that suggested a calamity had taken place. The calamity in question was that her food dish was empty in the middle. Not actually empty— there was plenty of kibble around the edge of the dish.

"Oy, what a crisis. What a tragedy. For God's sake, Binah… there's still food in there." I spoke over her air-raid siren wail, and shuffled the bowl so that the empty space was covered up. "See?"

Binah sat down on the kitchen floor and primly wrapped her tail around her feet, the very tip twitching over her toes. She glared at me with clear affront.

"There are starving cats in Rome that would fight you to the death for this kibble, Binah." I made a sound of disgust and bent down to pick up the dish. Bad idea: when I stood back up, the world swayed. My head was pounding, and my vision pulsed.

The meowing resumed, pitched high with excitement as I pulled the kibble box from the pantry and made a volcano of food in the middle of the bowl. Binah was throwing herself bodily at my legs by the time I set it on the floor, wincing as my thighs cramped and my back seized. When I stood back up, I had to wipe my forehead clean of sweat. My muscles were shuddering, like I'd run a marathon. I'd overdone it, and needed to take care of myself. Food, water, coffee... and the seed packet I'd found, the one with 'Zealot' written on the label. The dream had reminded me of it, and I knew better than to ignore those kinds of dreams.

I ended up getting most of the way through making an open-faced sandwich when curiosity overpowered me. I poured myself a cup of coffee, went to the bedroom to get the seeds, then took both outside to the weedy, hard-scrabble yard that passed as our garden. There were a number of cracked pots with old potting soil in them, so I dragged one inside and took it to the kitchen sink, dug around in it, and planted the seeds in the dampened soil.

Then I waited, not entirely sure what to expect. Marijuana? A magical beanstalk? Nothing?

The pot sat there, dirty and mossy, the soil undisturbed. It seemed 'nothing' was the answer.

"Huh." I drained my coffee, which tasted just as bad as the cup I'd gotten while I was out, then washed the cup and my hands before getting back to my sandwich. I'd found a Ukrainian deli where I was unlikely to see any of my old cronies and had gotten myself some *salo*[6], one of my few guilty pleasures: pork fat cured with salt and garlic, eaten raw on heavy rye bread. It was a Ukrainian stereotype and I knew it, but *salo* was at least part of why I'd never been motivated to take up my mother's faith. I liked mine with sharp pickle, horseradish, thin slices of fresh raw garlic and parsley. I was most of the way through restoring some calories when a sweet, narcotic smell pushed through the strong savory odor of garlic and forced me to look back toward the sink.

Flowers that resembled foxgloves nodded from long green stems, growing and stretching so fast that they changed position as I blinked. The smell grew stronger with every passing moment, clouding my head. The sandwich fell from my fingers to the counter. In the back of my mind, I was sure I should have been worried about what was happening, but after my next breath, couldn't bring myself to be concerned.

The walls swam as I stumbled to the table, groped toward a chair, and slithered down into it. My eyes grew

---

[6] ALSO A STEREOTYPICAL UKRAINIAN FOOD, HENCE THE TOUCH OF GUILT.

heavy. I closed them, lulled by the smell, and on the backs of my eyelids, an image began to form. The outline of a woman, her body made of sparkling motes of colored light. She was plain but confident; petite, with a bob of brown hair and a strong Southern accent. Georgian, maybe.

"Norgay? GOD, I hope the Phitonic coding Zealot taught me works. Anyway, it's worse than what we thought. They have the MahTree, AND they found someone who knows where to find the Shard. Her name is Lee—Lee Harrison. She's a cenote diver and archaeologist, which means you were right and the Shard is probably south of the border."

"I don't know much about Harrison, but I know she's not as strong-willed as the other Keepers. She's a plain-Jane human with no special training other than being tough as old leather, and Bishop WILL find the Shard if he has the chance to interrogate her. She was captured, then escaped, and was caught by the Templum Voctus Sol—because of course, they're looking for the Shard as well—then recaptured from them. Her last known location was the holding cell at McKinnon Funerals, 115 Sutphin Boulevard, in South Jamaica. If you can get Zealot and RUBICON or the Irregulars in before the 20th, you might still find her there, but be careful. Bishop's serious about finding this Shard. He's sent Men in Black… Gen 2 and 3, possibly some Gen 4 Silencers."

I watched in awe, confused, but fascinated. The hallucination had solidified. I was watching—and hearing—Agent Kristen Cross speak earnestly and urgently, as if toward a video camera.

"I haven't heard anything about the other Keeper, but I suspect he's been taken to Delta Site. I'm still trying to get a location for

you, but it seems like no one below PK-RATCHET clearance knows anything about the Icebox other than it's somewhere cold."

"Bishop is gunning hard for the America-Korea link. The current theory is the Templum Voctus Sol and Odaeyang are both connected to the Church of the Voice. The meeting in Quantico was almost all about how to bring them in or erase them. He doesn't want to meet the Deacon—he just wants him dead, along with this 'Soldier 557' lieutenant of his. It's honestly terrifying, sir. I don't have any firm evidence, but the way that things have been around here recently, it feels like command is preparing for something. Something big."

"I'm going to do my best to learn more about Delta Site and see about getting those plans you asked for in my last brief. Information to come, assuming something hasn't happened to me. If you've got this report in hand, then the meeting with Zealot on the 25th went smoothly. I'll keep you updated as I can—it'll be easier once Bishop has left town. Keep GOD underfoot, sir."

The smell abruptly faded, and the vision faded into a hazy, ghostly negative as the plants drooped. The color drained from them, and their leaves curled and browned. I blinked rapidly, squinting against the sudden glare as I rose to my feet and stumbled off to find a notebook to jot everything down in before I forgot any of it.

I was still furiously scribing when Talya appeared in the doorway, hand resting on the frame. I was muttering to myself, a hand twisted up through my hair as I frantically wrote a list of bullet-points.

"Rex?"

"Shh." I didn't risk glancing away. *Lee is a 'Keeper', knows something about a 'Shard'. Link between American TVS*

and Korea Odaeyang with Church of the Voice and Deacon? Vigiles
(?) held meeting on this, want to bring down Deacon (?).

Talya wandered across in silence, curious as any cat. She sat down, and Binah leaped from the floor to the table to greet her.

"Meeting with 'Zealot' was supposed to be on the 25th... same day as the blood rain." I looked up, setting the pen down, and found the girl looking back at me. "Incredible."

"What?" She was jiggling in her seat with barely-controlled curiosity.

"I just saw something. In the pots, over there." I said in Russian, and waved irritably toward the sink. "Something I don't think I was supposed to see. Now I have to find my sandwich."

She blinked as I rose and shuffled off, still a little woozy from whatever cocktail of drugs and pheromones had been used to pass along Agent Cross's report.

"Rex? Are you alright...?"

"Zealot," I said, getting my plate and taking it back to the table. "Someone named Zealot. Someone else named Norgay. The FBI agent that was murdered, the one the Vigiles are threatening me over... I don't think she was murdered by the Templum Voctus Sol. She was spying for someone, Talya. I think she was killed by her own people."

"Uhhh..."

I waved my hands, frustrated by my inability to get my point across. "I can't explain. What did you want to ask me?"

"Uh, nothing. I came to tell you something." The gears were turning in Talya's head. She was young, naive, but she was smart and logically-minded. "I think it might have something to do with what you're rambl- uh, talking about, actually. It's about MinTex."

I chased the mouthful of sandwich down with cold coffee. "Go."

"Okay, so, get this." She leaned forward conspiratorially. "MinTex is a shell company registered in the Bahamas. Pretty standard corporate tax haven stuff, right? But from there, it gets really weird. The company is registered to 'Max Sterling' who is apparently the CEO of the 'Spartan Trading Group'."

"'Max Sterling'? Slightly better than 'Fayk E. Nayme', but not by much." I narrowed my eyes, thinking back. "There is no Spartan Trading Group in the *Organizatsiya*, or that I've ever heard of associated with it."

"Right. Well, Max doesn't exist, obviously, and Spartan's address is in Delaware. There's this one address these kind of companies all use, 1209 North Orange Street. There's like... hundreds of thousands of companies registered there."

"LLCs don't have to disclose their directors or board if they're registered in Delaware. We used to use privacy services there all the time. So it's a dead end?"

"Well, hold on. I did some digging on the Max Sterling alias and Spartan." Talya held up a finger. "Spartan is itself a shell. Their PR presence consists of an automated phone service. They're apparently an oil and gas consultancy, whatever that means, but they don't have any employees."

"A holding company for a holding company for the *Organizatsiya*."

"Right." Talya's uranium-gold eyes were shining with the thrill of the chase. "Now, get this. I went looking for anything that might be owned by Spartan or Max Sterling. Spartan is indexed on Wall Street, even though they don't actually produce anything. Their shares go up and down based on pure speculation, and I guess some dodgy brokering so that they look like they're actually doing something."

"That one was one of Yegor's primary duties for the *Organizatsiya*," I said. "Managing dodgy brokers."

"Yeah. So, me and one of my friends, we, uh, paid a virtual visit to the brokerage that manages Spartan's stocks. It gets a bit speculative here, but the brokerage only has one agent, and he also happens to manage funds for this super-conservative Catholic PAC, 'The Future of America'. My friend told me that TFA is basically the re-election machine for the President of the North Carolina Senate, Sebastian Hart, and HE is-"

"Gearing up for a presidential run next year," I finished. "Well, well."

Talya nodded, bouncing nervously in her seat.

I thought over that while I eased back, wincing. "So MinTex might not belong to the *Organizatsiya* at all. It could be the child of a more established corporate-government alias, and used to launder the money gained by trafficking children. But… that's incredibly risky, from a cold, hard business perspective. Sergei couldn't have been doing this for long."

"Why?" Talya cocked her head.

"Because Lily and Dru were disciples of the Deacon," I said. "And I'm fairly sure now that the Deacon is at war with the Vigiles Magicarum. Like I said, I saw something I wasn't supposed to see. A report, coded into those dead plants by an FBI agent who was working for someone called 'Norgay'. There's two opposing sides involved here: the Vigiles, led by someone named 'Bishop', and the TVS, led by the Deacon."

"Deacon and Bishop?" Talya rolled her eyes. "But I guess that makes sense. MinTex was only registered a bit over a month ago."

"So Sergei—or Sergei's proxy, Vanya—was working for the Deacon, but he turned on him and began working for the Government instead," I said. "That must have happened while we were still searching for the children. Fascinating."

Talya nodded, eyes wide and serious.

I took a bite of sandwich, and shook my head. "If your theory bears out, I believe we've stumbled on the proverbial can of worms."

"If you want to pursue this, I need more information," Talya said. "I need to know who the major donors of the PAC are, so I can look into them. If I could get bank information, then we could confirm that money's being exchanged between the PAC, Spartan, and MinTex…"

I grunted. "Can you and your friend 'virtually visit' these records?"

"They don't have any records on the Internet. I'd have to get on a LAN, a local network inside of their office. Or, you know, a filing cabinet." She wrinkled her nose.

"Then the next goal is to locate the premises of the PAC, and hope it's local," I said. "A list of donors would be useful *kompromat* to have against the Vigiles, Sergei, and possibly Hart as well."

"I already know where it is," Talya said. "It's weird, though. The PAC's HQ is actually a funeral home, so it might not be the right address..."

I frowned. "115 Sutphin Boulevard?"

Talya paused, hands fluttering. "Uhh... yeah. How'd you know?"

"Same address as the place I heard about in that report just now. The Vigiles are keeping someone there. A woman, name of Lee Harrison" I said. "So you're right, and if I'm hearing you correctly, all roads lead to the Vigiles Magicarum."

She picked her nail with her teeth, brow furrowed. "So if the MinTex-Spartan-TFA trail and the Lee Harrison trail lead to the same place, and the Vigiles are involved with your old *Organizatsiya*... then they must have known about the abuse of the children?"

"You hired me because the police weren't turning anything up. Seems like there was a reason for that."

Talya paled. "But the Deacon's name and the people on that computer that you found…"

"A name is easily faked," I said. "Someone interested in framing the Deacon could readily just use the name or title in text messages. And remember… Soldier 557 killed Lily and Dru Ross, correct?"

"And we never… oh." Talya's eyes widened. "You think they betrayed the Deacon? And he had them, you know, whacked?"

I snorted. "Yes. That also explains why Soldier took out Falkovich. I'd wondered about that."

"The Vigiles. Wow. Ayashe's going to love that." Talya shook her head in disbelief, picking at her lip. "You… you don't think she knew, do you?"

"I'm not sure," I said. "But I doubt it. Ayashe fancies herself to be a white knight battling the forces of eldritch chaos. Kristen's report implied that most Vigiles agents are in the dark about the higher-level activities of the organization. That makes perfect sense to me—it's how we used Sixers."

"Sixers?"

"*Mafiya* associates," I answered. "They usually thought they were doing one thing when they were actually doing another."

"Maybe we should get Lee and try and explain all this to Ayashe, then?"

Lee was a 'Keeper', whatever that was. I frowned. "I doubt Ayashe will listen. If Lee's still in that funeral home, then the place will be under lockdown. We can try to pull her out, see if she can corroborate, but our focus should be gathering more information and obtaining evidence. My bet is that the TVS were running children down to Texas for years, and the Government made a deal with Sergei to take over the business. Sergei decided that trafficking the kids wasn't bringing him enough profit… so he sanctioned some of them to be killed for the organ trade."

"Ugh." Talya rubbed the bridge of her nose, screwing her eyes shut. "Well, I'll try to find something I can hack into from the Net first. I just… People can be so awful, Alexi. I don't know why anyone would do this."

"Because they believe you're either a winner or a loser. Men like Vanya and Sergei look at other people in black and white. Weak or strong. Success or failure. They think they're playing a great big chess game, and everyone is just a piece on the board. They frame everything through a lens of lack. Zero sum. If I win, you lose."

"Is that how you think?" Talya cocked her head.

It was a question asked in innocence, but the answer was not an easy one. I glanced down at my nearly untouched cup of coffee. It smelled bitter and muddy.

"I grew up being taught that this is the way of the world," I said, framing my words carefully. "But after learning a lot about myself and what I care for, I made the decision to leave. For a while, I didn't know how, but fate caught up with me. You have to understand… when you're 'in'—especially when you're born into it—you grow up thinking life is a zero-sum game. So I suppose that I do still think that way, sometimes, but it used to be all the time. It's not anymore."

"That makes you a good person, you know."

I snorted. "Don't count on it."

The girl's expression was troubled now, her features sharply drawn. "You know... I worry about becoming that way. Like, by joining the Club. Jenner's a wonderful person, I mean, you know that... but now that I'm looking to be patched in, I'm seeing the other side of it. She's really ruthless. I think she's killed people, like... not because they were bad people, but because they were in her way. Do you think so?"

I knew so, but I wasn't about to tell Talya that. I leaned forward a little. "It doesn't matter. You can't ask questions about it in the open like this, though, and you sure as hell shouldn't talk about it with me. I'm not part of the Club. That's part of being involved in a gang—the business of the gang is no one else's business. If you mine for information like that, they'll think you're a snitch."

"Well, I'm not-" she stammered.

"I know you're not. But that's the definition of respect in this kind of place," I said. "You don't ask about people. You judge them by what they do, and keep your thoughts about them to yourself."

She frowned, rolling one of her lip rings around and around. Talya had worked for the Smithsonian as an I.T. Coordinator before this. She'd been part of the Four Fires, the 'legal' Weeder community group that had turned out to be rotten to the core. 'Street hardened' was not a phrase I'd ever associate with Talya, no matter how many tattoos or piercings she got.

"I guess I expected it to be more honest here, you know?" She said, shrugging. "More open than the Four Fires."

"It is more honest overall. And you're right: Jenner's good people. But don't talk about her business, ever. Not even with people you trust." I had a sip of coffee and nearly spat it out. I'd made my coffee the same way every morning for twenty years—strong black drip that could melt a copper penny, no sugar—but ever since the alcohol cravings had started, it tasted like swill. I wanted it anyway. Fucking Yen. I set it aside and concentrated on the food, pausing as I heard the roar of motorcycles coming up the drive from outside.

"Speak of the devil." Talya brightened again. "I better go out. Jenner will want me to park her bike. But Rex?"

"Uhh?" I grunted around a mouth full of *salo* and rye.

Talya's face flooded with a smile. "Thanks for the advice. It's, I guess I'm still getting used to the way things work."

"Jenner and Zane know that. They won't involve you in anything out of your depth." I waved her off with a little shooing motion. "Off you go."

She smiled, and then scampered from the room. The bikes outside were revving in place, a sound that did nothing to help my headache. Grimacing, I set the last bit of sandwich down and had only just started to rise when I heard Talya's piercing scream from outside.

CHAPTER 17

I hadn't been stupid enough to leave myself unarmed after last night. I had the Wardbreaker holstered under my parka, and a knife, which I pulled as I barreled through the house to the outside.

The yard was wet, a fine mist of rain floating and steaming in the headlamps of dozens of bikers, a mob of unwashed leather and diesel roaring in the yard. Talya stood between an injured man lying on the ground and the growing semicircle of bodies and machines. The man was unconscious. Both his hands had been cut off, the stumps of his wrists badly cauterized and tied off with fishing wire.

"I don't care who you think you are!" Talya was shouting, mantling protectively over the injured man with her fists balled up in front of her. "You're a fucking mongrel!"

The guy looming over her looked like a skinned bull. Seven feet tall, close to four hundred pounds, he was muscular in a way that was neither attractive or functional. Veins crawled up along his reddish, freckled arms like worms. He had a thin-lipped mouth on a crocodilian face, and tightly curled, short hair the color and texture of rusted steel wool. His eyes were flat black pits, communicating nothing but cruel indifference.

"What the hell is going on here?" I shoved through the fringes of the pack, brandishing the knife at any upraised hands, and joined Talya to face him down.

"About time someone with balls showed up," Bullhead rasped. His voice was very deep, but so dry that it was always on the edge of cracking. Very few people had a voice like this, the color-texture of crumbling tar, but this man did. "Otto was just about to fuck Little Miss Piggy here and see if he could bait out Tranny with a bit of squealing."

Talya's lips peeled back from her teeth with a snarl, her pupils constricting to slits. I was about to step back when the door to Strange Kitty flew open and the Twin Tigers boiled out of the club with a small army of bikers, punks and rivetheads.

"Speak of the devil, and she shall appear!" The man to Bullhead's left spread his arms, hands open. He was tall and skinny, with a faded dirty-blond mohawk and an unpleasant air of entropy. "Our favorite little slanty-eye whore!"

Jenner sneered. "You forget to take Otto's cock out of your mouth before you came here, Dogboy? You sure sound like a guy talking around a mouthful of dick. Get the fuck off my property."

"Came to deliver you something," the big guy rumbled. The words coming out of his mouth, their tone, didn't match the complete lack of life or affect in his features. It creeped me the hell out. "But then Otto ran into your puppy dog. She a new member of the Little Girls' Club?"

Talya smiled, her voice laced with sugary venom. "Go out into traffic and play a nice long game of hide-and-go-fuck-yourself."

Jenner grinned. "Hah! You heard the girl. And stop talking about yourself in the third person, for fuck's sake."

While they traded barbs, I assessed Otto and his subordinates. Dogboy wasn't a Blank- I wasn't sure what he was, but something was off about the way he held himself. Too stiff, too… dead. The old man standing to Otto's right looked like he'd come from a hobo camp and picked up a lot of roadkill on his way into the city. He was shirtless, skinny-fat, with a pot belly and weather-worn skin. He wore countless necklaces, his chest decorated in several pounds of beads, bones, feathers, chains and rings, most of which hummed with Phitonic charge. A mage: one of the crazy street shaman variety.

"This everyone who's come to back you up? Jeez. Looks like you're a few men down," Dogboy said. His voice had a harsh purplish crackle to it that lifted the hair on the nape of my neck. "How's life been treating you since Mason died?"

Jenner's face went very still. "Pretty fucking good, actually. Now, in case you didn't hear me, I told you to get the hell out of my yard."

Dogboy leered at her. "I bet it's tough having to manage everything without a man behind you."

Jenner looked as grim as I'd ever seen her. "You've got five seconds to turn the fuck around and leave. One."

Dogboy laughed, flashing fangs. That solved that mystery. He was a vampire... but what was Otto? A Weeder of some sort, apparently. But Weeders were alive in a way that almost defied description, as if they carried more energy, more vitality than a normal person. I let my vision slipstream, peering at him, and recoiled at what I saw. Otto's aura slithered over him like a caul of pulsing grubs, a deep red-violet.

"You don't fucking get it, you little bitch." Dogboy abruptly sobered, hands on hips. "News travels. You don't get to play pretend any more. Give it up. This city belongs to-."

"Blah blah dur hurr me big man, whatever." Jenner talked right over the top of him. She could exceed him in volume and pitch. "You wanna take it? Come and dance, little boy. I'll eat your fucking heart right here in front of your ballet troupe."

A storm was brewing in the ranks on both sides. Zane waited like a pillar of expressionless brown marble, arms loosely folded. Big Ron glowered at the intruders with one thumb hooked into his belt and a shotgun over his other shoulder. Neither man spoke.

"Snow White and the fucking Seven Dwarves." Dogboy sneered. "You don't belong here anymore. No one cares about your stupid laws, and no one's going to save you when Otto drags you off by your fucking hair and-"

Jenner bristled like an angry alley cat as she advanced on him and shoved his chest. Dogboy caught her wrists inhumanly fast. Before he could do anything about it,

Jenner pivoted her hands inward to break the hold and kicked him square in the crotch with strength far beyond her size. As he buckled, she caught his hand and threw him to the ground by it. She didn't let go: Jenner stepped over his arm, twisted it as he swung at the back of her knee, and broke it at the elbow.

Dogboy hadn't even finished his scream of agony before the Nightbrothers roared and closed in on us in a wave of unwashed leather and metal. Someone barreled toward me, a pipe raised over his head. I hit him with the glass breaker end of the knife, knocking his arm down before slamming the hilt into the side of his helmet. He was just human, and the blow sent him stumbling. Another man came in from my right, lunging straight into Zane's foot. He took the kick to the nose, and sprawled back into the dirt.

In the chaos, I saw Otto deliberately push into the brawl and make a beeline for Talya, who was fighting two men with the help of a couple of punks only a few years younger than she was. I shoved the reeling biker in front of me, knocking him to the ground, and struggled through the pack to join her.

"Come at me, dogfuckers! *Cái thằng chó đẻ*[7]!" Jenner screeched as she kicked over the nearest Nightbrothers bike with her full strength—her real strength, the superhuman strength of an Elder shapeshifter tigress. A thousand pounds of iron, leather and chrome toppled to

---

[7] 'SONS OF BITCHES!' RATHER MORE RUDE IN VIETNAMESE THAN IN ENGLISH.

the ground over Dogboy's legs as he struggled up, elbow and wrist twisted and useless.

Every muscle in my body screamed with fatigue as I fought to get to Talya before Otto did. He had the look of a snake cruising toward a particularly juicy mouse. In theory, Talya was more than capable of defending herself: she shapeshifted into a prehistoric lion the size of a school bus. The problem was, unlike the other shifters in the Big Cat Crew, that lion was not under her control. Her *ka-bah* would be angry, hungry, and not capable of telling friend from foe. The fight would turn from a brawl into a bloodbath, just like that. Even worse, Talya wasn't looking in his direction.

"Fucking- *CHET*!" My curse cut short as I spotted movement out of the corner of my eye and reflexively shielded myself. A wire-wrapped baseball bat hit the thin magical barrier and bounced back into the face of the surprised man who'd swung at me, but the exertion had already cost me. I felt like I'd pulled my remaining energy out like an unraveling thread.

Otto grabbed two of Jenner's human punks by the backs of their heads and cracked their skulls together. He dropped the skinny teenage boy, picked up the other girl by her neck,, and bodily threw her at Cliff. As they went down, Zane spotted the same thing I had.

"Talya!" He bellowed over the noise, fighting his way across the yard. "Talya, head's up!"

"Talya!" I called in time with him.

Talya finally turned around. She lit on to the four hundred pounds of hurt that was stalking toward her, and her eyes widened.

Big Ron lifted the shotgun, and fired a round into the air. The sound was deafening, echoing through the compound and up and down the street beyond the fence. Abruptly, the fighting stopped. The shaman stopped doing whatever he was doing, hands poised. Even Otto froze in place, shoulders hunched.

"All y'all want this to get heavy?" Ron bellowed. "Really? Because it's about to git heavy!"

"No need." Otto sneered, and turned to Jenner. He was more than capable of looking down at her, the Goliath to her David. "You and me, Tranny. How about it? You win, Otto leaves. Otto wins, you forfeit your title in New York."

"You're *Khayty*. Outcast. You don't get to set terms, and you don't get to lay a hand on OUR *Malek-Kab*, pigfucker!" It was Zane who stepped up, muscles pumped, skin flushed.

"At ease, boy." Jenner said, waving him down. She was grinning from ear to ear. "Yeah, you know what, that suits me just fine. But Zane's right—you're the invader, asshole. You don't get to set the terms. I do."

Otto's lip curled on one side. "Otto don't take orders from chinks."

Jenner jerked her head. "Shoot him, Ron."

Ron didn't hesitate. He aimed and fired.

The street shaman threw himself in front of Otto like a trained bodyguard, gibbering something I didn't understand. The buckshot pellets bounced and... *skittered?* Each pellet fell to the ground as a cockroach. They shot off through the legs of the crowd, disappearing into the gravel. Nice trick.

"Saved by the bagman," Jenner said, cocking her chin. "You got lucky this time, Otto."

The shaman began to move around his boss, chanting in an unfamiliar—possibly made up—language. The barrier he wove formed a circle that strengthened with his passing.

Otto barked a hoarse, humorless laugh. "You can't shoot Otto and make him go away."

"This gun begs to differ," I said, opening my jacket to show the Wardbreaker.

The shaman saw it, and his eyes went wide and wild. He pointed and shrieked. "Cursed!"

"You're not the only one with a spook, shit for brains," Jenner said, crossing her arms. "Consider it a warning shot, and let's work this out like civilized were-things."

"Whatever," Otto grunted.

"Yonkers Power Station, Halloween. Two nights from now. I set the terms, you show up for the fight," she said, watching him through narrowed eyes. "No posse, no bullshit. And I'll show you what it means to be an Elder."

Otto laughed again: an awful, forced, clicking laugh. "Fine. That'll do."

"I'll be making you say that back to me through a mouthful of smashed teeth," Jenner said. "Now get the fuck off my land before we blow you off of it."

"Get out of here!" Someone from the back of the Tigers pack yelled, and then the shouting broke out in earnest. Every Tiger began to yell at them, forming an improvised riot line. Dogboy snarled, fangs bared, but he was drowned out by the sudden unified wall of sound. Zane, usually quiet and controlled, was shouting at the top of his lungs, and I added my own voice to the mix as we drove the aggressors back towards the driveway. Several Tigers mounted their own bikes and revved them to life, herding the scrambling Nightbrothers forward or to the side to avoid being run over. Dogboy hauled his motorcycle off the ground, spitting a seemingly endless torrent of sexist, racist vitriol in Jenner's direction that was cut short when Ron fired a second warning shot.

Jenner stood straight, impassively watching the chaos around her. I drew up beside her, not saying anything. Her eyepatch had been torn off during the fight, revealing the deep red scar and empty socket on that side. Sirens were howling in the distance, and getting closer at a rapid clip.

After several minutes, the forward line straggled back into the yard, clapping each other on the shoulders and buzzing with excitement. Jenner drew a deep breath, and lifted her voice to be heard over the noise. "Alright, everyone! All weapons, out of sight! Cliff, Skinner, take the car and get Rob to the hospital!"

I cocked an ear and listened to the pitch of the approaching squad cars. They were regular old red-and-blue sirens, not the warbling howl of the Vigiles' purple and white ones. "A word?"

Jenner grunted. "After this is sorted out. Go put your piece away—I don't want anyone hauled in tonight."

I inclined my head and withdrew, joining Talya at the door. We rushed back inside to hide any contraband. The knife went into my locker, the Wardbreaker into a hidden pocket in my suitcase made for this exact circumstance. There was no hiding the blood outside on the gravel no matter how much dirt was kicked around, and everyone was still roughed up by the time five cops marched up the driveway, scowls in place, radios chirping. Zane patted Talya on the back before breaking off to join Jenner as she faced them down, hands on her hips. Talya and I stayed by the house. The less of a chance they had to see me, the better.

"Wow," Talya said, her voice close to a whisper. "Rex, this is so awful."

I nodded, watching the body language of the officers.

"Rob Polawski. That guy they hurt?" Talya's voice thickened a little. "He... he was driving our truck tonight. He was a hopeful, you know? Not even a member of the Club yet. I don't know him that well, but he was always so nice to everyone. He has a daughter."

A chill passed through me. "What truck?"

"The truck taking the guns we found to Miami." Talya reached up to tug at one of her lip rings. "I wish Mason was still here. No one tried to start anything with Jenner when it was the pair of them working together. I don't understand why this is happening."

"Like I said. Most people in this business play hard." I folded my arms, frowning. "I don't like this one bit."

"Why?" Talya looked over at me. "I mean, obviously, but..."

"Otto is a Morphorde," I said.

"No," she replied. "He's still a Weeder."

I arched an eyebrow. "You can tell?"

Nervously, she nodded. "But there's something wrong with him. Something wrong with his Ka-Bah. When he was walking toward me, I looked him in the eyes and I saw... I saw..."

"What?"

"NO-thing," Talya whispered, shaking her head.

What I saw was a DOG, but we were at the stage of mincing semantics. I nodded, and when Zane returned to us, I stepped forward.

"Zane. I need to tap you for a job," I said. "Do you have B&E experience?"

Zane glanced back at the police circus in the drive. "Plenty."

"Enough to go do some work at short notice."

"Maybe. Depends on the site."

"Commercial."

"Ooh, are you guys talking about breaking into that funeral home?" Talya perked. "I could go!"

"No." Both of us said it at the same time, then looked at each other. Zane followed it up, stepping forward to lay a hand on Talya's shoulder. "No, Kitten, no way. You're still too green for that kind of shit."

"I have to learn somehow." She scowled. Even that managed to look kind of cute.

"Yeah, but the time to learn isn't during a live run," Zane replied. "Come inside, both of you. Jenner pre-approved any missions related to finding the missing kids, as long as one of the Big Cat Crew knows what's going down. When do you want to do it?"

"Tonight," I replied.

He froze. "You're kidding me."

I shook my head. "If we go tonight, there's a slim chance we'll find what we're looking for. Every day that passes is a day where the evidence we need could be erased."

"The place is crawling with cops, the Vigiles are on the way-"

"Which means they're distracted," I said, staring at him. "Believe me when I say that I'm in no mood to go and do this on such short notice. But we're pros, aren't we? We have to do what we have to do."

Zane rubbed his face and grimaced. "Do we have an address? And why are we breaking into this place?"

I looked to Talya, and the pout disappeared as she realized she was supposed to be contributing. "Yep! We have an address! That's... uhh... that's about all, though. I need you to get me some computer equipment."

"Talya and I have both got pieces of the MinTex puzzle, but we need to get records to work out the rest," I added.

"That's the company that was handling the money for the kids, wasn't it?" Zane's brow furrowed as he thought, popping his lip under his teeth. "You sure it's the place?"

"Verified and triangulamated." Talya saluted.

"A funeral home. Fuck." Zane shook his head. "Should be easy, at least."

I shook my head. "Don't count on it."

Talya got a funny little smile for a moment, looking between us. Zane arched an eyebrow.

"I was just wondering. If like, something happened... Would the cops that are guarding the place be like: 'Hey!'" She made a pistol out of her hands, sighting down. "'You can run, but you can't formaldehyde!'"

The pair of us stared at her for several seconds before Zane groaned and began to chuckle, shaking his head.

"Like, even if you guys were at a dead run, it might be tomb much for you to handle." She grinned, perfectly unashamed of the pain she was inflicting.

I regarded her flatly. "You're fired."

"Jesus Christ, Kitten." Zane couldn't look at her, still laughing. "That was bad. That was real bad."

"Yay, I'm bad! And fired! I'll uh... I'll go write my shopping list! So you know what to get! All those computers look the same, haha." Talya bobbed with a little curtsy, and with a last anxious look at the strobing lights at the other end of the yard, scurried off into the house.

CHAPTER 18

Two hours later, me, Zane and Binah cruised up along a quiet street in South Jamaica with our headlights off, rain pounding down on the roof of the car. McKinnon Funerals was contained in an old rowhouse next door to a Catholic outreach center, and they and the other houses facing Sutphin Boulevard watched over the narrow, tree-lined street like a parade of old Victorian ladies. McKinnon was the last house on the block, a corner lot with a large greenhouse-like sunroom protected with a tall, spiked iron fence. It had a small parking lot, and a garage entry around the back. The front door faced a small sunken courtyard. It was pretty and leafy, and looked like the kind of place you'd find small yappy dogs, wool quilts, and potted poinsettias.

Zane groaned. "Well, this looks like a fucking piece of cake."

"Don't be ridiculous. This is going to be a tough job no matter how we stretch it," I replied. "It's heavily guarded. Cameras everywhere. There's probably police bunked in every one of these rowhouses. The only thing we have going for us is the weather."

The bigger man stared at me blankly for a moment, then shook his head and got busy pulling on his ski cap. He'd come out in soft clothes, easy to tear if he had to shapeshift. Skateboard sneakers, loose gym pants, a dark crewneck sweater.

"What?" I said.

"I was being sarcastic, dude."

"I am not a 'dude'," I replied. "And I'm in too much pain to be able to tell if you're being sarcastic or not. As it stands, it took me years to understand that people didn't mean they thought something actually resembled a piece of cake."

"Is this a second language thing?" He arched a thick eyebrow, slinging a bandoleer over his shoulder. The tools were spaced a few inches apart, and muffled with bunches of fabric staplegunned to the nylon band. Zane, for all his well-spoken politeness, was as much a professional thief as I was.

"No. It's a 'people don't say what they actually mean' thing." I had my own toolkit, a duffle bag the right size for me to wear like a backpack when required. I opened the door, slinging the bag over one shoulder. "Here's a good example—when people say 'what's up?' I mean... is that a philosophical question? A literal inquiry? People would ask me 'what's up?', and I thought I was supposed to guess the correct answer. 'Oh, well, the ceiling is 'up'. The sky is 'up'. Why the hell are you asking me this? Am I living in a Doctor Seuss book?'"

"Huh." Zane followed me out onto the street while I held the door for Binah. I was dressed like a utility worker in dark blue coveralls. Together, we looked like the kind of guys who could very well be here to fix a failing mortuary fridge late at night. Not exactly a foolproof disguise, but the best we had on such short notice.

"It's worse when people are trying to make friends with you," I continued, holding still while my familiar leapt to my shoulder. "Like, say you come up to me while I'm reading the news at the table in the morning, and you ask me: 'What are you reading?' My default response is to tell you the truth. *The New York Times*, *The Washington Post*, whatever. But that's not what you're asking. What you're actually asking is: 'Hey Alexi, tell me what interests you in the newspaper so we can chat about it.' And if I don't remember that you're speaking code, it comes off as cold and disinterested, even though it's the truth."

Zane nodded slowly, sucking his lip under his top teeth. "You know, I never thought of it that way."

It'd been Vassily who'd explained that particular thorny chestnut to me. My throat twinged. "People say that a lot about the way I see things."

The pair of us fell silent as we came into range and faded into the shadows. The first thing we did was scope the front yard. We were within twenty feet of the door when the hairs on my arms and the back of my neck stood on end, prickling with every quiet step. Magic thrummed out across the yard… power with an oddly familiar resonance, like the work of a street artist I'd seen over and over, but didn't know the name of.

"Wait a second," I whispered aloud to Zane, then turned my voice inward to Kutkha. *"Kutkha, what the hell is that?"*

"A ward," he replied, without a trace of mockery. *"A very powerful ward."*

"This is by the same person who did up Semyon's apartment. I'm sure of it." Astounded, I crouched down in the shrubbery, reaching out toward the core of energy that howled from the center of the door. It was a different type of ward than the one that Semyon had received to protect himself. That particular ward that had made him so confident that instead of fleeing the city once he learned there was a hit on him, he'd run to his apartment in Manhattan. As I mapped it out—it was so complex that it looked more like a vortex than a geometric figure—I realized something else. I had run into this artist multiple times.

Long ago, I fought and eventually killed a rival spook: an Israeli mage, Eric Kovacs. Kovacs had been a curse specialist, a Hexer. He'd had a strong, hard-to-sense ward on his apartment window. I'd fired a round from a sniper rifle right into it, and the glass hadn't even cracked. I hadn't made the connection at Semyon's house, but thinking back, I was sure that it was the same mage. This ward was less aggressive, but just as advanced as both the previous ones I'd encountered. It was the kind of magic that could persist for hundreds of years, the product of intense formal training given to a prodigy. Six years ago, I'd failed to bust Kovacs' protection. I'd only busted Semyon's because I had the Wardbreaker and a human sacrifice ready to go. I was all out of sacrifices, and if I used the Wardbreaker, I might as well paint 'ALEXI WAS HERE' on the wall in bright orange letters. I didn't really believe Keen, but I wasn't willing to take the risk now that I was on his radar.

I opened my eyes and exhaled thinly. Kovacs had been working for the Manellis, though that was some years ago. Semyon was an FBI informant. If Semyon had answered to Agent Keen... then it had to be a member of the Vigiles who'd made these wards. Right?

"Alexi? What is it?" Zane whispered. He was much larger than me, and in the darkness of the garden, he looked like a hunched gargoyle.

"They have a snitch ward on the place." I shelved the mystery for the time being. I'd have to think on it later. "An alarm. We can't get in here. If it's all the way through the house, we're out of luck. Let's see what we find behind the building. It's a funeral home; they'll have a garage where they deliver the bodies."

The business of funeral homes was the business of discretion. Every one of them needed a staging area where fresh cadavers were delivered before embalming and display, preferably without anybody on the street knowing what they were transporting in and out of the building. We hopped the fence and stealthed around the corner through the garden, where we found a continuation of the spiked fence with a solid gate with a sign. *'Property of McKinnon Funeral Home: Authorized Personnel Only.'*

"Here we go..." I whispered, going to a knee. I peered through the gap between the fence line and the start of the gate. As I did, I saw something stir: A leg, then a hand flexing on the barrel of a long assault rifle that gleamed with the same ghostly scarlet glow as the guns we'd taken from the scrapyard. I watched and waited as a heavily armed, heavily armored man strolled past and out of sight. What little I glimpsed was military-grade gear.

I grunted, letting the cat down to the ground. "I'm fairly sure those are Men in Black. Terrible amount of security for a funeral home."

"How're we going to get in, then?"

I thought for a moment. "Let's go around further, on the street. There might be a way in around the other side. If there's not, we're going to have to leave it at scouting and call it good until we have more firepower."

He gave me the thumbs up, and we made our way back out and into the street, careful not to be seen through the huge windows on the front of the house. We went around the corner of the block to see what we could see. On this side, the fence was tall and solid, an industrial fence with an electronic sliding door. The house beside it was an old standalone clapboard house with peeling paint. Small, narrow, with a tiny front yard, a chain-link fence and a narrow driveway that ran all the way to the backyard. An eight-foot wooden fence separated the house from the funeral home's courtyard. The fence was bare for most of the way down, but the section facing the backyard was topped with razor wire.

"Jeez," Zane hissed. "This place is banged up like Fort Knox."

"It's do-able. I'll send Binah ahead." I crouched down, motioning to Binah with my hand.

"You can do that?"

"We'll find out."

Binah had been ghosting us with eerie willingness, and obediently padded up when I made the chin-scritch motion to her. Instinct told me I needed to touch her with bare skin, not gloves, so I pulled them off and bent over her, caressing her head and flanks, rubbing her ears, pressing my mouth to the top of her sleek head. With little effort, I felt it—the spark of consciousness, the connection between magus and familiar. A familiar, Kutkha had told me, was the incarnation of your soul in a non-human form. I was about to find out how deep that connection ran.

I drew a breath, let it out, and recessed into my core: The temple where I meditated. The temple is what is commonly known as a thoughtform, a visual interface for my psyche. In my old way of looking at magic, the temple was an astral niche shaped by my will out of Yesod, the next-densest layer of reality that was intermeshed with Malkuth, the material or earthly reality. As my understanding of magic had become more flexible and fluid, so had the thoughtform. After a few minutes, I was there.

The entry to the temple was down a short flight of sandstone steps, and in through a metal door that opened into a huge bell-shaped chamber. The immersion was so complete that I heard the marble floor ring out beneath my shoes. I smelled salt water, and here and there, traces of honeysuckle drifting on the cold air. The temple was faced in black granite, with a smooth polished ebony floor set with a plain, unbroken silver ring. The entry point was in the east; to the south was a nasty creeping lichen that was eating its way through the stone and trying to burrow through it. That was how my imagination visualized the

Yen. It was much more entrenched than I remembered it... like mold that was working its way through a loaf of bread. For time being, it was placated by the fight at Strange Kitty.

With one eye on the Yen, I began to search with my imagination for the iconic entryway of felines everywhere: a cat flap. When I found it, I crouched down and looked inside. There was a tunnel beyond: the psychic link between me and Binah.

"Will she understand if I ask her to look for an entry large enough for a person?" I turned to look over my shoulder, knowing Kutkha would be there.

My Neshamah sat on a gilded silver perch on the other side of the chamber, his plumage simmering off into the air like an indigo heat haze. Kutkha was in his usual shape, that of a peacock-sized raven with a long sweeping tail. His tenebrous body was the color of the night sky, and his burning, brilliant magnesium eyes were currently closed while he stood on one leg, grooming the feathers of his head with the other foot. "Yes, my Ruach. I will make it so."

I focused on what we needed her to do, imagining the request as a mouse cupped in my hands. When I could feel its heart thrumming against my palms, I released it through the image of the cat flap and watched it scurry away before I stepped back out of meditation. I immediately had the odd sensation of looking back at myself from the ground. Somehow, I could both see Binah, and see Binah watching me. It was as confusing as it sounded.

"Okay, girl," I whispered. "Go find us a door."

Binah's ears pinned as she slunk off into the night like a ribbon of smoke. My head throbbed. I had to close my eyes, too dizzy to move as a fraction of my awareness left with her.

The cat made a beeline for the standalone house, hopping the front fence into the yard. She sauntered down the path with her tail held high, then scaled the tall wooden fence adjacent to the small compound where the guards waited. Through her eyes, I was able to see inside. It was nothing but a square of bare concrete and a couple of marked parking spaces, both empty. There were two guards, both of them dressed like SWAT on steroids. They were carrying rifles that spat magic in Binah's vision, sucking the air toward them. There were sigil patches on the guard's uniforms that did the same thing. One of them glanced at Binah as she strolled along the edge of the fence, but he paid no more mind than that.

Binah leapt lightly from the fence to the roof the garage, sniffing at the corrugated iron sheeting. I breathed deeply and evenly, waiting until she shimmied down the other side. There was a tiny backyard there, mossy and neglected, that was framed by the neighbor's fence line on one side, the back of the garage on the other, the rowhouse, and the wall separating it from the next rowhouse over. Binah wound through chipped lace metal tables and dead pot plants to a pair of double steel doors set into the ground at an angle. They were chained together by a thick, rusted chain and padlock. The basement entry.

"Clever girl," I murmured, squatting back on my heels. I rubbed my eyes. "Alright. There's a way in. Cougars are good jumpers, aren't they?"

"Yeah."

"Boost me up. I'll cut the wire and get over. Then you follow in cougar form."

Zane grimaced.

I eyed him back. "What?"

"Nothing. Guess that's how we're going to have to do it." He rubbed a hand over the reddish fuzz on his head. "Let's go."

We followed Binah's trail down the driveway. The people who lived in this house had put heavy drapes on their windows, the better to block out the sight of hearses pulling in and out of the funeral home. We crept to the gate leading into their backyard, where I crouched to pick the lock, wincing as I jarred the injured side of my ass. When the lock popped, I got a small can of WD-40 and gently spritzed the hinges and latch before opening the gate and crab crawling inside.

There was always an odd sensation of pressure when you passed a physical barrier like this one, the Will of the residents who had made this their home. It rippled over my skin all the way to the fence. "Okay. And for the love of GOD, please boost me up with the right leg."

"Why?"

"That *pizdets*[8] Vigiles sniper took me down with a rhino dart, is why." I got my wire snips ready, and waited for him to crouch and lace his hands. When he did, I stepped up. He lifted me like I weighed nothing, and I was weirdly conscious of how close his face was to the backs of my legs as I got to work on the wire, snipping out a wide section.

I pushed the wire into the funeral home's yard, resolved myself to the agony that was about to follow, and pulled myself up and over as quietly as I was able, which made it sound like a fat raccoon was hauling a pizza box over the fence. I dropped down and stumbled to one knee as my glute quivered and then gave out on me, throbbing painfully. Binah watched me from beside the double doors like a statue of Bast, her tail wrapped around her feet. I'd always figured that cats spent a lot of time judging their owners, but now I had an empathic link to one, I knew for certain that they did.

Abruptly Binah's eyes widened, and her ears flattened to her skull. She scrambled away under one of the patio tables as a huge feline shadow fell over the backyard. I turned to see a puma the size of a pony balancing gracefully on the edge of the fence before he bounded down to join us in the yard. He was carrying a tied bundle of clothes in his mouth and was still wearing the bandolier.

"Zane?" I said, warily.

The big cat looked up at me wildly, gray-green eyes shining in the dim light reflected off the clouds. After a

---

[8] WHORE, CUNT. LIKE 'KHUY' (DICK, FUCK', IT'S USED AS AN INTERJECTION.

tense standoff, the puma dropped the bundle, licked his chops, then yawned. He sat down on his haunches.

I nodded, and went to the double doors. They were warded, but not with anything I couldn't deal with using the arcane tools I'd brought with me. A bit of sulfur, a few muttered words, and a lock pick, and the lock was off. I greased everything and gently pulled the chain from around the handles, laying it aside, then looked over at Zane. "Okay. Are you changing back?"

The puma flattened his ears, and motioned to the door with a paw. Not sure what he wanted, I squinted. This time, he pointed at me, then the door.

"Right." Only slightly less confused, I opened the door and slid down into darkness.

CHAPTER 19

The doors led to a flight of stairs with a dead end at the bottom. The door to the basement was boarded up, which explained the lack of wards. I got a crowbar and tested the strength of the nails. They were old and rusted in, but after several minutes work and some WD-40, I was able to crack open a big enough hole to climb through. A wave of humid, bad-smelling air roiled from the dark space beyond. It wasn't the acrid, violet oily-sweet stench of DOG. It was... cold. Gray. Toxic, in the way that mineral tailings or chemical slag was toxic. A nasty metallic taste filled my mouth as I slipped inside.

"Jesus Christ," Zane hissed from the stairwell. "What are they keeping in there?"

"Smells like acid. Batteries, maybe." I switched the penlight for a larger flashlight, holding my knife in my other hand. The beam of light revealed rows of steel shelves filled with coffins wrapped in plastic. Black coffins, rounded coffins, baby coffins. They were stacked from floor to ceiling in rows. It was a big room. "What was the matter back there?"

"I don't like changing when people are around."

"Why? It doesn't bother me in the slightest."

"That's not the point."

Which reminded me. There were things I'd wanted to ask him back in the house, but hadn't been able to. Considering anyone who might overhear was already dead, this coffin-filled basement was as good a place as any to humiliate myself.

I drew a deep breath, and turned back to look at him. "On a semi-related note, Zane, I needed to ask you something."

"Like?" He regarded me suspiciously.

It was a simple question, but I had to deliberate on the words. I shifted my weight, frowning as I tried to make them come out, and couldn't on the first couple of tries. "How... exactly...?"

He arched an eyebrow.

"How can, uh... I mean, how did you know you were gay?" I looked up at him, brow furrowed. "I-I mean, I don't mean to put you on the spot or anything, but..."

Zane looked down at me in growing disbelief. "Rex. We are in the middle of a goddamn break-in."

"And...?"

He rubbed his face. "We're in a funeral home. I smell dead people, okay?"

"Well, why do you think I'm asking you here?" I hissed. "You think I want anyone listening to this?"

Zane screwed his eyes shut and pinched the bridge of his nose. "Okay, look. Is there a point to you asking, or are you just, like, curious? Or...?"

I wanted to tell him what had happened with Angkor, then Christopher. I wanted to... but the words stoppered up again. "Look. Just answer the damn question, and we can move on. How did you know you were gay?"

"Well, uh... you generally know you're gay when you're attracted to other men," Zane finally said.

"Attracted how?" I frantically searched back for how I'd felt around Angkor and Christopher. "Attracted to companionship? Or magnetically? Or does it have to be... you know... genitals?"

He stifled a laugh. "It's not any one thing, man. It's not like there's a form you fill out to get your Gay Passport. If you like dudes, you like dudes. It's that simple."

"Don't you have to, well..." I dithered off.

Zane stared at me. "Have to what?"

"Well, I mean..." Flustered, I gestured in strangled silence with the flashlight, the beam crazing off the walls and ceiling. "Aren't gay men... different? Somehow? I mean, made differently?"

"Okay. These are REALLY uncomfortable questions, alright? Like, borderline homophobic bullshit uncomfortable." Zane made a sound of exasperation.

Homophobic? *Frightened* of gay people? That actually sounded... well, fairly accurate. I was weighed down by a lifetime of guilt and confusion that felt to me the same way this basement smelled and tasted. I remembered the way I'd lain awake in the dorm I'd shared with Vassily, jealously disgusted by the sounds of awkward teenage sex coming from his side of the apartment. I remembered the way Angkor looked at me, the stir I'd felt in my jaws when he angled his head just the right way. The taste of salt on Christopher's neck. The way I'd felt when he... ugh.

I sighed. "I know they do. The words aren't coming out the way I want them to. I just don't get it."

"If you weren't my friend, I'd have punched you by now," Zane said. "You know that, right?"

"I didn't mean it that way." I slashed a hand down. "Look, I'm not trying to piss you off—I'm trying to understand something."

"You're doing a pretty good job of the former. So let's just-"

"Let me put it this way," I cut him off, rubbing my hands over my thighs. They were clammy inside my gloves. "The word I grew up with for 'gay man' is literally just *pedarasti,* and that's what everyone I knew thought being gay meant. My father, my grandmother, my friends. And before you jump my shit, I'm not saying they're right. But the most consistent thing—one of the only things everyone in my life all agreed on—was that being gay meant you were fucked in the head. I don't know how to talk about this! I'm trying... I'm struggling to find the language just to ask questions about it."

He rolled his eyes in disbelief. "And I'm saying this is a conversation we really don't need to be having while we're balls-deep in a B&E. In a funeral home. With dead people."

Suddenly, I snapped. "I fucked around with a priest last night, alright?"

Zane's eyes widened. He opened his mouth, closed it, deliberated for a second, then winced.

I began to pace. "Look: This, this… this YEN has been making me do weird shit. It makes me want to drink, and I can't stop it. I… saved this guy's life, we were riding a combat high. He brought brandy in to help us calm down and one thing led to another… before I knew it, he was on his knees and I was… I was-"

"Woah there. Hold up a second-"

I turned on him. "And it's not the only thing. I was supposed to be meeting Angkor for dinner the night he vanished. A date, alright? I asked him on a date. He stood me up."

The angry defensiveness had drained from Zane's expression, replaced by something worse. Pity.

"So this is why I'm asking you. I *know* you're not fucked in the head. You don't have a Yen. You have your shit together. I thought, I thought maybe hearing how it works for you might help me… sort this out."

"Huh. Yeah, what you're saying you went through, like… I never had that." Zane frowned, but it was a different kind of frown now. Not anger—or at least, not anger at me. "I mean, I grew up in the liberal college part of Oregon, so there was no pressure one way or the other, really. Mom was a Hawaiian hippy, Dad was cool with everything except racism and heroin." He jerked his shoulders in a shrug. "Started looking at other guys when I was just a kid. Found my first boyfriend in high school, and it just kind of went from there. Everyone knew, but I was a big guy and a football star, so no one was willing to fuck with me about it."

"What do you mean by 'looking'?"

"You know, like, checking them out. I figured it out at the beach." His lips twitched at the corners. "Lots of hot guys and not much in the way of clothes, you know?"

I'd lived near the beach too, but I couldn't say I'd spent my youth staring at other boys. Mostly, I'd tried to avoid 'looking' at all.

As the silence dragged on, Zane shrugged again. "So, the thing with the priest. Did you like what he was doing?"

My chest swelled, and only at the last moment did I realize that I wasn't supposed to yell in here. I flushed from hairline to collar as I spluttered. "That's, I-"

Zane held up both hands. "You don't have to like, legit tell me, but if the answer is 'yes', that's the answer to your question."

"But I don't think I *did* like it." It was my turn to frown. "We were tipsy. I mean, he didn't actually do anything to me. I made him do things to... him. And he was angry and upset afterward. Said he'd 'relapsed'."

"Well, yeah," Zane replied. "Collar queens—like, gay priests—are twisted up in some serious denial, you know?"

He had a point there. "I had no idea what I was doing. It just... happened. Same with Angkor, until he showed his true colors. You know he hit on me the first night he woke up, after we rescued him out of that silo?"

"Doesn't surprise me," Zane said. "He's hit on me, too. I'm pretty sure he'd fuck anything that looks at him for a straight second. Not that there's anything wrong with that."

So I wasn't the only one? I was well aware that I wasn't exactly a dish, but knowing he'd also flirted with Zane was just indignity atop indignity.

Zane inhaled deeply. Audibly.. He was slightly less tense. "How about we finish this job, go to a bar and wrap this up later? I want to help, but I'm pretty sure there's bodies in this basement and I really want to get out of here, okay?"

It was easy to forget how uncomfortable other people got around bodies and coffins and the like. "Just tell me one thing. You don't like... lose anything, do you? By coming out gay?"

"Like what?"

I thought about it. "*Sila*. Your *muchestva*." I knew the words in Russian, but not their direct counterparts in English. "Strength, virility, I guess."

Zane laughed, choking the sound with a hand. "Only thing you lose coming out is caring about what other people think, man. I can introduce you to the scene if you want, but before any of that, you and I are going to have a talk. We need to have the safety talk, and some of the like, ah, 'parley'. You know. The codes."

Safety talk? Codes? I'd hoped speaking to him would have alleviated my concerns, but now I felt more anxious, not less. "Alright."

"We good?"

"If anyone hears about this, I will kill you." I paused. "And them."

"Don't I believe it, too." He snorted. "Don't worry, it's cool. I won't tell anyone."

It wasn't 'cool', because that aura of pity hung around Zane like a bad smell. I knew he was trying. For now, given the circumstances, that was good enough.

We moved quietly between the rows to the other end of the room. The shelves took up about two-thirds of the basement. In the other third near the door, there was a plastic card table and tools on hooks on the walls, along with three plastic 80-gallon barrels. The lids were hammered down, but a crust of astringent black goo had bubbled up around the seals.

I wrinkled my nose. "Well. Now I know how the Men in Black 'ensure your safe departure' from any given location."

"The fuck is going on here?" Zane rarely swore. "Are these-?"

"Bodies, yes. That smell is sulfuric acid. I would've expected better from the Government, to be honest. Lye is better for dissolving corpses, and it's a lot cheaper."

"Shit, shit shit." Zane was breathing a little harder. "What do we do?"

"Keep your voice down. There's nothing we can do," I said, moving to the door. "Those bodies have been in there for days. They're nothing but sludge by now."

The door leading up inside was warded, and I could sense intuitively that it was linked to the main defense of the house, the vortex of power inscribed on the front door. I frowned. "Well, this is the end of the road, unless we can muster up a significant sacrifice. Even then, I'd be leaving an incriminating trail behind us."

"Magic ward, right?" Zane said. "You know, I could try busting through it in cat form. The magic won't hurt me."

"No. It's not made to hurt. It's made to alarm." I rubbed my jaw as I thought. "You know, I'm betting that the guards patrol in here. They may have some way to go in and out of the locked doors: a token, a talisman. If we can draw some attention and surprise one, we might be able to get our hands on it."

"About the best I can do is meow really loudly."

I shook my head and looked again at the table. My eyes drifted to the barrels... and then it hit me. I smiled.

Zane watched apprehensively as I went to the barrel closest to the door. "Go find me something I can use to spoon some of this out. Plastic or glass, not metal. And a crowbar. There's one on the rack over there."

"Uhh-"

"I know what I'm doing," I replied, examining the barrels with a flashlight. The light didn't penetrate the plastic.

Zane handed me the crowbar first, and I dutifully used it to pry up the lid on the first tank. When it came up, so did the stench: a horrid rotten-egg-and-rust smell. There was a corpse in here, barely anything more than a suitcase-sized lump of blackened flesh. The acid wasn't pure enough for what I needed, so I tamped the lid back down and tried the second, and then the third. Third time was the charm. The body had only been in there for a day, at most, and the acid was still clear enough that it could be used to burn through wood and metal.

Zane had managed to find a mason jar somewhere. I cleaned the dust and dead flies from it, set it on the table, and composed myself for magic.

"Hold your breath as long as you can," I said. "We'll retreat to the back of the room. And whatever you do, don't interrupt me. Not for anything."

The big spells weren't always the most useful. Smaller magic had its merits, such as when you had to move something, but not touch it. I lifted my hands and concentrated, waiting until I could feel the threads and currents of Phi around us, and then waved gently. The jar wobbled, lifted, and then drifted to the barrel. I motioned down, and held the jar in the solution until it filled. The acid burbled and hissed, but it didn't dissolve the glass.

It took more effort to keep the full jar steady against the continuous downward pull of gravity, and as I worked, I had a small epiphany. Phi followed the direction of gravity, but not the gravity of Earth: it followed the gravity of the nexus of the GOD organism, the I of GOD. Suddenly, my telekinesis was a lot smoother as I guided the jar to the door, and as it drew closer, the ward remained inert.

The mage who created these works of art was thorough. I was sure that the paneling, knobs, and hinges were guarded against force, magic, fire, and physical contact by living things over a certain size: burglars with screwdrivers or crowbars, for example. Chemical contact without human contact had not occurred to the caster, at least not for this part of the door. The acid bubbled and frothed, releasing white hydrogen gas as it trickled down.

I held my breath against the fumes. My eyes were pouring, stinging and red from the steam rising off the metal. Once the jar was empty, I set it down on the floor—carefully—and went to the barrel and fixed the lid down before retreating. Zane was gagging at the back of the room, nose buried in the crook of his elbow.

"Now what?" He snuffled, voice thick with mucus.

"We wait," I said. "Not for long. They're melting those bodies in lab-strength acid. If I'm correct, then in a few minutes time, that door will just fall off."

"It's going to make a hell of a noise."

"It's the best we can do," I said. "We need one of those sigil patches they're wearing to even be able to get into the house."

Zane and I both took deep breaths of the relatively fume-free air at the rear of the room, then hustled for the door. The wood had sunk in and blackened. As we reached it, the top hinge gave way and the door slumped in its frame on an angle. Soon, the second hinge was pulled out of the sizzling wood as the cellulose decomposed. It began to lean forward: I reached for the air around it with my Will, pulling it back toward us. The artificial breeze carried the stink of sulfur, but the door fell back in toward us instead of out onto the stairs.

"Huh?" We heard a man's voice from the next floor up.

I turned the flashlight off. We got into position beside the open door, me with my knife, Zane with the crowbar. A few seconds later, a light jogged down the stairwell, bouncing off the walls as the patrolling guard clattered down, rifle up and ready. He burst through the doorway, and as he swung toward me, I caught the muzzle of the gun, pushed it up, and stabbed him in the left armpit as hard as I could.

Three things happened at once: The knife hit an artery, and white chalky blood gushed from around the hilt under high pressure, pumping in time with the Man in Black's heart. He kneed me in the balls, and Zane swung the crowbar like a baseball bat across the back of his neck, sending him sprawling on top of me as we went down together. Zane staggered away, and before I could call for help, he threw up.

"Zane, don't- GOD dammit!" The Man thrashed as he bled out, semi-conscious. I pushed him off and tucked my hands under my armpits, rocking. I didn't feel the acute groin pain where it was supposed to be: the nerves down there had some weird arrangement with my hands, and the blow briefly paralyzed them and made them throb with weird, tingling pain. "Zane, they can track you with that! Don't leave anything behind!"

Zane looked back at me, panting. His skin was usually a dusky cool brown. He had turned a weird shade of bluish-brown gray. "I can't fucking help it! Can't you smell that?"

The Man's corpse began to flop, then bubble into gray goo. Zane blanched, and before I could stop him, he covered his face, still retching, and bolted up the stairs, tripping in his haste to get away from the decaying homunculus. I flailed around in the mess for a second, then sighed, gave up until I recovered my composure, then started over again.

When I got to the top of the stairs, I found myself in the funeral home's garage. It was a large underground space at the end of a ramped driveway, big enough to hold five cars side by side. There were four vehicles here, but only one was a hearse. Two were nondescript white vans that hummed with magical and electrical resonance, while the other was an honest-to-GOD cement mixer truck. This vehicle had the strongest resonance out of all of them, vibrating with odd energy that set my teeth on edge. It wasn't the kind of energy that I associated with DOGs or Morphorde, per-se. It was more like... radiation. Zane was as far away from that truck as he could be. He leaned on the hood of the hearse, struggling to keep his breathing steady.

Frowning, I slung the dead guard's rifle over my arm, letting it hang from the strap. "What the hell happened down there, Zane? You said you were-"

"I am. Just. Fine." He cut in, voice rough from puking. "But that... that thing. Rex, it smelled like Hell. Like, like dead... GOD, I can't describe it. This whole fucking place smells like that."

I frowned. To me, the MiB didn't smell like much of anything. Their blood and the gray goo was relatively inoffensive compared to the usual array of bodily fluids expelled during a kill. Curious, I turned inward, looking back to Kutkha. In my mind's eye, the raven Neshamah hunched on his perch, feathers fluffed.

"What do you think?" I asked silently.

"I think that something is terribly wrong here," Kutkha said.

He wasn't wrong. There was an eerie, unsettling feeling to the place that had nothing to do with it being a funeral home. I looked around and tuned in, walking a circle around the cars. There was a row of steel freezers against the far wall, fridges where they stored bodies before taking them to the embalming room. Across from them was a small office, unlocked and open, that had rows of screens with camera feeds, and an elevator used to transport a body and its attending staff to the upstairs floors. Well, to the second floor: it only had one button. There were stairs, too: a narrow, steep stairwell behind an unlocked door. I opened it and looked up inside. They looked like they skipped the first floor as well.

"So where do we go to get this computer information Talya wants? Upstairs?" Zane asked.

Possibly? But... no. I swung back, nose twitching, and found my eyes drawn back to the freezers. There was something odd about them, a break in the pattern. There were three freezers, and each had three vertical rows of cadaver trays. I saw the shadowed lines of each door, the brightness of the buttons, and the negative space around them more than I did the freezers themselves... but it was the sound which led me over. Or more accurately, the absence of it.

Zane said something, but his words were an unformed blob of color as I focused my senses. Curious, I touched the handles of the pull-out trays. The rightmost fridge had a fine hum that buzzed my fingertips through my gloves, making them twitch spasmodically; the center one did not. The center and the left-hand freezers weren't humming, even though they had live lights and appeared to be on.

"What are you doing?"

"Facade," I grunted, pressing the button locks and tugging on the tray handles. None of the middle three trays opened. When I tried the left-hand ones, yanking on the middle handle caused all three to shift slightly. Turning one or the other locks on or off didn't result in anything opening. I was vaguely aware of Zane drifting over to join me as I peered over and around the switches and buttons.

"You know, I can help with anything scent related...?"

Annoyed, I waved him away as I tracked the faint glint of fingerprints on the burnished steel, the way the white fluorescent light was twisted by the tracks of oil left by countless hands. Cops wore gloves by default, but their hands simply smeared the grease from the sweaty fingers of those who didn't... and with a couple of mishaps, I was able to figure out the sequence.

"Locker one's 'Occupied' alert on, lock button left on 'Lock'; middle locker unlocked, no Occupied light, lower locker's light on, unlocked, temperature lowered to..." I tapped the temperature button, watching the digital display as we went from 72 degrees to the 60s, 50s, 40s. I put my ear to the door and listened to the way the faint electronic whine from inside changed as I skipped through the 40s, getting loudest around 42. When I found the right percentage, there was a deep 'clunk' from inside the false meat locker. "42.5 degrees."

"No shit." Zane watched on from behind me with folded arms. "Stupid question. Why didn't you bust the lock with magic?"

I swung the heavy steel door open, revealing a Mobius strip-like trigger ward that encircled a small device, an unremarkable beige box with folded wires protruding from neatly drilled holes its base. "That. I don't know what it does, and I don't want to find out."

CHAPTER 20

A short flight of stairs lead into something awfully like an industrial maintenance corridor, the kind that had no place being in a house like this. I had a strange feeling of familiarity as we passed underneath a humming doorframe into what should have been the homey interior of the first floor, but was instead a kind of in-between mezzanine porch plus basement, a basement of pit cells dug into the earth below us. They were small and narrow and powerfully warded, and definitely not regulation standard.

"What in the living hell?" Zane pulled down his balaclava, and padded ahead of me. "This is some kind of... holding center?"

"I wish I could say I was shocked." I sniffed before I did the same thing, scenting the oily pink odor of bleach, the iron tang of blood, and the musty perspiration and mildew smell that always seemed to accompany spaces where people exerted themselves. Locker rooms, dance floors, torture dungeons: they all smelled the same.

I kept the Uzi ready in my hands as we descended hollow steel steps at the end of the mezzanine. The place was deserted. We scanned the cells—all empty—and then tried the doors that faced them on the other side of the corridor. They were not warded but they were locked, an issue quickly and easily solved with bump keys. The doors were on rollers and slid across, instead of pushing in… a detail that made sense when we opened the first one. The doorway fed through a plain device that resembled an airport metal detector. It was studded with pieces of black stone, and had a bone-chilling, alien aura. Beyond the funnel was a familiar sight: the interrogation room where I'd had my chat with Agent Keen.

"I can't." Zane shook his head, swallowing. "Whatever that thing is. I can't walk through it."

I stuck my hand out into it, and immediately felt a swooping dampening of my senses. My ability to sense the wards behind us muted, like a volume switch turned down. For a person like Zane, whose body was enmeshed with that of his puma-form Neshamah, the disruption would be very physical. "An anti-magic device. Interesting."

"This is creepy as hell, Rex." Zane backed away from it, moving to the next door. "Let's find this shit we need and get out of here."

We had a look at the other rooms. Two were interrogation rooms like the first one; one was an office. There was no computer, or even filing cabinets. The last was the torture dungeon I'd suspected was here by the smell. It superficially resembled the one we had in the lower level of the AEROMOR office warehouse, with a tiled floor and a drain to hose the room down. They had facilities for foot torture—if you were torturing someone to a confession or a revelation and also didn't want them running away, you generally stuck to the feet.

"I wonder if Ayashe knows about this," I mused aloud.

"Jenner warned us about the *Deutsche Ordern* puppeting the Vigiles, but I don't think I really believed her until now." Zane hung back, brows furrowed. "They're like boogeyman stories for little Weeders, you know?"

"No one has really explained to me what they are."

"They're like... descendants of the Teutonic Knights via Nazi Germany and the old Catholic church," Zane said. "That's what Jenner and Karim say. They're the only two Elders who are old enough to remember them when they were operating in the open, now that Michael's dead."

"I see. Well, the Men in Black will check in on this room soon. We have to get moving." I made sure the rifle was ready to fire. "Let's try upstairs."

The stairwell to the second floor opened up into a Victorian Gothic hallway. We stepped out cautiously into a heavy, dead silence broken only by the distant thundering of the rain outside. Thick carpet, dark line wallpaper, Empire furniture and chandeliers. They couldn't have made it look more like a funeral home if they tried.

"Elegant, but oppressive," I murmured.

"Ugh." Zane's lip curled. "This place makes my fucking skin crawl."

It was a safe bet that the computer was in the manager's office, and that the office was behind one of the *Staff Only* signed doors. "Let's search. I'll take the odd doors, you take the even."

Zane grunted, and broke off down the hall.

The first door on the left was a bathroom, the second a store of cleaning supplies. The third, which was locked, was labelled *Embalming Room*. I bumped the lock, oiled the hinges, and pushed the door in. There was no alarming smell from inside, but after a moment, a strange, oppressive, creeping sensation passed through my skin, the primal feeling of entering into the den of something large and dangerous. Normally, I'd heed my intuition and not go in. The problem was, the computer and documents Talya needed were possibly in this room, or in an office attached to it.

With the Man in Black's rifle in hand, I waited to the side of the door a couple of seconds before stepping inside. There was no one in the room, but the lights were on. I checked for cameras, didn't see any, and eased down on the trigger. The embalming room was clean, clinical and tidy. Everything was in its place, clearly labeled: 'Makeup', 'Catheters', 'Drainage', 'Prep'. The tables had been washed down, the mortuary tray blood-free and shiny. The body cooler was built into the wall on the far side of the room, across from another internal door. One of the freezers was empty; the other had a red light. Occupied.

I went to the mortuary freezer, and was just about to unlock it when a toilet flushed from behind the door across the room. I reflexively spun around and pulled the trigger, shredding the door with a burst that emptied a quarter of the clip. The enchanted gun made barely any sound, a rattling *thud thud thud*, but chips blasted out from the holes and into the air in a cloud of dust. I froze, breathless, as a heavy silence fell over the room. After several seconds, a runnel of blood crept along the floor from beneath the remains of the door. Red blood.

When the dust cleared, I opened the remains of the door to reveal a fallen man in a suit—an ordinary, non-bulletproof suit. He was unremarkably middle-aged, neat Ivy League hair, and now very dead. He was still twitching, pants crumpled down around his knees. He had a radio that chirped and clicked. I turned him over with my foot, and my heart sank. He was wearing an FBI badge. A Vigiles badge.

"Shit." I'd just killed a fucking Federal Agent in cold blood. Accidentally. Reflexes, in this case, were accidental.

"Feeling a little highly-strung today, my Ruach?" Kutkha asked.

"The first time you've spoken to me since we got in here, and it's smartass bullshit." Where there was one Agent, there was always another. I couldn't search him—not without contaminating the scene and giving investigators ammunition to track and prosecute me. At the same time, couldn't they do it anyway? Adeptus Varma had magic capable of reconstructing crime scenes. *"What attracted your attention?"*

I felt, rather than saw, my Neshamah's wry smile. *"The sensation of impending doom."*

I swallowed, turning, and looked over the room. The only other thing of interest here was the freezer. If the dead agent had been watching this room, it was entirely possible that whatever was in there was not actually a body.

"Is it an immediate doom, or a deferred sort of doom?" I sighed, and shouldered the rifle while I went to the meat locker, unlocked it, and pulled out the tray.

The stench of putrefaction punched me in the face like a tangible thing. I staggered back, coughing, and squinted at the body with watering eyes. The freezer wasn't cold, and there was no way this body was here for embalming. The flesh had peeled away and partly liquefied. The woman—by the hair and the remains of her breasts, I was sure it was a woman—was missing her eyes, which had melted in their sockets and tracked down both sides of her face. Her neck was swollen and puffy, inflated up around her jaw, and her tongue was grossly swollen, forcing her mouth into a silent rictus scream.

"Fairly immediate," Kutkha replied.

CHAPTER 21

Varma's illusion hadn't prepared me for the extent of the horrific, degraded ruin that was the remains of Agent Kristin Cross, but I was sure that was who I was looking at. Her face was barely recognizable. All her remaining flesh was soft and fish-like, bloated with rot, and black ichor leaked from the gaping wounds in her neck. I'd ever only seen a couple of corpses this bad. Frank Nacari, back in Brighton Beach, and Moris Falkovich in Hunts Point. It was more than just physical ruination. The horrified expression, the black slime crusting the wounds, the way that she just somehow felt *wrong*. Violation was a characteristic of Morphorde kills, and whoever – *whatever* – had done this clearly hated women, and this woman in particular. Was it personal? A vendetta? Or just Morphorde?

I thought back to what Agent Mattson said about what had killed her. Some kind of toxin, they thought, or magic that replicated a toxin. Was there a residue left behind? Something I could use to track the killer? Even if Soldier 557 hadn't killed Kristin, it wasn't like I had any better leads.

I searched around the room until I found a thick needle and syringe, took them back to the corpse, and slid the needle into a squishy patch of decayed flesh on her neck. The gunk drew into the tube like brown-black custard. When I had a sample, I took it back to the counter and squirted it into a small plastic jar with a yellow lid, like the kind used to collect urine samples, trying not to breathe in the smell.

Squorch.

I paused, the syringe still in my hand, as a soft wet sound popped the bubble of silence around us. I turned just in time to see something shoot through the liquefying remains of the Agent's belly, darting like an eel.

"No. Oh no. No, no no." I lunged back at the freezer and unceremoniously slammed it closed. I had my hand on the locking mechanism when it slammed open again. A prehensile tentacle whipped out and around the edge of the freezer. The steel handle hit me in the gut and sent me stumbling back into the edge of the surgery table.

"I said 'NO', GOD-dammit!" I lunged forward again, recoiling as the creature tore itself free of the corpse, sending liquefied tissue slushing off the tray to the floor. It fell off the roller bed in a clumsy heap.

I backed away, not turning around. It wasn't a DOG... it was some kind of giant insect-dinosaur death machine. Its color flexed and shifted under a coat of reeking black ichor. It was six-legged, eyeless, with a long snout and a rounded shell that reminded me of a pill bug. It was a bit larger than a human torso, and the tentacle was actually a tongue that darted in and out of a tube-like, toothless mouth. The tongue waved back and forth warningly, and the blind head swung unerringly in my direction as I put the table between me and it. I was about to break away when a horrific sound rumbled through the floor, though my bones and the nerves of my teeth. It was not a sound you heard with your ears: in fact, sound was drowned by the curtain of sonic white noise, rendering ears useless. Worse, it wasn't just booming through the material plane. It was rattling the Phi around me, shaking the metaphysical structure of the room—and the metaphysical structure of my body along with it.

My vision turned to static and I crumpled to my knees, gasping as the air shook. The burst relented, and I had enough sense to throw myself and scramble away over the floor on my hands and ass before it boomed again. This time, the sound crushed me down to the floor. It was like a hand pushing me down against the ground. I rolled over onto my belly, pulling myself arm-over-arm toward the door.

The creature staggered around, throwing its head and its tongue—a good six feet of barbed, sticky flesh—like a bullwhip. It smashed trays and cabinets, pulled a door off one of them and slammed it into the surgical table, crumpling three inches of steel like tin foil. I froze as it bowed its sightless head and began to slide its tongue over the ground in a serpentine wave. I was almost to the door when the next crushing wave of sound emanated from it. It dragged me helplessly to the ground. Worse, I was getting a migraine: the edges of my vision crawled with aura, like heat haze. When I tried to grasp my magic, the energy slid through my control like sand vibrating through a sieve.

I pushed against the wall and watched the creature unerringly stumble to the bathroom. It lashed out with its tongue, roping around the dead Agent's legs and dragging him across the floor like a winch. The Morphorde—it had to be a Morphorde of some kind—was drooling copiously. The corpse went in feet-first, and whatever its saliva touched disintegrated into goop. It took seconds for the body to disappear, not minutes. Seconds.

When the creature paused for a breath, a bang and a shout broke through the wall of white noise. The door kicked in, nearly hitting me in the face, and three Men in Black opened fire from the doorway. They were oblivious to my presence, focused on the Morphorde.

"We got a Streetsweeper!" One them yelled over the magically silenced gunfire. "Echo, Echo, Echo!"

The Streetsweeper responded with sonic. It's normal pulses of echolocation had been debilitating: the weaponized form was agonizing. I clamped my hands over my ears, trying to block out the intense vibratory pain. Through watering, slitted eyes, I saw the Men in Black stagger, screaming silently in the sonic bubble, and then the Streetsweeper lurched forward, slashing with its tongue at the MiB closest to the front. I was expecting it to pull the MiB's legs out from under him. The Streetsweeper wrapped its tongue around his waist, and cut him in half with it. It dragged the man's torso toward itself, leaving the legs to topple over.

"Fuck!" I swore, unable to hear myself. Involuntary tears poured down my cheeks. I forced my eyes open and half crawled, half dragged myself to the door. I was slightly better outside in the hallway: I got my feet under me, stumbled in the direction I'd seen Zane go, and nearly ran into him as I rounded the corner.

"What the fuck is happening!?" He shouted, one hand clamped to his ear, the other carrying a bag of dismembered computer equipment.

"We need to get out, now!" I grabbed his arm and pulled him forward, toward the inner stairwell. Going back the direction we had come was suicide: there was no escape through the garage. "There's a Morphorde in there!"

"We have to stop it!" Zane shook me off, yearning back toward the sounds of shooting and screaming. "We-"

"We don't have the tools or the manpower for this!"

"I'm the tool for this job!" Zane snapped. "That DOG could kill everyone in this neighborhood!"

"It's not a DOG, and I'm telling you that I just watched it cut a supersoldier in half with its GOD-damned tongue," I snapped back. "A supersoldier who just called for backup, and they'll shoot *you* as readily as they'll shoot *it*."

"Cover me, then." And Zane dropped his gear, shedding his clothing as he ran for the now-quiet room and transformed .

Bravery was one thing; recklessness, quite another. I cursed bitterly, checked that I had enough ammunition in the rifle, and ran off after him.

I screeched to a halt in front of the broken door to find... nothing, save for pieces of warped metal and plastic, the guns, and the MiBs' goggles and headsets. They had been vomited in a pile near the mortuary table. The Streetsweeper was nowhere to be seen. Zane was pacing around the edges of the room, huffing and sniffing.

I flinched, aiming up as I looked around wildly at the ceiling, the corners of the room, then toward the bathroom. The only sign of the dead FBI agent were his effects: a tie clip, the cover from his notebook, his ID card and an assortment of other small, inorganic items. Everything was gone, including the blood.

"It could be in the bathroom," I said to Zane.

The cougar ignored me, shoulders hunched as he—she?—paced back and forth. I went to the bathroom and opened the door, staying around the wall. The toilet was mangled, as was the wall. The large industrial air vent overhead had been torn out, leaving a gaping black hole. The plaster around it had clearly been gouged by claws. Fear mingled with relief, until a thin wailing sound pierced the air from outside. Sirens, the warbling cadence of the Vigiles Magicarum fleet vehicles.

"Zane!" I went back out. "Zane, we have to go!"

The cougar growled at me, and when I took a step forward, she bunched and hissed. My heart sunk. Zane had changed once already, and shapeshifting burned a lot of calories. He hadn't been able to eat in between changes, and his Ka-Bah had gone feral.

Suddenly, I was pissed. Furious. "Your fucking action hero complex is going to get us killed or worse! Snap out of it!"

The big cat reared onto her back legs, hissing and striking at me with a paw. I slapped it aside, grim-faced, and then punched Zane's Ka-Bah right in the side of her head. It wasn't going to hurt her, but it seemed to shake something loose. Human awareness returned to her eyes, just before I seized her by the scruff and pulled her toward the door.

"Move it!" I let go at the threshold, and broke into a limping jog. The puma followed on my heels, ears flat to her skull, tail held low.

Lightning flashed through the windows; rain pounded the door, the glass, and the garden outside. The street beyond pulsed with purple, blue, red and white lights. The Vigiles and NYPD were working together. They'd cordoned off the street in front of the house to stop curious onlookers from getting closer, while entry teams mustered out in front of the house, visible as dark lumps through the sheeting rain. Conscious that the Streetsweeper could still be inside, I hustled into the parlor, then beyond that to the sunroom door. The sunroom was a greenhouse-like structure full of stacked chairs and folded plastic tables. The marquee was longer than it was wide, and ran down the side of the house to the corner of the road, where another door led out into the garage entry. The two sentries were gone, but the gate and garage were open. Voices rang out from inside: voices, then screams.

"Well, they found the Streetsweeper." I kept a hand on Zane as he flattened to the ground. "Don't even think about it. We're getting out of here."

Zane growled, bunching as I got ready for the sprint. We broke out into the open at a run, which slowed to a trot and then a standstill as the sky turned red over our heads, and a deep, sonorous moan rolled through the air. It made the ground rumble and the dirt on the ground dance.

My heart sank as a familiar, shuddering ripple of dark energy washed over me in a crawling wave. The hair on the back of my neck prickled, and the rain—already chilly—turned icy. Behind us, something hard, something I couldn't see in the dark, punched through the top of the sunroom like a bullet, the sound of shattering glass breaking through the roaring storm.

"Run!" I took off as fast as my legs could carry me.

Darkness deeper than night fell over New York city like a blanket. The streetlights were dulled. The troopers out on the street didn't even notice us as we pounded through the hail thundering down over the city. I kept anticipating the smell of blood, but instead, a nauseous, rotted odor began to saturate the air, as half-seen shapes—some the size of my thumbnail, others as large as my hand—rained down on us and scuttled away through the rancid water. We were sloshing across the thin torrent that was racing downhill along the street when the quality of the rain suddenly changed, turning rancid. The reek of human excrement suddenly dominated everything.

I swore, wrestling with the car door, and threw the bags inside first. Zane got in after them, and I slammed the door closed, turning back to the street as the cougar wrestled with whatever had stuck to her fur.

"BINAH!" I called out to my familiar, and threw a hand up to generate a magical shield against the filth and bugs raining from the sky. "Binah!"

The sky rumbled, and the water on the ground shuddered. As the sound cleared, I heard her: a faint panicked meowing coming from the house beside the funeral home. She'd gone to their garden. I ran over and vaulted the front fence, weathering blows against the shield. There were bugs in the sludge. Large, cockroach-like bugs with spines and needle-sharp pincers swarmed up my boots and over the cuffs of my coveralls, trying to burrow through them and into flesh. I slapped them off as I struggled not to throw up at the wretched violet-and-tar brown stench of their ichor, and vaulted the fence into the garden. "Binah!"

Binah was fighting for her life on the front deck of the house, trapped inside a circle of insects. A cockroach the size of her head leaped at her, chittering. She spat and struck it away, and jumped up to hang on the screen door with a hiss.

I thundered onto the wooden floor and stomped on the first line of bugs, grinding them under my boots as I fought toward her. The bugs popped and burst into foul-smelling fluid, and the insects still alive swarmed the gooey mess, sucking it up and increasing in size as they did so. I had to drop the shield to grab Binah and haul her out the door. Her claws pierced my shirt and the flesh beneath as she clung, terrified. I wrapped myself around her and ran back out into the rain.

Bugs now made up the majority of the movement on the road: scuttling, drowning, fighting, eating one another and growing. They surged and splashed around my feet like schooling fish as I ran back, doing my best to shield my cat from the blows overhead. Zane had changed back, pale and scared as he threw open the door and took her from my hands. He picked the biting cockroach creatures off her like oversized ticks while I pulled others out of my hair. The sounds of people screaming, crying, and the sharp rapport of gunfire rang out from around the corner. Car alarms, sirens... chaos, just like the meat storm.

I dove into the car once most of the crawlers were off, slammed the door and plucked out the ones that had embedded their proboscises through the denim and into skin. I was bleeding from dozens of tiny punctures.

"Jesus fucking Christ." Zane pulled one out of my hair and threw it out the window. "What the fuck?"

"This is bad," I said, thinking back over what Kristen Cross had said in her report. "Very bad. A second harbinger. It has to be."

Zane looked as exhausted as I felt, but he still had the energy to scowl. "Yeah. But a harbinger of what?"

Tiredly, I watched the insects pound against the windshield and splatter, their bodies splitting into bugs the size of mites that were washed away by the water. "For once in my life, I'm not sure I want to know."

CHAPTER 22

We got back at 3 a.m., exhausted. I'd only been up for seven hours, but it had been one hell of a night.

Strange Kitty was closed, and the yard that had been a warzone only hours before was now cold, wet, and still. I could smell the bugs, but no longer see any on the ground.

Zane had left for home, so it was just me and Binah. I burst into the darkened clubhouse, thinking I'd be here alone, but was surprised to see Jenner's bony shoulders at the bar. She had her back to the empty room, hunched over her drink. A battered AK-47 lay on the counter near her elbow. She wore no jacket: just a loose faded black tank top that had definitely seen better days.

"Jenner?" I called out to her.

"Ehhn?" She started up a little. She sniffed the air as she turned and focused on me, bleary-eyed. "Oh, Rex. Yo."

Her voice was heavily slurred. Grimacing, I crossed to the bar. The craving for alcohol simmered behind my concern, peaking as I got closer and smelled the fumes wafting off the bar counter. My mouth was ashy and parched, tongue sticking to my palate, and it smelled good. "Where is everyone? Are you alright?"

"I'm pissed off, is what I am." She put her glass to her lips and threw back whatever was in it. "The universe needs to let the fuck up for a day."

"Tell me about it." I tried to stay back from the bar and banish the craving. "Did you see what was going on outside?"

"I sure as shit smell it." She hawked in her throat, grimacing. "Figured it was the shit garnish on top of the shit sandwich that was tonight. Started getting ready for the end of the world yet?"

"Bugs just fell over the city," I said. "Everywhere."

"Thought that's what I smelled." Jenner shook her head. "Dunno if you saw the news. Miami just got wiped off the map by the biggest hurricane on record. They thought it was gonna head for the Bahamas, but it turned and hit Florida. Hurricane Samantha. Next one's heading our way - they were saying they expect it to hit on Halloween. Category Four. They're calling it the Perfect Storm."

"That's the night you fight Tiny, isn't it? Otto Roth?"

"Yeah."

In the silence that hung between us, I took the seat next to her.

"Did your man make it? Rob, the driver?"

"No. Blood poisoning got him." Jenner scowled. She had taken off her eyepatch, baring the scarred ruin of her eye. "I got too cocky again. Now another good man's dead, and we're screwed."

"They took the truck?"

"Damn right they took the truck. My fucking truck, and my fucking guns." Jenner slammed the empty glass back to the counter. "Now I have to answer to the fucking Crazy 8's down in Miami, assuming they didn't drown like rats. The floodwaters are up to the goddamn traffic lights. I shit you not."

"The only way the Nightbrothers could have known where to hijack the truck is if someone told them the route," I replied. "Who knew?"

She glowered at me. "What're you trying to say?"

"I'm not *trying*. I'm telling you. You have a rat in your ranks. So who knew where the truck would be?"

Jenner stiffened with tension for a few seconds, grinding her teeth, and then sunk down to lean on the bar. She slid her hands up through her hair.

"Ron and Zane," she said. "Talya. A couple other crew. It might not be any of 'em. We went on another wiretap hunt while you were gone. Found one inside the pool table. I dunno how they found time to drill the hole, but there it fuckin' was."

"I doubt the Vigiles sent the Nightbrothers in," I said. "Though given what Zane and I just found, I'm not discounting it. It's still more likely to be someone you know and trust."

"Yeah." Jenner shook her head. "Fuck me, Rex, I know we got problems here. There's factions in the Tigers, you know. Cliques. The old boy's club, the guys that fought with... with Mason in Vietnam, they aren't happy with how I'm runnin' things. You heard Ron the other day."

"I did." Eyeing the rack of bottles, I took a seat on her other side.

"Some of the boys blame me for all the dying last month. Some of them think we Weeders can't be trusted to protect them. Can't say I blame 'em." Jenner shook her head, her hair slipping over her cheek. "We got new recruits training up, but Dogboy fucking nailed it. We're low on manpower, and it's screwing with people. I think... I think they'd have rathered it was me who'd died, 'stead of Mason."

"Don't say that," I said. "That's ridiculous. What happened tonight demonstrated their loyalty to you."

"Nah. Bikers jus' like to fight. Zane is good... yeah. The Big Cat Crew is pretty solid. It's just though... fuck. I don't even know." She fumbled for the bottle on the other side of the bar counter. "Fuck feelings. Fuck Otto. Fuck storms."

"You need to slow down a bit," I said. "I can smell your breath from here."

"My liver needs to work out too." She uncapped the bottle - bourbon, as usual - and poured herself another. "You want one?"

My mouth itched, and before I could help myself, I'd spoken. "Yes."

"This'll put hair on your chest." She leaned over the bar, snagged a beer glass, and dumped a tumbler's worth of bourbon into it. I took it with a sinking feeling in the pit of my stomach. It smelled sour, but my body mechanically lifted the glass to my lips. It tasted pretty much how it smelled, and as the sense of satiation flooded through me, I made myself set the glass down. One mouthful was enough, I tried to tell myself - and the Yen.

Jenner didn't seem to notice the struggle, but then again, she was drinking out of the bottle. "So hey, Rex, between you and me, there's something else."

"Go on."

"The Malek of Austin made me an offer." She gazed up at the war memorabilia above the mirrors that hung behind the bar, frowning. "Guy by the name of Starfish. Me and his right-hand girl, Cassie Bones, have a history together. Good history, mind you, nothing bad. She runs a Weeder warband down that part of the South."

"And?"

"Cassie and Starfish have wanted us to band together and merge gangs for years." Jenner sighed, and puffed some of her fringe out of her face. "We always said 'maybe one day'. We've always been pretty proud up here, you know? Wrapped up in our own business. Well, I spoke to Cassie again a couple days ago. She's begging me to take the boys down and join her permanently."

"Are you thinking about it?" My fingers were playing around the glass, flirting with it. The amber liquid looked like honey, and the smell of it was becoming more enticing by the minute.

"I can't deal with it right now, because of Otto fucking Roth." Jenner snarled under her breath. "I'll kill that fucker on Wednesday night. I'm going to have to kill Dogboy and Gator, too."

I brought to mind my clearest memory of Dogboy: the sight of his bared fangs. "Dogboy is a vampire?"

"Correct." She lay her face down on her arm, pointing up at the ceiling with the other hand. "I dunno, Rex. I'm rambling. I'm pissed off at Cassie for turning the thumbscrews on me, but I know she means well. I think… I think maybe she's got a good idea? But I can't just fucking *leave*."

I thought for a few minutes. "I think we should."

"What? And abandon Strange Kitty?" She hawked in her throat. "Fuck that, Rex. Fuck. That. I can't let Otto get his greasy fucking paws on my land."

"I'm worried that they were counting on you saying that, Jenner. This fight is bad news," I said.

"It's a fight. Been in 'em hundreds of times." She shook her head. "They aren't gonna outfox me."

"You know he's not normal, don't you? Otto is Morphorde."

"Don't have to be Sherlock Jones to see that." Jenner didn't look up. "'Course he's fuckin' Morphorde."

"Then why not hit him and his club Tuesday night? Burn them out." I frowned. "You said it yourself. He's *Khayty*, an outlaw, and he won't respect the rules."

Jenner began to chuckle. I watched her, perplexed, as she pushed herself up and turned to face me, a delirious drunk smile on her lips.

"That's where my favorite spook comes in, doesn't it?" She said, exhaling a cloud of sweet, boozy breath. "Let's go out back to my room."

I wasn't sure I wanted to, not with her like this, but the tigress resolutely slid off the stool and weaved toward the red door. I almost took the drink with me, but forced myself to leave it on the bar and followed at a wary distance.

Jenner staggered to the room where she occasionally slept and collapsed onto the bed. "I told Otto he can only bring two of his crew with him. And I know he's going to bring Dogboy and Gator."

"Gator's the spook? The old guy?"

"Yup." Jenner arched her head back against the pillows. "Now, Otto isn't going to just bring those two along. He'll bring his gang and hide them, but we're going to set up before they do. We'll lay a bunch of traps."

She was definitely drunk. Exasperated, I looked away from her. "Jenner..."

"Don't you 'Jenner' me. I was in the Viet Cong. My last life, I fought in World War Two while your parents were still in diapers, and I know what I'm talking about," she snapped.

"Fine. Traps. What kind of traps?"

"Laaaaandmiiiines." She stretched the word out with satisfaction. "Well, remote-control proximity mines."

I slouched deeper into the beanbag and rubbed the bridge of my nose. "And what, exactly, do you intend to do with the bodies and-or severed limbs that result? Not to mention the noise. Are you going to fight off the National Guard by yourself, too?"

"You stopped a bunch of bullets at that junkyard," Jenner said, leaning up to look at me. "Can't you create a buffer to diffuse sound?"

I looked up and blinked at her. "You're serious."

"Bastard wants to take MY land," she grumbled. "I'll fucking show him, Rex. Can you do it or not?"

"Well... in theory, yes." I regretted the words as soon as they came out of my mouth. "But-"

"Buuuuut?"

Proximity mines. "I'd need a large blood sacrifice to ward a whole area like that. And where in GOD's name are you going to get proximity mines?"

"Pfft. I already have 'em. This is America, son."

"So... you're going to lay literal landmines. And dig them up once you're done, I hope."

"Bitch, I can smell the individual fucking pheromones in your sweat when I'm shifted. I can smell where we hid the landmines."

"Then can't Otto?"

"If he's an Elder and he knows they're there, he could. But he isn't, he doesn't, and he won't." Jenner rolled over onto her side and squinted at me, as smug as any cat. "Why do you think I chose that site?"

I rubbed my hand over my mouth. "Running water... isolated, derelict, smells like old machinery, but isn't so polluted as to be advantageous to a Morphorde."

"No more than any other place in this filthy shithole of a city." Her dark eyes glinted. "So once he does the big reveal, we blow up a mine. The whole lot of them'll piss themselves. Even big bad bikers are scared of the dark, Rex. The shit they can't see terrifies them."

"I can probably contain the sound of the concussion with the right ward," I said. "But I can't do it now. I need to sleep."

"Sure." Jenner was looking pretty sleepy as well - and not nearly as drunk as she'd made out to be. "You've been pushing too hard again."

"Me? Never." I snorted, and rolled my eyes as I got to my feet. My back, knees and hip cracked, and I winced.

"Yeah. You." She pushed herself up to recline. "What's eating you, son?"

"All sorts of things." Even though she hadn't made any move toward me, I had the sudden urge to step back and away. "The Vigiles, mostly. Tomorrow night is my deadline."

"Don't worry about 'em. If we have to squirrel you down to Texas to hide out with Cassie, we will." Jenner waved it off. "What else?"

"It's not that simple," I replied, frozen in place: half forward, half toward the door. "Have you spoken to Talya about what she's discovered about MinTex? The link between the Russian Mafia and government?"

"Yeah." Jenner scowled, foot twitching like a restless tail.

I began to pace, glancing at the walls. Was the room safe? "I have a theory as to what's happening, and it's not good. Do you know what a 'Shard' is? And what a Shardkeeper does?"

Jenner's face became mask-like, carefully neutral. "Maybe-yes. Depends who's asking."

"Is this something in your book of laws? The Ib-Int?"

"The Ib-Int isn't a book. You get all the information during your first shift." She frowned. "Why're you asking?"

"The Vigiles and the TVS are both looking for a Shard. They're at war over it." I laced my hands in my lap. They were shaking - with fatigue, with the need to go out and finish my drink, with overstimulation. "I think Angkor is working for the Vigiles, and he was captured by the TVS. He gathered the intel he needed from us and left after the blood rain signaled him to do something. He may have murdered the Vigiles agent Ayashe was upset over, Kristen Cross, and gave me to his handlers. They knew exactly where I was that night. They knew where to stage the setup. I think they want me to take the fall for Kristen's death, because they murdered her. She was a traitor to the agency."

Jenner peered at me owlishly. "How'd you figure that out?"

"I found a report Kristen had recorded for a third party," I said. "She explicitly recounted the conflict between the TVS and the Vigiles, and mentioned their pursuit of the Shard and the people who know its location. She said one was in prison, one is on the run, and one is dead."

"Yeah." Jenner grimaced. "Michael."

I paused for a moment. Michael had been someone I'd met only a few times. The leader of the Pathfinders and the true Elder of New York, he had been a tall, imposing, priest-like man. Bald, monastically calm, he'd died a horrific death the same night that Mason had vanished. "You think that's why he was murdered?"

She nodded. "Yeah. I *know* that's why he was murdered."

"So what is a Shard, then?"

"It goes back to the myth of our creation," Jenner said slowly. "The short answer is that a Shard is a piece of GOD's skin. A piece of Eden that got flung out when GOD was fucked by the Morphorde and stuck in a single cell of its body, like a splinter of glass."

Eden? Here? "I…"

Jenner's eyes burned with an orange-green halo as she fixed on me. "We know there's a Shard here. All of us sense it, instinctively, the first time in the first life we ever shapeshifted. For me, that was back near the end of the Crusades. I knew that the Crusaders and the Muslims were fighting over the wrong chunk of land right from the start. The Shard's not in the Middle East. I don't know where it is, but Michael did, and he took that secret to his grave. The TVS probably wants it for their own fucking loopy reasons, but I can tell you why the Vigiles does - because they're run by the fucking *Deutsche Orden*. They're the last real Templars, and they're still searching for the Holy Land. The REAL Holy Land."

"So tell me about them," I said. "The *Deutsche Orden*."

She lay back, her hands laced behind her head. "Well. It starts all the way back in 1190, the year of the founding of the Teutonic Knights. They were a pack of fucking bastards. They started out as thugs enforcing the tolls at ports in Germany, you know."

"Interestingly enough, my *Organizatsiya* started out the same way," I said. "Though we never received a knighthood."

"Hah. Well, back in those days, if you had a dick, a sword, some money and a bunch of friends, you could go to the church and turn your protection racket into a knightly 'order' as long as you promised to kill Muslims and Pagans. There's a bit more to it than that - lack of roadside hospitals, mostly - but that's the bare bones of it."

"Cynical, but accurate." I shuffled up, and leaned back against the wall.

"The Teutonic Knights raped and burned their way through Eastern Europe, killing every GOD-damned wizard, Weeder, Feeder and funny-looking animal they found, and established Prussia on the graveyard they built," Jenner continued. "They ruled it for a long time, but lost everything when Prussia turned Lutheran. The hardcore Crusaders retreated to the Holy Roman Empire and set up as specialized supernatural critter-killers. They called themselves the *Venator Dei*, God's Huntsmen. Most of the Teutonic Knights branched off into this hamstrung honorary knighthood thing that exists today, but a hardcore group kept going as the Church's supernatural hit squad. They worked all through the Inquisitions - *all* of them - and split off into advisories that went around the world. The *Deutsche Orden* boomed under Hitler. After the Second World War, they gained a foothold in the US."

I rubbed my lip thoughtfully.

"They play at being Protestant over here, but they're whatever denomination they need to get their way. The *Deutsche Orden* got mixed up with politics, found their way into Government, and they backed Reagan, then Rutherford. These fuckin Nazis got Rutherford into power so they could get their tentacles into the CIA and the Army and the FBI, and then they killed him."

I frowned. The 1983 assassination of President Rutherford by a sorceress had been the instigating event behind the formation of the Vigiles Magicarum, as well as the event that had brought magic into the modern American consciousness. Before then, magic was the world's worst open secret. Everyone knew it existed, in churches and cults, in dark tarot parlors and Spiritualist seances and Occult fraternities, but everyone hid it from one another, afraid of what would happen if they came out. The revelation that Presidents had a secret astrologer in the White House at all times, and always had - the 'Special Advisor to the President' - to inform their decision-making had scandalized the public when it had come to light. But even then, it had sort of existed as a weird, subconscious social thing. Rutherford's death and the Vigiles' creation had made it real in a way it hadn't been since the fall of Alexandria.

"So the *Deutsche Orden* is possibly the inheritor organization to the Thule Society," I said. "Nazi Germany's occult elite."

"The Thule Society basically *is* the *Deutsche Orden*," Jenner said. "There's a super-religious old guard at the core of then, the Order of Saint Peter, and the rest of them are occult-ish Nazi mystics and American Exceptionalists. They don't believe anything supernatural is HuMan. Supernatural *anything* is exclusively the work of 'dark forces', and all mages, shapeshifters, and anything not a plain ol' HuMan derive their abilities, personalities, and form from demons."

That explained Keen's attitude, and the statue and paraphernalia in the Judge's oratory. "The others don't sound like they believe you."

Jenner groaned. "They don't. They don't get that the Order won't be happy until every last one of us is dead. Their whole 'Agent-Adeptus' setup is them using fire to fight fire, and once the wildfire is put out, they'll extinguish all their torches."

"She may be coming around," I said.

"Don't count on it." Jenner shook her head.

"Well, that's food for thought," I said, easing up. "But if I don't sleep, I'm going to throw up."

"Go." Jenner waved airily, covering her face with her arm. "Leave me here. All alone, in the cold."

"I'm sure you'll survive." I sat up and stretched.

"Hey, life is more than just survival." She lifted her wrist from over her eye to glance slyly at me. "You know, you'd be great to snuggle. Big broad shoulders."

"No, but thank you for the compliment." Suddenly prim, I half-turned toward the door.

Jenner laughed. "You'll loosen up one day, when you find the right boy."

I was grateful my face was turned away from her. "I... well..."

"Angkor isn't worth you worrying about." She was mumbling a bit now, already falling asleep. "You should get to know Zane better. You could climb that boy like a palm tree, mm-mmm. He'd give you the time of your life."

I blushed so hard I thought I was going to pass out, and began sidling toward the exit. "And on that note, it is well past my bedtime."

"Me toooo," Jenner replied.

Only once she had rolled under the covers and started snoring did I begin to feel sick at the smell of stale liquor, and left as quickly as I was able so I could get into bed.

Even though my eyes would hardly stay open, I found myself staring at the ceiling of the bunk above my head. My brain was trying to process the day, skipping from Doctor Levental to Sergei, then to Christopher, the MiB, vampires, crooked senators, Streetsweepers, bug rains, and wiretaps. The ruminating became cyclical after a while, and I was on the cusp of sleep when I finally realized something.

Sergei. Wiretaps. The Wrathling he'd used to cut me from my magic - the Wrathling who was probably destined to take the place of my soul when Sergei cut the cord. He had summoned the creature back to himself and learned where I'd been. Which meant he knew I was staying with the Twin Tigers, and probably had a record of everyone else I'd come into contact with while I was carrying the parasite.

Including the guy who'd kept me fed while I was homeless. Rahul Ali Wheeler.

CHAPTER 23

Jenner was right. The Universe needed to let the fuck up for a day.

My face and fingers tingled with numbness as I hauled myself out of bed and looked over at the clock. 5:30 a.m. Just sitting upright left me feeling light-headed and nauseous with exhaustion, but if Sergei was working back through everyone I'd had contact with, then he'd either found Ali or would find him soon. He'd kill him just to prove a point. He'd leave me no solace, no friends, nothing except the certainty of my servitude to him. It was the way of the *Organizatsiya*, as relentless and terrible as the *GULAGs* that spawned it.

Ali was my responsibility, and my body was going to do what the fuck I told it to do. I dragged myself up and out to the kitchen, forced down a plate of fried eggs and steak, and chased it with the rest of the bourbon and a B vitamin. I had a headache coming on, but the bitter smell of coffee turned my stomach. If the Yen kept screwing with my palate like this, I was going to have to start taking caffeine pills. It could make me drink, but damned if I was going to let it decide which vices I kept and which ones I didn't.

After my first real meal in days, I felt slightly more awake. I shaved cold and spent a while in meditation, staring fixedly at The Chariot until I felt like I had control, then went to my locker and loaded for bear. Guns, knife, my new armored suit, fresh gloves, a clean tie. By the time I was done, I looked almost human.

Binah trailed after me as I prepared, her tail arched inquisitively over her back. When I was ready, I crouched down and stroked her head and flanks, lowering my head enough that she could stand up, her front paws on my knees, and groom my forehead and the tip of my nose.

"Not this time, girl." I got up and checked her food: two days' worth, with the kibble box readily accessible on the top of the locker in case of emergency. "You keep an eye on the place. I'll be back before you know it."

I left her on the bed and closed the door to the barracks. Her anxious meowing followed me through the house, echoing between my ears all the way to the car.

It was freezing cold, dark, and sleeting. The chill drilled into my knees, and they were aching by the time I reached the alley where I'd camped like Hobo MacGyver for most of the fall. Ali lived in the shitty part of The Bronx, which was saying something, given the state of The Bronx overall. Most of the apartment buildings here were gutted hulks, while others had been torched and were now nothing but piles of rubble. Ali's E-Zee-Pawn was an ironic bulwark against the surrounding urban decay, the second of a strip of six structures that still stood among the wreckage. The alley ran between Ali's and the building next door, an empty bodega with smashed windows and broken, empty shelves.

The only sounds were those of distant traffic, and plastic bags rustling in the wind. The place was dead. E-Zee-Pawn was shuttered, the windows beyond the grate broken and crazed. People had been trying to break in and steal his inventory. The sign on the door was turned to 'CLOSED', and my gut began to churn. Ali lived above his store in a small apartment, and he was a creature of habit. Every morning, he walked to a better part of town, got coffee and a sub from the same store, walked back and opened up at 8:45 a.m. There was no reason for it to be closed at 9:30 on a Tuesday morning.

"Shit." A tremor passed from sternum to navel, an unpleasant nauseating thrill. I drew my knife and went down the alley, sniffing.

The dumpster where I'd lived was still exactly where I'd left it, turned on its side against a limp chain-link fence at the other end of the alley. It was still remarkably clean. The screen door that led into the narrow two-story building was ajar, and the solid door behind it was also loose. The lock had been gouged out of the wood with a chisel. I instinctively longed for a gun, but the knife was safer. The DOGs I'd been fighting for months used firearms to reproduce and heal. I still didn't understand why or how, but I'd seen it enough times that I was willing to take it at face value.

I pushed the door open, and walked into a wall of stench. The cloying smells of old meat and piss hung on the air, scents that twisted my stomach. Normally, I didn't have a problem with the dead... but it was all too easy to flash back to Mariya's apartment smelling like this.

I recoiled from the entrance, a hand over my face, and squeezed my eyes closed. I didn't have to go in. Realistically, there was no reason for me to go inside. I knew I should find a payphone, call the cops, and let them handle it... but this was my fault. Ali had been kind to me, and I'd led wolves to his door.

My shoulders sagged, and I backed away to lean on the opposite side of the alley, struggling to stay with my senses. Ali and the doctor were good men, men who'd done nothing wrong by Sergei in any personal way... men who had offered me their assistance, help and resources when I had been at my most desperate. They hadn't deserved this.

I gulped fresh air, and forced myself to open the door and cross the threshold. The short concrete corridor inside had an interior door that led into the storefront and a flight of carpeted stairs leading up to the living quarters on the second floor. There was only the one apartment in this tiny building: he had no neighbors. I trudged up, dreading what I knew I'd find, hoping that he had at least been able to die quickly. That really depended on who Sergei had sent to kill him.

The stairs led to a door in an alcove. It was dirty and old, made more homey by the protective hamsa pendant on his door and the hemp welcome mat outside. This lock had been opened more carefully: there was no damage, and the door was closed. There was no point in knocking. The smell told me there was no hope of anyone alive being at home.

Picking locks with magic was something I could do, now. I put a hand over the lock and concentrated. A thin thrill of power lanced through my fingers, and I felt for the tumblers, lifting the pins and holding them up as I worked the doorknob with the other hand. After a couple of seconds of effort, the knob turned. I held it while I worked on the deadbolt, which was more difficult... but after a minute or so, I felt the lock turn and clunk, and the door opened.

Wait. The deadbolt was locked? I froze before entering, ticking off the possibilities. If I were interrogating someone, I'd lock the deadbolt, too. Same if I was worried about being interrupted. That meant that the murderers had escaped through a different entry... and maybe they'd arrived through a different entry, too.

The stench of rotten flesh was overpowering. Eyes watering, I stepped into a hallway that creaked with age. Ali's house was lined with cheap pea green carpet that went halfway up the walls to a wood-paneled edge, where it was replaced by faded wallpaper. The hallway was neat, but the walls were stained yellow.

If Sergei had ordered the hit, I wouldn't rule out the chance that he'd hired another spook already. There was a possibility of magical traps. If there is one thing I am not, it is incautious, so I sketched a sigil and murmured a command word in the fetid stillness of the hallway. "*Chet.*"

A fragile-looking web of kinetic energy spun itself ahead and around me in a sphere, Phi rippling like a sheet of tiny stars as I found the sustaining point of the spell and held it. I was tired, and the shield was thin. It wasn't going to take more than one hit, but it would be enough. With my guard up and my knife turned back in my hand, I followed the sound of buzzing insects to the kitchen. There was no door, and the worn wooden frame had gouge marks. I rounded the edge of the doorway, knife and spell at the ready. Just in case.

It wasn't as bad as I expected. It was worse.

Ali had clearly been dead for days, if not weeks. He was pinned to the wall beside his refrigerator, body sagging off the cutlery that skewered his limbs. Butter knives, not even knives with a point. They'd been rammed through his wrists, calves and ankles. I couldn't tell what had killed him. The window had been left open, and his corpse was crawling with maggots, flies, and ants. He'd had large chunks of flesh torn from all over his naked body, gaping holes scissored out of his dark skin. Something in his mouth glinted gold.

My heart sunk. Ali had been a kind man. Street-hardened, full of private pain, but kind. And they had reduced him to this flyblown hunk of meat

"Ali. My GOD." Sick with anger, I edged forward and used a fork to gently pull his jaw down. The object inside spilled to the floor with a thump. It was a gold Zippo. I picked it up with a dishcloth and rubbed the ichor off the monogram. 'V.S.L', in Cyrillic letters. One of Vassily's old lighters, taken from my house. I curled my fingers around it, hand trembling as my intuition began to pound at me from behind the fury... the wordless voice of my Neshamah, which suddenly swelled into a scream of warning, just before a shotgun blast took me in the back.

.

CHAPTER 24

The shield took the worst of it. The barrier absorbed buckshot with less difficulty than a single high-powered round, but the force of the blast sent me sprawling. I bounced off the edge of the sink and staggered against Ali's corpse, dragging it down off the wall. It didn't fall, and that took me aback just long enough for his cold, rotted arms to clutch me in a bear hug and pull me forward against his chest.

I shouted wordlessly and shoved myself away from him, even as the time dilation of adrenaline hit me. Several details imprinted themselves in a single moment of terror. The first was that the maggots infesting Ali were not white, but orange. The second was that his stiffened frame was inhumanly dense, like hardwood, and drier than it looked. The third was that someone was behind me, and they had anywhere between one and five rounds left in the shotgun.

Ali's jaws unhinged soundlessly and he lunged forward to bite me. The MiB suit saved my neck. His blunt, gore-covered teeth slid off the weird toughened fabric, unable to pierce or tear it. He was obscenely strong.

I gave up trying to get him off of me, and instead grabbed him by his waist and swung us both around just as the shotgun filled the small room with explosive white noise. It cut my vision and made my hands seize painfully. Ali didn't even flinch as the shots hit him, but they made him break his vise-like grip around my body. He lunged for me with teeth bared as I stumbled back, threw up a hand, and barked the word for fire. "*Aysh!*"

The magic responded like a striking snake. There was a weird sub-audible screech as my Will bent reality against itself like a match against sandpaper and used the friction to explosively ignite the dust in the air, a flashbang that burst my eardrum. Ali shoved away from me and the sudden flash of intense heat and light that washed over us and the room. The fire ignited his ragged clothing and hair. It also hit the walls. The greasy wallpaper went up in flames with a roar.

Behind him, Vera threw the empty shotgun and fled down the hall with an inhuman sound I never hoped to hear from a human throat again, a cross between a scream and a hiss in two voices - one human, cracked and dry, the other terrifyingly alien. The thing wearing Ali's face reeled out of the kitchen with a deeper version of the same sound, rolling against the walls to put himself out. I lost track of him: the tiny kitchen was full of smoke, and the flames were already licking at the ceiling. My only way out now was the window. I threw it up, awkwardly pulled myself through, and kicked down at the bloody sink to find some kind of leverage.

There was the sharp bang of a silenced pistol from behind me, then searing pain as Vera unerringly aimed, fired, and shot me in the ass through the curtain of smoke and flame.

"Fucking piece of horse shit!" I snarled in Ukrainian, pulling through and out onto the gutter ledge as the next round grazed me, scoring the suit and skipping off my hip. The further I got away from her, the wider her margin of error. For a marksman as good as Vera, any margin of error drastically increased my chance of survival.

I was on the ledge between the first and second floors. There was no fire escape. It wasn't a massive drop, but my injured leg would crumple when I hit the ground. I'd smack face-first into the pavement before I had time to roll.

The decision was made for me when Vera vaulted the window onto the ledge with inhuman alacrity, pistol in hand. Her hair was smoking, skin flaked with ash, but otherwise unharmed. She screeched at me, lips peeling back from top and bottom rows of razor-sharp iron teeth. The only way was down.

"*Chert*!" I channeled my fear into a shield and leaped off the building.

My hope was that the shield spell would soak my fall in the same way it soaked the momentum of a bullet. What actually happened is that I hit what felt like an invisible cushion of air about two feet off the ground that depressed and then sprang back, flinging me forward and up. I barely got into a roll in time, tumbling over myself on the asphalt. A round struck the ground half a foot from my nose, sending asphalt flying. I scrambled up as more bullets struck the ground around me, then dove for cover behind my car as three louder shots blew holes into the empty street. A much larger gun. A sniper rifle?

I heard a thump from across the street, then two more shots. I pulled the Wardbreaker and a compact mirror out of my bag and looked out around the edge of the trunk, mystified, just in in time to see Vera stagger up to her feet like a broken puppet. Dust poured from two large holes in her torso. She clutched at her gut, trying to hold it in like blood.

The rifle cracked, and Vera's form blurred as she practically teleported away from the plume of dirt as the next round struck the pavement instead of her. She moved so fast that I caught my breath, astonished.

Vera hissed, a high whistling, banshee keen, and fled down the alley. I listened to my heart thudding against my ribs, panting with pain and stress. Ali's building was now his funeral pyre. Smoke billowed out every entry and exit, flames licking out from the windows. There were no sirens yet, but somewhere nearby, there was a sniper.

I squinted at the ruined apartments, but couldn't spot anyone in the black, gap-toothed windows. Warily, I rolled over onto my good side, and as silence reigned, reached back and felt around where I'd taken the bullet. The jacket and pants had technically stopped the round, because the suit material - and the slug - had punched into my glute. I was looking at a puncture as deep as my little finger instead of a five-inch tunnel and a perforated bladder, but I didn't dare pull the material free until I got to my medical kit.

I crawled around the car to the doors opposite where the sniper's rounds had come from, gritting my teeth as I opened it and hauled my first aid kit out onto the road. The shaking was so bad that I could hardly get the bag open, let alone the gauze wound pads I needed.

"Ohh... now this brings back memories. You, my sweet bargain-basement virgin, up against the side of a car on a ruined highway after thinking you could kill me. Me, breaking your wrists, my cock in your mouth."

I froze, my breath catching in my throat, and turned around on my knees to find a very small man standing barely an arm's length from me on the road. He had to have been exceptionally handsome once, with features and a bone structure that evoked a Platonic ideal of HuMan form... a form which was decaying and patched, like a porcelain doll that had been dropped, shattered, and glued back together again. He had a huge fall of matted white cornrows and a scrabbly, stained Fu Manchu mustache the color of dirty bone. His dark red-brown skin was scoured with open sores weeping grayish fluid; his cheeks were concave, the fine straight nose dividing the sunken pits of his eyes, but it was the eyes themselves that caught and held me. They were wide violet pools encrusted with frothy black muck, like pond scum. The NOthing screamed at me from those eyes. His pupils were Black, empty gnashing mouths. In them, I saw the Rape of Eden as clearly as I'd dreamed it.

I blanched, recoiling from him against the open door. "What the fuck?"

"Exactly! The first time we fucked! Remember?" He grinned with a mouth full of snaggled, dirty teeth set like pieces of broken glass in his gums, a leer that abruptly transmuted to a thoughtful scowl. He scratched his cheek.

"Ahh... wait. No... different story. That was someone else."

My eyes narrowed. "Listen to me, you little punk. I don't know what the fuck you're on, but-"

"You're a different Alexi," he rasped, craning his head forward. A wave of stench, the sour smell of rotten fruit, hit me like a slap to the face. He sniffed, deeply. "I see, I see. Well... I could get that bullet out for you if you'd like. Suck it right out of that tight little ass of yours."

I'd jumped from the fire into the creepy Morphordian frying pan, apparently. I felt back for the car door, the gun pointed away from him. The Wardbreaker didn't feel right in my hand. It felt... pregnant. Too heavy, stirring with a sick energy in the presence of this man. "No, thank you. I'm very grateful for your assistance, but my gratitude will have to suffice."

He sucked his bottom lip, and let it go with a last, lingering look at the blood pooling underneath me before he sighed. "Oh no... I can't leave. This one is a messenger, my silver-eyed boy. You've been invited to a party. A 'do'."

It took me a moment to realize that he was speaking fluent Russian. "I... who *are* you?"

"Don't be an idiot. I'm glorious." He gathered his long mane of ratty braids and slung them back over one shoulder. There were bruises all down his neck, the imprint of human teeth, and ragged punctures seeping a pewter-gray fluid down his throat. Vampire fang punctures. "Come with me? I make a great date."

"Go with you where, exactly?"

The stranger smirked, a grin like a broken windowpane. His teeth reminded me very much of StainedGlass, and my skin crawled. "To church. That's where you usually find Deacons, is it not?"

My gut chilled. "The Deacon?"

"The only one who matters," the man said. He suddenly seemed more lucid than before. "He wishes to extend his hospitality, in the traditional sense. A favor repaid, a professional inquiry made."

I wasn't sure I wanted to know what the favor in question was. "By hospitality in the traditional sense, you mean a guarantee of protection and goodwill?"

The stranger looked up at me, lips parted. "Absolutely. Hospitality is taken very seriously, on my Father's life. Oil for the wheels."

My eyes narrowed. In the Eastern European tradition, hospitality was a big deal. If formal hospitality was invoked, it was respected, even for enemies or rivals: at least, for as long as you were inside the quarters of the host. If someone hosed you down on the street outside the door, that was your bad luck. "Why does he want to see me?"

The small man smiled a different way, and it transformed his face. He still looked like he had leukemia with a dash of leprosy, but suddenly, his thin face was... almost winsome. "Why, he wants to ask you to kill somebody, of course. Someone you don't like very much."

"Who?"

"That is the Deacon's business." He flashed me another crooked, charming little smirk. "I might have the answer, but I'm so weak... a swallow of your blood, given freely, might restore my memory?"

My stomach wobbled, turning with revulsion. "No. No blood. And I want a guarantee of safe passage to and from this meeting."

"I suppose these are terms that can be agreed to." The small man looked me up and down. "The ruined chapel on Charlotte Street is where you shall be received."

"When?"

He flashed me that fractured, broken-glass smile. "Alexi, Alexi... that's a dangerous question for a Temporalist. When-ever you arrive, of course. He will intersect you. Or... I could take you now."

"I'll take the car. Alone."

"I could make the ride so much more pleasant." He took another step forward, nose still working. "No boring New York traffic with me in the jump seat."

"Thank you, but no." I resisted the urge to lean away from the man in front of me. "Leave."

He smacked his lips, but there was no saliva in his mouth. Without another word, he turned and padded away on dirty bare feet, hips loose, back straight. The way he walked was incredible, and... eyecatching. Sensual, inhumanly fluid. It was impossible not to notice, even with the pain and the brainfog and the panic.

I rubbed my eyes and snorted out the rotten fruit smell, and when I looked up again, he was gone. The back of my neck crawled as I got my first aid materials together, doused three gauze pads in wound powder and saline, and then slowly, carefully pulled out the trapped suit material from my buttock, snarling with agony. I was going to have to go to an urgent care center with some stupid excuse - like falling on a spiked fence. With Ali's corpse-blood all over my suit, the likelihood of infection was beyond my ability to treat.

"*I'm glorious.*" I repeated his words, dragging myself up and into the car. I groaned as I eased down to the seat... and then it hit me.

Glory. The gematria... the old-fashioned speech and custom, the diminutive, childlike height. The stench of DOG on the wind hit me too late. Soldier 557 was already gone, vanished into the city like a bad dream, and with him my last hope of appeasing the Vigiles Magicarum.

CHAPTER 25

It's amazing how much time to think a trip to hospital gives you. While I lay on my face and let a doctor pick over the bullet puncture and a week's worth of minor injuries— the result of an unfortunate household moving accident involving a spiked iron fence, I told them—I brooded on the best way to screw Sergei into the ground, get one over the Deacon, and survive my seven o'clock appointment with Joshua Keen. I was supposed to be helping Jenner set up for the fight, too. Fat chance of that. I was still lying pantsless on the table when the Men in Black arrived.

These MiB were trying to disguise themselves as normal people. Instead, they looked something like window mannequins. Artificial hair poked awkwardly out from under the brims of their hats. They had makeup on, intended to give them a more life-like appearance. It made them look more like airbrushed crash-test dummies, or bad cross-dressers.

"Mister Sokolsky?" Agent Tweedle-dee asked from just inside the doorway.

"You're early." I made sure that the starched white sheet covered my ass. "And in case you hadn't noticed, I'm in hospital."

"Mr. Keen sent us to collect you, Mister Sokolsky," Agent Tweedle-dum replied in the same lifeless voice. "There has been a development. He desires you to be briefed on the changes to your assignment."

While he talked, Tweedle-dee stared blankly at the suit hanging over the back of the chair beside my bed, obviously confused and possibly disturbed by the sight of it. Maybe it had belonged to the guy who shared his nutrient tank once upon a time.

"What? Would it offend Keen's delicate sensibilities to mingle among the hoi polloi?" I replied. "He knows I'm here. Why doesn't he come and pay a visit?"

The Men in Black blinked, both of them, at the same time. My skin crawled.

"This is only a mission briefing, Mister Sokolsky," Tweedle-dum said. "Please don't be unreasonable."

"What part of my having an injury requiring IV antibiotics and professional care makes me 'unreasonable'? How about you go back to Mister Keen and tell him that I'll meet him in a neutral third-party location, and he can update me there?"

"We have orders to take you to the mission briefing."

I struggled with the urge to roll my eyes. "Then I express my deepest regrets, but I will not be traveling with you in the corporate hearse today. Where does he want me to go?"

The MiB glanced at each other, as if unsure what to do about someone who didn't respect the sanctity of 'orders', then looked back to me.

"We can dispatch an escort," Agent Tweedle-dee said. "If you would prefer."

"It would be a great waste of taxpayer resources," Tweedle-dum added helpfully.

Fucking hell. I was trying to keep a low profile at this place. Somehow, I doubted the arrival of a full Vigiles SWAT team and a cavalcade of identical homunculi was going to keep me out of the staff room chatter here. I'd left the Wardbreaker in the car, but stashed my backup pistol under the bed while the nurse had been out. It was tempting, throbbing with power barely six inches away.

"No. Submit to this." Kutkha's contribution was a push of sensation, wordless, but easily understood.

I made a face. *"What do you mean 'submit'?"*

"Mister Sokolsky? If you don't comply-"

"I mean 'submit'," Kutkha said. *"And have faith."*

"Look, I'm very familiar with what your sort does to people like me, alright?" I gestured down at my sheet. "Can I at least get some clothes on and get the needle out of my arm?"

The Man looked down at my elbow. "You will receive a cannula in the interview room. If you already have a cannula in place, you should leave it in to avoid risk of infection."

"Oh yes - infection is my number one priority while in custody." *Oy gevalt*, but these things were stupid. "Turn around."

"We cannot let you out of our line of sight."

Annoyed, I threw the sheet back and stood, careful to cover myself—in the front. "Then you can kiss my supporating ass the whole time I get dressed."

I disconnected the cannula from the IV and capped it off, got dressed, and then limp-shuffled out with my collective fourteen feet of bodyguard. People stared at us on the way out—at the Men, at the way I was walking—but no one stopped us. One of the Men in Black held the door to their black Cadillac open for me, polite to a fault, and we motored off.

All Cadillacs smelled faintly like cigarette smoke, and this one was no exception. The windows were black. Not just tinted—opaque, fathomless black. As soon as I was in, the driver pressed a button and a screen between their side of the cabin and mine darkened. It turned into a black mirror that didn't allow me to see where I was being taken. Wincing at every contact with the seat, I wrapped my arms around myself, leaning against the door, and watched my reflection on three sides. There was nothing else to do but wait.

We drove for close to an hour before I heard a gate open, and then the clunk-clank of our car going over speed bumps, heading in. I frowned, trying to keep my weight off the bad asscheek while the car curved around and came to a gentle stop. There was shuffling, doors opening and closing. The back door opened to reveal a wall of soldiers in new tactical gear. Three inscrutable, unidentifiable men, masked by high tech headgear and visored shades, were waiting with handcuffs at the ready. Two carried M-16s on bandoleers, while the other one had his weapon in his hands.

Submit. I grimaced, and held out my wrists.

To my surprise, I wasn't blindfolded—just cuffed. They helped me out into what appeared to be a parking lot, and formed a triangle with me at the center. While the one on my right frisked me, taking my knife and the gun I'd brought into the hospital, the lead spoke in a voice made harsh and mechanical by the mask over his face. "Mister Sokolsky, we ask that you remain positioned between us at all times. If you deviate from our path, you will be a designated security risk and dealt with accordingly. Do you understand?"

I regarded him sourly. "Perfectly."

We formed a neat, symmetrical column, following a narrow pathway defined by strips of yellow tape on the ground. There were cameras everywhere, and wards, and guards—none of whom looked as intentionally inept as the Men in Black. The Men loomed over them, but the unobtrusive soldiers standing around the building, fingers at rest beside their triggers, were a far greater threat than Keen's errand boys. They'd respond to any crisis as a team, as if linked by telepathy—and given who I was dealing with, real telepathy was entirely within the realm of possibility.

The elevator was smooth and silent, activated by a palm print and retina scan. It was fast enough that my ears popped: agonizing, with the burst eardrum. There were no numbers over the door, just a single amber light that burned during the ascent. We stood in that sterile little room for what felt like half an hour before it slowed, lifting my stomach and dropping it back down in the seconds before the doors opened, and I was escorted into a soaring lobby.

There were no windows here, but there was a lot of glass. Concentric walkways ringed a slender standing stone in the center of the chamber. It was about eight feet tall, a glossy black plinth that stuck out of a circle of carefully groomed river stones. As soon as we passed the threshold, I felt my magical ability depress. The magic in the compact submachine guns my security carried faded into nothingness. The crawling embers in the metal were gone, even though the engraving was still visible to the naked eye.

"What's with the rock?" I said, jerking my head toward the plinth.

None of the stormtroopers and neither of the Men replied. The one in the lead opened a waist-high glass gate—also manned by a masked guard—and we started our corkscrew path to the next floor up.

I was admitted into the kind of office seen anywhere in the Financial District. Silver trim, white walls, a very dark lilac carpet that was almost gray, a stylish desk, fake bamboo in a pot. There were six people in the room. Joshua Keen was standing with Tomas the Magical Forensics Guy and one other man I didn't know. The stranger waited by the end of the desk, arms crossed, seeming generally unimpressed, while Ayashe sat on a chair in front of it. She had her hands fisted on her knees, her face a stiff, polite mask. Almost immediately, she met my eyes, gaze heavy with silent warning, and gave a tiny shake of her head. The other two people were both guards who left as we entered, taking position outside the frosted glass doors.

"He didn't give you any trouble, I hope?" Agent Keen said. His voice seemed a little more nasal than last time, but he was just as supercilious.

"No, sir." The MiB to my right said.

"Good. Wait outside."

"Yes, sir."

The two Men left, and the room became slightly less oppressive. Slightly. Ayashe's fingers loosened a little.

"Might as well break the ice," I said. " Because I was busy getting a wound packed and I'm very unhappy to be here. What the hell was the rush?"

"You might want to be more polite in professional company, Mister Sokolsky." Keen angled his head toward me. "Especially given recent developments in the situation you were assigned to—and failed to produce on."

Jesus. Talk about throwing your hand. "Except that I *have* produced a result. I'm meeting Soldier 557 tonight."

The corner of Keen's eye twitched, the only readable sign of his displeasure. "You mean to tell me that you, in three days, accomplished what an entire agency hasn't been able to do in months?"

"He came to me," I said. "Synchronicity, you might say."

"And what does Soldier 557 look like?" Keen arched a thin eyebrow. "Describe him to me."

"Short, dark skin, white hair, leprosy," I said. "I don't know what he is, exactly, but he's not human. He's got the requisite skills, he's-"

"That is not our man." Keen's momentary concern evaporated. He perked right up. "Emmanuel, play the tape."

The stranger moved off, as mechanically compliant as the Men in Black had been. He switched off the lights, pulled the blinds across the windows, then fiddled with the VCR and projector on the desk. I crossed my arms, hanging away from the group to better see them all at once. Ayashe still looked like she was sweating bullets, like maybe she was up for trial—not a position I'd ever expected to see her in, and one that made me irrationally angry. I didn't like the way the men surrounded her, like a wall of swords. If anyone was going to kick Ayashe's ass, it was going to be Jenner or me, not some Nazi Stormtrooper asshole.

The video started up, showing a crisp black and white feed of Judge Harrison's study. I frowned, suddenly curious.

"You will understand once you see this," Keen said. "Now watch."

After a few seconds, a shadow passed across the floor, the silhouette of an opening door that was followed by a person sweeping into the room. They were tall, dressed in a broad-brimmed fedora and long coat, and stopped and turned as Judge Harrison followed them in, his arms open in greeting. Despite the danger, I felt a small rush of excitement. A Man in Black? Maybe I'd been right after all.

The scorn I'd been mustering died on my lips as the guest took his hat off. It was Angkor.

Keen glanced at me, but I was well in game mode by now and my face had settled into a stiff mask. We watched Harrison motion to the seat across from his desk, radiating a kind of manic excitement as he bustled around the room. Angkor accepted the seat with his usual grace. He casually took out and lit a cigarette. We could see his face and the back of Judge Harrison's head. There was no sound and no color, but Angkor was an expressive conversationalist, gesturing with his hands. The whole time he was speaking, Harrison was, slowly, carefully opening a drawer on his desk. A revolver lay on top of the papers, and as he reached for it, Angkor's hands moved in what I knew was an arcane gesture.

The gun was forgotten as Harrison clumsily jumped up, knocking his chair over as he staggered to his feet and then fell to his knees. He had his hands pressed over his groin, struggling to get his legs under him again.

"Pause it," Keen said.

Emmanuel paused the video mid-frame, just as Angkor was getting up to pursue his mark. His face was clearly visible. He looked hard, focused: the face of a professional killer at work.

"So, as you can see, he is neither short, dark, nor leprous," Keen said brightly. "Which means that you officially have no-"

I laughed, a short, derisive bark. "That isn't Soldier. That's Angkor. He hates the Deacon more than you do."

As one, the four of them looked at me.

"But never mind that," I said. "I'm finished here, right? So, throw me down the well or burn me at the stake or whatever it is you're going to do, and get it over with."

"I *told* you that's who he was," Ayashe said. She sounded like she was fighting the urge to get up and punch this man. "I told you his name is Angkor, and that's wrapped up with the TVS somehow, but we don't know how. I subbed the report-"

"I don't care about one non-human's report on another," Keen said. "But the corroboration between your knowledge is interesting enough to delay your detainment. What can you tell us about him?"

"Excuse me? *Excuse me*?! I am a GOD-damn Federal Agent!" Ayashe got to her feet, and froze as the two men at the door—like automata—pulled sub-compacts from their jackets and aimed them at her.

"You're an animal who can't control herself." Keen was as calm as the eye of a hurricane. "As you just demonstrated. Sit down."

She stared at the weapons in disbelief. "I don't know who the hell you think you are-!"

Keen didn't even reply: he just jerked his head, and the Men in Black opened fire.

Instinct threw me to the ground, and Ayashe as well—but there was nowhere to run, and nowhere to hide as the shorter, better equipped Men advanced in the sudden vortex of sound. When my vision cleared, I saw Ayashe on the floor, wheezing and wild-eyed as she bled across the regulation-gray carpet. She had dozens of wounds, holes punched out of her limbs, torso, and even her neck… but she wasn't dead.

"Take her out," Keen snapped at them. "Sandbox transit. And make sure she regenerates. The Director will want to review her before processing."

Processing? I watched numbly as the Agents crossed the floor. Ayashe was still struggling. With wounds that would have instantly killed anyone else, she struggled as they grabbed her arms and dragged her away. She stared at me in desperation, white eyes huge in her dark face. They carried her into the waiting arms of no fewer than ten guards who had materialized outside the room at the sound of gunfire.

"So." Keen took his glasses off, wiped flecks of Ayashe's blood off with a handkerchief, and then set them back on his nose. "What *do* you know about the man who killed George Harrison, Sokolsky?"

I was still down on one knee on the floor, ears ringing. The blown eardrum that had just started to heal had that fuzzy feeling again, like someone was holding a pillow against that side of my face.

"Well." I cleared my throat, fighting to not look at the smear of blood leading to the closed door, to ignore the way my heart now rattled behind my ribs. "He's Korean. He's a Biomancer, a mage who uses-"

"I'm well aware of what biomancy is. Who does he work for?"

"Not the Deacon. And apparently, not for you. Which leaves another branch of Government, himself, or…"

"Or?"

Or he goes around calling himself 'Zealot' and working for a guy named Norgay, I thought. "I don't know. I thought he worked for you."

"That isn't very helpful, Mister Sokolsky."

"Angkor was careful never to tell us anything about himself," I said. "But what I do know is that he isn't Soldier 557. And I can hand you the Deacon and Soldier, together, tonight—but I have to be at the meeting."

"That won't be necessary," Keen replied stiffly.

"Except it is," I said. "Because he didn't give me a time."

"I'm not following."

"The right time for him to arrive is the time I'm there. If I'm not there, it's not the right time. He's a Chronomancer. I wasn't joking when I said the meeting was an act of synchronicity."

"Fucking warlocks." Emmanuel was churlish, fatigue written into his voice and the lines of his face. "Can't you just meet up like normal people?"

"We wouldn't be mages if we did," I replied.

"How convenient for you this is the case," Keen said. "And where, exactly, will we be escorting you?"

"You won't be 'escorting' me anywhere," I said, thinking quickly. "Because he won't come if you do. You'll let us meet and set up around us. Then you can take him out."

"Where?"

I snorted. "Why on Earth do you think I'd tell you that?"

"We can rip it from your mind if we have to, Mister Sokolsky." Keen looked down his nose at me. "You seem to believe you still have a choice."

"By the time you get someone in with enough power to mine a Phitometrist of my ability for information, the Deacon will have sensed the disruption in the magic he's worked to arrange this meeting," I replied. "And that's it. He'll vanish. And given that he's mixed up in the chase for Lee Harrison, you really, really don't want him to vanish, am I correct?"

It was a reach on my part, but the way that Keen's already tense face sharpened, and the way that Tomas and Emmanuel both slammed the shades on their expressions was enough to tell me that I'd found the right button to push. I also knew that, by pushing it, I'd guaranteed my execution. Unlike Ayashe, I couldn't take twenty rounds and live—but unlike Ayashe, I hadn't believed them capable of humanity to begin with.

My eyes hooded as I got to my feet. "You're wrong. I do have choice. You need me capable of deciding when I'm going to go see the Deacon."

Keen shook his head, and I froze as the MiB leveled their weapons at me. When I felt back for my magic, it simply wasn't there—not with whatever suppression it was they had on this place.

"We have Lee. And you are missing a key element to this," Keen said. "But you seem to fancy that you're a clever man, so let me ask you a question—do you know what *cordyceps unilateralis* is?"

"Cordyceps is a family of fungus," I replied quickly. "They're famous because of their ability to parasitize and control insects."

"Correct," Keen replied. "Much in the way that a demon has parasitized *you*. Or more accurately, what used to be 'you'. That is what demons do, as according to their nature. They parasitize human beings and turn them into vehicles, zombies so perfect that they maintain an illusion of humanity where there is none. There is, in fact, no 'Alexi Sokolsky' left in that hollowed out core where you may have once had a soul. Whatever it was that happened to you when you were young allowed a malevolent entity to seize control. It replaced that child with itself."

I stared at him. "You're nuts."

"You grew up into a warlock. Into a cold-blooded, unrepentant murderer without a conscience." Keen cocked his head. "A career criminal, a murderer, a thief, a liar, and now a Faustian deal-broker. Which is exactly what one would expect of someone who was possessed by a monster, wouldn't you say?"

"You're nuts," I repeated. "My abilities, my mysticism… they were completely unrelated to all of those things. I didn't have any choice growing up in the family I did, in the circumstances I did-"

Soldiers were massing at the door. Keen just smiled. "No, you didn't. And that is my point. *Deus Vult*, Mister Sokolsky—I'll get the Deacon eventually. On *my* terms. Not yours."

CHAPTER 26

The last thing I remember before blacking out was being pinned down by a team of guards, so many of them that I couldn't breathe. When I stirred out of the drug fugue, my IV was gone, my clothes were gone, and I was somewhere that smelled like rotting garbage. The cell was basically a metal box with bars on one side cemented into a pit in the ground. No bench, no bed, no toilet—I had a five-gallon bucket that had been sawn down to three gallons and a small stack of cheap, office-grade toilet paper. Everything was welded and locked together tight, and without tools, there was no hope of escape. All there was to do was listen.

Piercing female screams rang out periodically from somewhere deep within the building: the kind of raw-throated shrieks you usually heard from a woman during childbirth. It might have been Ayashe—it might not. My brain was scalpels and static, everything whirling and cutting, crackling and snapping. From behind the cold iron bars of my cell, I could hear unseen guards talking in between the sounds of torture. Their voices were quiet, but the gaps in their audible words were filled in by the synesthetic patterns that beat a tattoo in my mouth.

"Jeez she... out. Can't take much more of... surely," I heard one say.

"You'd be surprised."

"I am. Whatever she's got, they want it real bad."

"Don't think they're going for info, man."

"Speaking of screaming my head off: it's true. They're already stiffing guys their pay over in the Icebox. The brass says we 'eat too much'."

"Well, no shit. They expect men to be on their feet ten hours in the fucking tundra-" whatever he said next was cut off by the next scream. "- cutting corners. It's already biting them in the ass."

"Yeah, it's fucking ridiculous. They should put in more of those milkhead freaks if they want soldiers that don't eat anything. Speaking of them… that 'thrope they brought in been rendered yet?"

"Nah. I heard Cruz say something about needing one of the big digester trucks for her, like the ones they use for dinosaurs and shit, but I'm about ninety percent sure I saw them stick her on a helicopter to the Sandbox."

"I thought we *had* a big truck?"

"We did." The guard dropped his voice further, enough that I had to put my ear against the bars. "Like I said, all this bullshit with cutting corners is bad news. The truck's missing."

"Missing?" The other man hissed in disbelief. "Who the fuck let it out of their sight?"

"Must have been those older milkheads, because no one was fired that I know of."

"That is a grade-A fuckup. I dunno… can you like… undigest 'thropes? Maybe some of their friends took it to try and turn them back."

"Doesn't work like that. Not unless they come back like that Slimer thing from Ghostbusters, right?"

I listened to them chuckle in growing horror, thinking back to the heavily enchanted cement mixing truck at the funeral home. That had to be the 'digester' truck they were talking about. The 'milkheads' had to be the Men in Black, with their white blood. The Men dissolved into slime that left no residue, and that slime… was made from shapeshifters?

My stomach churned, and my head swooped dizzily as I crouched back on my heels and rubbed my face. The woman's screams continued as the guards' talk turned to football and gossip. Then, suddenly, they cut. The men who'd been chatting, trying to drown out the heart-rending pain in those cries, once again turned silent and professional. One of them checked in on his radio, while the other swept past my cell and looked inside. His face was masked, eyes shielded behind a reflective visor. After a second of scrutiny, he moved away.

There was another cry from somewhere not too far away—this time, a sound of rage. Both the guards in my corridor looked up, one immediately onto the radio. "459 to X-Ray, welfare check on Zone 3-6-"

He was cut off by the sound of a door being kicked in. The pair turned and opened fire with silenced weapons, still loud in the confined quarters of the tunnel-like corridor. Three bursts, as they advanced and covered each other—and then a yell and an explosion that sucked the air into the hall and popped my eardrums. The pain in my injured ear was like a stab to the side of the head. Wincing, I clamored forward against the bars of my cage, trying to see what the hell was going on.

Hell turned out to be a shirtless, bruised, bleeding woman who gunned down the men on the floor with the precision of an experienced hunter as she stalked out into the corridor. Her expression was blank with concentration, and she had blood all over her face and throat. Stocky, tanned, short-haired and square-faced, I recognized her immediately.

"Lee!" I called out as she turned in my direction. "Lee Harrison!?"

"Who the fuck-" she spotted me looking out at her from the small cell door, which was at knee-height to anyone standing. "No way. Is it... no way, it can't be."

"Let me help you get out!" If it was a case of mistaken identity, I wasn't complaining.

She was already running over, crouching down with a shuddering sob of pain. Lee had the strong, muscular build of a career adventuress, but they had fucked her up—her bare skin was covered in scorch marks from electrodes, cigarette burns, cuts, and deep, bloody bruises. With sweat-slick hands, she unlocked the cage by touching a sphere of black glassy material to a matching lock, which didn't unsnap so much as ooze around the heavy iron loop and reform. I tried not to boggle at it. When she threw the door open, she stopped, lips pursed.

"I thought you were… shit. Never mind," she said, the hardness of her eyes dulled with fatigue.

I scanned her warily. "I'll help you anyway. We have to leave, now."

"Come on." Even with the wild-dog look about her, she jerked her head in a nod and pushed herself back upright. I crawled out as she stumbled and sagged against the wall. All she wore was a pair of jeans. Her bare feet looked like hamburger, swollen and twisted with fractures. It was a miracle that she could still walk.

Rushed but not panicking, I frisked the dead guard, found a keycard and a single frag grenade on his belt. I swept up his gun just as the door at the end of the hall burst open. Lee saved my life for the second time: she yanked me around the corner of the T-intersection where she'd emerged as ten guards opened fire and turned the corridor into a blender. I helped her to run to the next door, turned and opened fire on the first man to make the corner. He ducked back around, winged, but not before he'd thrown the grenade in his hand.

"Come on!" Lee threw open the heavy industrial door and hobbled through. I caught up just as the explosive went off, deafened and numb from the concussive wave that hit the door as Lee slammed it closed. She hooked the weird glass lock on and closed it up, and we plunged our way forward.

Neither of us knew where we were going. I sunk my trust into my intuition, that strange cocktail of experience, sensory input, and raw psychic *knowing* that pressed me toward the surface. Like runners in a three-legged race, we turned another corner and found a filthy cargo elevator that worked with the keycard.

"We're not going to make it." Lee moaned, as the elevator began to lift. "This fucking thing's too slow!"

"You won't be able to do the stairs," I said. "This is what we have. Give me a boost up to the ceiling."

Lee growled with the effort, but she lifted me high enough that I could push open the trapdoor on the elevator and get on top of it. There'd be plenty of room to stand when we reached our floor. I reached down for her with both arms. "Give me the gun and grab on. Now... One, two, three, jump!"

She shot through the hatch just as the elevator slowed. I pulled the door up, handed her the rifle, and took the grenade in hand.

"Fair warning," I said. "We might die."

"Death is better than what these assholes have in store for us." Lee spat.

"Glad we agree." The elevator honked as it reached its floor, and I felt my link to the Art sweep back into me in a tidal rush. We were clear of the Vigiles' anti-magic field in the levels below. Still, this was no time for spellcraft: I pulled the pin on the grenade, waited until the doors opened, then threw it back down into the elevator.

The sound of it bouncing and rolling was drowned out by the hail of gunfire. The Vigiles guards had approximately one second to scramble, and at least one didn't make it in time before the explosion rocked the elevator in its shaft. Screams pealed up from outside, followed by the thundering of boots in the steel box beneath us. I looked up and around, and spotted our salvation barely six feet over our heads: the ventilation tunnel and the extractor that pushed the pressurized air from the elevator shaft into the engine room.

"Okay, one more big jump, and we'll make it," I said. "Stand on that hatch and boost me up."

Lee got on just in time, snarling with pain as the soldiers tried to bust up into the shaft with us. They fired at the roof, denting but not piercing the thick metal, as I clambered up to hang off the pipes beside the ventilation. I broke the vent off with the stock of my rifle, braced it, and shot up at the extractor until pieces blew up and out into the room above. Muscles burning, I dropped the rifle, swung up, and pulled and kicked until the fan dislodged into the floor above, raining metal down where Lee hung on grimly to the door. Then the elevator clunked and groaned, and began to descend.

"Climb up! Climb up!" I barked at her, scrambling up into the ventilation. "Climb up and grab the pipes!"

"GOD-fucking... DAMMIT!" Lee grabbed the counterweight as it shot up, swung crazily, and leaped out to clutch at the red pipes I'd used for leverage. She was weakening, and fast—but I caught her and pulled her high enough that she could hold on beside me.

"Just hold on, okay?" I turned, huffing, and gathered force at the end of my fist. "*Tzain!*"

The dust thrown up the shaft by the grenade was plentiful. I smashed the grate open with a long blade of bonded matter and pulled it out, throwing it down onto the elevator below. Puffing with effort, I swung up and in feet-first, hooking my knees over the edge of the floor above us. All those Soviet-era gym drills Nic had made me do as a teen were finally paying off.

"I'm losing it down here!" Lee called up to me.

"Hang on." I kicked the remains of the ventilator away, braced my heels under the solid edge of the rumbling elevator turbine, and bent back down into the shaft to clasp Lee's reaching hand. Something in my back popped as she climbed up my body and into the room. Panting, she pulled herself up and over, then helped me up before stumbling to hands and knees. But it wasn't over yet.

"This leads to the roof. It has to." I rolled over, made sure I could still bend at the waist, and got woozily to my feet. My half-treated bullet wound burned and throbbed with warning, but my legs held.

"I can't feel my feet." Lee shook her head. She was bathed in sweat, drooling blood from her mouth to the floor.

"We made it this far. Let's get out of here." I hesitated for a moment, then pulled my shirt off. They'd taken my clothes and given me a set of gray scrubs, no shoes. "Here."

Lee looked up woozily. When she saw what I was offering, she reached for it and knelt down for a few seconds. I turned away as she dressed. That she'd been half-naked up until now wasn't the point.

"Okay." I heard her get up behind me. "I can do it. You take the gun."

"No. You should," I said. "I'm a Phitometrist. I'm always armed."

If what the guards had said was true, then Ayashe was on her way to prison and whatever horrors awaited her there. There was no point in trying to look for her here. I felt a pang of regret as I swiped the card, counted, and kicked the door out into the howling wind outside, a word of power curled on my tongue. Visibility was fractional—it was pounding slushy, icy rain, and even the flood lights on the roof barely illuminated anything beyond six feet. The reek of garbage was overwhelming despite the cold. There were helicopters warming up somewhere, the *whop whop whop* of rotors audible over the continuous roar of the storm. The wind was so powerful that it flattened us both as we half crawled, half clung to the slippery metal on top of the building.

I knew nothing about Lee, but in the immediacy of the moment, there was complete trust between us. We kept our hands clasped around each other's wrists as we fumbled our way in the dark. The first helicopter rose over the edge of the building minutes later. We dove behind turbines as the searchlight flooded the roof, giving us a brief view of where we were: near the edge of a very large, bland building surrounded by mountains of trash. The ground was at least fifty feet down, but where there was an elevator machine room, there was a ladder. There hadn't been any stairs inside the machine room.

As I glanced in that direction, the door burst open and soldiers poured out. GOD, but they were fast.

Lee broke off before I did, racing for what I hadn't yet seen: the handrails of the ladder leading down. Head and heart pounding, I followed as quietly as I could, crawling on hands and feet as the helicopter's lights swept away. They were having a hard time staying level in the air. The wind swept the machine toward the other end of the building as surely as it tried to sweep our feet out from under us. Teeth chattering, Lee hung onto the ladder for a moment, then slid down. I followed, watching in nauseated fear as lights blazed up around the building, including one that splashed the wall right beside our descent.

The indignity of it, the hopelessness of it, pulled something up from the deep reserve of furious power that had always been at the core of my Self, the dark water that lay under the facade of the temple. I threw up a hand, power surging through my limbs, breathing life into a form with a sharp word of power. "*KAPH!*"

The light blew. The beam vanished as quickly as it had lit on us... and so did the next one along, then the next. Three were all the spell had in it, but it was enough to douse this end of the building in shadow. I heard Lee curse before she let go of the ladder and dropped the rest of the way to the ground. Five feet, no more than that. She hit the ground and crumpled with a stifled cry barely audible over the sound of sleet striking metal.

I heard gunfire cracking through the darkness. They were pot-shots, but a couple hit close enough that I had to snatch my hand away from the sparks. For a second, I thought I'd taken ricochet, but there was no damage evident when I dropped down. Lee was curiously still, head dropped between her shoulders. She swayed with exhaustion as I pulled at her. I got her arm over my shoulders, and began to run for the nearest cover.

The *Tzain* spell could cut as well as pierce, and I used it to slash open the fifteen-foot wire fence that surrounded the huge plant. Two layers of chain-link, a manned tower with lights sweeping at just the wrong angle... we plunged headlong into the darkness, slushing through the rotten slurry that ran from the towering mountains of garbage that rolled like hills in every direction.

My stomach curdled as we stumbled blindly into the narrowest valley between piles of landfill, staying ahead of the tide of law enforcement now sweeping every part of the yard behind us. We dropped into waist-deep, filthy water, waded through it, and emerged into a wet, filthy, warm mound that sucked at and scraped our legs. Our only guide was the faint orange glow on the horizon, the lights of the city.

Soon, we left the sounds of guns and dogs behind us. The helicopter was heading out this way—one of two now buzzing around the building, their searchlights sweeping in an expanding triangle around the transit camp. Lee was moving woodenly, staggering wildly whenever she lost my support. We broke through the trash mountains onto a path, another chain-link fence, and beyond that... water. Water, barges. New Jersey burned in the distance, the same baleful orange as a forest fire.

"Fresh Kills. We're at Fresh Kills, we have to be." I spoke quickly, struggling for breath. "Staten Island. How the hell are we going to get across the water?"

My reverie was cut short by the sound of the chopper breaking through the storm. Out of time.

"Come on! Final push! We can hide on a barge!" I tried to push off, but was jerked back by Lee's dead weight. She went to her knees where she stood. Confused, I stared at her, trying to figure out what had changed. Only then did I see the enormous bloodstain across the front of her shirt, the blood that even now was being washed away by the sleet pounding everything in sheets of gray ice.

Lee shook her head.

"*Kurva blyat!* Come on! You're strong!" I looked up as the helicopter buzzed by only a few hundred feet away. "You're a survivor! Come on!"

The woman's face set. She picked herself up, frustratingly slow, and stumbled off with me toward the nearest garbage delivery barge.

The barges that went between Fresh Kills and NYC were nothing more than huge, flat-bottomed steel trays guided by tugboats. They ran around the clock, crowding the wetlands around the dump in roughly divided lanes. They were slow, but they had numerous hiding spots—assuming you weren't crushed by an overfilled dumpster. Strangely, all these barges had their lights off, and there were no people milling around... and it wasn't until we'd made it another hundred feet that I saw the rust, the holes, the way that the scows were listing in the water. The tide around these derelict watercraft was utterly dead. We'd stumbled into a graveyard.

At a loss, I pulled Lee up onto the docks and into the closest shelter we had—a battered, gutted riverboat with half its roof caved in. There was dry space in it, and wood—not that it was safe to light a fire. I lay her down on the floor, and knew, as soon as I lifted her shirt to examine the wound she'd taken, that it was too late.

CHAPTER 27

"Bastards got a lucky shot, didn't they?" She croaked.

"Yes." I pulled her shirt down and sat back. The cold was drilling into my bones, and with it, a fatigue so profound that I felt like I was being sucked down into the ground.

Lee's eyes rolled, fixing on my face. "You... really look like him. Easy to mistake."

"Like who?" I frowned.

She regarded me in silence for several long seconds. "You look like Norgay."

My head rang empty with a sense of surreal futility. "Norgay? Norgay, from... Answer?"

"Yeah." Lee's breath rasped through bloody teeth. "You could be his... his cousin or something."

"I'd say that was the weirdest thing to happen to me today, but it's not." I sat back with a shrug. What could I say to that, really? "I know of him, and of Answer. Kristen Cross talked about you. You're the Keeper, the one who knows where the Shard is."

Lee winced as she shifted on her back, trying to find some way to lie comfortably. "Don't... expect me... to talk about it."

"To be frank with you, I don't want to know." I searched for a way to help her, and came up blank. All I could do was help her find a position that didn't hurt as much. "The people who know where to find the Garden tend to end up dead."

"Hah." Her eyelids fluttered. "Tell me something. You believe in God?"

"No. Not the Abrahamic one. I think..." Exhaustedly, I dwelt for a moment in memories of awe, of my moments of immersion. "I think GOD is beyond our everyday perception. That it lives and breathes around us, and like any living thing, it's mostly made up of microbes and water. We're the microbes. And I think GOD is under attack."

"The-The First War was n-not a war. It was a rout." Lee said, reciting slowly and deliberately, like a child reading from a book. "It came when the... with the first star to ever light the Mirror of the sky."

"It came when that star fell, screaming, to the White ground," I finished, the mnemonic cadence reminding me of my own visions in the months since Zarya had entered our world. "Never forget that when the Morphorde appears, the skies scream."

"So you're the real deal, huh?" Her voice was thickening, slurring, like someone who was fighting sleep. "Now... here's a story. My dad... big-shot judge. Joined the Teu... Teutonic Knights. One day, in '83, he takes me by the hands and tells me that he m-met an angel. Face-to-face."

"There are no angels, only demons." Kutkha's words from months ago returned to me. For some reason, they sent a cold, crawling thrill down my spine.

"He... he told me I needed to straighten out, prepare for the Tribulations." Lee continued. Her eyes were closed, her breathing labored. "I blew it off. Always cared more about the real world, like Mom. Dad had... lots of people coming in and out of the house after that. Visitors. Men I didn't know."

"Okay." My eyes were heavy as I sat back. Had to wonder where she was going.

"Didn't care much at the time." Lee's throat clicked, her voice gluggy from the fluid slowly filling her lungs. "I was busy working with the tribes in S-S-South America. Until J-July. D-Dove a new cenote. Deep... deep, beautiful waterhole, never touched. Reached the bottom, got sucked in through a cave system into... into Eden. Found... found crystals, everywhere. Beautiful... so beautiful. All white, silver, pink. Picked one up... got hit with all this... all this *shit.* " She choked out a small, bitter laugh. "Too much knowing. Scared me into a r-religious experience. Went back to Dad, told him. I didn't know he was wr-wrapped up with the V-Vigiles. J-Just thought maybe... maybe he was right. Fucker gave me to them."

"To the Vigiles?"

"Yeah." Lee's eyes closed. "Gave me to these freaks. First round of torture, no luck. I dreamed of a woman in a tree. She spoke to me every night. Teaching me...

reassuring me. Stopped the Vigiles freaks from getting in my head. One day, on transport, this little guy hijacked the truck. Took me somewhere in the f-forest. Leader called himself 'Deacon'."

"The Templum Voctus Sol," I breathed.

"They had... this Tree down there with us. The Tree spoke like the woman in my head. She was so small. So sad. These men, they were evil. Blind, didn't know they were evil." Lee's face rippled with momentary pain, and she grunted, shifting on the floor. "At war... with Vigiles. Spy told them I knew where the Shard was, so they asked me. Round two torturef-fest. Still didn't say a d-damn fucking thing."

A tree. A... MahTree? Kristen's message had said something about a 'MahTree'. At a loss, I took her hand in mine. "You're stronger than me, then. The Deacon kicked my ass."

"Hah." The touch seemed to help. She shuddered and relaxed again. "A guy came to h-help me. Pretty boy. Said name was Zealot. Worked for ANSWER."

"Answer to what?"

"Don't know. It's an acronym." Lee swallowed, trying to clear her mouth. "I knew 'em already. Big Dog, Norgay, they helped me in South America. ANSWER... helps the tribes. Weapons. Advice. Fight against corps, government."

"Was 'Zealot' an Asian man?"

"Yeah. Let me free. Turned back for the T-Tree. D-don't th-think he made it."

Angkor. I looked down, stunned into silence. "I know him. He did make it... we—me and my friends—we rescued him from the Deacon."

"Good. Vigiles picked me up again. I was stupid... hid for a while, slummed it. Went to a biker bar, talked to some bikers who s-said they'd take me to Mexico. Took me to the Vigiles instead." Lee's voice had lost its hard edge, softening as the life gradually drained from her. "Couple d-days ago."

Bikers? I scowled, and was about to ask her if any of them had been named Otto when Lee reached up and grasped my wrist with a callused, strong hand.

"Zealot's alive?" Lee asked.

"Yes," I said. "He is."

Her eyes were still closed. "Tell him from me. Seventeen. Thirty-seven. Zero Two point nine, north. Eighty... eighty-nine. Thirty-seven. Zero nine p-p... p-point two, west."

A chill passed through me. Coordinates.

"You have to t-t-tell th-them." She broke off into a weak, rumbling cough. The blood that bubbled at the corners of her mouth was bright red and frothy. "Tell them. The Garden. CIA wants it. To weaponize it. Tell them... ANSWER."

Then it was true. There was a Shard of Eden here, on Earth. I tried to imagine someone like Agent Keen or the Deacon walking on that pure, silver soil, plunging their hands into it and turning it gray and leaden. In my mind's eye, I saw it blacken at their touch, the fragile creatures that lived there recoiling from them, their bodies crushed by tractors and hard, black leather boots.

A tremble passed through my jaw, and after a moment's consideration, I stood. I went to one of the windows, punched it, and brought back a thin shard of glass.

"Repeat those numbers," I said.

Struggling for breath, Lee stammered out the coordinates a second time. I dutifully carved them into my arms, coding them along the way. I used the Glagolitic script, an ancient Slavic alphabet, substituting each number with its gematric letter association. I ended up with two lines of practically indecipherable code etched into my flesh. Lee's face was ashen by the time I finished. Her eyes wandered over the runes.

"Tell Norgay... They have the Mother. I can hear her. She's somewhere cold." She whispered.

"I will."

"Do you know... my father? What happened to him?"

"Dead," I replied. "Someone killed him."

She heaved with a racking, clogged-fluid sound, head lolling. "Good. F-fuck him. Fucking asshole... got me into this. Trusted him. He gave me to the c-cops. His... fucking... stupid... *cult*."

"Listen, try and save your strength," I said. "Try and relax. The round had to have missed anything serious for you to make this far. I might be able to stop the bleeding."

Her eyelids cracked open, unfathomably dark in the gloom of the boat. Glassy, distant eyes. "Don't lie.

Doesn't... suit a face... like yours. D-Don't worry. Death's... death's okay."

Lee's eyes didn't close again.

Some deaths, I could literally watch the soul slip its skin. It was like a ripple through water, or like the way that a TV's faint discharge stopped prickling the air when it was unplugged. Some people died hard, others died soft. Lee had it soft. I kept the vigil during her final dive, holding her callused hand between my thin-skinned ones. It took a while. The process of dying isn't as fast as the movies make it out to be.

Lee was a stranger to me, but in that one frantic hour, I'd felt the strength of her personality, her will, her... courage. She'd done something I never had. She'd fought for something: the cenotes, the forests, endangered species. For Eden. Things that could not even thank her for the work she did, and she'd done it anyway. And now, all that strength was gone. Her potential, the friendship we might have had, was gone. All because the *Deutsche Orden* wanted to use Eden as a weapon.

Once I was sure she was dead, I proofed Lee's body against necromantic revival, cutting out her heart and tongue with the piece of glass I'd used earlier and throwing everything overboard. The boat was old. I had the mental strength for one more spell—the one that could set the dry interior timbers ablaze. The oil-soaked hulk exploded as I stole out of the ships' graveyard. I swam doggedly across the Kill until I reached land, and began walking toward the lights of Staten Island's suburbia. When I was far enough away to look back, I saw the helicopters circling the boats.

Grief sometimes felt a lot like disgust. Exhausted, wet, and filthy, I spat it out on the road, and limped off to find a ride back to the city.

CHAPTER 28

I ended up stealing a boat, not a car, and had my first go at navigating a watercraft in what had to be the worst weather possible. The storm that had started with the bug rain had not stopped and showed no sign of slowing down. After what felt like hours, I ran aground somewhere up the Rahway River, stumbled my way through a park thick with young beech and elm trees, and found an empty parking lot on the other side.

This was bonafide New Jersey suburbia: clean, pretty family homes, no fences, no fear of crime. I stuck to the trees, following the sound of traffic. Fumbling my way along in the dark and the rain, I avoided the houses and found a gap between the tall concrete fences separating the 'burbs and the Turnpike. My heart lifted at the sight of it—cars slushing along in near blackout conditions, water pounding the asphalt. Somehow, I was going to make it… provided I avoided the toll booths.

I ended up borrowing a car from one of the quiet streets near the highway, but didn't go out onto the toll road. Instead, I followed Route 9 all the way to Jersey City, twenty miles or so, and left the highway before reaching the Holland Tunnel. Even from a distance, I could see the red and blue flashing lights. My escape had triggered a full-scale manhunt.

The best way to avoid getting caught would be to swim the mile across the Hudson, but I just couldn't do it. Exhausted, half-starved, I'd burned out my remaining energy to just stay on the road and not run off into the grass on either side. Instead, I swung into a Target parking lot, curled up on the front seat of the car like a shrimp, and slept a black, heavy, troubled sleep. I startled myself awake every five minutes, spasming at the ghosts of explosions, guns going off, screams. It was still dark when I woke up, which was disorientating, because the parking lot was now full of cars.

When I finally opened my eyes, I took some time to fumble through the glove compartment, under the seats, and around the transmission to see what I could dig up. The glove compartment had a fistful of singles and coins—change for the tollway—and more scattered coins around on the floor. There was a sweater on the rear seat, black leather shoes, and a peacoat in the trunk that was slightly too small across my shoulders, but at least gave me something to wear besides my prison pajama pants. I found another twenty bucks in the coat.

I tied the coat off like a bathrobe, got out, and went to do some shopping. Food—I was delirious with hunger—a pair of discounted blue jeans, a pair of socks, and a razor. The Yen wanted beer, but we didn't have the money for it and I was too tired to bother trying to steal a six-pack of something I hated. I shaved my head and eyebrows in the store bathroom, put the shades on, and headed for the train station with the last of my change jangling around in my pockets.

There were police at the station, but they didn't give me a second glance as I blended in with those taller than me. I was alarmed to discover that it was close to seven p.m. when I ran into my first clock. I had no idea what day it was, how long I'd been sedated in the Vigiles' holding cell, or whether I still had a home to go to. What I did know was that I had a car with all my things in it—wallet, gun, clothes—parked in an underground lot near an urgent care center not far from Hell's Kitchen.

An hour later, I slunk through the rows of vehicles, trying not to look shifty as I approached my sedan and picked over it, searching for bugs or traps. When it turned up clean, I blew a short sigh of relief, broke in, and turned the engine. My things were still here, including Binah's food dish. I didn't have the keys, but that hadn't ever stopped me before.

Every aching joint in my body was screaming the same thing, telling me to go home, get coffee, go to bed, get antibiotics, and heal the throbbing, hot wounds I'd taken: the punctures and scratches and bruises. I looked like a sick bird, panting and pale; I had a fever, shaking with the effort it took to turn my head and reverse the car out. But I was alive—and for now, free. If I wanted to stay that way, there'd be no return to Strange Kitty, no contact with the Twin Tigers, no going back home.

I drove to a Dominican bodega and bought up their stock of Ampitrex, the easiest antibiotic to find on the street. From a pharmacy, I got saline and peroxide, rubbing alcohol, and bandages. There was a clean scalpel in my first aid kit. Hidden down a dark street, I lanced the angry bullet puncture so I could clean out the pus and mud and pack the wound. There was a lot of both, but at least I'd had my shots at the beginning of the year. One of those other, unromantic details of hitman life – I always stayed on top of my vaccinations.

The miserable reality of my situation began to sink in as I worked. I was homeless, again. Without my cat— again. My final remaining possessions were at Strange Kitty, the last things I had, many of them irreplaceable. Photos of the Lovenkos, me and Vassily. My college photos, photos of my horse, the one or two pictures I had of my mother. Expensive, one-of-a-kind books— the Red Book first among them—and my personal grimoires. The Hammer. All of it was gone.

There was little point in pining. Keen wasn't stupid, and he'd made a career out of catching spooks like me. He'd have my things under watch, and as it stood, I'd already put the Tigers at risk. If the Vigiles caught me, I wasn't going to escape a second time. They'd mine Jenner's secrets from me, or Talya's. GOD, Talya wouldn't survive prison. No. It wasn't worth it. Precious as my things were, they were just things. And if I played it right, there was a way I could get them back, AND help the Tigers scatter before the net closed in.

I ended up wandering back into Manhattan, where I found a payphone not too far from the place where I'd busked tarot readings for money in August. I dialed the phone number for the club. No one answered the first couple of times, but the third time, Ron picked up. "Strange Kitty, whozzat?"

"Ron. It's Rex. Is-?"

"You listen to me, you fuck." Ron didn't let me get another word in, dropping his voice. "Jenner says you're out. You stood us up last night, and now the place is fucking crawling with cops because of you. You're an SOS now, okay? Shoot on Sight. You got that?"

"I want my stuff," I snapped. "Arrange a dead-drop."

"It's gone. They took your fuckin' cat, everything. Now scram."

"Ron, listen to me-!"

He hung up, leaving the phone buzzing in my hand.

I slammed it back into the cradle and leaned against the glass, battling down the wave of rage that threatened to drown me and send me out onto the street swinging at the first person to cross my path. Ron was lying. I *knew* he was lying. I wasn't going to get the chance to prove he was lying his fat fucking ass off.

"Piece of dog shit!" I snarled in Ukrainian, punched the side of the telephone booth, and stomped back out to the car. I climbed in, slammed the door, and got back on the road to... wherever the fuck I was going to sleep tonight.

Caught unawares, *again*. Homeless, *again*. Rage vibrated through my fingers, made them clench around the wheel so tightly it creaked. It took a few minutes to let the fury blow over, to simmer down, turn cold, and purify. Objectively, it wasn't as bad as last time. I had my wallet, a gun, some medical supplies, a change of clothes, some burner credit cards under IDs the Vigiles still didn't know about, cash they couldn't trace. Last time, I'd had nothing at all. I needed to calm the fuck down and think.

The cops would be looking for this car, so the first thing I needed to do was change rides. Then I needed to find a way talk to one of the other Tigers—Jenner, Zane, or Talya. But first, I needed to speak with the Deacon.

CHAPTER 29

The ruined church Glory had directed me to swelled out of the ground like a giant's ribcage, surrounded by shattered piles of scorched rubble. The ceiling was intact, but the walls were crumbled down around the thick pillars and iron frames that held it up. As I got out of my car, I noticed the rain was being replaced by snow.

The Deacon looked much how he had when I'd caught him and his merry men about to fuck and murder Angkor on an altar. He wore a clean but ragged robe that was a deeper shade of black-violet than the night outside. His hands were gloved, but thin and elegant. His face was nothing but a long, flat mask. It was the color of old bone, with three asymmetrical black slashes where eyes and mouth should have been: a mockery of a human face. He was waiting for me on the raised dais where the altar had been, standing beneath the frame of the church's rose window. It was now nothing more than a gaping hole in the wall.

"I hoped you'd come. And right on time, too," he said, once I was within easy earshot. His voice was level, well-educated and calm. "Did my herald advise you of my offer of parley?"

"He did." I came to a stop around ten feet away. "So now I'm here, and if I don't hear anything I like within a minute, I'm leaving. Parley away."

"A minute will not convey much. You can relax. Tonight, at least, I would speak to you as one of the Wise to a fellow magus."

With Lee's glassy stare burned into my memory and the location of the Shard carved into my arm, I wasn't much in the mood to parley with a child-murdering rapist, but enemies were sometimes better resources than friends. "Then speak."

The Deacon tilted his head at an angle and stared down at me. "The fall of human flesh over Wall Street and the rain of Philimites a few days ago. I don't know if you've followed the news since it happened, but the CIA—and therefore the Government—have declared that the former occurred due to an upper-atmosphere incident with a Chinese jetliner. I know for a fact this is false. The cause of the rain is known to me."

That gave me some pause. After a quick glance back over my shoulder, I folded my arms and waited.

"They were members of a cult in Eastern Siberia and the Korean peninsula," the Deacon continued. "They called themselves Odaeyang, or the Salvation Sect. Every member of their order was killed in what appeared to be a mass suicide. Their remains were sucked up by their ritual working and teleported to the Financial District of New York City. A well-staged dramatic incident, to be sure, and a pointing finger to those of us who know how to read these signs. Surely the intention of Mrs. Soong-mi."

South Korean? A nasty hint of suspicion curled through me, quickly crushed. "And the main event was...?"

"The transportation of an artifact from the West Coast to New York City," he said. "By *Deutsche Orden* operatives in the Vigiles Magicarum."

The Tree? "What artifact? Do you know?"

"I don't think that information is relevant to this discussion."

"I do," I replied, as inspiration suddenly struck a match and lit a deep, slow burn in the pit of my gut. "And I'm willing to trade information, quid pro quo."

"And what do you think you could possibly offer me?" The Deacon tilted his head to the side.

"The *Organizatsiya*, and Sergei." I kept my voice and expression level, but couldn't suppress a small, savage thrill of pleasure. "He screwed you over."

The Deacon didn't have facial expressions to distract me, so I could often read him better than most people. Without his saying anything, I knew he was interested.

"I'll give you names, locations, operational capacity, weapons, known businesses, their contacts. Accounts, dead-drop locations. A graveyard full of bodies. And if what you say is good enough, there might be more."

He paused for a moment, a pillar of black linen, and then gestured with his hands. "The Vigiles-*Deutsche Orden* brought back a relic of the War of Heaven."

"Which is?"

"You first. I know that AEROMOR is the main base of operations for the Russian *Mafiya*, but when my scout broke into the venue to look around, he found precious little of interest."

"Because their information is digitized and stored downstairs in an archive of floppy disks," I said. "They keep them in a safe near the interrogation rooms. Glory really needs to learn how to use a computer."

"I see." The Deacon digested that for a moment. "The relic is a Spur. It is a tiny fragment of the Spear used to pierce the Heavens in the first great battle between God and the Leviathan: a large, black stone, blacker than space. Coagulated evil. Anti-magic, anti-life, anti-itself."

I sucked in a sharp breath. "I've seen it. The Vigiles have something like that in their headquarters."

"Really?" There was genuine shock in the Deacon's voice. "And you were not driven insane?"

"They use it to suppress magic. It didn't really seem like... anything, really." Now that I thought about it, the stone plinth had almost pushed away attention. "They put it up in their building, built a little rock garden around it."

"If it fit inside of a building, then it is only a chip from the totality of the Spur." The Deacon descended the two steps leading down from the old pulpit, and to my surprise, he sat down on the ground. "Do you remember what I said to you on that night? The last night we fought?"

The night when you shot me and turned John Spotted Elk into a giant cockroach? "Most of it."

"I told you that I thought it was a shame that you would reject what the Father has to offer men like you," he said. "The power to rid the world of the unnatural and perverse; an understanding of the mechanics of fate and time. I was honestly feeling maudlin that night. You might not believe me, but the whole business with the children made me sick. I complained, but was overruled: my superiors tolerated it because they thought they needed Sergei. Now, we have the gift of hindsight."

How noble. I fixed my game face and squatted down where I stood, hands linked between my knees. "I'm more surprised that a man like you would tolerate superiors."

"I am in all ways a servant to powers I do not understand, Alexi. Pride goeth before the fall, and Father help any man who thinks himself equal to the power of Deity," The Deacon replied. "Those children were supposed to be taken for a higher purpose, to be trained into warriors. After the extent of the abuse came to light, Sergei Yaroshenko is now... out of favor. We were not involved in the pornography—that was entirely Sergei's business. So, tell me: how was he conducting this trade under the nose of the Vigiles Magicarum?"

Interesting, but at least half a lie. "They were paying him to do it."

"I had wondered. No… I had *known*, but it is always good to have more evidence. Do you have evidence?"

"MinTex," I said. "A shell company owned by a shell company owned by the Future of America. A PAC."

"A Traditionalist Catholic PAC affiliated with a certain up-and-coming Presidential candidate," the Deacon said. "How... elaborate."

"Made more so by the route of sale," I replied. "And their headquarters is—*was*—a safehouse used by the Vigiles. It got trashed the night the bugs fell."

"The Philimites. Interesting. Were you involved?"

I shrugged. "Expect to see my face on the news tomorrow morning. If I'm not in the top ten most wanted right now, I'll be shocked."

"It seems to be your destiny." The Deacon lay a hand on the ground. "You escaped me twice. You are the first to have ever done so."

"Am I supposed to be flattered?"

"I mean more that... that you survived was an extraordinary twist of fate. I didn't see it coming, and that means someone must have had a hand in your survival. Reweaving the strands of fate is... a very rare power. And it gives me hope."

"Hope doesn't really seem like something in the repertoire of a priest in a cult of the NO-thing."

"It is... " he looked up, and made a thin sound of exasperation. "More complicated than that. Tell me... can you imagine an enormous machine made from dead planets and people, fueled on the pain and suffering of billions of creatures within its walls? An engine that is fed on the blood of pure creatures, innocent creatures, who are tortured into insanity and then thrown onto gears that crush them for their decaying Phi? A great machine with a singular purpose: to carry and breed an army that will in their turn consume more worlds, capture more life, as it drills its way into untouched, unsullied parts of reality."

I felt Kutkha flinch, and then my gut chilled with a nasty, wrenching sensation. Dread... like a long-forgotten memory.

"Every night before I mastered my abilities, I dreamed some part of the end of the world. The visions varied according to threads of probability, but in every single dream, every single night for most of my life, these dreams ended in a vision of the Engine." The Deacon's shoulders hunched sharply. "Up until I found my... patron... I would only see parts of this machine. I was a ghost watching men being bred by giant insects, or women turned into chambers made of rotten flesh, forced to gestate monsters that ate them alive as they were born. It was all in glimpses. Disconnected nightmares of something so massive that the mind's eye could not behold it in its entirety. Then I met the person who brought this all together for me. They confirmed that the Engine is a very real thing, and that people who revel in pure nihilism and who believe they alone are chosen are calling the Engine to Earth. If an Engine passes through our world, all of us—all of us – will be combined into it. Me, you, everyone. Evil and good, child and elder. There is no mercy, no reward. Nothing."

I could hear the emotion in his voice now. He sounded... upset. Frightened.

"I won't escape this fate. Neither will you. Nothing can. And the, the *things* that come out of it..." The Deacon turned his face. If he had features, he'd have been frowning. "Only recently have I understood what's coming, and understood the extremes to which we must go to repel it from our world. You may have noticed, Alexi, that Life cannot stand before the Void. The Void, by its nature, is a mouth which devours living things. Glorious heroism has a place in fantasy, but in reality, the brighter something shines, the purer and more innocent it is, the more vulnerable it is to its antithesis."

A strange alien memory of the White Land writhing under an insectoid horde flashed through my mind, and I shuddered.

"Now, perhaps, you understand why we would take the young shapeshifters and magi. To harden them, to train them. We need an army to mount a defense, and the sacrifice required is great... but only the Morphorde can destroy the Morphorde, a force proportionate to the arrival of the Engine."

"Except that I literally busted you performing an actual HuMan sacrifice to the NO with an actual person," I said. I couldn't keep the disbelief out of my voice.

"Angkor is not a *person* by any measurable means, but I'm not pretending you didn't witness what you saw. Evil men love a cult, Alexi, and cultishness inspires loyalty. Everything you saw in Red Hook was nothing more than showmanship. We have to gather resources through all channels."

"You wanted to make DOGs out of those kids." My lip curled, but he sounded utterly sincere. "You were turning them and those men into fucked up monsters."

"They were already monsters. Rapists, thugs, murderers, racketeers. I would rather that we had our DOGs on leashes, don't you?"

I fought the urge to roll my eyes. "And Mason? What did he do?"

"He raped a communist girl in Vietnam and gutted her with a bayonet while he was high on heroin. He never told Jennifer Tran, and never would have."

"What? And he told you?"

"He couldn't help it. We locked eyes, and I saw his timeline laid bare."

"And Angkor? What did he do?"

The Deacon's silhouette shifted, mantling in a way that reminded me very strongly of an irritated crow.

"*It* is an agent for an organization bent on summoning the Engine to destroy us all," he replied, voice tense with anger. "That... *thing* is a pathological liar, a spy, a saboteur. Even its physical body is a lie, a mockery of all that God wrought from Eden. As far as I know, 'Angkor' was sent here as an agent by the international elements of our shadow government, and his mission intersects with the Engine in a profound way."

My knowledge on that matter was definitely not something I was willing to give up, seeing as he was still holding onto his trump card: the MahTree. I couldn't bring myself to be angry at Angkor anymore, no matter how disingenuous he was. Suspicious, annoyed, but not angry. Not after Lee and Kristen.

"Angkor and the *Deutsche Orden*-Vigiles coalition are all tied up together, though I don't know the details. You freed him before I could purge his influence from our timeline, and sure enough, the signs have started. Let me guess: he attempted to become close to you, didn't he? Friends? More than friends?"

"I don't think that's any of your business," I replied.

"You would be wrong, because a creature like Angkor doesn't have friends: it has tools, which it skillfully manipulates to achieve its ends. And I wonder where you fit into its strategy."

That concerned me more than I was willing to show or admit. "Was that all this was about? You wanted me to know about this Engine, slander Angkor, then make excuses for yourself and your activities? If so, we're done."

"I told you I contacted you to make an offer, actually, which I predict you will reject. Also, a warning – which you may or may not."

"Which is?"

"The Vigiles Magicarum do not answer to the FBI," he said. "Not at the upper levels. They answer to the CIA and the military, and all three organizations are infested by the Teutonic Knights."

"The *Deutsche Orden*," I said.

"Yes. These Crusaders are much older than this country. They are theocratic Illuminati with very definite plans for America and the world, and your shapeshifting biker gang has come to their attention in a negative way. You should prepare accordingly."

"Too little, too late," I said. "They're already onto them."

"Then you should prepare to mourn." The Deacon inclined his head, gesturing with his hands. "The Vigiles do not bother imprisoning shapeshifters. They force them to shift into their animal soul-forms, then render them down into their basic Phi and use them to create homunculi and other weapons."

My skin rippled with goosebumps that had nothing to do with the cold. Not that the Deacon was one to talk: I remembered all too well what he'd done to Mason. "I'd figured that out myself, but like you said, better to have evidence."

"The Wise are not any more fortunate. I have reason to believe they mutilate us." The Deacon huffed a testy little sigh, an odd sound from someone dressed like the boogeyman. "That is the default course of events. Unless a dramatic decision is made, I foresee you ending up in that men's mage prison the Government operates, and that is where my ability to see the future ends. There is something wrong about that place, Alexi. The arrival of the Engine is tied to that prison as much as it is tied to Angkor's presence on this world, but I don't know why."

"So what's the offer?" I knew he had to be lying, but was listening attentively now.

"A double hit in exchange for a great deal of money and a boon." The Deacon motioned with an elegant hand. "Whatever the *Deutsche Orden* is doing must be stopped for this world to survive... and that is where my hope comes in. I want you to find and kill the lynchpin, a man named Charles Bishop. He is the director of the Paranormal Special Activities Division."

"The CIA. You're joking." I arched an eyebrow.

"He spends a great deal of time in Seattle. My offer includes sending you to the West Coast with protection and weapons. Excellent protection. Glory is fully capable of enabling the assassination of a senior Intelligence official."

"Then send him in, if he's so good." I sniffed.

"Glory is exceptional in every way, but he is inhibited from striking directly at Bishop because of his nature," the Deacon said. "But when it comes to support, espionage, and protection, he is absolutely the best I could offer. After the events of the last few months, he has every reason to want to protect you, both for personal reasons and for reasons of duty."

"I noticed. He was filling his pants out like he meant it, so if you're trying to sell me on this, you're failing miserably."

"By putting my best man at your disposal? Well, that isn't intended to be your incentive. Your reward is a separate matter," The Deacon crossed his ankles and leaned back. "I doubt money over a certain quantity is of much interest to you, and so I have a singular offer. I am willing to grant you an act of magic at great expense to myself: The chance to go back in time and undo—or do— a regret. Loss, humiliation, a bad mistake, an error of judgment… anything that could have been avoided with hindsight."

I was glad I was sitting down. A swooping feeling of vertigo passed through me like a current. The feeling of *if only*.

He pressed on. "I believe we all have things we wish we could change, and within limits, you can. It has to be something within the last year or so, and it will be difficult and potentially dangerous... but to avoid the arrival of Hell on Earth, I will make the sacrifice and sign a contract in blood, if required."

A tremor ran through my jaw. "And who's the second mark?"

"Angkor. Every single precognitive vision I have had features him prominently. He must be removed from this timeline."

Of course. I clambered up to my feet, lips pressed together in a tight line. The Deacon also stood, and his robes fell around him in a way that resembled skin more than cloth. "Alexi, I beg you to think about this carefully. Now that Odaeyang is gone and the Spur discovered, the final events leading to the summoning of the Engine have begun. We have less than twenty-three hours to decide. Any time after that, and it will be too late to swing fate. The Spur fragment is already attracting calamity to this city."

"I make my own fate." I jerked my head up in acknowledgment. "We're done here."

"If you won't kill the abomination, then at least consider Bishop," he said. "It won't earn you my magic, but we will pay for him. Handsomely."

If nothing else, that part of the deal was worth thinking about – assuming that the rest of what I'd just been told wasn't complete and total bullshit. "I'll think about it. And if I need to contact you?"

"You will always know where to go at the right time."
And with that, The Deacon turned away and strode into
the nearest cluster of shadows. I felt a ripple of energy,
unpleasantly cold, and then he was gone.

CHAPTER 30

The fragments of information I'd picked up over the last three days—GOD, had it only been three days? —flitted around one another as I mechanically searched the dark streets for a good mark. It was already time to change cars. I used to think it odd that the ex-cons in the *Organizatsiya* boosted cars so easily and so frequently, but now that I knew the law was searching for me, I was starting to understand why they did it.

I ended up jacking a couple of sets of license plates from abandoned, non-functioning cars, and took a plain Volvo station wagon parked outside a run-down warehouse in Hunt's Point, something old enough to not be missed and with enough room to lie down in the back. With tools, I could move my gear, swap the plates, and boost the car without an alarm within ten minutes, skills honed by over a decade of practice. I could have started the engine with magic, but high-speed hotwiring was a skill worth keeping sharp.

Dissociated and thirsty, I drove a loop and checked back, searching for tails. None—yet. I relaxed fractionally, enough to start trying to put everything I knew together.

The numbers written on my arm felt like an afterthought compared to everything else, the reality of what I—we—were facing. Kristen Cross, Lee Harrison, her father, the Shard of Eden—Kristen had mentioned that, too—this MahTree. Bishop, Odaeyang, The Deacon, Soldier, Sergei, Harrison, the Nightbrothers... and Angkor. They were all connected somehow, but the links just wouldn't fall into place. There was too much fuzz, too many missing pieces. Some of them were in Talya's hands, some of them in Otto Roth's, and the rest was all on Angkor, wherever and whoever he really was.

If I triangulated what I knew, then Angkor was working for a third party—ANSWER—in opposition to the Vigiles and the TVS, who were busy pulling at each other's collars as they fought over the Shard, the MahTree Lee described, and probably this Spur, as well. I could assume Angkor had killed Harrison's father as a last-ditch attempt to find her.

I was willing to bet real money that the bikers who'd taken Lee in were on the Vigiles' payroll. Bikers stomped people for looking at them funny, but they didn't hand people over to the police. My leap of faith was that the Nightbrothers had done it, but there were a lot of bikers in New York, and there was even more police corruption.

We needed the information on that hard drive Zane and I had pulled out of the funeral home. I needed to find Talya, and therein lay a problem. I didn't know where Talya lived, her phone number, or her haunts besides the clubhouse. There was one roundabout way I could possibly communicate with her, but I couldn't do anything about it until the morning.

Stress beat on me in waves as I pulled into a patch of shadow by the side of the road and cut the engine. It was time to make the final switch, exchanging the plates of the stolen car for the ones from the abandoned car and taking the fresh set for my own ride, completing the shell game and ensuring my anonymity.

A shell game. As I worked, that phrase repeated itself over and over in my head. For a time, I paid the echolalia no mind, screwing the new plates on as quickly as I could comfortably work and fighting not to freeze at every little sound. After a while though, I began to think. *Shell games. That's what this is, isn't it? There's a prize under one cup that's being shuffled around and around the empty cups on the table. But who's the one hiding their hand?*

There was no magic bullet, no epiphany as I got into my newly disguised car. When I tried reaching back to Kutkha, it was like trying to grab at a shadow through a field of snow. At a loss, I touched the wires to start the engine, and considered where to spend my night. I wanted my bed, familiar smelling blankets, my cat sleeping behind my knees, and a chance to rest. What I *needed* was a place where no one would find me, where I could hide from the unholy trinity of the TVS, the police, and the *Organizatsiya*. Somewhere like... *A gay bar?*

I tensed in my seat as a thrill passed through my nerves. My mouth went dry, my pulse lifted, and suddenly I remembered that I was thirsty: very thirsty, and hot. I slowed for a red light, looking around at where I was. Still in Manhattan, headed south. I fumbled across the seat for my water bottle and took a swig, trying to clear the nasty antibiotics-and-pus taste in my mouth.

No one would think to look for you in a gay bar. Alcohol, cigarettes, sex... who'd think to search there for someone like you?

The water did nothing to ease the parched feeling in my mouth and throat. This was the Yen talking—it had to be. I tried for Kutkha again and slipped, unable to focus on anything as the light changed, drawing me toward Lower Manhattan, Greenwich, and East Village. I knew them by reputation. East Village was where the *Organizatsiya* went gay-bashing—or went to find dick, because who knew? My understanding of how my people worked had been crushed up and thrown away, like a dirty tissue. Maybe my fellow Slavs were all self-loathing, hypocritical pieces of shit.

When I squashed down the flash cravings for alcohol, different cravings surfaced. The taste of ash. The salt on Christopher's throat. Now *that* was a bad idea. If I went to a gay bar, I didn't have to do anything but get a drink, placate the Yen, and cool my heels until I figured out what how to play this. Try and contact the Tigers, flee the city… I was too tired to think about it. My head pounded. Without any idea where I was actually going to go, I headed for Greenwich Village. Tonight was a Tuesday, and it was cold and wet... there wasn't going to be anything too crazy happening.

Traffic leading into the village was backed up, not that unusual in Manhattan. It wasn't until I found myself in total gridlock that I realized what I'd gotten myself into: a riot. Gangs of people surged and ebbed around each other on either side of the road, neither side willing to give up turf. On the left, there were furious, sign-and-baseball-bat waving protesters. The signs they carried left no illusion as to why they were here. 'HOMOSEXUALS ARE POSSESSED BY DEMONS!' screamed one. 'AIDS, Hell, Salvation!' screeched another.

On the other side of the road—and on the road, in places—a motley group of teenagers, men in leather, men without shirts, women in overalls, women in tutus and Bohemian flowing clothes and sequined frocks, punks, and a mixture of other people were trying to get the protesters to back off by throwing bottles and cans at them.

"You made the plagues come! You made them come!" A woman's furious voice broke through the racket as I rumbled past down the road. She sounded like Ayashe when she was angry, the same jagged candy-cane red spike of noise. She kept shouting as the crowds drowned her out. The police were slowly making their way up toward the nexus of the fight, but with the people spilling out onto the street like this, no one was going anywhere fast.

When I found a place to pull over, I got out and walked back down toward the angry, chanting mobs, moving to join the crowd of counter-protesters. They admitted me without so much as a sideways glance. I fell in beside a pair of men holding hands, giving their fingers up and over to the zealots challenging their existence. The religious were blaming them for... what? AIDS? The Philimites? Dead, hacked-up bodies falling out of the sky?

Movement ground to a stop somewhere on West 10th Street. The pavement was full up, and I was half-blind from the noise, unsure of where to go. Wincing, I tried to piece together the signs through the television-snow effect of my synesthesia, and pulled around with a cocked fist on reflex when a loud squeal erupted by my other ear. I turned in time to see a tall, bearded nun go stumbling past me, knocked off her spike heels by a tubby, balding man in a 'JESUS SAVES' bowling shirt. She—he?—caught themselves on their hands before their face hit the pavement. The old guy was sweating, looking for a way to run. I jerked my shoulders and stalked forward at him, reaching under my jacket, and he backpedaled.

"You some kind of fucking coward!?" I dialed up my accent, but didn't pull anything out except my hand, fisted around an imaginary weapon. He didn't wait to see if I was holding anything or not: scrambling, thick lips quivering, he fled to the safety of his pack.

"*Khuy tebe v zhopu!*[2]" I shouted after him. "That's what I thought, *suka*!"

"Oh my goodness, thank you so much." The nun had recovered, frantically smoothing her—his?—dress down. They wore screaming scarlet robes, a habit, sequined gloves, and makeup straight out of a Coney Island funhouse... but they were clearly a nun. "I usually see that sort of thing coming. Ugh, what a mess."

"No worries." I stared, trying to make sense of exactly what I was seeing. "Do you... do you know where's a good place around here to get something to eat? Maybe a room? I've never really been here before-"

"Oh! First time in the Village? Well, didn't you just pick a *wonderful* night to visit!" The nun leaned toward me in a wash of perfume, reached down into her collar, and pulled out a pink and white brochure with the aplomb of a magician pulling a card out of their sleeve. "Try the Ninth Circle or Uncle Charlie's, honey. And take this."

I did, too startled to argue. "Thank you, Miss... Mister..?"

"Sister, and I'm spreading the good news about the Rubber Habit!" She reached out, and before I could stop her, cupped my hand with both of her gloved ones. "Now, you make sure you have a read of that before you go trading, alright? And thanks for standing up for me."

"Uhh..." I took it, glancing down at the cover image: a conga line of nuns, some with mustaches, habits drawn up above their waists, feather dusters jammed up in... yes. "No problem."

Sister Ruby leaned in, mock-kissed me on the cheek, and sashayed back into the fray like some kind of strange Valkyrie. I watched her leave, blinking, and then down at the pamphlet, *Play Fair*.

Numb but curious, I found a wall, leaned back, and opened it up. A pair of condoms in silver packets tumbled out from inside. My face flushed hot, and I furtively picked them up and shoved them in a pocket out of sight before I began to read. About three pages in, I realized that the Sister hadn't been a nun at all—she'd been an angel. Every uncomfortable, humiliating question I might have had for Zane had an answer here.

It was like a studio light fading in. Gay people had... literature? Policies and procedures? Community information? Community? Nuns? Bearded nuns with glittery red eyelashes, sure, but they seemed to perform the same role as educators. Suddenly, it was me who felt strange, because I was less normal than what was written about in *Play Fair*, and less prepared for the maelstrom of Lower Manhattan than a man in six-inch heels and a wimple. But at least I had some rules to follow, some guidelines to stick to. The very last paragraph was about guilt, and seeing it written somehow made me feel better about being here.

Head pounding, I glanced at one sign down the road. At first I thought the place was called 'Ooo ooo ooo-9', until I saw the part above that read 'Ninth Circle Steakhouse' and the name clicked. A steakhouse. That had to be a gentler entry into this world than a bar. There'd be tables, food, a place to sit down and think about what I was going to do.

My illusions were quickly dispelled on entry. The Ninth Circle did not smell like steak. It smelled like beer and vomit and male sweat. It was painfully loud and painfully crowded. The bouncer didn't even notice my arrival, probably because he and everyone else were watching a naked man with a jockstrap on his head mixing a drink with his cock on top of the bar.

Right. Not a steakhouse. I turned around and barreled straight into the broad chest of a very drunk man who had tottered in the door behind me. He put his hand on my shoulder to steady himself, and by the time I recovered from the accidental shove, the riptide of people going in and out of the narrow, dark room had almost dragged me to the bar. As soon as the smell of alcohol hit me—really hit me—I felt my whole body yearn toward it.

I battled my way to edge of the counter, some distance away from the cock-tini party, and stood up on the rail so

I could be seen. A dark, curly-haired man came bustling up, but instead of asking me for my order, he grinned. "Meow meow, fresh meat. You cross the street to join us tonight, church boy?"

"No," I said. "Can I-"

"You wanna Virgin Mary?"

The only way I could hear him was because his words were a different shape to the deafening background noise. Eyes closed, I held up a ten. "No. I want something very sweet, very sour, very strong. Lemon. You got anything like that?"

"Sugar, I will blow your fucking mind." The bartender plucked the note from my fingers.

He'd barely moved away when someone bumped into my right hip. I cracked watering eyes, squinting at a man who could have walked straight out of a Hitler Youth poster. Blond side-part, blue-eyed, clean-cut, in a beige greatcoat, polished high boots, and an armband with a pink triangle on it instead of a swastika. He flashed a grin and said something I didn't catch. I grimaced, shook my head, and tried to ignore him while I waited for my drink.

The bartender brought back something icy cold and bright yellow, and the vivid blue smell and taste of lemon cut through the musk of the bar and gave me something to focus on that wasn't the pain in my ears. I ignored Nazi Boy and pushed off, shouldering through the forest of taller men toward the back of the room.

Across the room from the blaring jukebox was a staircase leading down and to the left. It opened into a smoky lounge that was quieter and less crowded than the upstairs. The crowd was diverse, and when I found a place to stand, I could readily identify the different cliques. There were pretty boys, preppy boys, blue collar toughs who looked almost exactly like the dock workers and auto mechanics I'd grown up around, and barflies with sweaty untucked button-down shirts and gold chains. All of them seemed profoundly uninterested in me. I found myself feeling both grateful and increasingly self-conscious as I searched out a dark corner to hide and furtively drink my lemon mystery drink.

The bartender had done what I'd asked him to do: strong, sweet, and sour. I was shaking with a revolting amount of need as I sucked it down and the muscles along my spine unknotted. Some clarity returned, briefly, before the alcohol hit and I flushed with heat from my socks to my collar. The drink didn't last long, and I knew, with a sinking feeling in my chest, that this time, one wasn't going to be enough to make the Yen recede. It wanted more, and it knew I was injured, stressed out, pent up, and now, homeless. It was going to get what it wanted.

The guy behind the bar down here was a heavyset, bearded man with no shirt and a permanent pout. He looked at me quizzically when I slunk over.

"Stolichnaya," I said, reluctantly, thumping the glass onto the bar. It was the strongest, nastiest thing I could think of, the one most likely to make the Yen screw off for the night. "Two over ice."

"You're new," he replied, moving to the shelves. "What's your name?"

"Konstantin." On the occasions that I'd gotten magic work outside of the *Organizatsiya*, that was the alias I'd always used. "And not much of a conversationalist."

"Ooh, is that Russian? You sound kinda Russian."

"Ukrainian." While he poured, I glimpsed my reflection in the mirror. The gray hair made me look old, which was probably why I wasn't going to get much attention. Even as I thought it, though, I saw Nazi Boy cruise down the stairs and circle around behind me like a shark nosing its way toward blood in the water. He had a riding crop tucked up under his arm. I kept half an eye on him as the bartender brought me my drink.

"Well, I'm Paul. You may not be chatty, but let me tell you—I could listen to that accent of yours all night. You get beaten up out there? You look pretty rough."

"No." As Nazi Boy came to close in, I sighed, and braced to be hit on.

"Isn't it illegal to let old guys in here, Paul?" he said, wrinkling his nose as he pulled in beside me. "I thought there was a rule about that."

"Hah! There should be a rule about letting your loose ass in here, Troy. Age is in the miles, right Kon?"

Insults it was, then. I ignored them both, and threw back the first shot of vodka. It was sour and tasteless, made drinkable only by the ice, and I shuddered my way through the swallow.

Troy wasn't the type to give up. "Why do you have your shades on in the dark? Are you blind, old man?"

"I can see you wear your dick size on your armband." I swirled the ice around in my glass.

Shirtless Pete barked a derisive laugh. "Quit trying to hustle the new guy, Troy. Jeez."

Troy giggled, and melted into a sensuous, hip-jutting pose against the edge of the bar, bringing the riding crop around onto the counter with a smack of leather on wood. "Hey, *I'm* young enough that I can still get it up. Can *you*?"

I was beginning to reconsider my burgeoning sense of self-identity. If boys were this annoying, then I was less interested in men than I thought. "Not for you. Go away."

"It's okay. We're all twenty-three here, right? Right, Paul?" Troy looked to Paul for approval, but he was studiously washing an already-clean glass and leaving us to one another. There were people behind us watching from the pool table.

I shook my head, resolving to finish my drink and leave, when I felt a hand slither down my back and over my ass. I reached back and grabbed the boy's pinkie. His eyes widened in the second it took me to yank him around by it, use that one finger to torque his entire arm as I turned, and put him to his knees in front of me. He blinked, stunned, but not as stunned as he was when I took the riding crop that he'd left on the bar and cracked it across his face.

The sound cut through the music and plunged the room into sudden stillness. Troy looked up at me with naked shock, blue eyes startlingly bright against the red welt spreading over his pale cheeks. He hissed and fought to free his hand, so I cranked the finger lock harder, making him bend forward at the waist with a stifled sound of pain. "Look at me."

"Agh! Let go!"

"Look at me, you little shitwipe." I didn't raise my voice above what I needed to, jerking him against the joint. He finally peered up at me, eyes watering, and I jammed the crop up under his jaw, leaning down. "Don't touch me. *No one* touches me unless I say so. Do you understand me?"

He snarled. I let go of his finger and shoved with the crop at the same time, throwing him off balance. He sprawled on his ass, the long SS-style coat tripping him up, and awkwardly clambered to his feet.

Like most men, Troy was taller than me, a fact that seemed to occur to him as he put a gloved hand to the welt on his cheek and looked down at me.

"You hit me in the face!" His eyes narrowed. "Bitch, I have to *work*."

"You should have thought of that before you went for my wallet, Princess." We were drawing a small crowd—all the blue-collar guys in their coveralls and jeans and a couple of older barflies. I snatched my vodka and threw it back. Diluted and very cold, it was slightly more tolerable.

The boy clearly didn't know a thing about fighting, because he came at me while I still had the glass in my hand. I dodged his swing and clocked him with it, then followed up with the crop as the circle of men around us cheered lustily. I beat him with it all the way to the edge of the pool table. He got in one good kick: the polished spur on his boot caught me in the side of the knee and almost put me down, but I hopped through it, huddling close and fast, and smashed him across the jaw.

"Yeah! Get him, shorty!" someone called out.

"Get him! Put him on his knees again!"

It wasn't a fair fight. It ended when his wobbly fist clipped my cheek and I weaved in under his guard, slamming my knuckles up under his sternum. It drove the air from his chest and bent him double. He gasped as he slid into a loose-limbed kneel and clung to the front of my slacks. I reached down and thrust my fingers into his thick hair, pulling his head back so he could see my face and cocked fist.

"Do it! Smash him!"

"Hahaha, oh man, look at that guy..."

The boy's eyes were dilated and hazy. His face was flushed, bottom lip swollen. He licked his mouth, choking back a short, hysterical laugh. It took me a moment to realize why. He was hard, cock straining against the front of his riding breeches. He was much, much larger than Christopher. I felt his girth pushing against my ankle as he ground forward.

"You *like* it." The blow he'd taken to the mouth—I didn't remember hitting him there—slurred his words. "You like it, *don't* you?"

My fist shook, and my jaw wound taut.

"Hit me." His eyes were half-lidded, like he was drunk or high on more than just pain. "Please... Sir?"

Sir. The word was like a shot of adrenaline straight to my cock. The foreskin was trapped over the glans, as usual, burning and tearing every time the exposed tip jostled against the inside of my clothes.

"Yeah! Do it!"

"Fuck his mouth!"

"Do it!"

My blood surged, and before I knew what I was doing, I reached down and jerked my belt forward and up, undoing it one-handed. The men around us bayed encouragement, and I felt Nazi Boy melt against the front of my thighs. His mouth was wet, banged up and swollen, lips an inviting crimson cupid's bow. I pressed a gloved thumb over his bottom teeth, sliding it into his mouth, and felt him moan and sag into the grip I had on his hair.

The Yen was leering at me from behind my eyes, feeding off the hot, Red energy of the men behind and around us, a shield wall of grins and hard, eager bodies. I'd never realized that lust had a smell. It was exactly the same as the way a man smelled in the moment before you pulled a trigger between his eyes.

"Please!" I couldn't hear him, but Troy's lips framed the word clearly enough for me to read. He was aroused to the point of combustion, hanging on the moment I freed my cock and pushed it between his lips. "Come on, you sadistic fuck!"

I hesitated at his words, the way the Yen echoed them. This wasn't what I wanted. I didn't know what I wanted – not really – but whatever my first time was going to be, I didn't want it to be this.

"You're right. I'm a sadist." I shoved his head away from me and spun around, pushing through the pack of drooling catcallers to the exit door.

The howls of disappointment followed me all the way outside. I slammed the door behind me, wincing on every step. It was still raining, and there were no people out here. It was lit by the second-floor windows overhead on both sides, and a red light strip that turned the shadows cast by the trash cans and dumpsters into black voids.

I staggered into the nearest doorway and collapsed against a dry wall while I fumbled to relieve the pain downstairs. I was in agony, all because I'd let some goddamned hustler rile me up. And why? He'd hit too close to home on the issues with my dick, even though getting erections didn't seem to be the problem. I knew, now, without a doubt, that something was wrong with me. Most of my life, I'd just blown it off, or assumed that other men experienced the same discomfort to a lesser degree. But neither Troy or Christopher showed any sign of pain when they were rubbing up against my legs. Something wasn't right.

Swallowing, I closed my eyes, wrapped my hand around my cock, and slid the foreskin back into place. The pain relented as suddenly as it'd begun. I shuddered, relaxing against the wall.

The windows above me were open, venting a noxious oily pink smell into the night air. Someone was talking loudly on the phone. I tuned into the conversation, searching for a distraction. A nasal New Jersey accent carried out on the heavy, damp air.

"Yeah, look, okay. No, I believe you, but I just have to make sure. Like, if I'm going to tell this guy where to go... yeah, they're not the kind of people you fuck around with, Carmine. You're sure that's where they'll be? And you're sure they've got that houseplant?"

Carmine? Houseplant? Still panting, I froze back against the wall and pulled my hand out of my pants, scrambling to redo my belt.

"Alright, and you're sure? Okay. Good. Dad knows how to get in touch with the Deacon. What? No, of course not, no one's here... I'm at that fucking fag bar across the bridge to drop off Silvo's snow and pick up our cut for the month. Cool it, and get in position for when that Soldier fuck comes calling, okay? Can you, uh, work some hocus-pocus to figure out who's going with the Russkies to do the handover?"

I glanced across the alley. The window was across from the dark doorway. I swallowed, then tried to relax the muscles down along my spine and weaved out into the red light like a drunkard, using the wall to guide my way. I sagged into the doorway and looked up.

The man upstairs was bullish and slovenly. He had a heavy, sensual face, hair down to his collar, and wore a pale pink business shirt with the top two buttons undone over a gold necklace and a thatch of chest hair. He was scowling, pacing beside the window with a cigarette between his stubby fingers. He had a cellphone the size of a brick jammed between ear and shoulder, and a scar that twisted up from the corner of his mouth to his ear when he turned to the left. A weird, twisted smile curled my lips.

Perhaps there was a GOD after all.

It was Celso fucking Manelli.

CHAPTER 31

At first I couldn't believe my luck—but then it dawned on me that I was exhausted, already on the run, and I'd left my gun in the car. The cops were hunting me, and I needed to keep a low profile... but it didn't sound like Celso was going to be at the Ninth Circle for long.

Heart racing, I kept moving down the alley to see what I found at the end. As it turned out, that was a parking lot. A parking lot with a red stretch Humvee parked across three spaces and a bored driver sitting inside. He was reading a magazine and smoking out the window, hands visibly trembling.

According to Doctor Levental's information, Celso never went anywhere without bodyguards. I was willing to bet they were inside with him, and the driver was holding the fort alone, a gun resting on the seat beside him. I wasn't sure I had enough energy for magic, but I needed to find the strength for it. Hanging back in the shadows, I drew a deep breath, held it, exhaled, and closed my eyes as I lay a hand on the wall beside me.

The distant music pulsed rhythmically around me, making the Phi in the air throb and whorl in slow, stately dances. The building itself was charged with the sexual release, frustration, passion, love, and despair of its many residents, turbulent and heady, and after my experience with Troy, I was looped into it. I drew on that energy, pulling it through my right hand and into my body.

I found one security camera, which I disarmed with the same word of power I'd used for Yegor's office—*Kaph*, the regal letter of the open palm. When I felt the tension discharge and the camera fail, I focused on the driver. He was scratching his arm and neck, picking sores in his flesh with his nails. He had the junkie itch.

The man glanced up as I weaved toward the car, disheveled and visibly intoxicated, and reached across to the passenger side seat. I held up my hands to show I was unarmed, and called out. "Hey man, you look bored. You looking to score?"

"Maybe." His eyes narrowed. "What're you selling?"

"Good clean girl." I'd never been high in my life, but had known enough tweakers that I could fake it in a pinch. "Only got a couple hits left. Three Jacksons for both."

The man's throat worked. He wasn't desperate yet, but he wasn't going to turn down the chance to grab a couple of baggies and run. "Sure. Bring it over here, I'll have a look."

He kept his hand low as he turned to face the door, and I knew he wasn't holding his wallet. I made a show of pushing my jacket back and fishing around in my mostly-empty hip pocket on the way over. I pretended to palm something small, keeping my hands where he could see them, and turned slightly as I approached the door. I turned so that I was almost side on and hunched in. "Here, make it quick. *Tzain*."

He lifted the snub-nosed pistol he'd been concealing beneath the window, mouth twisting in a sneer as he armed the threat behind it. The spike of condensed matter around my fist took him in his open mouth and punched out through the back of his head in a narrow wedge-shaped spray. His eyes rolled, and he toppled to the seat like a ragdoll.

'*Tzain*' was quickly becoming my favorite piece of Phitometry. I looked back to make sure no one had seen what had happened. Some people were lingering far back in the alley in the darkness, but they were oblivious to what had taken place. I shoved the dead driver over onto the passenger's side, gingerly picked the gun off the floor, and frantically wound the window before anyone caught us.

All the windows were one-way, mirrored on the outside. A black screen of plate glass divided the front and rear passenger seats, no magic. The car itself had magic worked into it—alarms and defenses to stop locks from being picked or broken. The decor was all cherry-themed. Cherry-scented mirror hanger, cherry carpet, and now cherry-colored goop all over the place. I found the keys on the seat underneath him, and sure enough, it had a custom cherry-shaped metal keychain with a scrawl of steel text.

"The Cherry Popper," I muttered. "*Bozhe moy*. You have *got* to be kidding me."

The driver was glassy-eyed, bleeding out from the back of the head. I felt like I was being watched while I used his blood to draw on the screen and windows: precise letters and symbols I'd memorized to build Jenner's sound insulation wards.

About fifteen minutes later, Celso came out from the back of the club with a pair of bodyguards, one in front and one behind him. I pulled a glove off and rolled the window down enough to get my hand out to give them a thumbs-up, then wound it back up and started the car with blood-stained keys.

I heard them load in, and jumped when an intercom in the dash crackled. "Take us home, Paulie."

Instead of driving off, I locked the doors and pressed the button that rolled down the screen between driver and passengers. Then I braced Paulie's hand-cannon against the top of the seat. The first guy was sitting with the back of his head to me. He didn't even have time to turn around before I put the barrel to his skull and blew his brains out across the men in front of him. The sound triggered momentary panic. Celso and his other bodyguard scrambled for weapons and door handles, then simply stopped.

Covered in gore, they stared open mouthed at me, the now-glowing sigils, and their friend as he slowly slumped forward in his seat.

"Before you do anything stupid, I'd like you to know that I have had a very bad week, and I am not in the mood for anything other than prompt, courteous compliance." I spoke slowly, calmly, coldly. "Hands where I can see them."

Celso wasn't some inexperienced street tough, and neither was the blockhead sitting beside him. They were shocked, but I could see them sizing me up as they slowly raised their hands.

"Good." I braced the pistol on the back of the seat to keep a steady aim. "Now. It's storytime. What the fuck is going on with this 'Tree'?"

"Tree...?" Celso repeated numbly.

I gestured with my free hand. "Trunk? Branches? Some leaves, maybe? You too stupid to know what a tree is?"

Out of the corner of my eye, I saw the other wiseguy start to go for his jacket. I shot him in the chest—the right side of his chest. The sigils absorbed the sound of the shot, as well as Celso's shout of terror when he flinched and scrambled across the seat.

"You crazy fuck!" His voice had risen a full octave.

"Tell me who is doing what with the GOD-damned MahTree." I kept the gun trained on the bodyguard as he slumped, clutching at the bloody hole in his jacket.

Celso purpled. "Do I look like one of those fucking guys that makes fucking poodles out of shrubbery, asshole? You can't fucking shoot me anyway! Go ahead, try it! See what happens when my spook's-"

With a small amount of effort, I burned some energy and made the sigils on the cabin roof flare with bright violet light. He glanced at them, the words dying on his lips.

"Your spook isn't as good as me. Wrong answer." I shot his bodyguard a second time—this time, in the leg. The guy screamed.

The color drained from Celso's face. I turned the gun on him, and he shrunk back against the seat.

I stared at him. "It's a Tree from Eden, isn't it?"

"Kill me," he rasped. "I ain't tellin' you nuthin'. You can kill me, but *they'll* eat my fucking soul. I'll go to the Father like a man."

The gravity in his words chilled me. I noticed the necklace that was framed by his open collar. It wasn't the usual Catholic crucifix, now that I could see it up close. It was a pendant with the eye and cross, the symbol of the Templum Voctus Sol.

"Then I suppose we'll be doing this the hard way," I replied, and aimed at his knee.

He lunged forward at me, trying to grab the pistol from my hands. I pulled back, dragging him forward. I yanked his head over the screen and smashed him over the skull a couple of times. He snarled, flailing for me, until he accidentally grabbed the remains of Paulie's face and flinched, horrified. The brief distraction was all I needed to strike the big nerve in his neck. Celso went down like a sack of hammers.

I shoved him back into the cabin, opened the door and let myself out, closing it behind me and getting into the back cabin. The wounded bodyguard was struggling to get his gun again, but a sharp tap to his chest was enough to discourage him. I used my knife to cut off Celso's shirt, hit him a couple more times when he came out swinging from his brief KO, and trussed him up with torn, wet strips of fabric. I searched him for weapons, took everything I found, and turned to the bodyguard.

"You." I pointed at him. "You tell this man's father that the Yaroshenko *Organizatsiya* did this. You tell him that Nic Chiernenko and Sergei Yaroshenko have declared war on your family, their allies, businesses, and associates. You hear me?"

He made a thin, raspy sound, helpless fury burning in his eyes.

"You tell him that the Russian *Mafiya* is going to kill anyone who gets in their way," I said. "So he'd better try get us first, next time."

With that, I opened the passenger's side door and kicked him out to roll around on the wet asphalt, then went back around and started the engine.

First, I headed for the docks. The waterfront was quiet on a Tuesday night, with old warehouse hulks and ruined buildings. Celso's car was basically a tank. I drove it straight through a chain-link gate into one of the brownstone shells, cut the engine, and had a proper look at the back. There was cleaning gear in the trunk, along with handcuffs, zip ties, baby wipes, a first aid kit, and rubber dishwashing gloves. They were the mark of a professional. One never knows when one has to cap someone in one's fancy limo, after all.

I cleaned up as best I could, rolled the bodies in the dirty towels, and left them underneath some rubble. By the time all that was done, Celso was awake and furious, ranting at me from behind his gag and squirming around on the floor of the passenger cabin. I kneecapped him for good measure, and stuck him in the trunk.

My plan to get in touch with Talya had been to go to Zane's gym in the morning and talk to him about everything that was happening. I doubted Ron had shared our brief contact with the others. Zane probably knew what Talya had found on the computer drive. If he didn't, he could get me a meeting with her so she could tell me herself. We could put everything we knew together into a comprehensive picture. Celso complicated that slightly— but on the other hand, presenting a captured TVS agent was a good way to convince Zane of my sincerity.

The gym where Zane trained was an unassuming, grungy little joint in Bushwick, a garage converted into a training circuit for cage fighters and boxers. Zane was both of those things, and he trained every day for anywhere between thirty minutes to an hour at six in the morning. I brought the hulking Cherry Popper to a slow stop out front at half-past five, backing it up into place, and cut the engine. My stuff was in here, retrieved from the stolen Volvo and stashed on the now-clean front seat. Celso's car provided me with a weird sort of camouflage for now, a car so distinctive that no one was likely to assume I was in it until word had gotten around, and even then. I cracked open the driver's side window to vent the lingering raw meat and piss smell in the cabin, and waited.

Sure enough, the familiar deep blue and red rumble of a large motorcycle appeared at about ten to six, purring its way up the cracked road toward us. The Harley cruised to a stop a couple of bays down. Zane was already staring at the car as he pulled his helmet off, astonished. "Rex...

Where have you been? And why the hell are you driving a pimpmobile?"

"I thought I'd try my hand at something new." I tried to stay casual in the hope he wouldn't notice just how nervous and angry I really was. "It's called 'The Cherry Popper'. I'm not even joking."

Zane squinted at me. "How is the, uh, 'Cherry Popper' related to you being AWOL for two days? Jenner's been going nuts wondering where you are. Did something happen?"

"What?" I braced an elbow on the edge of the window to lean out. "Jenner... what has she been saying?"

"Just worried about you going missing. First Angkor, now you." Zane frowned. "Why? What's going on?"

Well, well, well. Ron *had* lied to me. "Get in, and we'll talk. I need you to direct me to Talya's house so we can pick her up and go somewhere private. I've got company in here."

"Company?"

"Celso Manelli. I picked him up in Greenwich Village. This is his car."

Zane blanched, green eyes widening. "You... picked him up in Greenwich? Celso *Manelli*? The *mobster*? Why?"

"He's a high-ranking TVS member, that's why," I said. "So we'd better get this sad excuse for a car somewhere discreet."

"There's nothing about this car that's 'discreet'," Zane said. "Okay... look. Me and Tally are staying at a safehouse right now, alright? There's an auto shop underneath. How about we ride there together, park the car inside, and put Celso in the basement so you can talk to him?"

I nodded. "Perfectly acceptable. By the way, is there a stove there? Like a camp stove or something?"

"At the shop? There's a lab. I'm sure they have a stove."

"Wonderful." I pulled back in the window and started the car. The Hummer coughed back to life, drowning out the faint sounds of Celso's thumping in the trunk. "Oh, and by the way, I have to pick up some sugar."

Zane eyed the Cherry Popper with deep suspicion. "You mean you want to go cruise around Hunts Point a while before we take it in?"

"No. I mean, literal sugar." I paused, thinking. "And butter. I need about a pound of each."

"Sugar and... Rex, I swear to GOD. You always manage to make my life that bit more surreal. You know that?"

"Well, the idea is-"

"I don't want to know. Come on. Let's go home." Zane pinched the bridge of his nose, then turned and stomped back to his motorcycle.

CHAPTER 32

The Humvee handled like a refrigerator on wheels and barely got thirty miles to the gallon, but we thankfully managed to avoid any accidents on our way to Jamaica. The safehouse wasn't particularly safe, and it wasn't really a house, either. It was a dilapidated apartment over a mechanic shop. The Twin Tigers MC had an affiliated motorcycle repair shop that was a legit business, owned and operated by Cliff. This place was not that repair shop. 'A&J Motors' was for cars and meth. It handled all their stolen cars, taking them in as functional vehicles and reducing them to collections of parts. They had an adjacent scrapyard guarded by two bullet-faced pit bulls. They ran up to the fence and barked alarm as Zane got the garage door open and guided the lumbering car inside.

It seemed appropriate that the Cherry Popper barely fit in the building, but we squeezed it in. The bumper was flush with the closed garage door, and the trunk pushed up against the workbench at the back of the stained concrete room. The door into the building was on the right, so I got out on the passenger's side.

"Okay, so, I guess I kind of want to know about the sugar," Zane said, shuffling past. "Because I was thinking about it, and… well, you know. Curiosity got the cat and everything."

Speaking of cats. I concentrated for a moment, eyes closed, and sagged with relief as Binah's presence kindled in response. She was upstairs.

"Curiosity *killed* the cat," I replied. "Thank you for getting Binah. Where's Talya?"

"You know Binah's here?" He turned to look back.

"She's my familiar: of course I know she's here. I'll take Celso downstairs – can you bring me a pot and some water? I need to get it boiling. I only need about a cup."

"Sure." Zane shook his head, contorted himself around the end of the car, and disappeared upstairs.

This particular act of revenge was far, far more satisfying than the hit on Yegor. Celso Manelli had been the one who'd gunned down Mariya in her shower. He and Snappy Joe Grassia had gone to her house to kidnap Vassily. On whose behest, I still didn't know. I was going to find out.

I popped the trunk, having to force it up past the edge of the workbench. "Good morning, Celso. Bright and fresh as a daisy, I hope?"

"Yrmm fckin psychmm!" Celso was a mess. He'd pissed himself overnight, exacerbating the misery of being tightly bound with swollen, shattered knees. His hair was ropey with dirt and sweat. "M' frrkin kll mmrrh!"

"*Oy*, such language. You have a big, big, BIG day today, so you had best put on that thinking cap and get ready for breakfast." I hauled him out like sweaty, stinky luggage and dragged him to the door by the ties on his ankles.

Zane dutifully returned with what I needed – sugar, butter, a medium-sized pot and a cup of water—then stood by the stove I'd found with an expression of long-suffering disbelief on his face. He helped me get Celso up and tie him to a sturdy chair, one limb at a time. Once he was secure, I pulled out my knife and cut his clothes off. All of them, including the trashy zebra print thong he was wearing. I held it out to Zane between pinched thumb and forefinger.

"You really need someone to do your underwear shopping for you, man." Zane held the smelly wet rag out as far from his face as he could on the way to the trash can.

Celso was wild-eyed now, cursing from around his gag. I cut it off, and the screeching began. "You little fuck! What do you think you're doing? Do you know who I am!? You gonna fuck with me, you little twink?"

I looked him over. "Well, we *were* at a gay club."

"What the—you lookin' at my cock or something? Is this what gets you off, huh?" Celso's rage melted to sneering mockery. "You gonna play with it, huh, faggot?"

"I didn't bring my tweezers," I said.

Zane actually barked a laugh from across the room, already on his way out the door. He didn't laugh very often.

"Fuck you! You don't scare me, pussy little dwarf piece of shit!" Celso spat at me. "My whole fucking family's gonna be after you! My dad'll fuck you up! Do you hear me!?"

"Your father is irrelevant to me," I replied, setting the pot on the stove. I poured in the water, then the sugar, then turned the heat up.

The big Italian jeered. "Whatcha gonna do, tough guy? Make me some candy?"

I smiled thinly. "We're going to start with your knowledge of the Templum Voctus Sol and the Teutonic Knights, the *Deutsche Orden*."

"Go fuck yourself."

"Frank Nacari was murdered in August," I said, stirring the sugar around. I put the spoon down, and began unwrapping the butter. "As I understand it, he was murdered by Jana Volotsya, at the time the representative of the TVS in New York. I understand that the Yaroshenko *Organizatsiya* worked for the TVS before changing affiliation to the *Deutsche Orden*, but what about you?"

"Wait," he said. "I know you. I fuckin' *know* you. You... you're the Russian Mafia spook, aren't you?"

"Yes."

He leered. "I gunfucked your whore of a sister, asshole. She was your sister, right? The old bitch in the apartment over the cafe?"

I stayed outwardly composed, but for that, I'd hurt him regardless of how he cooperated now. "Mariya died suddenly. One entry wound. Nothing much to tell."

"Oh, naw, bro. She was screamin', and cryin'." Celso brayed with manic, nervous laughter. "Too ugly to fuck, scarecrow bitch-"

I marked those 'facts' down for later. They'd be useful—*after* I'd gotten what we needed. "I knew you were there. Thank you for confirming what Snappy Joe Grassia told me."

"Hell yeah I was there, and I'd have fucked her if she didn't look like a dog's ass." He laughed again, cutting short when the part about Snappy Joe finally hit him. "Wait. Joe? *YOU* killed Joe?"

"That's right." I poked the butter around, then added the next quarter pound. "The woman you killed, Mariya, raised me and my sworn brother. My mother died when I was young, and Mariya took over the job for Vassily and I. He was the man you kidnapped, by the way. The sick one. He also died."

"And you think I give a fuck why?" Celso was breathing heavily, worn out.

"Because one of the things Mariya was passionate about was cooking," I replied, tapping the spoon on the edge of the pot. "She ran a café, and she insisted that 'her boys' knew how to take care of themselves. Do you know the boiling point of human flesh, Celso?"

"I know your dead mom was a whore!" Celso spat in my direction, but he was dehydrated and running out of spittle. Most of it ended up in his own chest hair.

"Human skin burns at one hundred-sixteen degrees Fahrenheit. The tissue is damaged, then redness, swelling, and pain results. At one hundred-twenty, the nerves give way with terrible pain, and then they die. At one hundred-fifty degrees, you suffer third-degree burns within one second of contact. Skin falls off, bones and nerves are damaged beyond repair, and if you do manage to survive – assuming, of course that less than 10% of your body has been burned – you scar so badly that you barely look human anymore."

"Fuck you!"

"Sugar begins to boil at two hundred-ten degrees," I continued breezily. A pleasant caramel smell had begun to fill the room. "But the boiling point is only the first stage of making candy. You see, sugar doesn't lose heat very well. The longer you boil it, the more water evaporates from it and the hotter it gets. So the first stage, which is the stage you use to make syrup, is two hundred-thirty degrees: almost twice the temperature required to burn human flesh."

"Wait," Celso said. "Hold up just a second."

I wagged the hot wooden spoon in the air. "There's five stages of the candy making process, Celso, and it's important that you know them all. Soft ball, at two hundred-sixty degrees; hard ball at two hundred-eighty-five, soft crack at three hundred, hard crack at three hundred-fifty, and then caramelization at four hundred-ten degrees." I looked up at him. "Four hundred and ten degrees, *suka*. Imagine how that's going to feel when I pour it over your dick."

The sugar and butter was at a rolling boil by now. Celso had gone a nasty shade of red.

"We just started to boil. From here, it takes about fifteen minutes to reach four hundred degrees. That's how long you have to tell me what I want to know. So let's start with John Manelli's relationship with the TVS. When did it start?"

"How about you go fuck yourself with that spoon?"

I got a ladle, and used it to skim a little of the bubbling oil and sugar mixture. When I turned with it, he flinched, but then steeled himself, snorting like a bull. I walked over, and flicked the ladle at his chest.

Sugar burns hurt. A lot. Celso yowled, and began to struggle and thrash against the steel frame and the handcuffs that bound him to it. While he wore himself out to a panting, shuddering, bleeding mess, I strolled back and continued stirring. "What year did John's relationship with the TVS start, Celso?"

"Fuck you!" It was higher pitched this time, shrill with pain and uncertain fear.

"You can stop this, Celso," I said. "You don't have to go through this. But we've reached soft ball stage, and it's time to test the sugar again. Wouldn't want to burn it."

"No! No, you fuckin' – STOP!" Celso rose and thumped back against the chair to no avail as I bought the next ladle across. This time I got in close and poured the thick, superhot liquid over his skin, across his pecs and down over the top of his soft belly. He howled in agony.

"You can stop this," I repeated, going back to the pot. "Do you smell that nice butter toffee scent? It's already almost time to test again."

"Okay!" Celso half wheezed, half sobbed, his breathing ragged. "Okay, look —"

"The timeline of TVS involvement with your family, boy." I turned with the ladle in hand to find Celso staring at me, eyes wide with mingled terror and fascination.

"They'll know." He had a look of disbelief, like he couldn't believe he was breaking down under the pressure. The sugar solution was still stuck to him, slowly pulling the skin off the deep, peeling burns on the shoulder and chest. "They'll tear my soul to shreds. I'll go to Hell."

"And I'm thirty seconds away from pouring that pan of molten sugar over your body, starting with your pathetic, tiny, unprotected sea slug of a cock. Then over your hands. Your face, into your mouth. Then I'm going to intubate you. Are you a big boy, Celso? Do you know what tracheal intubation is?"

He shook his head, face milk-pale under his stubble.

"Tracheal intubation is where I punch a hole in the front of your throat and put a piece of hollow tubing inside so that you can keep wheezing away while your mouth is full of bleeding, swollen burns." I stopped in front of him, staring him in the eyes. "And then, with you blind, emasculated, unable to open your fused, rotting mouth, I'm going to care for you. I'll cleanly amputate the things that fall off, make sure you stay alive. And when the scars are all healed up, I'm going to send you drooling and limping and crying back to Daddy. Do you think your family will love you when you look like that, Celso? Remember what they did to Vincent after his accident?"

Celso was crying now, his eyes puffy and red. His gaze was rooted to the ladle. "Oh GOD no, please."

I flicked the ladle at him. The big man shrieked, lashing his head back and forth. He only belatedly realized there was no pain. The ladle was empty.

"It's not them!" He cried, voice roar. "It's just me, okay?!"

I cocked my head. "Explain."

Celso licked his lip. He was perfectly abject now, trembling, bathed in sweat. "So there was this... this thing that happened. Back in '82. My dad says he was visited by an angel, like, an honest-to-God angel. Her... his... *their* name is Mu-Munificence."

Munificence. Munificence was a synonym for 'generosity', but the name sent a cold, crawling thrill down my spine.

"I swear on my mother's grave she's real," Celso said. "But she's not an angel, not really. She protects my Family. I always knew something about her was screwy, though, like, because she's tied up in drugs and with the cops. She's got black hair. And she's blind. Angels aren't blind."

I frowned. "So what's your point?"

"She told my dad that he was a strong man, that his prayers had been heard. She told him that the time of Tribulations is at hand." Celso was talking eagerly now. "That the Rapture was coming in less than ten years' time. And she said that GOD loves kings, real men, the faithful. If it wasn't for her, we wouldn't be where we are today."

The Tribulations? Same thing this 'angel' had told Lee Harrison's father.

Celso kept on babbling. "She told my dad to take over the dope trade so that we can cut it off, kill all the scum bringing it into the city. People like you, all the fuckin' commies and gooks and fags, all the ones screwing up the world. We got rid of one guy. Uhh... what's his name... Brukov? Rodney Brukov, I think. She found a guy in the Russian Mob that was willing to turn him over."

Rodion Brukov had been my old boss in better times. He had been a fair but ruthless man, a true *Vor v Zakone*. He'd died a miserable, lingering death. "Who betrayed Brukov?"

"Jesus, I can't even say these friggin' Russian names. Greg? Grig? Solensky or something. He was a real bum."

"Grigori Sokolsky." I wish I would have been surprised, but I wasn't.

"Yeah! That's the guy." Celso licked his lips. "But like I said, I knew something was screwy the whole time. Angels don't get wrapped up in fuckin' dope. Dad was getting weird over time, too, like... erratic. Angry. He didn't want anything to do with us or the guys on the street. Spent all his time praying, going to these secret meetings with spooks from the Government. I think maybe he had something to do with the hit on the President."

I waited, letting him talk.

"Frank and Rob found that Fruit thing out in the bay a couple months back. It was bad news from the start." Celso was nervous now – nervous and angry, but not at me. In some deep, dark recess of his mind, he'd wanted to rant about this for months. "Dad said it was a holy relic and Munificence told him we had to bring it to her, but the thing killed a couple of guys. Then Frank and Rob went missing. Frank turned up dead. I dunno what happened to Rob."

I did. "So what's your role in this?"

"I called bullshit," Celso said. "Decided I'd have to take over the Family. It was, like, becoming a cult, you know? One day, Carmine like, calls me, tells me he needs me to meet someone. He takes me to this place in the woods, spooky as hell. And I met an angel. A real one."

"How do you know she was what she said she was?"

"My little finger was missing," Celso continued. "Providence cried on it, and it grew back right then and there. That's how I know she's the real deal. Her priestess, like, she lost both her legs. Providence gave her her legs back. She told me Munificence is a demon that's deceived my father, and I had to take the Family back. She... she showed me things. Horrible things. Wonderful things. She taught me how it really is, showed me all the codes in the Bible, all the secrets hidden in it." His face suffused with childish wonder.

"What does Providence look like?"

"How do you think an angel fuckin' looks? She's beautiful. Tall. White hair to the floor, perfect pale skin. Beautiful... just beautiful. I can't even describe it. She has these *eyes*. They suck you in, and you can hear *Him*. The Father."

From one cult to the other, then. A picture was beginning to assemble, and it was grim. "And the Deacon? When did he appear?"

"He came from Chicago when Jana was killed by some crazy spook," Celso replied. "He's real good. Loaded and connected, a good leader... he had to go stealth though, you know, for his safety."

"And the Tree?" I regarded him levelly, taking the bubbling pot from the stove.

"It's a Tree from the Garden of Eden," Celso breathed. "It's only small, though. This crazy gook cult got hold of it in China or somethin'. The Deacon found out, took it from them and brought it here. Then the Feds somehow learned about it, and *they* took it, so we took it back. Then the Russians we'd brought on turned traitor for some fuckin' reason, so they stole it and they're going to hand it over to the Vigiles tonight. Those fucks... when I learned my dad was working for the fucking Feds and the Deep State, all those wacky child-fucker Satanic assholes, I just lost my shit. I mean, like, you know who runs the Vigiles, don't you?"

"No idea," I replied drolly.

Celso's eyes burned like coals. "The CIA runs them. They're not human, man. They're these *reptiles*. Aliens, here to destroy the world."

And with that, we were just about done. He'd veered off the necessary course, which meant he was running out of useful info. Save for one last, specific thing.

"Where is the Tree being intercepted?" I asked, moving back to the stove.

Celso looked like he was about to refuse, until I picked up the ladle. "A warehouse. East Hangar Road. Great big warehouse right at the end of East Hangar Road. You gotta get to it from the service lane on I-678. They only let trucks in though, so..."

"Carmine's taking some of his cowboys there?"

"I-I dunno. He's gonna put a call through to someone who handles that shit better. This is the GOVERNMENT we're talking about, man." He squinted at me. "Who the fuck *are* you, anyway? Whose side are you on?"

"Eden's." I pulled my knife and threw it. The blade flew end-over-end and plugged Celso in the chest with unmistakable finality.

CHAPTER 33

Binah was banging on the back of the safehouse door and yowling like a banshee by the time I got to the top of the stairs, then launched herself at me like a furry cannonball when I let myself in. I caught her as she leapt up, spluttering as she rammed her head, flank and tail against my mouth. "That's my—pfft—girl."

"Eee! You're *alive*!" Talya pushed away from her desk in the den, and before I really had a chance to brace myself, bounded over to shower me in affection much the same way as my cat.

"Uhh… yes?" Awkwardly, I interposed the roll of caramel between us. I'd let it cool on a sheet of baking paper while cleaning up downstairs. "Here. I thought you'd be the one who'd most likely eat this."

"Oooh. That smells great!" Talya didn't seem to notice how stiff my back was as she took the candy from my hands. "It's warm. Did *you* make this?"

I couldn't help but smile at her, and as Binah wrapped herself around the back of my head. "I did. It's leftover from my business downstairs."

The girl regarded me with wide, innocent eyes. "What happened to the rest of it?"

I'd used the rest of it to seal Celso's nose and mouth, and to cauterize his stab wound so that he didn't bleed. Still, I didn't want to put her off her food. "Secret wizard business."

"Well, trick or treat, I guess." Talya laughed, and peeled back some of the wrapper to gnaw at the toffee as she went inside.

Zane was working out here instead of going to the gym. Shirtless, he was shadow-boxing near the window. The converted office was cozily run down, complete with some fresh Halloween decorations for the season. Both Talya and Zane had big camping backpacks sitting on the floor. Something in my chest unknotted when I saw my bags and suitcases piled carefully against the wall behind them.

"Where's everyone else?" I looked between the pair of them.

"We're all bunkered down in different locations," Talya was quicker on the draw than Zane. "Jenner's had to make a difficult decision for us."

I reached up to scratch Binah's chin. "Please tell me she's throwing the fight and you're all relocating?"

"Uhh." Talya winced.

"No," Zane said heavily. "We stay and fight. The match with Otto is tonight, and we're going to send the Nightbrothers packing. After that, we're going to ride down to talk with Starfish and Cassie's crew, wait until the heat's off, and come back."

I sighed. "So she's letting her pride get the best of her."

Zane shook his head stubbornly. "This is our city. Our city, our problem, our responsibility. It's taken Jenner two decades to get some respect from the other M.C.s in this country, and if we run from Otto, we won't ever get that back."

"I won't argue. But I'm worried there's something we're not seeing." Resigned, I searched for a chair and fell into it, too stiff to properly bend my knees. Finding Celso had given me a shot of fresh energy, which was now well and truly spent. I hurt. The infection was still there, brooding in my flesh and only just barely put down by the antibiotics I'd started. They were working, given the reduction in fever and the sour metallic taste in my mouth, but I'd be on them for days.

"You look like shit," Talya said. "You want some coffee?"

"Yes." It was going to taste awful, and I didn't care. "And whatever you have to eat. I've had a hell of a week, and Jenner needs to know about it. But I can't go to the fight tonight."

Talya paused in the doorway to the kitchen, looking back. Zane stopped mid-exercise, fists up, knee lifted to his chest.

"Why?" Talya asked.

"The short version? I have to go and head off some bad, bad business." I sighed, sitting back. Everything achęd. Just watching Zane working out hurt. Binah hopped onto my lap, and her paws seemed to find a deep bruise wherever they went. "The long version is that I was captured by the Vigiles, again, and they're gunning for me with everything they've got. I'm nuclear right now, and I need to get out of town."

"Yeah. We saw someone that looked a bit like you on the T.V. They're forecasting a Cat 4 hurricane, too." Zane let off a flurry of short, sharp jabs, turning sideward into the last strike. "Whatever you tell us will get to Jenner. She's holed up with Ron and some of the other guys."

GOD, where to start? I lay a hand on Binah's back. The sensation of relaxation that she offered me was intense enough that my eyes stung for a moment. Not tears... just relief. "Well... firstly, what we found at the funeral home is just the beginning of something much, much larger."

"You're telling me," Talya called back from the kitchen. "I cracked that hard drive you guys got."

"And?" I looked to the door. It was so dark that all the lights in the house were on at eight a.m. in the morning. I watched Talya's shadow track back and forth through the swaying bead curtains.

"You first. I'll have to show you."

Right. "The FBI agent who was murdered was spying for someone. A group called ANSWER." I turned back to Zane. "Any of you heard of them?"

"ANSWER. Yeah, I have," Zane said. "Well, the name. Michael said that if we ever met an operative from ANSWER, we were supposed to treat them as if they were *sen-sun.* Kind of like, uhh, 'brothers-in-arms'. Allies by default."

"That seems to tie into what I've learned about them." My gut rumbled as the smell of coffee began to fill the house. "Angkor is a member. He goes by the name 'Zealot'. His breakaway and disappearance has something to do with ANSWER's business here, which depending on who you ask is either about saving the world or destroying by summoning something I've heard described as the 'Engine of the Morphorde'."

Zane eased down from his fighting posture, a silhouette against the window. "I don't know what that is, but I don't like the sound of it. You sure he's not a V.D agent?"

"The Vigiles Crusader spook from the CIA that forced me to work for them didn't recognize him on video," I replied. "They kidnapped me again, made me watch a security tape taken from the last murder scene Ayashe took me to. And they gunned down Ayashe in cold blood right in front of me and dragged her off full of holes."

"What?!" Zane paled.

"I overheard some guards saying she'd been taken to the Vigiles prison. Well… one of them. They have two, I think: The Icebox, and the Sandbox," I continued. "So I don't think she's dead. Just as well, because I learned what they do to Weeders while I was in custody. You remember how you threw up when we broke into the funeral home?"

"Yeah," Zane said cautiously.

"They have a way to render Weeders into their elemental Phi," I said. "Using something called a 'digester truck'. That truck we saw in the garage was one."

"Render." He repeated the word numbly, dropping to crouch on his toes. "Render, like what? Like soap? You mean to tell me they're pulling people's fucking souls apart?"

"And using the resulting matter to create homunculi," I finished. "Yes."

Talya returned with two cups, one for me and one for herself, and a small plate stacked with a shapeshifter-sized serving of reheated pizza. I normally didn't eat pizza, but I needed the calories. She took a seat while I dug in, her face tight with anxiety.

"You know, the Elders always tell us stories about the Crusaders and witch-hunters," she said after a couple of pieces had disappeared. "They're like the boogeyman, you know? Some part of me, like… can't believe someone could really do a thing like that."

"People can be the worst Morphorde, Kitten." Zane shook his head grimly.

"I know that," Talya replied, brow creasing. "Don't talk down to me like I'm dumb. I'm *Unangan*. My grandma spent like ten years in a concentration camp. What I meant is that I don't believe a person could look someone's *kabah* in the face and think 'hey, I wonder how I can turn this into magic playdoh'. That's a Morphorde thing."

Zane looked a little chastened. "Right. Sorry."

"I got out of the Vigiles' transit house," I said, starting on slice number four. My stomach felt like a bottomless pit. "Escaped with another woman they'd captured. Lee Harrison."

"She's been on the news, too." Zane sat down, stretching his legs out in front of him. "They're saying you murdered her."

"The Vigiles did." The pizza turned to ash in my mouth. "She was… a courageous person. I wouldn't be alive if not for her. She escaped, and came back for me. Admittedly, it was only because she mistook me for someone involved in ANSWER, a man named Norgay."

Talya cocked her head. "Norgay as in Tenzing Norgay? The Sherpa?"

"I suppose." I shrugged, forming my next words carefully. "I didn't learn much from her except that some bikers apparently turned her into the cops when they recognized who she was. She was tight-lipped, as much so as Angkor. Following that and my escape, I met with the Deacon."

"You weren't lying about having a hell of a week. And bikers?" There was something in Zane's voice that was off, and I frowned. "She probably ran into one of the cop M.Cs. There's a couple of crews who are cops or ex-cops that do rides and take over bars."

"You *met* the Deacon?" Even Talya was squinty-eyed about that.

I held their gazes, steady as the dawn. "The Deacon thought he could recruit me, because as it turns out, the Templum Voctus Sol is literally at war with the *Deutsche*

Orden. He claims he's foreseen the end of the world because of the arrival of this Engine and that Angkor and ANSWER are acting to usher it in and throw us all to the NO."

"I assume you refused," Zane said. A statement, not a question.

If I was honest, it was less cut and dry than I would have preferred. I didn't trust the Deacon as far as I could kick him, but I had no solid reason to doubt the core of truth that braced his weird opinions about Angkor. The Deacon was irrefutably right about one thing: shit was getting weird and bad, and fast. The events of the last four months were building to *something*. I had no doubt that 'something' was nothing good.

"Of course," I replied. "I've been fighting the TVS for months. I never told you what drove me from the *Organizatsiya*, did I?"

"No."

"A Gift Horse showed up in New York," I said. "Her name was Zarya. She arrived in a great big shell, a Fruit or, as Angkor called it, a Rind. She was being held captive by the Manellis, and against my better judgement, I got involved. Jana Volotsya was the first TVS member I met: a sorceress, and possibly the TVS leader in NYC prior to the Deacon. She knew that Zarya's Rind was here and circulating in the underworld, but not where, so she instigated a gang war by murdering one of the Manelli Family shotcallers to see if he or someone else would slip the location."

I hadn't expected either of them to really know what a Gift Horse was, but both Talya and Zane blanched a little. They looked at each other.

"We know," Talya said, looking back to me. "About the Gift Horse, that is."

Zane nodded.

"What? How?" I glanced between them sharply.

"We felt it," Zane said. "And about a month after that, the arrival of something else. These are… I guess you could call them 'sacred', in the sense that they're important and supernatural."

"Our *Ka-Bah* talk to us across the barrier of our consciousness," Talya said, her voice crisping to an academic cant. "They can reach over when we're asleep. We don't really 'dream': we talk to our Ka instead. On the night the Gift Horse arrived, everyone I know had the same conversation with their animal."

"*The Mare is here,*" Zane said. "*The Fruit of the Pure Lands has arrived.*"

"Then a Tree of Life," Talya said nervously. "Zane, is it even okay for us-?"

"I know about the MahTree already." I couldn't keep a note of irritation from my voice. The hoarding of knowledge was a terrible problem with Weeders. They were almost like a strange sort of occult hive-mind. "Lee told me."

"Then she wasn't close-lipped enough," Zane replied. "No one should know about this other than us. It means the creatures of the Pure Lands are under threat."

"I don't think they are," I said. "I think… based on what I know of GOD and my own knowledge of how bodies work… I think that the Gift Horse's arrival is something akin to an immune response. Because this has all been going on a lot longer than just her being here. Celso was saying that plans have been in motion since the mid-80s, at least. What else do you know?"

They looked at each other again.

"Stop it," I said. "For GOD's sake. Literally. I'm a big boy now, and I can handle forbidden knowledge."

Talya bit her lip and looked down. Zane regarded me levelly with green eyes too light for a face as dark as his. Cat's eyes.

"The Deacon's right," Zane said. "The world's gonna end soon. We've known it for ages."

That threw me for a second. "Wait... what?"

"We all do." He shrugged. "The Weeders, that is."

"And you... didn't think to…" I gestured with a piece of pizza. "*Say* anything?"

"Even if people believed us, it'd just cause problems." Zane grimaced, and rubbed the back of his head. "We know because of Talya."

Talya stiffened, her hands fisting on her lap.

"I have to start from the beginning to give you the right context." Zane turned his hands up, and when he began speaking, it was in the rhythmic cadence of a storyteller who had memorized lines told to him by another. "The Pure Lands were the skin and virgin flesh of the YESbeast. They took the form of endless forests made of glass that embodied all colors, a giant prism that constantly reflected itself. Our Ka roamed these forests in ecstasy, feeding and transforming, living among the branches of the great Trees who breathed fresh life into our kills. We hunted in innocence of death. It was a great *everything*, and no being went without. Then the Morphorde came."

"There were two great wars for the YESbeast. The first was an invasion, in which a full quarter of the Beast's flesh was spoiled. The second was when the forests, now aware of mortality, fought back." Zane let his eyes hood. "Eden lost the Second War. The Pure Lands were destroyed and shattered, introducing Separation, Time and Form into GOD. All the Weeders who will ever live came from that final act of destruction, tiny shards of Edenic memory and primordial form floating free inside of the YESbeast."

Talya nodded. "They bond to HuMans during birth in place of a normal soul, appearing at random on every world in every Cell of the YESbeast's body. When the world is healthy, the only Ka that incarnate are small animals, prey creatures like the Pathrunners. As a world sickens, more of our souls are drawn to the world, like an immune response. The Ka get bigger and meaner. You start getting tiger shapeshifters, lions, rhinos."

"People like Jenner and Ayashe," I said. "And you, Zane."

Zane nodded, arms folded across his broad chest. "Yeah. When a world is dying, about to be drawn into the hot zone of the Third War, then the big guns arrive. More and more shapeshifters appear, and they're the badasses, the ancient Ka who fought the armies of the Morphorde. We're talking like... dinosaurs. American lions, like Talya. Megafauna. Giant snakes, giant eagles. When Talya arrived in New York and sought out the Pathfinders, we knew that shit was about to go down. There's others that have been appearing, too, all around the world. Cassie's one of them. So is Starfish."

"So you knew, too?" I asked Talya.

Talya nodded. Her eyes were dark and troubled. She was picking her lip, something she ever only did when she was nervous.

I drew a deep breath, and sighed it out. My plate was empty: eight pieces of lukewarm pizza had barely even made a dent in my appetite, but the grease at least made the coffee more palatable. "Well, that settles that then, I suppose. The jury's out on whether or not Angkor is to be involved in summoning this cataclysm, but my gut tells me the Deacon is full of shit on that front."

Zane scowled. "Well, you know what they say about good intentions."

"True." Tiredly, I motioned to Talya. "So, in light of all that, will you show us what you found? You might have the final pieces of the puzzle."

"Oh! Sure!" Talya brightened a little, and pushed her office chair back to her hastily-set up workstation. The desk and table she had set up groaned under a collection of beige steel and plastic equipment, which included two monitors and several pounds of cables. "This whole thing is huge. I was going to report to Jenner tonight."

Zane didn't even bother getting up. He just crawled across to kneel beside her, watching over her shoulder. "You were careful to cover your tracks with all this, right?"

"Hey, don't try and teach your grandmother to suck eggs. Of course I was careful." Talya fondly patted one of the whirring beige boxes that cluttered up her desk. "Mister Tunnels here means I don't even use my own internet connection."

"Mister Tunnels?" I stared at the box in confusion.

"Yeah! He gives me a new phone number every time I dial into my university. Among other things!" Talya was typing in lines of commands on a blank black screen. She hit a key, and a great big 'NeXtGen' logo written in lines of dots and dashes spooled out, then disappeared before a virtual interface unfolded. It was bland and officey: blue background, gray boxes, buttons with symbols on them.

I blinked, glancing at Zane. He shrugged, so I slumped back and stroked Binah's flank. She stretched out under my hand with a yawn before she curled back up, her front paws hugging her face. "How did you get into this kind of work, anyway?"

"My dad worked on the missile programs in Alaska. He was right there for it all, like, in the 50s and 60s," Talya said. "Mom lived on the islands, so I spent some of the year with her, and some of the year with dad on base. I always had a head for numbers and code, so I ended up getting a scholarship to Berkeley and it all sort of went from there. I was just really lucky to be in the right place at the right time, to be honest."

I watched her navigate deftly through the desktop to a series of logged files, curious and mystified at the same time.

"Okayyy… Where do I start?" Talya bit her lip, eyes scanning the screen as she selected a group of files and opened them. "Well, the first thing is that I've confirmed that The Future of America is a PAC basically owned by Spartan Corp, or more accurately, that 'Max Sterling' is the PAC's Chief Operations Officer. But the whole thing is so *weird*. Like, the Donor List. Look at these names."

I leaned forward and narrowed my eyes to read the spreadsheet she'd brought up. "Matim Harad'bak. Letiaat Suul'ah'fa. Prida Ul'khish."

Zane scowled. "They look like fake Middle Eastern names."

"I know, right?" She scrolled down, past the weird nonsensical names to a list of more typically Western-American names. "I looked them up, but they aren't names in Arabic or any other language I can find. But I was able to look up a few of these guys."

"Charles Bishop," I murmured. "Well, well."

"Do you know who he *is?*" Talya said.

I recalled the Deacon's blithe explanation of his role in government, and grimaced. "Unfortunately, yes."

"Nope." Zane shook his head.

"Charles Bishop is the Director of the P-SAD," Talya said. "The Paranormal Special Activities Division of the CIA."

Zane rubbed his hand over his stubble, scruffing it. "Damn, Kitten."

"So, uhh, I did some *careful* digging around on him," Talya continued. "And I couldn't really find much of anything that wasn't just a government 'meet your director' type profile. Someone I know on USENET told me he was involved with the Stargate Project during the Cold War, but no one knows how. He's a major donor to the PAC."

I rubbed my palm over my mouth, thinking.

Talya gave a musical little sigh. "So, it turns out that only some of the money The Future of America gets goes to Sebastian Hart. Some goes to Catholic charities and other organizations... umm... there were two that really interested me."

"Go for it," Zane said.

"The first one is the Catholics Against Cults foundation," Talya said. "They're seriously anti-supernatural, and they're also leading this big campaign around the Church of the Voice of the Lord."

The final stroke. My heart sunk, and I felt vaguely ill as I thought back to what I had done with Christopher, the memory of his unnaturally blue, piercing eyes looking at me beseechingly from the floor. "That cinches it. Pastor Christopher Kincaid is the Deacon."

"Woah, wait a second." Zane leaned back, arm resting over the other knee. "Where'd that come from?"

"A few things." I sat up and leaned forward, swallowing the pizza-flavored gorge rising in my throat. "Firstly, I interrupted a government hit on him. Men in

Black were breaking into the church late at night. They murdered the security, and I just happened to be there. After I saved him, he told me that he'd been losing time... that he'd been having fugues where he passed out and woke up without any memory of what he'd been doing or where he'd been."

"Shit," Zane said. "You didn't tell us that."

"A lot has happened," I said. "I've left a great deal out. Anyway, the guy I had downstairs, Celso, gave me some names. Providence and Munificence. Munificence – I think – backs the Manellis and is in opposition to the TVS. I'm fairly sure Providence, whoever or whatever it is, heads up the Temple."

Zane snorted. "Those names sound Southern to me."

"It was implied they weren't human. They seem to inspire fascination and worship in people." I sighed, trying to remember what Christopher had told me.

"You think that Providence thing got its claws in him?"

I nodded, slowly. "But I don't think he's being subjected to the role willingly. There's another thing. Jana, the demonurge woman who headed up the TVS's rituals before the Deacon... when I killed her, her body disappeared. She died on the 14th of August. Christopher told me his first fugue event was August 17th after he came home from a trip to Chicago. The three-day waiting period has a great deal of occult significance. It's why vigils for the dead are traditionally three days and three nights long. I think Providence, or someone associated with

Providence, did something to him to turn him into the Deacon."

"That's horrible," Talya said. "You mean he doesn't even know what he's doing?"

"Jana was a demonurge, like I said." I rubbed my eyes, thinking. "So he's quite possibly possessed by... something. Now I think about it, his appearance bears a superficial resemblance to Jana's Neshamah."

"Her what?" Zane asked.

"Jana's soul. The souls of mages have a form, too," I replied. "Hers was this tall, thin, robed figure, a DOG that was trying to look like an angel. It was all white and gold, not black and violet, but in terms of height, bearing, general appearance... there is a resemblance."

"Yeesh." Talya grimaced, then cleared her throat. "Okay, the other organization... umm... do you know anything about Sebastian Hart?"

"Other than that he's running for office?" Zane asked.

"Yeah. Hart is ex-military. Like, ages before he got into politics, he started a private military company, Graystag Securities Group," Talya said. "A LOT of the PAC's money goes to Graystag, which I'm pretty sure is illegal."

"Laundering," I said. "Has to be."

"Graystag are really specialized," Talya continued. "They provide security exclusively for mining and resource exploration operations. These are the fuckheads that evict native peoples from their lands when companies buy the oil rights out from under them. They have a big operation in South America at the moment."

"That explains why Sergei switched sides," I said, grimly. "The CIA are the essentially the gatekeepers of the international drug trade in this country. They protect a bunch of the narco chiefs in exchange for access to anti-Communist militias. If Charles Bishop used Graystag to gain control of the Cali cocaine operation in Columbia, he would have the *Organizatsiya* over a barrel. About sixty percent of all our money comes from warehousing coke and crack."

"And you said the Deacon was fighting a war against Charles Bishop," Talya said.

Zane's brow was furrowed in thought. He wasn't a stupid man, but he didn't have the same mercurial ability to make leaps of logic that Talya had. "Providence is behind the Deacon... so who's behind Bishop?"

"That's a very good question," I said. "The *Deutsche Orden*, I assume. And they may be allied with Munificent, based on what Celso was saying. If that's true... he also implied that they were involved in the presidential assassination."

"Yeah." Zane let out a tense breath. "Shit. This is way over our heads."

"Yeah." Talya bit her lip. "But it's kind of personal, you know? The kinds of things companies like Graystag do to First Nations people are just awful."

"Indeed." I regarded the spreadsheet thoughtfully. "But Zane is right. This is way over our heads."

"We have to be able to do *something*," Talya said. "We can tell Jenner and Ron, at the very least, and see what they say."

"Something's going on with Ron," I replied. "I don't trust him."

"Don't diss him to me," Zane said. "Ron's been in the club since the beginning. He was Mason's war buddy. His passing upset him about as much as it upset Jenner."

"He lied to me," I said. "He told me Jenner didn't want me at the clubhouse."

"He probably thinks he's protecting her," Zane said.

"Ron's kind of... old fashioned?" Talya made a face, and shrugged.

I made a sound of amusement. "Chauvinistic, you mean."

"I'll talk to him about it." Zane stood up from his crouch, stretching his back and knees. "He listens to me. I think if he knows how deep this all runs, you'll be the least of his problems."

I wasn't convinced, but I didn't really know the guy well enough to say how accurate the assessment was. "Well, I'm getting a hotel room and sleeping for today. And then I'm going out."

"Alone?" Talya's brow furrowed. "The last time you did that, we didn't see you for days."

"I have to. You all have to get ready for the fight with Otto, and if I'm caught... it's better that only one person be caught." I drew a deep breath. "I can't help but wonder why Otto picked now, of all times, to come and make an ass of himself."

"They just smelled blood in the water." Zane shrugged.

"They came from Chicago," I said. "Given that Jana tried to kidnap me and take me to Chicago, and Christopher started having his episodes after coming back from the same city, I'm not willing to put it down as a coincidence."

"But that doesn't mean it's *not* a coincidence," Zane said, shaking his head. "Assuming it's not connected until we have evidence is reasonable. Chicago is a big city. Linking them up is magical thinking, Rex."

I arched an eyebrow, staring at him. He wrinkled his nose. "What?"

Talya burst out laughing, but it took Zane longer to figure it out. "Oh... right. You're a-"

"Magician, yes," I said.

He flushed a dark reddish brown, and jerked his shoulders back. "Okay, you got me there. But let me tell you something: no hotel. You stay with us here, where you're safe."

"If the Vigiles find me-"

"Magic doesn't work on us," Talya said. "They can't track us down. That's why they're so big on keeping tabs on young Weeders."

"Any magic they've put on you won't point to us," Zane said. "Being around us offers you some protection."

The offer was tempting. I was queasy with fatigue, the kind of exhaustion that no amount of coffee was able to help. The Yen was going to be the monkey on my back soon, and I didn't trust myself at a hotel bar, unsupervised. Besides that, we were already close to the airport here. By the description Celso had given me, East Hangar Road had to be close by.

"Come on, Rex." Talya got up from her chair. "You've helped us heaps of times. Let us help you, for a change. When was the last time you slept?"

"Haven't slept in... months, it feels like." Frustrated, I rubbed my eyes. "Okay. But if anything happens-"

"We'll bail out the windows and land on our feet like cats," Talya said. She offered me a hand, and I smiled faintly as I accepted. Like Jenner, Talya was disproportionately strong for her size. Physical strength among Weeders had more to do with animal form than anything else. "Come on. You can take Zane's bed."

"Thanks, Kitten." Zane rolled his eyes as he bobbed back up to his feet.

"Well, he isn't going to sleep on my Hello Kitty bedsheets, is he?" Talya turned her head as she tugged me toward the hallway. "He has to sleep on the *man* bed."

"The man bed," Zane echoed drily.

"Yeah! Sandpaper duvet, rock for a pillow. The mattress takes steroids." She let go of me to flex and make a face. "It means you wake up *angry!* Pumped! Hurrr!"

"If your bed is softer, I'll sleep on the Hello Kitty whatever-it-is," I replied.

"She might be too badass for you," Talya said. "Not to like, boast or anything, but you have to be pretty badass to sleep on Hello Kitty sheets."

"Kitten," Zane said, looking up. "You're about as badass as a jam doughnut, okay? I'm just saying."

"Kittens can be badass." Talya pointed at her own face. "You see these eyebrows? These are the eyebrows of a badass. You just wait until tonight when I ride in and I'm like: 'Get out the way, bitches! It's the Purrminator!'"

Zane and I cringed at the same time: me by rubbing the bridge of my nose, him by palming his entire face.

"Yeah! You heard me!" Talya pointed at him, then caught me by the sleeve and pulled me away to my repose, giggling all the while.

CHAPTER 34

A full-length mirror took up a corner of the dusty bedroom where Talya left me alone. I approached it side-on, gathering the fortitude required to look at myself, and was hardly disappointed by how revolting it was. My face was pale and jowly. I had grown a stubbled mess of gray hair over my scalp and jaw. My nose was slightly crooked. When I peeled off my clothes, I found swollen masses of bruises, inflamed cuts, and the puncture wound. Peeling the clothing off had ripped off a few of the scabs, and blood oozed out of at least ten inflamed cuts, lines slashed down my body. Twisting carefully, I was able to finally make a real assessment of everything. It looked bad, but not as bad as it probably had a couple days ago.

I climbed into a hot shower, letting the spray pound the bruises on my back, arms and chest, then went back to the quiet hush of the bedroom and flopped out onto the creaky bed. The air smelled like old paper. The peaceful silence was surreal.

"Why do I care so much, Kutkha?" I sighed the question aloud. "The Tree, these Government assholes... none of it is my business."

"Perhaps the better question is: what makes a man stop caring about such things?" He replied. *"What is it that makes beings like Sergei, Yegor, and the Deacon? What is that which makes men unaffected by the sight of something awe-inspiring or horrific?"*

Good question. No matter how many hits I'd pulled or how much shit I'd seen, that sense of wonder in the face of the Mystery had endured. I'd dreamed of the Garden several times now, and each time I'd seen it, it had changed me. I was in awe of it: of GOD's skin, the incredible expanse of great, prismatic Trees. I could remember details with intense, supernatural clarity: their sighs and whispers, the way the MahTree's leaves carefully and gently reached out and brushed the delicate glass-thread creatures that swam around them. Zarya had been born to one of those trees. Maybe the MahTree the Manellis wanted WAS Zarya's mother. I couldn't say why, but the way I'd felt around those trees was the same mix of emotions and instincts I'd felt when I'd rescued the first of the Wolf Grove children, Josie. They made me feel... protective. Fierce, even.

I'd rescued Zarya for a whole number of reasons. At first, they were purely selfish. I'd been driven by the pursuit of the Mystery, the Source and promise of power. Six months ago, I might have been too jaded to care about people fighting and dying over a tree. But now, I cared. I cared a lot. Yegor's words had stuck with me, no matter how hard I'd tried to brush them off. While I'd been wrapped up in the ecstasy of the occult all those years, battling my pride and pretending I didn't love Vassily, I'd been protecting a pack of traitorous, child-abusing fucks. I'd killed for them.

"I don't know," I admitted aloud. "I don't know what it is that makes someone stop caring. But I have a question, and I'd appreciate an answer."

"Speak."

"Is my attachment to this, the need to find this Tree, tied to my other lives? The ones that came before this lifetime?"

There was a pause. *"Yes and no. It is most connected to the ones that are operating simultaneously to this Now."*

It was rare to get such a straightforward response from Kutkha. "Simultaneously?"

"You are not ready for that story, my Ruach." Kutkha sounded... anxious. *"But one day, not really that far from now, you will be."*

Part of me wanted to argue. The other part of me wasn't willing to. Kutkha wasn't some absurdly patronizing shade—he was my Soul, with a capital S. If he said I wasn't ready, I probably wasn't. If I could prove myself able to learn and understand, he would teach me.

Sleep hit me like a speeding truck. One second, I was drowsing off, and the next, I woke into darkness. The clock told me that it was eight p.m., and twelve hours had passed between blinks. I still felt like shit as I pushed myself upright, spent a couple minutes scratching together the energy to move, and got out of the warm nest of blankets and cat to start my night.

The first order of business was getting rid of Celso. Zane and I drove him out to the swamps in the pounding rain, where he was given a Viking funeral in a shitty stolen VW Beetle and left to burn in a greasy plume of black smoke. Zane dropped me off at the shop. I borrowed a motorcycle and raingear, loaded for bear, and left Binah with a full bowl of food, a clean litter box, and a note for her care in the event I didn't return.

East Hanger Road had an airfield on one side, and rows of huge cargo warehouses on the other. It dead-ended into a massive industrial park at the end, a desolate expanse of asphalt and prefabricated steel shelters, cold semis, and hangars. With the lights off and the cover of darkness, I cruised to a stop behind a large row of signs near the fence line. I could see a line of motorcycles parked deeper in the yard. Bingo.

With a heavy sigh, I cut the engine and took stock of what I had. The Wardbreaker, a spare knife—not my preferred one, the Vigiles had taken that—a spare bullet-resistant MiB suit, but no familiar, a fever, and very little energy for this spur-of-the-moment infiltration. Wearily, I checked over my gun and made sure I had spare ammunition and a clean silencer, then double-checked the rest of my tools. Exhausted as I was, I knew I had to follow this up. The immediate payoff was being able to give Jenner good intel when I finally got in touch with her. But it wasn't just that: my soul was whispering to me, telling me that this was important. That it was all important.

The only ways in or out of the building were through the loading docks or the door at the short side of the warehouse. I wasn't too keen on simply strolling in through the front, so I went around back, mounted the steps up to the loading dock furthest away from the front door, and fiddled with the lock at the base of the roller shutter. When it popped, I greased the door's rollers and opened it just enough to slide underneath.

The warehouse was lit down at the other end, but those lights didn't reach this end of the rectangular building. It was dark enough that I could safely crawl in, gently shut the door, and slip down behind a stack of plastic-wrapped pallets. From here, I could get a sense of what I was dealing with.

The pallets nearest me were full of garden mulch, soil, and fertilizer. The warehouse was cavernous, and the stock varied from dock to dock. I began the slow, quiet course down to the other end, ears cocked and eyes keen, and eventually began to pick out 'AEROMOR' on a number of the pallets and crates.

I was almost at the end of the building when heavy footsteps thudded right above my head. They were inside the warehouse office, one of those shipping-crate offices mounted over the cargo area. My pulse skipped, and I ducked down as several pairs of thick boots scraped against steel grating.

"Where the fuck are they?" The first voice was deep, masculine, but throaty. There was an odd rough strain to it, like the end of a crow's caw... as if his voice would give out at any moment. Otto Roth. "What time is it?"

"Five past midnight," the next speaker sounded nervous. It was Dogboy, his vampire lieutenant. "They said they'd be here zero-zero sharp with the Feds. I don't know what's keeping them..."

"Otto Roth doesn't like it when people are late." Otto's voice dropped to a dangerous rumble. "Otto thinks the cops should have gotten their motherfucking pot plant and left by now."

"Yaroshenko's the Master of the Fifth Choir, man. He's not gonna stiff us... it's probably just traffic or something.

I was still, but couldn't suppress a bitter smirk. *You clearly know a different Sergei Yaroshenko than me.*

The shadows wobbled across the concrete, cast long by the studio lights that beamed overhead. The hair on the nape of my neck prickled. There was something really off about Otto.

A few minutes passed, and then the rapport of a metal door opening and slamming echoed through the building like a gunshot. Ears cocked, I listened as shoes rang off the hard ground. Two pairs.

"Hey there, Joshy!" Dogboy called out, striving for cheerfulness. "Looking sharp, as always!"

"No need to be cute, Dogboy." A stiff, formal Gold Coast lockjaw accent. I tensed. It was Agent Keen.

"Where are the Russkies at?" Otto, this time.

"They're finishing up their business outside. Now, where is she? Is she safe?"

"The plant's upstairs," Otto said. "We put Christmas tree decorations on it for you."

"I'm so glad we chose associates with such a wonderful a sense of humor," Keen replied. "We are not pleased with you, Roth, and in no mood for antics."

"What's not to be pleased about?" Otto didn't even bother to hide how smug he was.

"Apparently you felt the need to sow your oats with Kristen," Keen said, each word formed sharp and cold. "Now, a Streetsweeper is loose. Would you know anything about that?"

"Otto knows the bitch got what she deserved. If you want a janitor, he ain't your man."

I tried to look around the crates to see faces, but sunk back down as the door opened again, hinges squealing. The conversation died as the newcomers joined the assembled. One set of heavy boots that rang with a recognizable cadence, and two other pairs of feet that were, by comparison, whisper-soft.

"How's it going, Nic? And, uh, *Advokat*, right?" One of the other bikers stepped forward to greet the current *Avtoritet* of Brighton Beach. And his *Advokat*, too? GOD, how I wanted to put a knife through Nic's neck.

"Not bad. Otto. Dogboy." It was Nicolai who replied, his dry scarecrow rasp heavily accented in English.

"Heard there was trouble in your ranks, Nic," Otto said. "One guy murdered. Other guys leaving."

"Yegor knew risks. There is always risk of playing this games." Nicolai sounded... exhausted. His English was normally better than that.

"Well, to business." Joshua Keen now sounded distinctly uncomfortable. Dealing with the riff-raff was out of his element. "The handover, first of all. Let me see her."

"Go get the plant," Otto ordered.

Unseen feet stamped off across the floor, and the room fell into the uneasy tension between merchant and customer. Keen was too uncomfortable to let silence reign. "At least you got her. If you've hurt her…"

"Ain't done nothing to the plant. Ain't like it got any holes to fuck."

"Charming. Did the cult give you any trouble?"

"Nah. We nabbed it while your guys were getting slaughtered upstairs," Otto said. "Never send boys to do a man's job, I say. You ever figure what happened up there?"

"No idea," Keen replied. "We lost contact with the team. The final report was that ST-1 was chasing down a suspected undesirable inside the auditorium. This 'Deacon', perhaps, though he was supposed to be occupied elsewhere. You had the Tree, and thus we ordered withdrawal."

They were talking about the Church of the Voice raid—they had to be. Stunned, I focused on my breathing, trying not to let it speed. There was only one reason the Tree would have been at the Church… and suddenly, Glory's remark to me made a great deal more sense. *'A favor repaid.' It was Christopher. I'd stopped the Vigiles from taking out the Deacon.*

A terrible feeling of mingled dread and sorrow swept over the room, a wave of pure emotion so powerful that it lifted the hairs on the backs of my arms and brought an involuntary sting to my eyes. The air itself was wracked with weeping as the men who'd gone returned, huffing, and set down something heavy on the floor.

"Ahh… yes. At last." Keen's voice became soft and reverent. "You could have cared for her better. Look at her. She's half dead."

"Sorry, but gardening isn't Otto's specialty," Otto replied. "Fork it over."

If they were moved, I couldn't tell. The Tree's pain, her terror and confusion beat through the air of the room. Her agitation became my agitation, the same internal desperation I'd felt when I'd first found one of the kids used in Sergei's movies, or when I'd heard Binah's stricken wails from the cage where she'd been imprisoned. My face began to burn with smoldering anger, like a seam of coal under the skin of my cheeks.

"All in order," Otto said after a minute or so. "So, got anything else you need done after tonight?"

"The fight is the most important thing, but I've brought along two new 'challenges' for both of your organizations to consider after you've completed tonight's objective. We're offering them at above-average market rates," Keen replied.

Fuck. *Fuck*. I *knew* it was too good to be true.

"Another agent screw the pooch?" Otto asked, voice thick with dark humor.

"No. There was only the one." Keen cleared his throat. "I am going to emphasize again that tonight's events must *not* turn into a slaughter. We want the Twin Tigers M.C. absolutely routed, but we want them alive. You will occupy the therianthropes while we bring them to ground. Do you understand this?"

"Pretty sure I do," Otto replied drily.

"If you can bait them to slaughter some scum, that would be beneficial. We need a case that will make the headlines."

I listened on in growing shock. Otto had been working with the Vigiles all this time. And 'A case that made the headlines' would be the kind of event that would justify rounding up every damn Weeder in the city, and probably a number of spooks, too. On top of the 'Staten Island occult sex murderer escape' story they were running about me, Keen was setting up a GOD-damned pogrom.

"We have hashed out job already. Everything is planned. Give hit files," Nic said.

"The first target is probably going to be more difficult to find than the second." Tomas still had that dead, recorded-message voice. "We don't know much about this mark. Goes by the name 'Zealot' or 'Angkor'. Everything we know about them is in that file you're holding."

"Oh, I know him," Nic said. "When we work for Deacon, I remember… uhh… 'seeing' him. He's a freak, eh?"

"Looks like a fuckin' princess to me," Otto said. "No sweat."

Nicolai laughed, a harsh croak of sound. "You do not know how true that is."

"Do not underestimate him. The first party to take them down gets the reward," Keen added. "But we emphatically want this one *alive*."

"It is not 'hit' if you want person alive," Nic replied. "It is 'catch and carry'. More expensive. And this one is a powerful spook."

"So be it."

Otto was beginning to sound impatient. "Who's the other one?"

"This man," Keen said. "Dead or alive."

"*Chert poberi.*" Nicolai grumbled in Russian. For him, it was equivalent to 'fucking hell'. "Alexi. No, we cannot kill him. My *Pakhun* wants him. We been trying to find this piece of shit for months."

"Then we can take him to Mister Y?" Dogboy said.

"Unacceptable." Keen's tone was very stiff. "We need him dead. If you can't do it-"

"No, you don't understand." Dogboy sounded worried. "You know who the head of their outfit is, don't you?"

"I don't care," Keen replied stiffly. "He's-"

"Sergei Yaroshenko is the Master of the Fifth Choir, man. You know what that means, right?"

"His status doesn't put him above the needs of humanity. That's all I need to know, and as I was saying..."

"You'll get your wish, Agents, believe me." An unearthly voice, silent until now, spoke from somewhere behind Nicolai. A voice as dry as old grave dirt. "What Nic isn't saying is that Lexi here is scheduled for induction into the Choir. And I assure you. It's a one-way trip."

... *No.*

CHAPTER 35

"I'm sorry, I don't believe we were introduced?" Keen was using the voice rich snobs reserved for 'the help'.

"Because I'm not why we're here, Agent."

No. My hands were turning cold and clammy. I thought I heard a bell going off somewhere, ringing relentlessly inside of my own skull.

"I assure you that you will gain absolutely nothing from challenging the Vigiles, Mister..?"

"Lovenko." The thing that had been Vassily ground the word out in only a vague approximation of his voice.

My legs went out from under me, and I slid down the side of the pallet as the ringing spread to my face and hands and my mouth filled with the taste of iron. *No, no, no.*

"Hey... did you hear that?" I couldn't tell who was speaking now. One of them. I put my face in my hands and stared at my palms, struggling to stay quiet, to not hyperventilate.

"Well, Mister Lovenko, we are employing your people for this task, and if your '*Pakhun*' is not willing to abide by the terms, then we are quite capable of finding someone else to handle the job."

"Keith Richards over here has got a point. This guy is Tran's friend," Otto said. "She's on edge already. We could push her over with him as bait."

"Guys, seriously. I swear I can hear something."

Distantly, I knew I should have cared. But the world was cracking, falling apart, and with it my sense of reality. Self-preservation. Everything. I was used to being the tough guy, a street soldier... but I felt exactly like the eight-year-old boy watching his father come up on him with a crowbar in his hand and intent in his eyes. My intuition began to pound at me, shouting from behind a locked door: the formless voice of my Neshamah, which suddenly swelled into a warning cry as magic flushed over me in a rippling green-tinted wave.

Life magic, I realized. Tomas wasn't a 'forensic specialist' after all.

"Fuck!" The sound of weapons being drawn finally galvanized me. Mind numb, body acting on training and reflexes alone, I pushed myself up and sprinted for the next row of cover as shadows rounded the line of pallets where I'd been hiding. But my heart wasn't in it—it had been torn out before I'd even started to escape.

A round took me in the back: a small caliber bullet. The armor in the back of the suit jacket took the brunt of it, but I felt something crack and shift in my chest as I sprawled to the floor and struggled to turn on the men closing in on me. But I only had eyes for one.

Vassily was a walking corpse. Pallid, his skin flat, white, and waxy-smooth. Tattoos floated beneath the translucent, papery skin of his hands. His cheeks and eyes were sunken, hair dull. There was no blood under the skin to even pretend at an appearance of life... but he was walking, talking, and his flat blue eyes burned with predatory intelligence.

Dogboy was the first to block my view: he'd dropped all pretense of humanity, rushing at me with a barbed tongue and needle-sharp fangs extended. The need for survival finally kicked in, but too late to stop him. He leaped on me from a distance, taking us to the ground. I drove my fist up under his sternum with a shout. "*TZAIN!*"

The vampire's eyes bugged, and he coughed up a gout of orange blood as he tumbled off, clutching at the huge punch-dagger hole I'd rammed up through his undead lungs and heart. I scrambled up to hands and a knee, only to find myself held at the point of two guns and two swords. Keen and Black held both expertly— longswords in their right hands, pistols in their left. Their aim was steady, flawless. The guns glowed with hot red sigils.

"Perfect timing." Joshua Keen muttered. He sighted down the barrel at my head, and squeezed the trigger.

"No!" Vassily shoved Keen just as he fired, sending the bullet wide. When Keen brought the sword around,

Vassily snarled bestially, lips peeled back to bare top and bottom rows of razor-sharp iron teeth.

He'd... *saved* me? The lizard part of my brain kicked in with a surge of futile hope as I got to my feet. I rose straight into a fist that decked me across the jaw and sent me sprawling to the floor. A human punch wasn't enough to take me down—but Vassily was no longer human.

I kept my guard up around my head, but there was no strength left in my arms. Vassily bent down and wrapped his hand around my throat. He lifted me up by the neck, squeezing hard enough that my pulse thundered behind my eyes and my vision shot through with red. As I struggled to prize his fingers off my throat and gasp a breath, his eyes glittered with something like excitement.

Dogboy coughed and rolled to hands and knees, drooling putrid Phi onto the floor. The burned wax smell was similar to Sergei's, but not identical... and my mind fixated on that stupid little detail as I was surrounded by a circle of guns. Some pointed at me, some held back the Agents from shooting me like a dog on the street. Nicolai was one of them. He was looking at me strangely, but I couldn't make sense of his saggy, jowly face. He looked much older than I remembered.

"This is why Otto likes dealing with the Church. Nice case of deliverance," Otto remarked dryly. He had a Magnum in his hands, but he hardly needed it. Vera was behind him, both of her revolvers aimed squarely at the heads of the Templars. She would not miss if she fired.

"Vera shoots faster than you. Back away," Nicolai said. "This is our *Organizatsiya*'s business."

I was struggling not to pass out. In desperation, I kicked out at Vassily's knees. I might as well have kicked the side of a boat, or the wheel of a truck. His flesh was unyielding, like cordwood.

Something in Keen snapped. He flushed scarlet with rage. "Put him down and give him to me!"

"For free?" Dogboy snickered. "You gotta be joking."

Keen brought his pistol up to fire at me. He hadn't completed the swing when Vera fractionally moved the muzzle of her left pistol to one side, and fired around Vassily's shoulder. I thought I was hallucinating when I saw Keen dodge the round by moving his head to the side, but sure enough, there was only a line of black powder where the round should have clipped his cheek.

"Calm down, all of you. We need him first," Otto said. "Like Otto says, he's all up in Tran's cunt. So cut him up a bit and use him as bait., See how much easier it is to draw the Tigers out."

"Sergei is insist we take him home," Nicolai shot back. "For his... Choir."

Choir. I had no idea what he was talking about. Magic burned on the back of my tongue and behind my eyes, but the white lightning flashing around the edges of my eyes was creeping inward. I was on the verge of passing out when a bad smell cut through the odor of Feeder blood. Greasy, sweet... the cheap perfume stench of rotting flesh.

"Gentlemen, there's a way we can all get what we need." The way Vassily's dead throat ground out the words was a mockery of his smooth voice. "It's easy:

Agent, you come with us and supervise the procedure at my boss's warehouse. We'll put you up, you get to relax. Lexi will be under the Maester's control after that. He'll go with you and help you with the shapeshifters tonight."

Through the haze and tears, I saw Vera's gun barrels begin to darken. The black holes at the ends bored into my temples, voids in the sparkling, spitting tunnel of my vision.

"What? So your 'Choirmaster' can blackmail us with his continued silence?" Keen scoffed. "The Vigiles Magicarum does not negotiate with vampires!"

The pistols were oozing. Thin runnels of oily fluid poured from them and spattered to the floor. I gurgled and struggled, fear like spikes throughout my body. Vera noticed my baffled stare, brow furrowing as she broke her aim to look at the muzzle of the revolver. Everyone else seemed to realize the same thing we did at the same time.

"Demons!" Joshua threw his pistol away as lights overhead blew, raining glass everywhere.

Everyone got the same idea. Vassily dropped me and turned, seemingly unconcerned about my being behind him. I coughed, heaved for breath and rolled back, putting as much distance as I could. My first thought was to run; my second was that I couldn't leave Vassily.

"*Semych*! For GOD's sake! Stop!" I shouted at him in our native Ukrainian, as the DOGs' insane shrieks and giggles filled the building. "Get the hell out of here!"

He looked back, and for a moment, his expression flickered to something more familiar, the reflex double-take of spotting a friend in a crowd. Only for a moment.

Magic pulsed around us, and the smell of Sergei's blood cut through the noxious stench of DOG.

"Stay there!" Something alien spoke through him, inhumanly guttural. He bared his teeth like a barracuda, eyes gleaming with points of orange fire, and ran to face the DOGs with nothing but fangs and fists.

"Look at all these idiots!" Glory's voice boomed through the warehouse like a cheerful claxon, punctuated by bursts of automatic fire. "You're an idiot! Aaand you're an idiot! You get some too!"

Tomas had taken cover, but Keen was fighting, grim-faced, pale and focused. His sword-hand blurred with inhuman speed as he dodged and weaved too fast for my eyes to follow, giving him the appearance of disappearing in pulses. There were bodies on the ground, and screams. Fuck this. I clumsily got up, stumbled back on the turn, and ran for my life, ignoring the shouts and sounds of pursuit.

No. It was crazy, I was crazy, heart thudding so loudly that even the rapport of guns firing and DOGs howling seemed distant and far off. I was so completely dissociated from everything now that I forgot my wounds, forgot the Tree, forgot everything as I raged against the unreal horror of Vassily talking, on his feet, still dead. The door was ahead of me, at the end of the warehouse, and I ran for it... only to come to a screeching halt as Glory casually strolled out in front of me.

"Soldier 557," I said, weakly. "What a surprise."

"That's me!" The small man was dressed exactly the same way I'd seen him last time—dirty tank top, black sweats, no shoes. He was carrying an assault rifle that was too large for him. Covered in dust, he looked like a child soldier out of a dystopian vision. "Come with me, and we'll clear the scum, tough guy. I'm here to rescue my Mother."

Shock laid over shock, and I actually found myself listening as the warehouse descended into chaos. "I... *what?*"

"My Mother." The craziness in his haunted features drained away. "I'm a Gift Horse, Alexi."

Without the madness in his eyes and the rictus grin, I could see it and smell it. The Phi that made him, spoiled into that rotten fruit smell. The ruin of his beauty. "The Tree. The Tree is your Mother?"

"What? You think I've been working for these Morphorde because I want to?" The small man's violet eyes were raw with pain. "They captured her. They've tortured us. Please... help me."

I began to stutter out an answer, but Glory pounced on me and knocked me down before I could reply. Weapon fire burst over our heads where I'd been standing. Disoriented, I rolled over to see something out of a nightmare. The fluid DOGs had merged into three bigger creatures, one of which crashed over a biker while he screamed. Keen was fighting off a DOG like a gladiator; Tomas was casting green bolts similar to ones I'd seen Angkor use... but the true horror was thrashing around in the center of the warehouse. A centipede. A black, glistening centipede the size of a subway car. Slack-jawed, I watched it fall on the nearest DOG and scoop it into its mouth with mandibles and other disgusting, venom-dripping parts of its mouth. It ate the screeching thing without pausing. Holy fucking shit.

"There's more where that came from, losers!" Glory cackled. He dashed past me, leaving me in front of the momentarily open door. It was about to be blocked by the cluster of abominations that were following in his wake.

I fled in the other direction this time, skidding behind a stack of pallets. As a huge shadow fell over me, I threw myself out toward the next row. A huge, pincered tail smashed down on the stacks of potting soil I'd been cowering behind only seconds ago. The centipede thrashed around to face the largest of the DOGs with a dreadful, rattling wet hiss.

Glory skipped along the tops of the cargo with incredible agility. I tried to keep up, but the broken ribs and the tightness in my bruised throat made running difficult. When Glory threw me his rifle, barely breaking step, I nearly dropped it. He bounded out into the fray, making a beeline for a huge planter, a blue-glazed pot that was shrouded by a sack.

I took cover and braced the rifle, watching numbly as a small wave of Morphorde rolled into the building. Cockroach-like insects, the kind that had fallen during the rain, flooded the building in a torrent. They joined the DOGs, who were being torn apart by the centipede. Mutated creatures lurched in after that, spiny horrors with no legs and too many mouths. Tomas had surrounded himself and Keen with some kind of field. The pair of them fought for their lives with gun and sword. The others were surrounded, but they were still battling on—and winning.

Several years ago, I'd seen a man burn to death from the inside out. Of all the deaths I'd ever seen, it haunted me most because of the way he'd been so calm, so completely stupefied by what was happening to him that he didn't scream, didn't seem to feel pain. I remember him turning to face me in shock, mouth open as if to speak, and belching flames with a look of confusion on his face. He didn't scream, didn't seem to feel any pain... not until the very end.

That was me, now. Mesmerized, bewildered, not even able to aim. I should have been terrified... but I wasn't. I wasn't anything. I stared as Vassily tore through a bloated mantis-like thing with nothing more than hands and teeth, spitting ichor to the ground. But Vassily, the Vassily I'd known, didn't fight. Not like that. He didn't move like, like-

"Run! RUN!" Glory's voice pierced the air behind me. I turned to see him carrying the shrouded planter. It had to have weighed three hundred pounds, at least. His muscles were straining, but he was managing it. Somehow.

Unseen strings jerked me up to my feet. The body still wanted to live, even if the mind did not. I dodged as something fell toward me: half a biker thrown over the cargo crates. He hit the wall, rebounding to sprawl across the aisle. A tumbled pair of legs still in jeans and boots, a rope of intestine stuck to the concrete. There was an explosion of soil ahead of us as the giant insect crushed one of the cockroaches, impaling others on its legs as it fought like some kind of fucked up Chinese Dragon. I jumped over the dirt and continued on, Glory panting behind me.

"Go!" Glory shouted.

He didn't need to encourage me. I rounded the last pallets and bolted for the door, struggling for breath. The Agents were outside, frantically trying to get their car to start. Keen was collapsed in the passenger side, his thin face a mask of agony. Black raised a hand behind the windshield, mouth opening, and I let off a burst straight at him on pure reflex. The bullets hit it with dull thumps instead of shattering, hazing the glass and causing it to crumble inward. The car reversed with a screech, and I followed it up with gunfire as the Agents fled.

Glory jogged past me in a trail of dirty white dreadlocks, bouncing around the corner of the building at top speed. At a loss, I followed him, only to skid to a halt as I saw his means of transport.

A horse. An honest to GOD horse, complete with a pack saddle.

"Help me get her up!" He looked back at me, violet eyes blazing and urgent. "We have to get her out of here!"

I'd taken too many hits to the head and heart to argue. Kutkha was pushing at me, wings beating a tattoo inside my skull, but my limbs seemed to move of their own volition. Glory was supernaturally strong, but he was too short to get the right leverage. I helped him arrange the pot in a saddle harness, the kind they used to carry the big drums during military parades. As I did, he desperately threw on layers of clothes: boots, a huge oilskin coat, a hat, scarf, and then a mask with a respirator.

Lifting and settling the pot took what was left of my strength. I stumbled dizzily against the horse's flank once it was done, gasping. Its vivid green smell cut through my fugue. I breathed deeply, and my head cleared a little... enough to hear the small, strangely familiar feminine voice that had been trying to pierce the haze of grief and shock all this time.

No! Get away! Ah-Lexi!

The MahTree didn't get another word in before Glory clubbed me over the back of the head.

CHAPTER 36

I am a man who usually makes good decisions. I'm correct often enough that I normally don't question my judgements, but the circumstances in the warehouse were not normal. This time, I'd blown it.

When I came to, we were still on the horse. I was tied belly-down over the back of the saddle as we galloped through long grass. Queasy, head pounding, I was steeling myself to find a way to fuck up Glory's day when the horse jumped, lifting me up against my restraints, and then slamming me back down again as we hit... water?

My body jerked with reflex panic as filthy swamp water swallowed us so quickly that it felt like we were falling instead of sinking. There was no bottom to this bog, only a void of freezing, empty space. The void howled like storm winds, a powerful current that flung the animal back and forth as it powered forward. I couldn't breathe—I couldn't *anything*, because all sensation of my body vanished into the intense emptiness of the fluid that swallowed us and then spat us back out again.

The water bowed up around us and exploded into a shower as the horse leaped up and clambered up out of a different pool of water. The place we emerged was dark, reeking of mold and moss, and chilly-damp. I heard Glory clicking his tongue to urge his mount to stay calm as it plunged headlong into a rushing stream, fording it up through an old, dank tunnel.

I was shivering like I'd been caught in a blizzard, too cold to move. Fuck. What the hell had I gotten myself into? I was gathering the will to struggle when Glory reached back with a hand, half-seen in the gloom. A weird, sweet, chemical smell stung my nose as I jerked my head away. The odor seemed to pass through me in a wave: my body flushed with heat, then numbness, and then sleep.

When I next stirred, it was to the uncomfortable sensation of wet skin against rough stone, the sounds of clicking and chewing, and the sickly smell of rotting, moldy meat. I was crumpled around the base of the MahTree's pot in the center of a dimly lit room, a bare stone-faced alcove that was connected to a much, much larger chamber expanding into darkness behind a set of heavy iron gates. The Tree and I were surrounded by black mounds that seeped blood and rot onto the floor. As my vision swam back in, I realized these heaving, buzzing, putrid piles were the rotting remains of animals. Mostly. Dogs, cats, birds, raccoons, rats, pigeons, and gulls were stacked around us, wall-to-wall. Several of the bodies, however, were human. Badly bagged and left to decay, they were eyeless, sagging sacks of flesh, their lips ripped away from grim yellow teeth. The room reeked with an oily acidic smell that was oddly familiar, an odor that resolved itself as I startled to full wakefulness. Scuttling, squeaking… the strange robotic, mechanical sound of chitin scraping against the floor. Philimites. As soon as I spotted the first one, writhing inside the body of a dead rabbit, I began to hear them all.

The air crackled with a low, silent scream, the room itself rent with the unadulterated grief of the MahTree. The leather bag was gone, leaving her as naked as I was in the middle of this carnage. She cast a subtle glow against the darkness pressing in around us, but she was visibly ill. Her smooth, flesh-like trunk was withered like an old parsnip, scored with deep lines. Her branches curled grayish at the ends, as flexible and mobile as hands. She had lost most of her silvery-pink leaves, and the few that remained were streaked with powdery tarnish. The Edenic soil she stood in was no longer silver. It was lead-gray and heavily oxidized, but still gleamed like pearl under the single lightbulb that hung over us.

For several delirious minutes, I slouched against my restraints in a state of stark disbelief. The fever was back with a vengeance, along with a deep, rusty pain in my joints and my neck. My chest throbbed, broken ribs stabbing inward on every breath. There was a metal gag in my mouth that held my tongue down, trapping it and removing all ability to speak. Shifting around on the sticky ground, I could feel my wrists had been handcuffed in proper metal cuffs. My ankles were bound by a couple of rows of zip ties. There was something around my neck. But besides the pain, I just… didn't care. I wasn't angry. I wasn't afraid. There was nothing but gravity, crushing me against the earth like a cold hand.

I sunk into the pain, and for a while I stopped fighting. Levental. Ali. Vassily. The monsters had gotten them. No one was going to come along and tell me it was going to be okay, that it'd be alright, somehow, that I'd defy the bacterial poison brooding in my veins and find some way, any way, to help Vassily or make it right. The Vigiles were going to round up the Tigers at that fight, and I wasn't able to warn them.

In the corporate world, you had fixers. In the law enforcement world, you had men like Joshua Keen. Ayashe had probably been reporting in innocence, unaware of why she'd really been recruited, of why she'd been allowed to exist as the only Weeder Vigiles Agent in the city. This had been his plan all along: to infiltrate, learn, divide, then conquer.

The Tree reached toward me with trembling branches, but I did nothing but stare at her. Every time I blinked, I saw Vassily's face, heard echoes of cavalier remarks about Weeders and digester trucks, saw Ali covered in wasps. I flashed on Lee Harrison's black, half-lidded eyes, and on Ayashe coughing her life out onto bland, lilac office carpet. And over it all, I felt the Yen inside me: grinning, wallowing in the horror.

"*Ah-Lexi?*" The MahTree's telepathic voice was small, feminine and breathy. Like Kutkha, she didn't speak the word so much as exhale the meaning into the front of my conscious awareness… a thought that you didn't think.

I shuddered and peered down and around us, trying to understand why we weren't being eaten alive. She and I were both contained inside of a magic circle inscribed in thick white chalky lines, a protective ward that was kept the Philimites away from us. Bugs bloated on meat would scuttle in, hit an invisible wall, and bounce back to rejoin the mass that had been lured in by Glory's offering.

"Ah-lexi?"

The second time the Tree called me, I looked up. The MahTree's remaining leaves rustled as she moved, her branches curling and uncurling like tendrils. Beckoning me.

"What?" I didn't have the energy to console myself or her.

"Touch me. Please." Her voice was pitiful, desperate. Needy. Like the pleading of a starving girl-child.

I felt a push, deep down: The same kind of protective urgency I'd felt when I saw eight-year-old Josie curled up in the corner of her cell, feral with terror. It was enough to pull me to my knees so that I could lean in. When I managed to reach up , she bowed toward me, her branches caressing my face and head. It was an incredibly tender, sensitive touch, cool against my feverish skin.

"So much pain," she whispered. *"You are in so much pain."*

"It's fine." Not really, but it was what it was. I was beyond caring about the dirt I'd ground into my wounds, so I sat back down, leaning against the side of her pot, facing the rest of the room. It was seething, hissing, pouring with Philimites that continued to test the magical defenses in increasing numbers.

The little Tree bent in against me, wrapping her boughs around my head and shoulders. She was quivering with fear and relief. I found myself relaxing, slipping down until the back of my neck rested against her small buttressed roots. The agony and tension of a dozen injuries ebbed away, second by second, until I lay in a warm daze. There was a rhythmic pulsing, fluttering sensation at the base of my neck, but it was far off and inconsequential compared to the waves of relief that surged through my body. *"Hey. What are you doing?"*

"Do not fear. You are suffering, and I can relieve your pain." The Tree sounded resolute, in her own, tired way. *"I do not have the strength to heal you, but I am able to do this."*

She smelled good: subtler than the Gift Horse, but just as unearthly and sweet. It was a smell that made me think of Zarya, and strangely, of Binah. I missed my cat. *"You... you shouldn't. You should be saving whatever strength you have."*

My words hung between us, as my eyes drooped and the Tree slowly surged back from her desiccation. It was as if she was feeding on something. On... what? My relaxation?

"Ah-Lexi. My son will be here soon." She spoke after a little while. *"He will Ruin me."*

"I won't let him." On that, I was sure.

"You will not be able to stop him." The Tree's words were like a bow across a violin, high and sweet and sad. *"This is the reality of what will happen."*

She was right, and I knew she was right, but it didn't stop me feeling resentful. *"We have to be able to do something."*

"There are times when we must simply submit to what comes. Sanity is the pursuit of reality." A soothing, shooting warmth

437

flushed through my body. It wasn't narcotic, because it didn't leave me feeling dull or sick, but it freshly tamped down the pain of my injuries. *"Can I ask you for something?"*

"What is it?" I drew a deep breath. My chest twinged, but the broken spur that pierced my lung was no longer painful.

"Hope." The Tree was breathing, too: a subtle swell and ebb I felt through her trunk. *"If you are willing to take a part of me with you... there is hope for my son. He is a sweet and gentle being, Ah-Lexi. This is not what he is. Someone has hurt him, exposed him to the NO and Ruined him. It is not his fault he is like this. If I am gone, he will never be healed... he will perish, and GOD will have lost another Stallion."*

Hope. What a novel concept. *"Whatever you do, I'm going the same place you are. But if it makes you feel better... "* I trailed off.

"Thank you." The small Tree was shivering harder than before. She was desperately, desperately afraid. *"I will give you my Rhizomes. But... I fear it will burden you."*

"Why?"

The small creature shuddered, leaves clinking like glass. *"You will take your story with you. I do not wish to harm you, but..."*

My story? I frowned, puzzled, and edged closer. *"What do you mean?"*

"Once, long ago, I knew a You." she insisted. *"When I was captured and imprisoned in a place without hope, it was alongside an Ah-Lexi. It is this story I carry, and this story I will impart."*

I rested my elbows on my knees, confused. Apparently 'I' – that being my other incarnations – had gotten around.

"It is a hard story, but in that, too, there is hope," the Tree continued. *"Perhaps the greatest of all."*

Kutkha was watching me in solemn silence from behind my own eyes. When I felt back for his approval or comment, there was nothing but the weight of his patience, his judgment, his expectation.

"Alright," I replied. We were going to die in this hellhole, or worse. What difference would it make, really? *"Hit me."*

The Tree's graceful gratitude rippled through me, fading off into something like concentration. I felt a momentary pressure at the base of my skull, and an electric current suddenly surged through my body. I barked a cry of surprise – there was no pain – as my body arched. My jaws snapped and locked as I blacked out in fits and starts, waking up to the brief realization that I could *feel* the fractalline map of the nerves in my body in technicolor as they lit up like Christmas tree lights, then passing out again.

When I woke, it was in a different place, a different time. And I was in Hell.

In the dank, cold darkness of this forsaken place, alike but so different from the room where my body lay, tiny mandibles rubbed together, exoskeletons chittering as they slid across one another. Countless Morphorde were tucked into the crevices, crooks, folds, crannies, and oozing orifices of HuMan beings. HuMans of every color and sex, forced by magic and violated biomechanics to stack and entwine with one another in a living matrix that comprised the walls, floor, and ceiling of this place. Millions of them.

I flew through this structure at dizzying speed, past the outermost walls of rendered, desiccated skeletons meshed together with metal and earth and into the bowels of this monstrosity. The twisted screams of countless people piped through vents and tunnels, channels and hallways. The flesh gave way to damp stone—the worst vision of a medieval past. Everything smelled like rotten blood and piss. Wet straw on the floor crawled with life and unlife, each consuming the other. Monsters leered, snarled, bickered and fought. The bodies of human slaves worked to death were abused by snorting, squealing creatures in the halls.

Calmly, my slave. A level, deep voice broke through the infernal whispering and the flickering, overpowering weight of memory. A man's voice. *This is an Engine of the Morphorde. You are brave and strong, and nothing is inescapable. Not even No-thing.*

The pressure and speed at which I moved through this place terminated in a room filled with dead, gray light. An emaciated Gift Horse Mare hung by one heel from a huge steel tree. She was nude, covered in weeping sores, and stared through me with piercing red eyes. Those eyes were the last thing I saw before the experience of the place condensed into a vortex of horrific, half-glimpsed visions. Of small, white-haired, dark-skinned men like Glory chained to dungeon walls by their hearts, pierced by chains dripping with their silver blood. Monsters, tearing at people around me, throwing them into pits and dashing them against walls. Packs of twenty or thirty Ruined Stallions gang-raping prisoners, prisoners preying on each other... and then my spirit burst into an enormous diamond-shaped chamber where a tall, cowled figure stood within the center of a glowing white and silver garden.

Half a dozen MahTrees were planted in square, rusted metal pots big enough to hold a fully-grown silver birch. They were leafless and sick. The air was torn with their silent weeping, their futile strain to reach one another with their naked branches over the head of the nine foot tall, black-robed figure who contemplated them. Its robe was short enough I could see their boots: cleated, bloody, the spikes dug into what could only be the soil of Eden. That figure sucked in the light around it, and when it turned, I felt a bone-deep, inescapable, wrenching terror. I felt the terror of a little boy watching his father advance on him with a weapon, of knowing, with full certainty, that he would be destroyed.

... You are brave and strong, and nothing is inescapable. Not even No-thing...

The MahTree let me go and I snapped back to my body. I tore away from her and vomited around the gag and onto the floor.

I was still puking when the slab-like iron doors across the room opened, and lights glared into the meat locker where me and the Tree were imprisoned. A deep rumbling sound rattled my teeth, and the reek of exhaust briefly overrode the smell of rotting meat as a truck slowly and awkwardly backed up toward us. It looked like a cement-mixing truck, much larger than the one that we'd found at the funeral home. A digester truck. The one that had gone missing.

The driver had little idea of what they were doing. The truck moved forward and back, angling weirdly, lurching, and then jerking to a stop. The cabin door opened, striking the edge of the entryway with a sharp bang, and Glory's angry cursing broke through the sounds of my retching. Unbound, I probably could have escaped. Tied up and surrounded by Philimites, head hot as memories continued to flood in under the surface of my consciousness, I could do nothing but watch the small Gift Horse as he broke open a panel from the side of the truck with a crowbar, swearing and muttering to himself, and pulled out a long hose from inside.

"He has come. You must flee," the Tree said. Her voice was… different. Clearer, the words formed with greater clarity.

"How?" The sickness was passing, but I was still tightly bound, dry-mouthed, and the pain was fading back in. Blearily, I struggled to kneel and groped for my magic. It was there, kindling deep in my belly. I'd barely formed the word of power in my mind's eye when whatever was around my neck turned hot and began to squeeze. I fought against it as my breath cut, but it quickly became unbearable, tight enough to almost dislocate my head from my spine.

"That's right! No juice for you!" Glory dragged the hose along the floor toward us, crushing bugs or kicking them aside as they swarmed away from the corpses in an excited, chittering mass. He delicately stepped over the edge of the circle, careful not to mar the lines, and the magic flexed and recoiled from him before resealing. I blinked, unsure I'd seen what I'd just seen as he lugged the hose in beside the pot and dropped it. It hit the flagstone floor with a thump. "What a sight for sore eyes you are. But it's done, nearly finished... nearly time to sleep."

The Ruined Stallion moved toward me with the same sensuous, fluid step I'd watched in the Bronx. He palmed my head as he unbuckled the gag, pulled it free, and threw it dismissively to the floor.

"You're sick," I said. "Let us help you."

Glory leaned in until his nose almost touched mine, and the violently rotten smell of corrupted Phi and old blood washed over me. His breath was fetid, and when I tried to turn my head, he caught my chin in his rough fingers. "You *are* helping. And I'm going to help *you*, Alexi. Listen to me... I'm going to tell you a secret. A very special secret, just between you and me. You see, I know you. I know you better than you know you. And I know that you have struggled, and fought, and that you hate feeling like this around me, don't you? You hate how beautiful I am, and what other men do to you. I've watched you fight it, just like I do."

The schizoid prattling was made more disturbing by his low, intimate tone, the way he stroked my skin and tried to gaze into my eyes. It reminded me strongly of Jana, the way her nipples had stood out against the front of her dress as she forced me to strip at gunpoint. "Glory, please-"

"You want to know my secret?" Glory hissed. "You? The *other* you? The *first* one? I know him inside and out...

and you want to know what he is? What his 'soul' turned him into? A slut. A whore. A filthy sodomite. You know that voice in your head? The one that calls itself 'Kutkha'? You want to know what it did to the *first* Alexi Sokolsky, the *original*? It made him a *slave*."

Calmly, my slave. Disturbed, I searched back for Kutkha, but found only a dark, heavy silence, as if a partition had been put up between us.

"You think... hahaha... you think I'm exaggerating, don't you?" Glory stroked my cheek, my neck, my chest. "You think I'm lying, don't you? No, no, no. I know you. The oldest part of you, the man who could have been so much, is a pathetic rentboy, whored out by his old, perverted Master to anyone who's willing to pay for him. He stole you from me and he *defiled* you."

I stared at Glory, perplexed, as he tried to stroke the Tree, who flinched away from him. He was tearing up as he refocused on me. "But not you, no... no, no, no. He won't get you. Because *I've* got you, right here. You and my Mother, at last. We're going to be free together."

Something occurred to me then. We *were* alone. There was no one else here: no TVS personnel helping him, no one driving the truck. I swallowed, eyes widening. "The Deacon... he doesn't know you're here, does he?"

Glory smiled, and for a moment, he was almost beautiful. "Oh no. He thinks he is my Master. A HuMan puppet in a coat of many colors, that's all he is. 'Lord of Time', hah. They all think like that, you know. Those Temporalists. They forget that time is less important than experience."

That cunning little bastard. "How long have you been using him?"

He flashed a crooked grin, almost bashful... an expression that abruptly fled his face as he cupped my cheeks in both his hands. His palms were clammy and cold, like frog skin. Hard, determined, the caress turned into a stranglehold as he stood, dragging me up with him. The wiry little Gift Horse might as well have been three hundred pounds of solid muscle. He pulled me around like a kitten as I struggled against his grip, pushing my face down into the tarnished soil. The Tree recoiled as he held me there, reaching down to cut the thick bands of zip ties constricting my lower legs. As soon as my legs were free, I kicked back like a horse with my better leg, snarling when I only found air. He slid up behind me, and for a horrified moment, I wondered if he was going to fuck me instead of kill me. I fought heedlessly, thrashing as the sick fruit smell washed over me, but he was still clothed. He bent over my back, sunk his sharp, glassy teeth into the meat of my shoulder, and ripped out a chunk of flesh.

Agony. I screamed before I could help myself, and with the fresh pain came a wave of panicked energy. Glory reared back, chewing noisily, and I struggled in outraged terror as he went back for a second mouthful, then a third. Blood poured down my back and onto the MahTree's roots as I pushed back against him, snarling.

The Tree meant me no harm, but I was still a Wise Virgin and she was a creature of Eden. She seemed to swell with a silent gasp. Glory chortled and muttered to himself as he messily fed on the meat of my shoulder, holding me down as a living sacrifice. My blood obliterated the tarnish on the soil and restored its silver sheen. I felt the Tree's trunk straightening, filling out. She kindled with luminous light even as her silent sorrow reached a fever pitch.

"Run. Please find a way." The Tree's branches curled inward like shielding arms as she fed greedily, unwillingly, on the blood that spread across her depleted soil.

When he was sure that the wound was large enough, Glory rolled me over onto my back and straddled my chest, pinning me awkwardly with his slight weight. He had a thin stiletto knife in his hand. He was healing, too: The white sores were shrinking, skin repairing, chest swelling as he drew a deep, clear breath. His muscles, atrophying with rot, were filling out. I bucked underneath him, trying to throw him off as he raised the blade overhead.

"It's time." Glory's expression was one of pure joyous mania, violet eyes glowing with mingled excitement and madness. "Goodbye, my sweet."

And with one sure stroke, he cut his own throat.

CHAPTER 37

Putrid, thick gray fluid burst from the Ruined Gift Horse's carotid, the spray explosion of a punctured artery. Glory's expression was one of orgasmic wonder as he pulled the knife down through his carotid and collapsed onto my face, spasming and rattling his way to a quick, violent death.

"Run! Run! Get away!" The MahTree's scream of warning cut through my shock.

The magic circle—an enchantment that must have been bound to his blood—failed around us as Glory choked to unconsciousness. Three things happened simultaneously: I slithered to the floor under his dead weight, slippery with rotten Phi. The hose leading from the truck shuddered, then began to pump thick white fluid onto the filthy ground, and the Philimites surged toward us in a wave of legs, spines, and sucking proboscises, emitting high, off-key shrills.

The cuffs on my wrists rattled and fell off as I slid into the puddle of mingled Gift Horse and rendered Weeder Phi. I struggled back to my knees again as the first bugs reached it and began to feed—and grow. The truck was

447

humming, the pump fueled by whatever trigger Glory had laid on it. I staggered up to my feet, and turned to see the Tree swelling, thrashing, and darkening to a nasty bruised purple color as her son bled onto her roots.

"*Run!*" She was fighting it, but the corruption moved through her like water being drawn up a syringe.

Still bleeding, I staggered past the truck, ignoring the sharp pinpricks of Philimite bites. I'd barely squeezed past the cab when the air around me darkened and warped. A tingling numbness gathered in my limbs, a sensation followed by waves of giddy, masochistic madness. The air behind me breathed on the back of my neck, wet and sticky, as a high-pitched shriek of insane, piercing laughter pushed me out into the room beyond the door, a void of space littered with rubble and trash, and lit only by the lights of the grinder truck.

Turn back. There was a small, mad, compelling voice in me, neither myself or Kutkha, who reveled as I limped out ahead of the squealing, chittering, screaming tumult behind me. It was manic, gleeful even. *You did this! You didn't stop him. You deserve this!*

"No!" I pulled at the collar—it had melted, losing its rigid shape as it oozed into a loose hanging loop around my neck. I turned and threw it back toward the door, only to glimpse a thick, fleshy limb—a misshapen, tentacle-like root—slither out of the door and up over the cab of the truck. The shrieks sounded like Glory. *He was still alive in there?*

The MahTree's empathic aura was weaponizing as she expanded, corrupted, and multiplied. The bodies had been tinder; the Philimites, my blood and Glory's were the matches, and the Weeder sludge was the fuel propelling her to rapid, agonizing growth. The air was wracked by her screeching, pulses of raw emotional energy that cracked like whips across my nerves, dulling them even as I wept and stumbled down a flight of broken stairs. I fell down the last couple, plunging onto an old train platform facing flooded tracks. There were a few small red lights at the ceiling level, flickering as the Phitonic storm above and behind me built to overwhelming force, pushing me down to hands and knees.

Go back! You made this! You killed Vassily! You deserve this!

"No!" Visions of the Engine quickened my pulse, battling with the hallucinations of the Yen. It was feeding me a movie reel of getting to my feet, staggering back up the stairs, and running to Her. I lost my sense of reality, feeling myself stand, feeling myself throw my arms wide as I went back to embrace the Tree, my body erupting ecstatically with shards of bloody glass. It was glass that fed off the putrid Phi, the desolation of the ruins, and my own hysteric, giggling exultation. My imagination had me dance madly through my own death as the Tree erupted with fruits along her trunk, like enormous lipomas, that burst and released skeletal figures who shambled to me and tore me apart. Wherever my flesh was pulled away, more Stained Glass grew, multiplying until I was a walking, jagged bomb, careening blindly into a wall and shattering into a fertile mess of new Yen.

The hallucination played over and over as I slapped and scratched at the ground with my hands, fighting the erotic, giddy self-destructive energy that surged through me. The Yen wasn't playing it subtle any more. It was wailing on me, pumping my veins full of adrenaline and endorphins. The MahTree's siren song built to a fever pitch, rattling the rotten subway tunnel and raining concrete and scree down on my head.

Jaws working, I lashed my head from side to side and clawed at the torn flesh of my shoulder with the nails of my other hand, crying out at the sharp pain that felt all too much like a glass cut. When I looked down, I saw them— the first protruding shards, growing from the wounds lie spear points. They vanished as soon as I blinked.

"No!" My hand, the walls, the floor were wriggling, and the train tunnel was full of a thundering racket that had been enmeshed with the harbinger moan of the Ruined Tree until it was almost on top of me.

In pure dread, I gaped as half a dozen huge, dark shapes burst out into view; apocalyptic horsemen tall in their saddles as their enormous chargers clambered and leapt up onto the crumbling platform. The one in the lead barreled toward me, only to pull up sharply on the reins. Sick as I was, details filtered in: The animal was eighteen hands or more at the withers and built like a tank. Thickset, powerfully muscled, with a horn the shape and size of a scimitar curving from the center whorl of its forehead. Split hooves, like a camel or a deer, zebra-like tail with a whisk at the end; it resembled a unicorn like a dump truck resembled a Ferrari.

The huge animal slid on the loose rubble, prancing as the rider reined her in and looked down. The rider's features were obscured by a sleek black helmet, part of a leather bodysuit that looked like something out of a movie. The opaque full-face visor was smooth and crystalline, like the eye of a praying mantis.

"Alexi!?" The voice was eerily familiar.

"We're too late! It's already started!" A woman called from behind.

The sound of my name jolted me out of the growing fugue of hysteria, bringing the newcomers into focus. Six riders, armed to the teeth and now struggling to control the cloven-hoofed animals who plunged and bucked with terror. They were crying out, high whistling squeals nothing like a horse's whinny.

"Zarya! Grab him and run! We didn't make it in time!" The first rider snapped, his voice hard and oddly familiar.

Zarya? A rider pulled up alongside me and reached a hand down. I was too sick, too numb, and too weak to take it. *That can't be right. Zarya's dead.*

"Come on, come on, come ON!" The rider vaulted to the ground, hauled me up under the armpits, and threw me over the saddle as the others turned back the way they'd come. The tunnel rumbled, and old instinct finally kicked in. I grasped the animal's stiff mane and held on as the rider pulled herself back up behind me, wrapped an arm around my waist, and pulled her mount around to join the others. Three of the riders, the ones now behind us, started shooting at the stairwell doors with weapons that sounded like airsoft launchers as we charged for the edge of the platform.

"I failed!" I gasped aloud, struggling against the too-strong arm around my waist. "Let me go! I failed her! They're all dead because of me!"

Humanoid creatures were pouring down the broken stairs: naked, twisted, masked by clots of ragged white hair, they brandished make-shift swords in their hands. I reached out for them, flailing back at the tall rider who held me, twisting with sobs as we angled for the edge of the platform and leaped out into the darkness. The moment of weightlessness took my breath away, and then the impact even more so. It jarred my chest, and I coughed up a gout of frothy blood onto the animal's neck. The pain stunned me into stillness so that I passively hung, too wrung out to fight.

The squadron of riders loped into the wet darkness of the underground rail yard, their animals whistling in terror as the ground and the roof shook. The rain of gravel had turned to chunks, heavy missiles that fell down around us as distant sirens pealed through the tunnels. A distant clacking sound was getting closer, and all of the animals fell into a column as we tilted left and raced down into a narrower, dark corridor. The horned horse-like creature squealed as it plunged, terrified, into the murk of the subway. There were no lights down here, but as we ran, I heard her hooves splash through water.

"*Ei-ei-ey!*" My captor called to her mount and bent us forward, her arm tightening around my waist. "Hold on as tight as you can, *bat'ko!*"

Bat'ko? There was only one person who had ever called me that, but Zarya was dead. I'd killed her.

Our mount made an unearthly vibratory sound. The powerful muscles of her forequarters bunched, hooves digging into the stone between train tracks as she shot forward and leaped out and up. My rider came forward and tucked her head down against my shoulder, both arms around my midriff. We hit water and plunged. The shallow pond swallowed us, pulling us into a void of weightless green Everything.

LoveYouLoveYouLoveYouLoveYouLoveYouLoveYouLoveYouLoveYouLoveYouLoveYouLoveYou...

It was cold. The vacuum howled like a cyclone as we fell, and then swam. Light blazed around the pair of us: Kutkha's energy shielded my body in a ball, a caul of blue-black light trailing from my body like the tail of a comet. Around and behind me, the rider was awash in green and white liquid fire that shimmered, seethed, and boiled. I couldn't speak, feel my hands, or breathe. The pressure of that great, singular sentience boomed around and through us, rattling every cell.

...LoveYouLoveYouLoveYouLoveYouLoveYou...

I was mad. Coming apart. There was no Alexi any more.

We burst out of water only slightly less filthy than the slurry in the flooded subway, still underground. It was warmer here, a heavy, dusty deep hush, like an old church. The animal struggled out of the pool, champing at the bit and rolling her eyes as she climbed onto dry ground. The others followed us out, forcing us to move up a flight of worn stone steps to make room as more beasts and their riders appeared out of nowhere.

"*Aiiigooo*, that was close." The rider right behind us brought his animal next to us, and reached out to me with a gloved hand. I watched it encroach, mystified. How was this possible? Hadn't I run back to the Tree? Wasn't I in the Engine? Where was Vassily? My wrist was taken in firm fingers. "Zarya, he's fading hard."

"I know."

"He might have Ruined the Mother. I'm-"

"I would know if he was Morphorde, Angkor."

What an awkward hallucination. Zarya and Angkor, here, together? Next thing, my mother was going to walk out of a wall with Binah in her arms and the Ukrainian flag draped around her shoulders. Strangely, I couldn't see anyone who was talking any more. The room had dimmed, the plants and walls and light blurring into each other.

"Breathe, *bat'ko*. We're almost there."

Breathe? How hilarious. My hands and face were numb, my vision a darkening tunnel. It was very important that Zarya didn't see the shards of glass I felt blocking my throat, so I reached up and pawed at my neck, trying to pull them free as the world swam and turned dark, then plummeted past me as I fell down a howling tunnel and hit bottom, landing on my back.

A sweet, painfully familiar smell washed over me. Warm, slender hands pushed mine away; lips covered my mouth and breathed for me, pushing air into the agonized swamp of my lungs. The flood of oxygen startled me up out of semi-consciousness, enough that I could open my eyes.

Zarya was gazing down at me, and her eyes were no longer blue. They were as white as winter skies, a piercing, liquid silver churning with bated power. The Gift Horse's fragile milk quartz skin had firmed and darkened, dappled in tones that ranged between marble white and a cool blueish brown. Her hair was still white, but cut shorter than it had been when I pulled her out of the womb of the Rind. It slipped over her cheeks, flossy and fine, hanging around her face. She had the kind of face that you could search and never be able to categorize, her features shifting from Arabic to Caucasian, Asiatic to African depending on the angle and the way the light hit her.

I stared at her in numb disbelief, mouth thick with the taste of blood. "Zarya?"

"Yes." She carefully scooped me up into a bridal carry, standing as if I didn't weigh anything at all. "Don't worry, *Bat'ko*—you're going to be okay."

CHAPTER 38

"He's got a punctured lung." Angkor's voice came from somewhere beyond my tunnel vision, oddly distant. "You should let me-"

"It's fine. I've got him," Zarya replied curtly. "Go tend your wounded—come and see me once you're free."

"Okay. Okay I'll... I'll be there soon, alright?"

I hung in the Gift Horse's arms as she carried me into a tent. The floor was covered in foam mats with reflective silver backs and army-style sleeping bags. Zarya lay me down and propped me up on the injured side. It hurt like a bitch, but the weird folded position made it easier to breathe.

Gasping, I watched her go to a large ALICE-style Army rucksack and rifle through it, searching frantically for something.

"Wh-whh?" Dizzily, I tried to move by myself and failed. Everything was heavy and fuzzy at the edges.

Zarya didn't reply, fussing with cotton and a small glass bottle. The sharp green smell of peppermint cut the sweet fragrance of Phi as she soaked the plugs and jammed them into her nose. She sniffed a few times, shaking her head.

"Peppermint oil. I'm sorry, Father," she replied thickly in Ukrainian, facing me. "You're still a virgin... the smell of your blood would knock me out if I didn't get this first."

Words failed me as we gazed at one another. She'd grown. In blue fatigue pants and a thin-strap tank top, she was a ribbon of lean muscle, almost seven feet tall. The weak, sick, fragile creature I'd Pacted on the floor of the Manelli's processing plant had died, and this Zarya had replaced her.

"You're alive." My voice was a wet rasp.

"Yes." She breathed the word like an incantation, and unseen power ruffled over my skin. "You fulfilled the Pact. I told you we'd see each other again."

I'd killed her, eaten her, and watched her vanish, but she was *here*. I reached out in shock, fingers trailing over her shoulder. As I did, Zarya cupped my face in gloved hands, smiling. Her eyes—now so much like Kutkha's— were wet with unshed tears. I stared up at her, wonder mingling with fear as that awful, hot night in August came rushing back in a torrent of imagery and sound.

My eyes brimmed with sudden tears. "Vassily didn't make it."

"I know." Zarya let go of my face, and grabbed the other thing she'd pulled from the bag: a dagger in a functional leather sheath. Vision swimming, I watched her pull the blade, and stared at the weapon in sudden hunger.

"They turned him into a monster." A wracking shudder passed through my limbs. "Z-Zarya, please-"

"This isn't for you." The Mare shook her head and set the edges between her lips. She pursed them as she drew the blade forward. The soft flesh parted like a peach, silver blood streaming from the cuts. I drew a deep, painful breath at the smell. High, floral, humming like a live wire, it cleared the air like a shockwave. Light seemed brighter, breathing became easier. She knelt down over me, and brought my head up so that I could meet her mouth with mine.

"It will be okay." Zarya's bloody kiss rolled through me like thunder, sheet lightning lancing down into my mouth to stab up behind my eyes, blasting through my gut, energizing every nerve. I could feel my heart squeeze, my cells regenerate, divide, and then die off according to some ineffable design.

My cock hardened and I stiffened with it, shaking uncontrollably through an ecstatic, painless release. The pain ebbed away, and in its wake was nothing but *Light!* and a deep, savage hunger. I surged up against Zarya, driven by instinct so powerful that I ceased feeling the rest of my body entirely. It was all mouth and greedy, swallowing throat. Everything vibrated, steadily building in both volume and power, consolidating into the sound of GOD's heart beating through time and space. It always said the same thing.

...LoveYouLoveYouLoveYouLoveYouLoveYou...

As the Phi put me under, I saw Kutkha in a nest spun of MahTree branches, his head tucked under his wing, and

I felt – and somehow, observed – the way that this Tree's roots had meshed through my body. Seams of light were braided along my spinal cord and the big nerves of my torso and legs like veins of gold in quartz.

The Rhizomes, I realized, not without a little wonder – and fear. What did this mean for me? For Kutkha? For the Tree?

Consciousness returned gently and slowly, like the rising sun. I was warm, soaked with sweat, and covered by an open sleeping bag. The bag was damp and dirty from the filth that had been ejected from my skin, a slurry of dirt, infection, and toxins pushed out by the flux of Zarya's blood. My shoulder was healed, the flesh that Glory had taken filled back in with new, silvery-pink tissue. The throbbing, infected wound no longer hurt. As I moved and stretched, there were small aches and pains. The muscle memory of the injuries lingered, the ache of freshly healed nerves adjusting to normalcy. I looked at the inside of my arm: the Glagolitic symbols I'd used to code Lee's coordinates had scarred over. They were faint, but legible.

"Zarya?" I called out to her in the thick silence. She wasn't in the tent, and it was zipped up—both layers. Puzzled, I started to get up and put my hand down on a pile of neatly folded clothes. They were approximately my size: a coverall and a t-shirt, underwear, and to my relieved surprise, a pair of thin leather gloves.

Once I was dressed, I pushed my way out of the tent into a camp that occupied a huge dilapidated building, a grand hall that was partly open to the night sky. Close to half the ceiling was missing, but the rain and wind that lashed New York never reached the camp. It hit a translucent energy barrier, an orange-tinted field that sparked and shivered under the icy assault of the storm. And just as well: the sky was a weird, sick grey-green, moaning and rumbling with spiraling clouds.

The only people outside were guards watching the entry and exit points. The futuristic workstations were now only manned by one person, a stocky, sandy-blond man in a black t-shirt and urban camouflage pants. He had his feet up on the black gun crates that served as his desk. He was ugly as sin from the neck up, fleshy and flat-featured, but he had the plush, muscular build of a Marine and the same kind of jarhead haircut. He was chewing gum and typing one-handed on a small, flat keyboard that didn't seem to have any keys: just patches of rainbow-hued light that lit up every time his fingers pattered over it.

"You looking for His Royal Whoreness?" The guy called out to me as I slowly wove my way toward him.

"Uh." I hung back at a respectable distance. He looked HuMan—but after what I'd seen, who knew? "Do you mean-?"

"Angkor?" He pronounced his name like 'Ang-gore', with the kind of hard accent that made me think of Chicago or Milwaukee. "Yeah. That's who I'm talking about. Last time I saw him, he and Zarya were off in the bushes together. But that was a couple hours ago."

Together? My gut clenched. "I see. And who are you, exactly?"

"Lieutenant COMMO Douglas Digger at your service, Sir." He saluted with one finger to his brow, not looking away from the flashing screen. An action movie...

no. A video game, because he was clearly interacting with it. But one so realistic that it was almost indistinguishable from a movie.

I stared at him dully. "Of the...?"

"ANSWER Cellular Scout Corps. COMMO division."

It was difficult not to stare at his screen in astonishment. "And they do...?"

"Technically, I'm the COMM's Officer attached to the Flying Fucks, which is the bulk of the Cellular Scout squadron you see before you," He pulled out a napkin and spat his gum into it, then reached for a bottle of crystal cola. "Realistically, I'm Angkor's substitute mom and a spittoon all rolled up in one."

I regarded this man—he really looked like a 'Doug', not a 'Mr. Digger'—with a deepening sense of madness. I wasn't quite convinced I was awake. "Right. You... have a history together?"

"I've been Angkor's COMMO for so long that I'm basically an armchair serial killer," Doug said. "The kind of shit I have to listen to over that fucking radio... Like, for his birthday once, I played him 'Happy Birthday to You' with a track made up of all the grunting, screaming Gift Horse murdergasms he's had over the years."

"Clearly I know less about him than I thought I did," I said.

"You're not the first person to say that."

Not Zarya, apparently. "Do you know where he is now?"

461

"Probably sucking something's dick. Go check down under the chapel," Doug replied. "First building from the rear exit, down the stairs. Watch out for the Tulaq."

Too-lack? "The what?"

"Tulaq. Big teeth. Flappy wings." Doug made a Tinkerbell wing motion with his hands. "If she gives you any shit, just tell her that Zarya and Digger say you're cool."

Tulaq. Right. I nodded stiffly. "One last question. Where are we?"

Doug arched his eyebrows, which made him look even more like a pug. "North Brother Island. The old sanitarium. Jeez, they didn't tell you anything, did they?"

"No, they didn't. Thank you." I nodded curtly and withdrew, shivering inside of the coverall. The craving for a drink was echoing in my head again... something strong and sour, like the way I felt about anything involving Angkor and Zarya, together.

CHAPTER 39

The chapel Doug described appeared at first glance to be solid after almost a hundred years of neglect. I slunk out under the eerie umbrella that covered the old sanitarium, the building where Typhoid Mary had spent her final days. I gazed off into the horizon, and saw the city bathed in thick smog... or smoke. From here, the devastation that had to be taking place could not be seen. It felt remote. Surreal, even.

The bare, dusty chapel had an air of sanctity that was unmistakable—a cool, sweet-smelling hush that fell over my shoulders like a mantle as I pressed in and went down a flight of stairs. Instinct led me unerringly to an arched underground room that was half excavated earth, half stone.

I opened the old door into a wall of humid heat: damp, hot air heavy with the smell of moss and lush greenery. Vines and roots clung to the broken remains of the chapel's basement. Radiant light broke through the ceiling in places, including the makeshift dais where a strange machine thrummed and pulsed with light—and life. It reminded me somewhat of an amphora, but it was much larger, and had a wet, silvery surface that rippled with motion just under the surface. Angkor sat in front of it on his bed, a thin air mattress, sharpening a small armory's worth of rainbow-hued knives with a whetstone. His head jerked up at the sound of the door.

"Alexi." He set the knife down and stood in alarm. He was still wearing the bodysuit I'd seen on him during our horse ride out of the sewers. "You're alive."

The sight of him made me feel oddly tired. Angkor was still beautiful enough to make my pulse pound. Full-lipped, sloe-eyed, his dark hair tousled from his helmet, my body responded to the sight of him with bittersweet hunger. I didn't know how I felt about that. "Angkor."

He approached me at a quick walk, searching my face as he closed in. I was about to say something – try to get angry at him, maybe – when he lay his long hands against the front of my shoulders and, after a moment's hesitation, pulled me into a stiff-armed embrace.

"I'm sorry I couldn't make it," he said. "Truly. Please believe me when I say that I couldn't find a way to let you know what had happened."

I breathed in the familiar sweet-spicy smell of his neck, and haltingly returned the embrace. "It's… it's not 'okay'. But I'll hear you out, 'Zealot'."

He stood back from me, hands still resting on my arms. "Who'd you pick that up from?"

"Kristen Cross's report to Norgay, whoever he is," I replied. "That was the first time I heard it. I figured out who it was when Lee Harrison died in my arms."

His mouth framed a silent 'O' for a moment, and the light in his eyes faltered as he scowled and looked down.

"Zealot of what?" I shrugged him off, not entirely gently. "There's already two parties of fanatics in this game. I don't know if I'm comfortable knowing there's a third."

He laughed, a little hollowly. "Zealots are a unit in a video game called StarCraft. It, uh, hasn't been invented here yet. Seven years from now."

I stared at him, puzzled.

"StarCraft is kind of a big deal in South Korea." He smiled sheepishly, and shrugged. "Like, it's a televised professional sport for people who can't play sports. It's a wargame with three factions. I was a Protoss player, and Zealots are one of the main Protoss units, so…"

I held up a hand. "What do you mean, seven years from now?"

"I don't know if you remember me telling you about Cells." Angkor sobered, and the subtle physical connection between us faded as he crossed his arms and rested his weight back on his heels. "Cells are planets, the 'cells' within GOD's mass. I told you I was a traveler between worlds. Well, that's true. Not all Cells are synchronous. Some are in the future or the past, relative to this world. The shortest explanation I have for that is that the closer a Cell is to the Skin of GOD, the more 'in the future' it is and the faster time passes. So to quote Arnie, I'm from the future. Make sense?"

"More than anything else I've had to deal with in the last twelve hours." I shrank into myself, grasping my own arm and squatting to rest on the floor. It wasn't just Angkor that made me tired: it was everything. It was the echoing rapport of the MahTree's screams, and the warring need to tell Angkor what had happened with Joshua Keen, and the Tigers, and... everything. "Look. I was pissed off at you for leaving without saying anything. I think I'm still pissed off, but not as much as I was. Not after talking to Lee Harrison."

"What happened to her?" Angkor squatted down, too. Like me, he could do it flat-footed. That lifted my mood, momentarily.

"She died," I said. "The Vigiles killed her while we were escaping their holding facility. Before you ask, I never met Kristen. Ayashe called me in to look at the crime scene after she was murdered by her own people."

"Shit. It *was* them." Angkor winced, looking down pensively at the ground. "Dammit. That means I screwed up even worse than I thought I had."

"Why? How?"

He gestured toward the city. "The MahTree. I was here because of her, all this time. She sent out a distress call and broadcast her position just before we arrived. I guess she'd been too weak to do it before then. Now she's Ruined. They're sending the military out to shoot her and bomb her, and you know what that does to Morphorde. She's going to get bigger, and she's going to burrow into this world like a metastatic cancer and we... I failed her. And you. Everyone."

"It's not over yet." I reached back to rub my neck. There were no scars, not even scabs, but somehow I knew that what I'd seen in my Phi-fueled dream was real. The Tree had given me something that was now part of my body, and it was something that could be used to help her. "And there's people who need us. The Vigiles set up Jenner and all the other Tigers at the fight they're having tonight."

"Tonight or last night?"

I paused for a moment. "What day is it? How long was I out?"

Angkor gave me a look that was almost sympathy. "It's the first of November."

"Shit." I breathed slowly and stared at the wall. "Then it's already over, and the Vigiles have them. We have to go and help her."

Angkor cocked his head to the side, biting his lip. "That depends-"

"There's no fucking 'it depends'. She saved your ass from the TVS. She housed you and fed you when you had nothing."

"It *depends* if we can even reach them." Angkor's head jerked up, eyes dark with warning. "You haven't seen what the Tree is doing to the city."

Even as he said that, a deep moan rumbled through the foundations of the building, and the amphora-shaped whatever-it-was flared, crackling with orange light. A familiar burned-crayon-wax smell cut through the room, sharp and chemical. Angkor didn't seem to notice: He reached down to a pouch on his belt, fumbling for his cigarettes.

"We're meeting with the commander of my division in about fifteen minutes," he said, reluctantly. "If he gives the all-clear, we'll look into it. If not-"

"There's no 'if'," I replied. "I don't care if you and your ANSWER division approve or not. I don't care if this 'Norgay' is the damn President. If you won't go, I will."

"ANSWER isn't part of the U.S. military," he replied, lighting up. His hands were shaking. "We're not even from this world. We're an interstitial paramilitary. Anti-Morphorde, pro-GOD. I'm not from this planet. Hell, I'm not even from this fucking time period. I was still a kid during 1991 on my home Cell."

"I don't care." I stood, too agitated to remain close to the ground. "They're my people – *our* people. We're going for them."

"I'll be holding off on a decision until I speak to the Director." Angkor shook his head, blowing a plume of smoke toward the floor. "No offense, Alexi… I like you, and I respect you, but I don't know if I trust you."

That hit me like a dull blow to the gut. "What? Why? What have I done that's untrustworthy?"

"An informant told me you were having your wrist twisted by the Vigiles." Angkor's face was hard, jaws tense. "I personally saw you break into the Church of the Voice carrying a Vigiles weapon, covered in human blood. Later, you were cooperating with Elij… Glory. I figured-"

"His name's Elijah?" The name made something ripple up along my spine, a weird tingling rush that prickled all the hair on my neck.

"Before he was Ruined," Angkor said, reluctantly. "His true name. Anyway. I figured you'd bargained with Elijah and the Deacon to get away from the Vigiles."

So much for not being angry. "You really think I'd deal with that child-murdering, child-fucking-?"

"I think you're a criminal," he said sharply. "From an organized crime family, who was being pressured to help a lawful evil organization he hates. Given the choice between two evils, I figured you'd do what it took to survive. It was a hypothesis."

"I stuck my neck out for you." Fury curled my tongue and made my hands ball up. As I took a step forward, Angkor bobbed up smoothly to his feet. "I fucking risked my pride, my self-respect, my reputation to try to get close to you. You saw me being raked over the coals by the *Deutsche Orden*, and you did nothing except make up bullshit about me in your head?"

"Alexi-"

"Do you want to know what the Deacon offered me to kill you?" I snapped my jaws together on the last word, advancing on him. "He offered me a trip back in time to save my sworn brother. Sergei's turned him into a fucking *monster*, and I could kill you and undo what was done to him, Angkor. If I said 'yes'."

"You couldn't." His face had drained of all expression.

"I won't," I said. "Because I don't work for men like the Deacon, or Joshua Keen. I'm sick of men like them, and I'm sick of cowards and liars like you."

"Don't speak to me like that." Angkor's voice was cold now. "You don't know the first damn thing about me."

"You're right. Because you hid it all." I squared up my shoulders, fighting the urge to close in and deck him. "The Templars got Lee and Kristen. They got Ayashe, and they've probably got Jenner, Talya, and the rest. So you can stay here and live with your fucking hypotheticals, while *I* go help them."

"Your crusade can wait twenty minutes," Angkor said. His voice was cool now, like polished metal. "Norgay wants to speak with you."

"I'm going whether you and your boy scout troop do or not. And I'm taking Zarya with me."

"That's Zarya's decision to make," he said, voice dark with warning.

"She'll choose me," I stopped, but didn't turn. "Because she doesn't lie. She cares about me, and I gave everything—EVERYTHING—that I gave a shit about to save her."

"If you waited just a few damn minutes-"

"You thought I was going to turn on my people. You're right, Angkor, I am from a fucking crime family. And you know what the fastest way to piss off a *brat'ye* is? Tell him he's a *suka* who rats out and betrays his friends." I did turn on him then, pointing. "You keep your mercenary, manwhore ass out of her bed and out of her life, and you stay the *fuck* out of mine. I'll do whatever work we have to do, and then that's it. You can go back to space camp and keep pretending like you're a real fucking person."

"There's bigger things happening than your journey of self-discovery right now, okay?" Angkor's face was as sharp as a knife's edge now, eyes blazing and furious. "The MahTree, the harbingers... If we can't work together, then you can leave. I don't need your approval to be Zarya's Hound, or to try and save your world before it rots."

'Zarya's Hound?' I was Zarya's Hound. I wasn't sure what was worse: that he'd gotten to know her when I'd never had that chance, or that I'd been rejected by him for a woman.

My face heated. "This is *my* fucking world, not yours, and I know what's coming for it. And no, I'm not telling you. I'll tell Norgay directly before I leave."

"Suit yourself," Angkor said. His features had tightened to arrogant aloofness. "I'm sorry. I thought you cared more about us than your pride."

"I spent twenty-nine years having the worst assumed of me. I'll fight for the people who don't." I hawked and spat, and with that, marched off back for the sanitarium.

CHAPTER 40

We found Doug loafing around t inside the main camp area. He was standing near his station to stretch his back, soda in hand, and casually glanced over as we approached. He looked a lot fitter than he had when he was sitting down. "Hey, Angkor! Norgay called about briefing. He wants Zarya to be there."

"She's busy," Angkor said crisply. I let him move in front of me, trying not to glare at him as he put his back to me. "Tell him she'll-"

"No can do, Sir." If Doug noticed anything was wrong, he didn't show it. "He's not on the line yet. Said to call when everyone you want to dial in is available."

"That will be me and Zarya," Angkor said. His tone was decidedly frosty.

"No," I said. "I need to speak to Norgay."

Both Angkor and Doug turned, staring at me like I had two heads.

"I have a report from Kristen Cross to deliver, and information from Lee Harrison," I said. "Norgay's ears only."

"Wait." Angkor held up his hands. "You can't have Kristen's report. Not unless she didn't code it properly."

"You mean the flower seeds?" I said.

Angkor frowned. "Those seeds were specially designed to pass a message on to only one specific person—my commanding officer. Kristen was given blank seeds and an enchantment to be able to send a message to him."

Then you didn't even get that right. "Well, they didn't work properly. I planted them and saw the message."

"That isn't good. Section Six better up their game," Doug drawled.

Angkor rubbed his face. "*Shibal no ma.* Fine. Whatever. Just don't embarrass yourself in front of my commanding officer."

"And if you want to tell him he's an asshole about something, you have to preface it like: 'with all due respect, Sir'," Doug added. "That's an actual rule."

"Don't encourage him," Angkor snapped.

"Well, with all due respect, Sir..."

"I swear to GOD, Doug, I'll never buy you crystal soda ever again."

Across the sanitarium chamber, I spotted a flicker of white: Zarya, mounting the steps as she strode toward us. I grunted. "She's here."

Angkor brightened and straightened, and I felt a powerful wave of jealousy as she saw us—saw Angkor—and smiled. "Okay, let's go get this over with."

It felt strange to be doing something as banal as arranging a meeting where Zarya was involved. She was so unearthly that I found myself feeling dissociated as the four of us gathered at Doug's workstation. Guards were posted at the main door to the sanitarium—something of a formality, given that the building's walls were full of holes and half the ceiling was missing. I watched on dubiously as Doug's fingers flew over the keyless keyboard, and he brought up a window on screen. It was very like what Talya had done on her computer, but... I had no concept of what I was seeing, really.

"So, who was snitching to you in the Tigers?" I asked them all, arms crossed.

"Talya," Angkor replied, not looking at me. "We were able to get in touch with her on Usenet."

"And believe me, *that* was a trip," Doug said. "Last time I used a phone to dial into a modem was... jeez, I don't even remember. It was like trying to use the Batmobile to talk to a dinosaur."

I sighed, exasperated. "GODdammit, Talya."

"She gave me her dial-in," Angkor said. "Ages ago. I got in contact with her and explained what was going on. She's a Weeder... she understands the gravity of what's happening."

"She's just lost her gang for doing this," I said. "No matter how well intentioned. She's a snitch."

"She's a first-generation incarnate super-predator, and she knows the stakes," Angkor replied curtly. "The appearance of super-predators on a world like this one is a really bad sign. Her 'gang' won't hurt over what they don't know."

"Assuming she's not already been rendered down into her component Phi by the Vigiles." I didn't want to look at him, even though it was tempting to stare at the way the suit hugged his figure from behind. The Yen was still goading me, forcing my attraction to him.

Zarya drew up beside us, her smile fading as she looked between me and Angkor. I was slightly mollified when she came to me first, leaning in against me and bumping at my jaw with her mouth before turning to Angkor. She slid her hands over his shoulders, and turned her face to nuzzle at the side of his head, and the fractional improvement in my mood was dramatically and thoroughly crushed.

"Okay, fix your makeup, ladies." Doug had another program up now. "We're encrypted, online and live in three, two, one. Good morning, Sir. Can you see us?"

"I can. Thank you, Officer." A deep, oddly familiar baritone spoke over the line. The screen was now black with a logo showing: a white circle outlined in green with an eight-pointed star in the center. "I understand we've escalated to Crimson status?"

Angkor bowed from the waist, hands in tight fists by his sides. "Yes, Sir. I'm sorry, I-"

"Scouts don't apologize, Zealot." Norgay cut him off quietly and firmly. "They report, evaluate, revise, and proceed. As it stands, you overcame amnesia via torture, the removal of your CTRL Device, and attempted to salvage the operation to the best of your ability. How long have you been doing this job?"

"Seventy years, Sir." He muttered.

Seventy? I gawked at Angkor in shock. Given his magic specialty, I'd been willing to believe he was fifty, but... well. I guess he'd lied about that, too.

"Your case file has sixty-five years of successful operations up until this point," Norgay said. "We will review the collapse of the mission with that track record in mind."

Angkor had shut down into military mode, still and self-contained. He kept his eyes down, and for a moment, I almost felt sorry for him. "Thank you, Sir. We will do our best for the rest of the time we're here."

"I do not doubt you." Norgay was all parts dry, crisp, and articulate. "We have escalated to an emergency scenario, but that does not mean this Cell is lost—yet. With a Mare onsite, not to mention the man standing to your left, there's still a good chance we can salvage the situation on a larger scale. Speaking of that, are you well, Zarya?"

I stiffened in place. Even without an image, I had the strangest, dizzying sense of someone looking out from that mostly-blank screen.

"I am." Zarya's tone was formal, but she was smiling and relaxed.

"Your uncle was displeased to learn you are associating with miscreants like Zealot and Digger," Norgay remarked.

Doug laughed. "Mischief managed, Sir."

Zarya flushed—her cheeks and throat turned a silvery metallic blue. "I-"

"-Didn't intentionally go there to wallow in Digger's kiddy pool, we know." The unseen man's voice warmed with a touch of wry humor. "So. Zealot, give me your briefing. Then I will pass on our latest."

"With Alexi present, Sir?"

"I have on good authority that men in his line of work are known for their discretion," Norgay said, amused.

I blinked, and considered Zarya for a moment. She was standing at ease, hands behind her back, like she'd done it all her life. Maybe she'd told him about me.

Angkor sighed heavily. "Agent Cross is dead. Alexi has reported that the second Keeper is dead. Our last Keeper is still MIA, and his radio is unresponsive. We don't know if he or Lee divulged the location of the Shard. I'm concerned that they extracted the information from Lee and then had her disposed of."

"No." I shook my head. "It was an accident. She caught a round when we were escaping the Vigiles holding facility together. They were torturing her, and she broke out and rescued me. We made our way outside into Fresh Kills landfill, and she was shot just inside the perimeter fence."

"Oh, yeah." Angkor grimaced. "You were there, weren't you?"

"If they were interrogating her, I doubt they managed to get her to talk about her discovery. She had a ferocious will," Norgay said. "Did you overhear anything of the sort, Alexi?"

"No," I said. "They were in the middle of torturing her. From start to finish, all I heard were screams. She broke out of the torture room."

"If they were trying to get her to bend with pain, I guarantee she held her silence. Which means that two of the three have managed to keep their secret, and only one remains."

"Who else died over this?" I asked.

Angkor pressed his lips together in a thin line.

"You have permission to answer his question, Zealot," Norgay said, after a couple of tense seconds.

"It was Michael." Angkor nodded stiffly. "The leader of the Pathfinders. You remember him?"

I did. Michael had been the Elder of New York before Jenner. We'd discovered him half-transformed and eviscerated in Lily and Dru's forest bunker. I'd only met him twice: an ebony-skinned, bald, austere man with kind eyes and a formal, controlled air. "Yes."

"He was the hereditary Grovekeeper of this Cell," Angkor said. "And the true Elder of the state. I figured out that the Templum Voctus Sol were the ones who helped John Spotted-Elk into his position, probably to put him in a position to learn where to find the Garden. He didn't. Michael took his secret to the grave."

I rubbed the inside of my arm thoughtfully as I listened. Petty as it was, I didn't want to tell Angkor the coordinates Lee had given me. She'd trusted him, but she trusted Norgay more. And so did I. "I see. And there's a third?"

"Yes," Norgay replied. "Continue."

"There was a second Harbinger event which allowed us to find the location of the Spur fragment."

"Where?"

"Wall Street," Angkor admitted. "The Vigiles are making use of a building there, and we've got people watching it already. Besides that, we found Kristen Cross's final report on the involvement of the *Deutsche Orden* with the Vigiles. Or, more accurately, Alexi found it... and he decrypted the message. Which is why he is here."

"You might want to let the eggheads in Section Six know," Doug says. "Tell 'em their magic beans didn't work properly."

"I'll be sure to do that." Norgay sounded distinctly wry now. "Alexi, has Angkor briefed you on our essential mission here?"

"No," I said. "I've been neck-deep in conflict with the TVS since August and the Vigiles since earlier this month, but Angkor hasn't told me a damn thing."

"That is precisely what he was supposed to do," Norgay said. "But I will give you the essence of it. The MahTree who you were being held captive with is a refugee. Zealot risked his life and soul to go into a warzone and save her and several other trapped Trees a number of years ago, patiently regrowing them from nothing but roots and Rhizomes prior to finding shelter for them."

I glanced at Angkor's profile. He was stony-faced, eyes forward on the screen.

"Rehabilitation was mostly complete when Zealot's location was compromised by a paramilitary cult affiliated with the TVS," Norgay continued. "*Odaeyang.* They took the Tree and brought her here."

I nodded. "To America, or to this 'Cell'?"

"To this Cell. The local chapter of this cult was wiped out during an international conflict with the Crusaders. Both organizations are interstitial, having a presence on multiple worlds. The *Deutsche Orden*'s East Asian chapter assembled a multinational strike force to intercept the Tree and brought her to the U.S., where they have the best facilities for Phitometry."

"They *tortured* her." Zarya finally spoke, low and furious. I looked over at her. Her hands were fisted by her thighs. "Her final cry was… it was…"

"I have no doubt she was terribly abused," Norgay said. "But to continue. The Templum Voctus Sol briefly had possession of the Tree, and she was recently reclaimed during a raid on the Church of the Voice here, where they are based. Zealot has been pursuing this Tree since she was kidnapped."

"I think I know who's behind the *Deutsche Orden* and the Deacon's cult," I said. Whoever this Norgay was, I was pretty sure he needed to know what Celso and Lee had told me. "Lee told me that she was handed into the

Deutsche Orden by her father, who was himself a Crusader agent. She told me that he was being led by some kind of supernatural being called 'Munificence'. I convinced another man to talk, too: the son of a Mafia Don who's been working in opposition to the Deacon. He said that the Deacon answers to an 'angel', whose name is Providence."

At mention of Munificence's name, Angkor's head turned like an owl's, skin paling. Zarya made a stifled noise in her throat. Norgay said nothing at all.

"I, uh... I feel like I'm missing something here." Doug scratched his jaw, turning back to look at me.

Me too. I nodded.

"Did either of them describe Munificence or Providence?" Norgay's tone had hardened now. Seriousness, not anger.

"No description of Munificence, other than that she's apparently blind and there was some confusion as to her gender. Celso said Providence was an angel. Tall, long white hair, blazing blue eyes. I thought she sounded like a-"

"Gift Horse," Zarya finished. "Yes. She's a Ruined Mare."

"You say 'Ruined' like a title," I said.

"It is, sort of." Zarya was clearly troubled. "We are fruit, *bat'ko*. What happens to fruit when it is not eaten?"

"It goes bad."

"Ruinicornu are bad fruit," she said. "Most are like Glory: Gift Horses who have been forced into a corrupt state. Providence and Munificence are... they were born that way. Morphorde-born. They are... "

"The seed-daughters of one of the Morphorde's Generals," Norgay said grimly. "Celebrity terrorists, you might say. They must be softening up the Cell prior to an invasion. That's the only reason Ruinicornu of their station would be here."

I swallowed. How much should I tell them? The glyphs on the inside of my arms itched. "I, incidentally, had a meeting with the Deacon. The short version of how is that he wanted to parley, and he asked me to kill Angkor and Charles Bishop, the head of the CIA Paranormal Special Activities Division."

Angkor's face twisted, and he looked away.

"Why?" Norgay asked.

"The Deacon told me that he has foreseen the future," I replied. "And that Angkor and Charles are instrumental in summoning something he called an 'Engine' to Earth."

Zarya made a low, throaty sound of stifled pain. "Oh, no."

Instinct told me to reach for her, comfort her with touch. I held off. Zarya was still a stranger: a stranger who was involved with Angkor. "Funnily enough, he didn't mention you, Zarya."

"A Temporalist can't see Zarya through time. She's a Gift Horse." Angkor did reach for her, and the stubble on the back of my neck bristled as she leaned into him and turned her face into his neck. "She's a wildcard, part of GOD's acquired immunity defense system."

Zarya's voice was muffled. "So are you. All of us are. Even this meeting is an immune response."

Angkor nodded, as stern as I'd ever seen him. "So… That explains why the Templum Voctus Sol and the Vigiles are both looking for the Shard."

Norgay grunted. "If an Engine is headed to this Cell, we will have to see what we can do about selective evacuation."

"What are you talking about?" I frowned, looking between them.

"Engines are troop carriers and planet-wreckers," Angkor said grimly. "The small ones are about the size of the Moon. Big ones can be larger than Earth."

"Can't this military force of yours do something about it?"

"No, *bat'ko.*" Zarya shook her head.

I clenched my teeth. "Well, we have to be able to do *something*. I'm not letting this thing just run over us."

"We will do what we can. Recovering the Tree is our absolute first priority, followed by the Shard," Norgay said. "I am going to call the group conversation here, however. I wish to speak with Alexi, Angkor, and Zarya individually and in private, in that order. You are dismissed."

"Understood, Sir." Angkor bowed again and bustling off away from me. Doug followed, and then Zarya, leaving me alone with the black screen and the eerie sensation of being watched by someone I couldn't see.

"Alexi Sokolsky," Norgay said wryly. "I've heard a lot about you."

"From Angkor?" I narrowed my eyes.

"And Zarya," he replied. "Tell me what Kristen had to report."

I recounted the facts I could remember—easier now that I'd been dosed with Phi and had slept. Norgay listened in utter silence until I concluded, and when I stopped speaking, he made a thoughtful sound over the line.

"Is that all?"

I looked down. "Lee gave me the coordinates to the Shard. She asked me to relay them to you, but before I say anything, I want to know why you want it."

"We will carefully extract it from this Cell and join it to a larger, independent Shard of Eden," Norgay replied. "Shards are fragmentary, as their name implies… they're used to rehabilitate MahTrees and other Edenic beings, but we have very little space and far too many Trees in the queue. Combining Shards into larger Edenic islands gives us space to work with, and means we don't have to risk creatures like Zarya and the Tree on Earth-like Cells."

"I see." I looked down at my arm, taking a moment to make sure I remembered the code accurately. "Seventeen thirty-seven, zero two point nine, north. Eighty-nine, thirty-seven, zero nine point two, west. The Vigiles are looking to weaponize it."

There was a pause as Norgay noted down the numbers. "Thank you. You have done a great service, but I admit that I'm curious as to why you decided to bear this burden."

Where did I start? The endless cycle of offense, violence, and revenge? The realization that I was eating my own tail all the time? The profound, bottomless exhaustion? I straightened my shoulders. "I'm tired of being nothing but a thug with a couple of magic tricks."

"Fair enough. I will let Angkor know that he needs to modify your memory, lest you are ever compromised and forced to divulge this information," Norgay replied. "Thank you. You have been an immense help. However, I wanted to speak with you about one other thing."

"Go."

"I want to offer you work."

My stomach tensed a little. "What kind of work?"

"Contracts, all expenses paid. You would be assigned Morphorde targets to take out using whatever tools you require," Norgay said. "You would have the full support of my organization, insurance, and are in no way required to subscribe to its philosophy provided you do the job."

He wasn't talking about medical insurance: he was offering me the paper trail that Ayashe had refused to provide. "Sounds too good to be true."

"It's not. Hunting Greater Morphorde is dangerous, thankless work. We can provide you with specialized training to deal with the kinds of challenges you would face as an operative."

"'We' being ANSWER?"

"'We' being C.E.I.D.R." Norgay spelled out the acronym. "CEIDR is the Cellular Espionage, Intelligence, and Direct Response agency within ANSWER's Intelligence and Research division. We have three main functions: we research, target, and either rehabilitate or eliminate key Morphorde operatives, and we root out any Morphorde attempting to gain a foothold in ANSWER and other related communities and organizations."

"What kind of 'Greater Morphorde' are we talking about?"

"Anything from organized crime bosses through to Ruinicornu like Providence and Munificence. Morphorde come in human varieties, as well as alien or monstrous forms. Your first targets would be the key players in this Engine business."

Alexi Sokolsky, interdimensional assassin? I smiled ruefully. I could see myself doing work like what he'd described—I'd taken hits several times a year, every year, since I was seventeen. Backed up by a powerful organization, with tools and expenses covered, all I'd have to worry about was staying alive.

I shook my head. "I want to, but I'm sorry. I can't."

"Tell me what's holding you back."

Brows creased, I looked down. "First thing is that the Vigiles have taken my friends. They're probably already dead, but I have to try and pull them out before they're rendered down for their souls. After that, I have to take out my old boss and put my best friend out of his misery. He's suffering."

"I understand," Norgay said. "Perhaps better than you'd expect. And I can see that the foreknowledge of the Engine weighs on you almost as heavily as these personal matters, so I'd like to make you an offer."

I was getting tired of the offers made by mysterious shadowy men. "I hope it's better than the Deacon's."

"We can offer support in retrieving your friends," Norgay said. "And it's not a purely altruistic act on my part. Most Weeders are our allies by default. We've been wanting to bust the Vigiles' holding center for months, and if you know the location…?"

"I do."

"Then something can be arranged," Norgay said. "And your second objective is to kill Sergei Yaroshenko, is it not?"

I froze in place. "… Yes. How do you-?"

"Sergei happens to be one of our high-priority targets on this Cell," Norgay said, "Would you like to know what information we have on him?"

"Yes. Everything."

Even without an image, I could tell Norgay was smiling. "Do you know the story of Sviatopolk the Accursed?"

"He was a pre-Christian Ukrainian prince," I said, heart sinking. "He killed two of his three brothers to take the throne, was deposed by the third—Vladimir the Great—and died in exile. You don't mean to tell me-"

"Sviatopolk didn't die in exile," Norgay confirmed. "Now, some of this is speculative, but I have an idea of his distant history. He was a Phitometrist—a necromancer, to be exact—and fully awakened into his magic. He knew his Soul and was in cooperation with it. My suspicion is that he attempted to sacrifice his Soul—murder it—and in the process, he became a vampire."

Murdered his Soul? His Neshamah? Being cut off from Kutkha was bad enough. The thought of him being hurt or killed... it made my stomach quake. "If he was, *is* Sviatopolk the Accursed, that would make him nine hundred and eighty years old."

"Nine hundred and seventy-two, actually. Sergei is the Thronos of the Fifth Choir on your world: the founder of a linage of vampires. Every Feeder in the Fifth Choir is descended from him, and are distinguished by their iron teeth and their feeding preferences for flesh and pain."

"I've never heard of a 'Choir'. I always figured a group of vampires would be a coterie."

"A group of Wrath'ree is a Howl," Norgay replied. "And given that the existence of Wrath'ree and that of Feeders is bound together, vampires throughout GOD refer to their collectives as Choirs. The leader of a Choir is generally referred to as the Thronos or Maester."

So that's what Dogboy had been talking about. "Do you know... if Feeders have free will?"

"All of the Furies—the Wrath'ree—who animate the Feeders in a Choir answer to their Thronos," Norgay said. "But they typically have choice. However, Feeders created from the dead are an exception to this."

"Explain." I regarded the screen stonily.

"That Feeder's Fury is under immense strain," Norgay replied. "It is generally a Wrathling—a baby Wrath'ree, you could say—and it animates the corpse by replacing the non-functional parts of the HuMan with its own Phitonic mass. To stay animate, it is constantly on the verge of starvation. Because of this, its will is weak."

"So it isn't even really Vassily at all, then? Just this Fury, this Wrath'ree?" Hope stirred in me. If it was just some ghostly creature using his body to look like him, that was much better than the alternative.

"That depends." Norgay sounded cautious, now. "It depends on whether or not Vassily's soul was still tethered to his body at the time of his raising. If it was, the Wrathling acts as a glue binding his soul to him. There is functionally no break in personality. If it wasn't, then the Fury will have essentially downloaded whatever neural mapping was left in the body, and will use that as a basis for a personality that is functionally similar to the original HuMan's. But it is a copy, and that personality will sharply diverge as the Wrathling matures."

"I see." I rubbed my jaw. "You... may or may not know this. But is it... do Feeders suffer from being what they are?"

Norgay made a soft sound—sympathy, maybe. "Not inherently. No more than any other thing within GOD, at least. And whatever you see or experience when dealing with Feeders, remember this: Wrath'ree are not Morphorde. They are the front-line soldiers of the Third War. Proud, ruthless, fierce, mercenary, and harsh they may be, but they are not evil. Wrath'ree will be the first ones to try to save your planet, and when the Hive arrives on your world, most of the Feeders, barring DOG-tainted characters like Sergei, will join them in battle. That includes your friend, if you can free him."

"I see." The information left me feeling numb. It was strange how hope could sometimes feel like mania, and other times, like anesthesia. "So you're wanting to take out Sergei?"

"He's an ardent, if mercenary, Greater Morphorde who is active on a number of Cells," Norgay replied. "So my offer to you is this: work for us, complete your trial mission, and your second guaranteed mission will be an assault on Sergei, his resources, and the liberation or euthanization of your friend with our full support."

"Assuming I survive."

"Assuming you survive."

There was no solid reason for me to trust this man. Agent Cross and Lee had fought for him, Angkor had thrown me away for his sake, but I didn't know Norgay from Adam. But without knowing that I'd taken the Tree's Rhizomes and seen the Engine, he'd hit it on the head. The knowledge *was* weighing on me, and without a leap of faith, it was going to bear down on all of us while I convulsed in the death grip of that old *Mafiya* life.

Whoever—*whatever*—Norgay was, he was holding an open door for me. One that wasn't haunted by Sergei, or my father, or Vassily. I'd settled for the zero-zero draw because I couldn't see outside of the cycle, but as Kutkha had told me, the road to understanding was long and bitter. Sometimes, there were forks in the path. On one side, the future stretched out into a familiar wasteland where I was destined to run in circles for the rest of my short, violent life. The other fork was dark, but it moved forward. Perhaps it led to what was right.

"Alright." I squared up in front of the screen. "Tell me what you need."

CHAPTER 41

My head was spinning by the time I left the computers to search for the others. Angkor, Doug, and Zarya were waiting behind the tents. Angkor was smoking, leaning against the wall, and didn't quite meet my eyes when I beckoned to him. "You're next."

He pushed himself up, and stalked off past me in sullen silence.

"*Bat'ko*, we need to talk," Zarya said once he was gone. "In private."

"Sure, leave me here," Doug sighed. "In the snow, in the cold. Alone."

Zarya laughed, a musical sound that gave me goosebumps on my arms. "You're *so* full of shit."

"Hey. My bowel problems are none of your business."

She wagged her head from side to side. "If you weren't addicted to sugar, the roadblock might ease up a little."

Doug barked a laugh. I bowed my head to him as we left. To my surprise, I felt Zarya's hand grasp mine, but didn't resist when she linked our fingers. It felt oddly natural to touch her... like a long-lost habit I was rediscovering.

"You have a good talk with Norgay?" Zarya asked, once we were out of earshot.

"I had an enlightening talk with Norgay," I replied in Ukrainian, staring at the ground. "Listen. Once you're done speaking with him, we're going to be organizing an operation to raid a recycling plant. I'm not going to have a chance to see you for a while after that."

"He asked you to take a job, didn't he?"

"Yes."

We'd reached Zarya's tent by the time I said that. She stopped and turned to look down at me. She was so tall now.

"You need to make up with Angkor, *bat'ko*," she said. "He's upset."

"Good. He dug himself into that pit when he pretended to care," I replied. "He should have trusted me. Now, I think he's hiding things."

Zarya held aside the tent flap so that I could crawl inside. "Hiding things? We're all hiding things, Father. How can you hold that against him when you commit the sin you accuse him of?"

She had a point, but it didn't stop me from feeling prickly about it. I entered the tent, and waited for her to join me before I spoke again, low and urgent. "He's lied continuously since we met. It's one thing to hide things, and quite another to actively deceive and suspect people of working for the enemy. He stood me up, he-"

"You have *got* to be kidding me." Her expression turned to astonished exasperation, and she shook her head violently enough to move her shoulders... like a horse. "You were stood up for a fucking *date*, and you're going to hold it against one of the best Hounds in GOD for doing his job?"

I wasn't sure what took me aback more: that she was admitting that she was also some kind of spy, or that she was swearing. "Zarya-"

"Have you lost your fucking mind?" She leaned in toward me and pinned me with the weight of her stare. "'Active deception' is my *career*. Are you going to hold it against me next?"

She had a career? "I..."

Zarya leaned away. "Am not thinking straight."

I frowned, looking down at the floor. In the dim light, I could see she'd left her knife out, the one she'd used to cut her lips. "The last time I saw you, I was pulling you out of a giant walnut. You were sick, you were weak... I thought you were a child. I didn't know you had a career. I don't even know what a Hound actually does, because no one has told me."

"I know you don't. Why do you think that is?"

"No idea," I replied. "And it's clear I don't know you or Angkor, either."

Her mouth drew to one side in irritation, an expression I saw every day in the mirror. "Of course you don't. Why do you think *that* is?"

"*I don't know!*" I finally raised my voice, but tamped it down to an angry hiss instead of a shout. "I don't know, and I'm getting sick of it. I lost everything when I came to your aid. Everything. I'm part of this, whether I want to be or not, and I'm not willing to be kept in the dark while-"

"You *are* involved," Zarya said. "And that is, if you think closely about it, precisely why neither of us can tell you everything. Haven't you ever concealed things from a loved one?"

Whatever angry thing I'd been about to say was cut off at the neck. "... Yes, of course I have."

Her eyes, liquid and inescapably eerie in their power to pierce me, to reach through me, closing a circuit in my soul. No... *with* my soul. "Have you ever lied to a loved one... because you love them?"

I couldn't move. I couldn't keep looking into those eyes, but I couldn't look away from them. The smell of the peppermint oil she wore in her nose plugs was quieting my other senses. Taste, smell... they were closed down, leaving all of their mental bandwidth to be commandeered by blazing Light. The Whole Color.

"I..." I froze, staring and transfixed. There was no way Zarya was an infant of her kind. Before her, I felt young, immature and awkward. "I... yes, of course."

"Why did you conceal it from them?"

"The work I did was dangerous. It shouldn't have involved them." I flushed, hearing the admission as soon as I made it. "But those were almost always about contracts—illegal, dangerous—or things that would have deeply upset or disturbed them."

"Or they were things that would have deeply disturbed you to confess?"

"Both. Sometimes." I was struggling not to edge away under the pressure of her focus on me. Her eyes bore into places I didn't want seen, places that were too painful, too vulnerable. It was a real pain, a kind of cringing that made me want to twist and wriggle away.

"Do you think the work my Hound does is any less dangerous? Do you even imagine it is?"

I readily recalled Norgay's brief description of what Angkor had done for the Tree, and sighed. "No. But it doesn't matter: he lied to me and he chose you. That's the end of it. I don't have to be his friend."

"You're upset that he's fucking me, and not you?"

I flushed a deep cherry-red. "Do you have to be crude about it?"

She turned her head back to stare me down. "It's not crude: it's straightforward. Because this is what that demand comes down to. You're jealous, and you don't want me and Angkor to fuck."

"It's... I..." I couldn't even find the words. My hands tensed, and I shook them out to try and stop them from cramping up. "No!"

"No what?"

"Last I knew, you were a child of your species and I... I asked him to dinner because I found him attractive, and because he was good to have around. I thought we had a lot in common and he... I thought he cared." I forced my hands still and stiff by my sides, but the spasms went to my face instead. "Fuck! I *know* this is selfish, Zarya, and maybe it doesn't upset you, but this is... it's terrifying, and I can't just stop being angry. Alright?!"

"Alexi." She crawled toward me and lay her hands on my knees. "You thought he cared about you, so when you found out that he's fucking me, that meant he couldn't possibly care about you?"

"I... don't know." My lips turned downward, the muscles beside my mouth and eyes jumping. "Not really."

"I mean, yes, you're right in the sense that, while I am not a Foal anymore, I am still a very young Gift Horse. Certainly the youngest Mare I know. But that makes me centuries older than you. Angkor is almost exactly the same age as I am."

"He told me he was fifty," I said, sourly.

Zarya bit back a laugh, catching her lip in her teeth. "He's *much* older than that."

I shook my head, trying to clear it. "So you aren't a baby."

"No. We are born in the Rind and we return to the Rind. Sometimes, they detach with us inside, and are carried on the currents to Cells like this one."

I nodded. "Norgay said you... had an uncle. Someone I knew? Or know? The other me? I figure that's where the 'Father' thing comes from, isn't it?"

"Yes. My father is another of your Ruachim. But you know you're changing the subject. You think Angkor can't care about you and me at the same time. That caring, that *love*, is a zero-sum game? That if you give your love to one person, there's nothing to give to anyone else?"

"I don't know if you... he could care about me if he's involved with you, no." The edges of my ears were burning now, I'd blushed so hard. "For most of my life, I only had the one friend. I cared about him to the exclusion of all else."

But that wasn't true now... not really. Not with Jenner, Binah, Talya, and Zane in my life. I knew it, and it embarrassed me more than what we'd been skirting around the entire conversation.

Zarya regarded me with that piercing white gaze again. "Vassily. You're talking about Vassily, and now that he's dead and worse, you can't be honest with him and tell him that you love him."

"Stop." I pulled away from her touch and looked down, at the walls, at the roof, anywhere but her.

"You wanted to be with him like Angkor is with me. Your feelings weren't those someone has for a friend, not even their only friend. And the thought of Angkor having sex with anyone else makes you think of all the times you heard Vassily in the other room with a girl... and wanted to be her."

My hands shook—but not with tics. With rage. "Zarya-"

She was up in my face, following me as I backpedaled. "And now you're coming angrily to me, that girl-"

"Shut up!"

"-and telling me to stay the fuck away from your man and not get involved with him."

I wasn't sure when the knife landed in my hand, or how I wound up on top of Zarya with the weird, rainbow-anodized blade buried in her chest. "SHUT UP!"

She stared down at the weapon like she didn't know what it was, or what it was doing there, then up at my face.

"You bitch! You lying *bitch*!" My hand wrenched the knife free and stabbed her again, driving it through her ribs. "You're lying! You're all fucked in the head! You're all...!"

Zarya barely even struggled as I ranted filth—vile, hateful, vitriolic filth—puking up the hundreds of conversations and arguments, the stupid, boring nights at the strip club, the locker-room talk and my father's bile about faggots and punks and fairies. I screamed about it, about the filthy house and even filthier school, about poverty and the rumors in the schoolyard, about the way I'd noticed Vassily's lips when I was no older than ten and had the skin burned off my back with cigars when my father saw us hug outside the school gate. And once the hate was out, the grief came in a wracking riptide of memory.

I remembered laughing hysterically with Vassily as a child, strange hiccoughing sobs from a throat unused to laughing. He was curly-haired, already painfully handsome at eleven years old, and he had me pinned by the arms and hips under our blankets while he roared like a big cat. We called the game "lions", because we both growled and meowed and pounced on each other, tumbling over the bed and often onto the floor. It always started with playfighting—it always ended with frantic, innocent pleasure from nothing more than friction. Neither of us knew what we were doing. Lenina did. One night, she caught us at it. We were made to sleep in separate beds, and were forbidden from speaking of "lions" ever again.

And we had obeyed. Lenina and Mariya's disapproval had pushed the desire and shame down into the darkness and drowned it. The dance between Vassily and me had always been there, submerged under my monastic iron will and his determination to fuck and drink himself straight. We got drunk together once—only once. He kissed me. I still remembered it, even though the rest of the night was a blur: his hands on my body, his mouth sweet with the taste of blueberry liquor, frantic tugging on my shirt in the dizzy moments before I passed out. When I woke, he'd acted like it had never happened. He told me the night was a blur.

Zarya was right—she was right about all of it. I was trying to find something in Angkor, and it had been denied me, again. I fell across her chest as she spasmed and gasped, weeping, confused by how wet my hands, face, and chest were. It took me a few minutes to connect everything: her glassy stare, the pour of silver blood wicking off into the air from two dozen punctures through her torso and neck, the click in her throat, the knife still buried in her heart.

For the first time in my life, ever, I froze over a kill. My GOD. I'd killed her. I'd lost control, and murdered her.

"Zarya. No. Oh GOD, no." I was shaking too hard to do anything except paw at her neck, searching vainly for a pulse, and then collapse next to her, tears streaming down my face. "No. No, please."

Zarya was beyond the point of being able to respond, mouth gaping spasmodically with soundless, agonal gasps. But I knew what she would ask for if she could speak.

"The Pact," I whispered, suddenly frantic. I grasped the knife hilt, swallowing, and pulled it free. The blade didn't catch the way it would have in a human chest. Zarya's flesh was pulpy and firm, like the flesh of a good, ripe peach, but it was blue instead of yellow or red. The sanctified, pure floral smell of her blood cut through the horror, the old pain, the new pain. Hunger overrode grief. Still choking with grief, I pushed her tank top up underneath her breasts, baring her sternum. I slit across and then up, and haltingly slid my hand in under her ribs until I found her heart. It was not difficult – her heart was enormous, easily twice the size of a HuMan's. Five arteries led out from it, and five veins in. I cut it free, hardly believing what I was doing, and brought the mirror-coated organ to my lips.

It was perfect. Hot. Sweet. Two mouthfuls, and I couldn't feel my face anymore. Another three, and the worst of my pain was gone, comforted by a perfect, total satiation. I was hallucinating in vivid color as I rolled to the side again and buried my face against her shoulder. Zarya was still hot to touch, almost feverishly warm. She was no longer breathing, or capable of breathing. Her chest was torn apart, heart gone, lungs pulled apart into indigo pulp. Shivering passed through me in waves, but I didn't pass out this time. I gained... distance. Clarity. I stepped back into the past.

It was a cool fall morning. The leaves had turned brown. I was young, eighteen, lunging Katerina in the round pen. Vassily was hanging on the fence while he watched us, his breath pluming frost into the air. Now and then, I twitched the lunge whip in Katerina's direction and broke her stride, forcing her to skid to a stop and turn back the other way. She was beautiful like this, a wild specter of a horse who snorted, bucked, and tossed her mane as she ran in loops around me without tack, bridle, or bit.

"Why do you do this?" Vassily asked me. "Run her around and around? Is it just so she can burn off steam?"

"No." I clicked my tongue and dashed the whip on the sand, urging her to a gallop. Katerina's hooves slid on the gravel, kicking them to dust as she bunched and surged forward.

"Then why do it?"

I didn't reply straight away. I let her run—let her flee—from the promise of the fearsome looking, eight-foot lunge whip. It had a handle that was taller than I was by several feet, and a tail longer than that. Despite its size, the whip was never used for striking. Once I noticed that she was breathing harder, I dropped it on the ground and held up my hands.

Katerina ran another lap before she noticed that the whip was gone. She slowed to a canter, then to a trot, a walk, then turned toward me, snorting like a steam furnace. For a moment, we watched one another. I could see her spirit in those big brown eyes, the galaxy swirl inside of the impassive marble surface of them. The space between us vanished, and as the connection was made, the horse lowered her head and ambled across to me. I reached for her, laying my hands against her withers as Vassily watched on in reverent silence.

"It's called 'joining up'," I said, quietly. "Horses are driven to run. They HAVE to run. They run for pleasure, for the joy of it, and they run to escape danger. They think when they walk and run. To come in here with me, with a stimulus like this, is a massive exercise in trust for her. She's scared of the whip—so she runs, and she fights, and she fears... and she waits, because she knows that when the whip is gone, I'm here waiting for her. She looks to me, and in that moment, she joins up with me. She submits to me. I submit to her. That way, we both know we can work together."

Vassily's face flooded with a smile. He grinned, blushed, looked down. "So you're her stallion substitute, huh?"

"No," I replied. "Stallions don't lead herds. Horses are matriarchal. Herds are led by the mares."

"So you're boss mare?"

I leaned against the arch of her neck, and breathed in the hay-and-sweet grass scent of her. "Yes."

Beside me, Zarya twitched.

It was her finger, brushing against my wrist. Then a tiny spastic tic ran through her neck, a fluttering against my face. It startled me out of my waking dream, and what I saw took my breath away.

The Mare's torn chest was filling with a clear, shimmering gel that swirled and coagulated through her tissues. Smoothly, rapidly swelling up from deep inside her torso, it rebuilt the flesh I had torn away. It was translucent at first, but quickly thickened and solidified until she was re-formed. Then, she lay still.

"Zarya?" My voice was a dry croak.

Flawless but inanimate, Zarya looked much like any other corpse... until I felt the life sweep through and around us. Her eyes suddenly kindled with light, opening wide. Ocean was in those eyes: fathomless, endless, and intoxicatingly, perfectly alive.

I couldn't move. Couldn't breathe. Paralyzed by awe, I watched as Zarya's chest swelled with a rattling breath that turned into a brutal hacking cough. She reached for me, and I took her in my arms and embraced her without any hesitation. No crawling skin, no embarrassment, no painful nervous tics. I felt like I should be crying, but no tears came.

"Try not to hit my lungs next time, okay, *bat'ko?*" There was a wheeze underneath the dulcet smoothness of her voice.

I hugged her tightly, and buried my face in her hair, against her neck. "I'm sorry. I'm so sorry. I killed you, I-"

"Did what I'd hoped you'd do." Zarya embraced me, chest to chest, holding me with the kind of raw, supernatural strength that told me she could have fought me off and snapped my spine over her knee if she'd wanted to. But she hadn't. "You're still young, *bat'ko*. I have to speak with Norgay. Angkor has told me they're finished."

"... Told you?" I pulled away a little, still resting within the circle of her arms. "How? Telepathy?"

She smiled. "He's eaten me enough times that we can speak that way."

"In any other circumstance, that would have been just a euphemism." I sniffed, looking down. Meeting her eyes had been hard before. Now it was impossible.

"It's not." The Mare stroked my face, the silver stubble that was growing in over my scalp. "Go talk to him. Apologize. Be honest with him. And... don't hurt him. Please."

She had a way of making 'please' sound like a word of power. I nodded. "Alright. And I'm sorry—I will never lose control like that again."

"I won't hold you to that promise, *bat'ko*." She smiled, cheeks dimpling. "Because I need to be Pacted. And because you love doing it."

"You *need* it?" Puzzled, I reached up to stroke her wrist.

"All flesh must be eaten; all blood must be drunk. But that's a story for another time. You need to go see Angkor."

Shamefaced, I began to pull away from her, but an impulse seized me and I bent down, almost putting my face to the floor, to delicately, chastely kiss her on the side of her throat. Zarya made a low sound of pleasure, writhing sensuously, then laughed and gently pushed me away. I bowed my head to her, and withdrew.

CHAPTER 42

The world outside the tent looked different than before. Brighter, fresher. I wandered back toward the command station in a daze. Doug was back in his seat. The screen with the logo was still up, so I beckoned to him to get a word.

"Don't worry—it's on mute." Doug called back. "He's waiting for Zarya. Is she... uh... alive?"

"Yes." The air moved over my skin like fingers. Every one of my senses was heightened: I could smell the age of the building, and the strangely clean, natural smell of everything. The light danced; I noticed the weathered laugh lines by Doug's eyes—and more strangely—the wary humor in them. Here was a man who used comedy as armor. "Did Angkor go back to his room?"

"He went out with the corrun, I think," Doug replied. "First field out the back of the building. Can't miss it."

I nodded stiffly, and withdrew with a last, lingering look toward the tent, where Zarya was only just getting out. "Thank you. For your discretion, as well as your help."

"Discretion is my middle name," Doug said. "Douglas Discretion Digger the… wait, no, 'dodecagon' isn't a numeral. There's actually no numbers that start with 'D'. Weird."

While Zarya began her conversation with Norgay, I went out under the Phitonic shield that covered the grounds. The building gave way to rubble and long grass. It felt remote. Surreal, even. Angkor was perched on a crumbling wall, watching the horned horse-like creatures – the corrun – as they dug brambles and roots from out of the mud. I was still far off when he half-turned his head. "Has he finished talking with Zarya?"

The extent of his extrasensory perception took me off guard for a moment. I stopped dead in my tracks. "Not yet." My chest tensed. It was one thing to talk about him with Zarya, quite another thing to face him like this. I lifted my chin and steeled myself. "I came to see you. And apologize."

Angkor didn't look over at me, but he was visibly tense in his legs and arms, muscles taut with readiness. "Well, I understand why you would be angry. So-"

"I don't apologize very often," I said, coming to stop barely an arm's length from him. "So please… accept it, and let me acknowledge that I'm not even thirty-one years old. I'm a jealous, bitter adult virgin who has no idea what he's doing, and that you did what you did because it was the best course of action available to you."

Angkor ducked his head and shrugged. He was smoking again, fidgeting unhappily with his cigarette. I'd watched Vassily smoke so much that I could read a man's moods from his hands better than I could his face. "Alright. I said some things I should regret, too. I'm sorry."

"It's fine," I replied. "If I couldn't deal with being pissed off, I'd have left Brooklyn years ago."

Angkor's whole face flushed with a brief smile. I looked him over, noticing for the first time how tired he really seemed.

"You know, Angkor, I want to trust you," I said. "Zarya does. She cares about you."

"She's a Gift Horse. To a point, she can't help it," he replied, still gazing at the corrun. "And I'm a mercenary."

"ANSWER isn't a mercenary organization, as I understand it."

"I'm a mercenary Hound." He shook his head. "The problem with a lot of what you said to me is that it's true."

"So come clean with me," I said. "Because I want to get to know you. But I can't trust someone whose motives and identity are completely opaque."

Angkor kept his gaze averted, his eyes little more than a dark crescent sweep of lashes against his golden-brown skin.

"Start with your real age," I suggested. "Nothing too serious."

"You really want to know?" He smiled and chuffed, amused. "Two hundred and twenty-six. Linear years, that is. I was born in 1987 on my own Cell."

That seemed impossible. "Biomancy?"

"Gift Horses," he said. "I met my first one when I accidentally found a Shard of Eden near the border of the DMZ. A Stallion. He was... dying. A relic of the Second War. I found him impaled on a spear, kept alive by his Mother's roots. They were locked in this weird co-dependent desperation..."

"And?" I folded my arms, realized it looked defensive, unfolded them.

"And everything before that isn't worth talking about," he said.

"I don't believe that, either." I came around, and sat on the wall beside him. "You've rescued MahTrees. They're ancient, fragile beings. That is not an unexceptional achievement."

"It was selfish, at first," he admitted. "I wanted to experiment on them. But then... I changed. A lot. I was a very selfish person when I was young."

I inhaled deeply, battling the disapproving voices of the dead, and lay a gloved hand on his thigh. Angkor jumped, and I pulled back uncertainly, only to relax when he covered it with his and pressed my fingers back down. The suit he wore was firm, about a quarter-inch thick in the reinforced areas. It made the lean muscles of his legs feel like smooth, matte satin.

"I can tell you something else," Angkor continued. "You probably don't want me as much as you think you do."

GOD help me, but I was shaking like a leaf. My anger had evaporated into the high-strung anxiety of a virgin. My awkward experiences with Tina, and whatever I'd done with Christopher and almost done with Troy apparently hadn't counted, when it came to my confidence. "I have no idea where you'd pull *that* assumption from, given that I've been ogling you the better part of two months."

He drew a deep breath and turned toward me, still seated on the wall, so that our knees touched. He kept his eyes down. "I'm intersex."

For several seconds, I processed the words. "Intersex?"

"Oh… right. It's 1991." He snorted, gaze still averted. "'Hermaphroditism' is probably the word you know, but it's… ehnn. Have you ever heard of adrenal hyperplasia?"

"No." I stopped trying to fumble for the language then, listening.

"It's a genetic condition. People born with it have what they like to call 'ambiguous physiology'." Angkor arched an eyebrow. "XX chromosomes, internal testes, and a perfectly functional body that was mutilated without my consent or knowledge. They didn't care that I'd be in pain for the rest of my life. I was put on female hormones, raised female, and wasn't able to set things right until I was nearly thirty years old and a Hound."

I blinked several times. "By 'set things right', you mean-"

"I had to regrow the organs that were cut off and out of me. Repair nerve damage, restore seminal ducts and break up the internal scarring," he said, glancing up at me with fierce, sudden pride. He made a slicing gesture under each pectoral with his fingers. "I had to remove *these*, because the hormones made them grow out. And two hundred years later, I know, without a doubt, that out of a thousand HuMans who've hit on me, I can only be who and what I am with *one* out of that thousand. Straight, gay, it doesn't matter. Because I didn't turn myself 'male' or 'female'. I restored myself to what I am."

He finished, breathing hard, and averted his eyes again.

"But you look male," I said. "So-"

"Above the waist," he replied. He was already a little distant again, removed from the anticipation of rejection. "And that's a deal breaker for a lot of people, especially men. Gift Horses... Gift Horses were the first to tell me that I wasn't just normal, but that I was *essential*. Before the Morphorde, everything was intersex or female. My body is Edenic, and I carry that distinction with honor. But if you're looking for dick, you won't find it."

I thought about it for a moment, trying to picture what he hadn't described as he waited in wary expectation. What I saw was the way the bodysuit hugged and lifted the right things in the right places, the length of his neck, and the elegance of his hands. They were opening and closing on his knees as he waited.

After a couple of minutes of observant silence, he cleared his throat. "So, if you've been wondering why I've been so cagey..."

Angkor trailed off as I leaned in and breathed in deeply against his hair. He was freshly fed on Gift Horse, and he had a luscious, intoxicating smell. Honeycomb and male musk, which—now he'd mentioned it—was milder than the body odor of many other men whose scent I'd noticed. When I slid my hand up over his leg to his hip, his lips parted and he turned to face me, dropping his foot down to the ground to half-stand.

"If that's the worst you were holding back, then whatever else you've been hiding will be distinctly anticlimactic," I murmured, struggling to keep some semblance of composure.

Angkor flushed, and then smiled: the smile that was peculiar to him and only him, where he pinched the tip of his tongue between his teeth as his expression flooded all the way to his eyes. "I guess I... I made assumptions about you because of who you are and where you're from. Not just about this. I'm sorry."

"Some of those assumptions are true," I replied. I had to adjust the way I was sitting now, and as I did, I realized that the usual tearing pain was absent. It gave me pause. "And I think you're sensible to be cautious. But the first thing you should know about *me* is that I don't care who or what someone thinks they are, how they look, or what they have between their legs. Anyone can talk. It's what they *do* that counts."

Angkor's eyes hooded, and he slid completely off the wall to the ground, pressing himself up between my legs. With me sitting and him standing, we were of equal height. My breath sped as he ran his hands over my shoulders, kneading them gently. They might as well have been carved out of stone.

"Second thing you should know is that I never relax," I said. My voice was a little choked.

"I'm sure I can do something about that." He leaned toward me, and brushed his open mouth over my cheek.

I felt something contract in my belly, deep down, a sensation not unlike the feeling that preceded ejaculation. Nothing came up, thank GOD, but I jumped and tensed anyway as Angkor ghosted his lips over my skin, angling his head to find my mouth with his. The blood beat against the inside of my skull as I hesitantly kissed him. It was chaste, at first, a dry press of lips that caused my chest to tremble and my hands to grip the edge of the wall. As I gained confidence, second by second, it deepened. I'd always thought kissing was odd, even gross... but as Angkor pressed the length of his body to mine, opening my mouth with his, I finally realized what I'd been missing out on all this time.

"We should go somewhere warmer," he murmured beside my ear.

"I… I don't think we have time." I was stammering like a teenage boy. So much for being the big bad 'don't you touch me' guy at the gay bar. "We have to go-"

"We've got twenty minutes. Zarya's starting up the plan for the extraction," Angkor said. "You need this."

He took me by the hand, and I let him gently pull me to my feet and lead me off to the nearest of the ruined buildings. The energy barrier protecting the encampment from the rain ended just beyond the limits of this building.

The sound of running water filled my ears as Angkor pinned me against the wall nearest to the doorway. He kissed me urgently, all hot, open mouth and roaming hands until I bit the side of his throat, gripping him with my jaws. With a small sound, he relaxed his weight into my teeth and let me take him to the ground. I fought visions of Christopher's guilt, seedy bars, Vassily, and my father as I palmed Angkor's belly and chest.

"How... how does this thing come off?" I swallowed, trying to find a zipper or snaps or something else, but coming up blank.

"It's enchanted, and alive. You have to ask it nicely." He flashed a crooked, charming smirk, and reached up to the high fitted collar of the suit. He hooked a finger under the firm, leather-like edge, and it split seamlessly as he drew down, as easily as if he'd pulled it through butter. I watched with astonishment as he pulled it off. The material turned soft, hanging from his limbs when it was deactivated, and he shrugged the top half of it off like a second skin. My mouth was dry as he lay back and shucked the rest off, slowly. He was nude underneath. By the dull orange light of the barrier, his skin was a beautiful rosy tan. I noticed the way the muscles of his belly tapered down to his hips, and my mouth began to water. He stopped just before baring his groin, looking up at me with eyes full of heat – and maybe a little suspicion.

"I'm sorry, I... really have no idea what I'm doing." I swallowed again, hands hovering. "I've kissed two people before you, and the first time she did all the work. The second time, I was very drunk..."

"I get it. I was a virgin until my mid-thirties," he said. "Try to relax."

My mouth itched with need as he leaned up, caught my lips with his, and rolled us over. The suit fell away from his body with a sigh, and when I stripped the rest down his legs, he didn't stop me. He kissed me deeply, deliriously sweet, tearing at my shirt as I reached down and fumbled with my belt. My hands were shaking too hard to get it, and when he pushed them away and down, I let him.

"Relax." He pulled my shirt up and lay it aside, kissing his way down my chest. It was like a trail of lights, nerves jumping under the press of lips hotter than fresh blood. While he worked my belt loose, I reached down and slid my fingers through his hair—and immediately realized that I needed the gloves off. It was a simple task made difficult—he was busy unbuttoning my fly—but when I freed them and ran them over his scalp, I gasped. His hair was fine, incredibly soft and glossy, laying over my fingers like fur.

Angkor murmured wordless encouragement as I pushed his head down. My face was burning hot, and I couldn't bear to look down at what he was doing. He wasn't the only one who was body-shy.

He paused, and lifted his head up under my hands before I'd so much as felt his breath on me. "Sorry to interrupt this, but I have to ask... do you feel tight at all?"

"Tight?" The question threw me, until I realized what he was talking about. My cock wasn't hurting for once. "Oh, that's-"

"Bound to be uncomfortable once the Mare's flesh wears off," Angkor finished. "Phimosis *and* frenulum breve. It's going to strangle you again once the Phi leaves your system. I can make it so it won't hurt, if you want."

"Yes. Please." I had no idea what he was talking about, but if it meant I never had another painful erection, I was there. "Will it-?"

"You won't even notice. Believe me." He dipped his face, lapping at the skin of my hips and then over the head of my cock. And suddenly, I realized why the guys I'd known had all made such a big deal out of this particular act... because the brush of Angkor's mouth made my spine arch and my hips buck.

He groaned as I pushed his head down, a sound that made my face burn even more. I pressed one hand to my mouth, the other twisted in his silky hair. The world focused in on that one point: the swirl of his tongue, the soft sound of his swallowing, his breathlessness. I looked down and was rewarded by the gleam of his eyes in the dark, watching me.

"Stop." My throat was tight. "I can't last."

"So cum." He lifted up just enough to whisper, lips gliding slickly over the head with every word. "Don't worry about it."

I nodded, entranced but anxious as Angkor groaned in the affirmative and began to suckle and stroke, tongue soft. I reached down with my other hand, fighting the need to buck, unable to stop it as the pleasure built to a peak and then overran.

For a moment, everything was perfectly still inside— gasping, wide-eyed, transfixed with blank pleasure—and then I sunk back down, hips jerking fitfully as the last throbs of release pushed out from my body into his.

"Good GOD." I looked down at him, panting with shock. "GOD, Angkor."

He licked his lips, and in the gloom, I could see his wicked smile as he crawled over me and bent down to lick my chest. It felt... incredible. There was no tearing, no constriction no pain. And I was still raring to go.

"Come here." I reached up to tug him forward. He'd avoided letting me see him from the waist down so far. "Show me how this works."

Angkor was suddenly shy in my hands, a shift in confidence I felt by the way he moved.

"Are you sure you-?" He half-whispered to me, leaning away a little even as he found his seat over my hips.

"I told you. I don't care." I reached down between his thighs, and pulled him against my shoulder by the back of his head. Angkor whimpered sweetly against my ear as I explored with a careful hand, curious and oddly excited. He was soaking wet and hard at the same time, and my fingers glided over and around what felt to me like the contours of an arum lily. His cock was a slender stamen just a little smaller than my thumb, hooded with skin and exquisitely sensitive. He writhed as I stroked it, clutching at my arms, and gasped as I roamed a little further down and accidently slid my fingers inside him to the knuckle.

"Please, please, oh GOD yes-!" Angkor clawed at my shoulders as I cupped my hand, thrusting with fingers and rubbing against his cock with the heel of my palm. My hands were very soft and very smooth from years of keeping them covered, and he came from that alone, crying out into my ear. The same dizzying sense of power I'd felt with Christopher swept over me again, but twice as good. When Angkor squeezed down around my fingers, my brain immediately transposed the sensation onto my cock—and the thin veneer of shame holding me back evaporated as instinct took over. I guided him over my hips, but he didn't let me rush. Acceptance had transformed him, and he teased and rubbed over me with the confident sensuality of a snake, the arch of his body a darker silhouette against the ceiling.

"GOD, you're beautiful." I couldn't quite believe I was doing this.

Angkor caught his lip in his teeth as he slowly angled the tip into himself, and carefully, deliberately slid down along it.

There was no way to describe that sensation, the feeling of being taken into someone else's body that way. I felt it through my hands—through my nails, clawing bloody crescents into his skin; through my teeth as I bit his shoulder and neck. I heard it in his passionate cursing, and his cries of anguished pleasure as he rode me with long, rolling strokes. There was no way to describe the breathless everything-ness, or the dark, savage thing behind my eyes that found a sadistic release of its own every time he whimpered under my teeth and nails, every time he moaned when I held him down and fucked up into him.

"AH-Yes! Oh GOD, GOD, Alexi!" Angkor dropped his head and wept against my shoulder, sobbing and pushing, hair hanging over his cheeks. His body was sucking at me, pulsing rhythmically in the buildup to a second, more powerful release. He angled to rub himself against my belly, and I couldn't hold back as he orgasmed: a shuddering, wracking, clawing climax that made him heave and buck. There was a burst of wet heat around my glans—him, then me—and then he bowed over my chest with his hands dug into the ground on either side of my head.

"Ahh-hhhaah..." He had his lip in his teeth, face flushed a deep rose gold. I'd never seen anyone in that state of abandonment before, and regarded him with something like wonder as he slowly, carefully rode out the very last of my orgasm and then pulled free with a soft laugh.

"How do you feel after that?" His voice was syrupy and thick as he rolled down beside me and flung an arm over my chest.

We were both soaked in sweat. I lay stunned, trying to adjust to the foreign sensation of physical relaxation. The muscular tension that usually held me together had lapsed. In its place was a floaty golden afterglow.

"I think I finally have an idea of what everyone was always going on about," I replied after a few minutes.

"Not bad, is it?" Angkor quietly asked, resting his head on my chest.

"No. Not at all." For as long as it had taken, I hadn't been worried about anything. Pain, tension, worry... it had all receded. "What did you mean when you said I'd be in pain once the Mare's flesh wears off?"

"A Gift Horse's blood can unlock almost anything." He drowsily toyed with one of the faint scars on my chest, rubbing his fingers up and down the keloid. It was usually numb, but I could feel the texture of his skin in my mouth. "Doors, physical and not. Cars. Avalanches. Tight foreskins. When you ate her, you took a Phitonic charge into your body. I drew on that to coax your skin to grow a bit."

"I see." I mulled on that for a minute or so, and reached up to absently stroke Angkor's hair. It was a strange feeling made stranger by the way he stretched and shuddered in response. "You know... I've never done this."

"This?"

"Touched someone without..." I trailed off, not able to find a word that didn't make me sound like an ogre. "Gently. I don't think I've ever touched another human being gently before."

"Why?"

"It hurt. Any time someone had touched me, growing up, it was painful." I stared up at the cracked ceiling above.

"Well... you knew a lot of Morphorde-infected people. Morphorde are anti-touch," Angkor said. "They hate touch and they hate sex, except when sex is used as a tool of war."

"My father was definitely Morphorde. But I thought everything Edenic was anti-sex, too. I had to be a virgin to safely handle Zarya."

"Edenic flora and fauna don't have a relationship with virgins because they haven't had sex. It's not really about physical sex at all, actually." Angkor replied. "It's more about... energetic self-containment. One of the best Hounds in GOD is seriously a superhuman-level slut. I'm not even joking. He's like the Alpha and Omega Slut."

I snorted. "Good band name."

Angkor made a low sound of amusement. "But despite that, the Hound I'm thinking of... Edenic things flourish around him. Eden loves sex. Non-penetrative. They're not big on penetration, but everything there feeds on pleasure. Basically all Edenic creatures are erotivores."

"Pleasure?" I pulled him against my side. The uncomfortable sweat on our skin would make it feel unpleasant, eventually... but not yet. "Zarya eats *pleasure?*"

"Why do you think she's sleeping with me?"

I blinked. "Well... I assumed it was because you love her."

He laughed drowsily. "It's because I'm an all-you-can-eat buffet and she was badly underfed. I love her as much as I do any Horse, but I'm a mercenary, like I said."

"Meaning... what?"

Angkor stretched languidly, nuzzling my skin with his mouth. "Most Hounds just serve one Gift Horse. I used to, but then I joined the Corps. My work takes me to places my first Horse can't go. He's kind of... childlike, and physically fragile. He spends a lot of time being babysat at ANSWER headquarters while I jaunt around the Theosphere. So I hunt when and who I can."

"So you don't love her?"

"Of course I do. But there's lots of different kinds of love, and as long as everyone's in agreement, they're all good." Angkor stroked the side of my neck and pushed himself up to an elbows. "We probably should go back. Zarya will be wrapping up. Norgay told me we're crashing the Vigiles' party as soon as we've put together the raid plan."

Part of me wanted to call him back down, to lie here and linger for a bit, but I was already feeling a different kind of urgency: the need to act, to set plans in motion. People needed rescuing and Norgay had a job for me to do, and Angkor and I would do this again together again... someday.

"Norgay said I needed my memory modified, to erase the true location of Eden." I sat up, watching Angkor's lighter flare. "We need to do that."

"He told me." Angkor drew and exhaled with a soft sigh of pleasure, and the smell of cigarette smoke briefly overwhelmed everything else, bright green in the orange-lit gloom. "I'll do it before we go back into camp."

"Good. I just hope we're in time to help the Tigers." I watched him stand, lingering over the curve of his back, the way the light slid over his skin. I didn't know what love felt like, but whatever I felt now was blue and bittersweet, a brief and brilliant pleasure. I had no idea when I'd see him like this again. "Assuming that Keen's plan to catch them was even successful. Jenner was going to put landmines in the ground."

"You can count on it, but the Vigiles Magicarum is also a bureaucracy, and a ritualistic one at that. We'll make it." Angkor turned to look back at me with his bodysuit hanging from his hand like a second skin. He was proud, fierce, beautiful enough to make me wish we had more time. "And if we don't, we'll kill every last one of the bastards."

For what felt like the first time in a very long time, I smiled. "Amen to that."

CHAPTER 43

We ended up having our war meeting around a fire, like a band of Mongolian raiders. The analogy cut even closer to the bone than that; the ANSWER personnel—they were not 'soldiers', I was told, but 'fighters'—were a motley of well-equipped troops, male and female, wearing idiosyncratic gear that, while functional, looked scratched and dinged up enough that it had to have been recycled. We were going up against the Vigiles with everything from spears to assault rifles and magical talismans. This alone eroded my lingering doubts about ANSWER being what it claimed it was: an interdimensional movement against the Morphorde. Some twenty fighters surrounded Doug's workstation, where we pored over maps in an effort to nail down where the Vigiles' holding center was. With my description of the ship's graveyard and the escape route I'd taken off Staten Island, we triangulated its location, and formed a plan.

My final misgivings were obliterated when our transport arrived and I finally saw the Tulaq. We went to the shore of the island to receive them. While we waited, I learned from Zarya that the process of jumping to a body of water and pushing through it into GOD's Phitonic bloodstream was called 'Riverjumping', and that corrun, Tulaq, and specially-bred horses of the Akhal Teke breed were some of the few creatures capable of it. She'd just finished telling me this when five beings the size of gliders burst out of the river, wings beating. They had far-reaching forelimbs; narrow, tense wings; and high withers that gave them a skulking, hyena-like gait as they clambered to shore. Water streamed from every contour. They almost looked like they were coated in plastic. Their feathers, which were shiny with wax, were gray-blue on their dorsal parts, darkening to a clay red on their flanks.

I was dumbstruck. Doug had warned me that they were intelligent, sentient beings, and that the feathers of a Tulaq's crest, wings, and tail were edged with razor-sharp carbon filaments that could slice HuMan flesh to ribbons. I stepped back when one of them passed quite close to me, pausing long enough for me to catch my own reflection in one of its huge eyes, and I smelled its weird, citrusy breath as it rolled its lips back from rows of pointed crystalline teeth. I jumped, startled, when it flared a portion of the dorsal crests that ran from either side of its skull and down the length of its spine, and as it tossed its head and skulked off toward the camp. I had the distinct feeling that it was laughing at me.

By the time we were ready, the storm had turned into a hurricane. The young trees outside the sanitarium were blowing almost flat to the ground. The rain was horizontal, the sky howling and red. The power was out, and New York was lit only by hundreds of thousands of car lights, sirens, helicopters, and backup generators. The site of the Ruined Tree was obvious from the air. The station Glory had taken me to was in the Lower West Side.

There the military had congregated around a howling black nexus, a collapsed city block at the eye of the storm that grew bigger and more voracious with every bullet they fired at it. A bunker was forming around the edges of the void... a concrete dome held together with crackling energy visible from the sky. The arterials were packed with cars full of panicking refugees: inert, glowing lines of scarlet light that snaked toward the city limits in every direction. New York was hemorrhaging out from the tumor swelling at its core. Even from here, it seemed hopeless, the fear meshing with my directive from Norgay and a tumult of confused feelings for Angkor and Zarya. They were riding on the two other Tulaq in our formation, each of us flying in tandem with the beast's bonded rider.

The plan was simple enough. The Tulaq would drop me on the roof, where I had twenty minutes to infiltrate the building using the route I'd taken to escape it. Whatever resources the Vigiles might have mustered in twelve hours to plug the elevator shaft weren't going to hold up to a forced entry by an experienced burglar with proper tools. The goal was to cause havoc: bust switches, short-out electrical devices and generators, free prisoners, draw attention, and cause a ruckus—at which point, Angkor, Zarya, the Tulaq, and a ground force with trucks and RPGs would assault the compound from the road and air. They were coming from two directions: the corrun cavalry from the swamp, and the trucks from the road. We had contingencies in place, but the quietest option was the first we'd try. The stealthier we were, the more likely the Weeders were to survive.

We flew hard, cloaked in devices that reflected light from the Tulaq's bodies and turned them into living stealth bombers. Their wings cut the rain and wind like scimitar blades. From the air, the recycling center was easy to spot: it was the only place in Fresh Kills that still had electricity. The lights blared out into the night sky. I tuned my binoculars as we swooped into view, searching for helicopters. There were none: *they* were grounded by the storm. The Tulaq—bullish and inelegant on the ground—could fly in the kind of wind and rain that would knock a helicopter out of the air. She and her rider soared easily around the spotlights and angled for the roof of the factory. Satisfied, I checked over my gear, trusting in the harness as we surged into a crosswind.

"Brace for impact." I thought back to Zarya.

"Understood. We're right behind you."

My stomach swooped as the Tulaq tucked her wings and dived. I braced my rifle and held on with my legs, trying to focus my aim over the head rush. She was so fast that the guards stationed on the roof didn't know what had hit them until we were quite literally on top of them. The squad of ten dropped to five as the Tulaq crushed one in her jaws, landed on another, slashed two with her foreclaws, and used her wing to slice one of the Men in Black in half. The rider and I opened fire to either side as soon as we touched ground, hosing down the remaining soldiers in a sweeping circle of armor-piercing ammo. Chalky white blood spewed across the concrete. Enhanced reflexes or not, there was nowhere for them to hide.

"My girl here wants to know what the hell these things are," the rider said. He had a thick accent, vaguely Middle-Eastern. "She says they taste awful."

"Dead macerated Weeder souls." I unbuckled my harness and dropped to the roof, then unzipped the front of my baggy riding suit and shed it like a snakeskin. It was made of special leather that the Tulaq's feathers couldn't cut. I wore ordinary, faded fatigues underneath, along with a tool belt and a shoulder holster. "That's why we're here."

"Fuckin' Morphorde." The rider hawked in his throat with disgust, and took the leather suit from me. He threw it over his mount's neck. The Tulaq spun and bounded away from me, launching herself back up into the sky with powerful beats of her wings and vanishing into the rain. I was alone.

"Touchdown." I ran to the nearest twitching corpse and raided it for a keycard, gas mask, and ammunition.

"Alright. COMMs copied in. Good luck, bat'ko. *"*

I ran another quick check over my weapons and tools, then took a moment to reach back in for Kutkha, and out for Binah. My heart sunk when I sensed her. She was alive in the building somewhere below, her anxiety thrumming through the energetic tether that bound us. After a couple more seconds, I could feel her pacing, hear her restless meowing, and, more distantly, the sounds of human distress that were agitating her. When I snapped back to my own body, it was like falling from a great height back into my skin.

The keycard got me into the elevator engine room. I kicked the door in, spraying the far wall with a suppressing burst that scattered paint chips and shards of brick across the floor. When the dust had settled and no one returned fire, I stepped in, closed the door behind me, and looked around.

The big motor and cables were motionless and cold. The electronic console showed that the elevator was on the second floor, the top of the building, and the ventilation grate that I'd busted during the escape had been replaced with a brand new one. That new grate was warded—with blood. I crouched beside it, frowning, and held out a hand. The magic hummed like a live-wire, energy that made the veins in my fingers and forearm buzz. It was a trap of some kind, a quick and dirty seal based on Paracelsus' Seal of Scorpio.

This felt personal. Scorpio was ruled by the nocturnal aspect of Mars. Intoxicating and dangerous, I'd been working with that particular kind of energy since birth. Scorpionic and Martial aspects were a powerful influence on my astrological birth chart, and the Vigiles had to know that. A Scorpionic ward pitted like against like. The design was simple, even classic, but the way it made the hair on my arm stand on end gave no reason to doubt its power.

There was a very good chance this ward was generally made to protect against forced entry, and specifically, entry by me. What it did was hard to say. It could secretly whisper to its caster, or explode in my face, poison me, or infect me with catastrophic sepsis. Given that it was drawn in blood, blood poisoning wasn't out of the question, either.

"Solidly made, but..." I sighed and shook my head, and immersed into the design. Carefully.

Every physical ward had at least one flaw: the alpha-omega point where the enchanter first touched the surface the ward was scribed on. There were several different methods to find this point. The easiest and most direct was a massive sacrifice directed into the matrix of the ward, which was akin to hitting a car battery with a lightning bolt. The energy swelled the ward, and if it didn't have a channel to shunt that energy away, it would burst from the pressure at the weakest spot. Most wards were made to conserve and gather magical energy to sustain their power, and if a mage was putting up a set-it-and-forget-it ward, a power sink was almost never factored into the design.

By itself, the Wardbreaker did something like a sacrifice. Using my blood and the kinetic energy it discharged when firing, it could surge a sigil, destroying it, or at least expose the alpha-omega point. Slowly, I drew the pistol from its holster, reading the sigil thoughtfully as I cocked the hammer back. There was no Phitonic sink to prevent surging, but there was a variable of some kind in place. Its purpose was inscrutable, but my guess was that it had multiple simultaneous reactions to being triggered. It seemed a little egotistical to assume that there was anything specifically related to me.

I used chalk and a soft nugget of copper—the pure metal—to circle the ward and buffer any explosive or venomous actions, then focused on the Wardbreaker. With a push of intention, the magic in my weapon kindled to life. Phi swept over it and up my arm like a hot wind. The energy tugged at my skin, pulling blood painlessly through the pores. It flowed between the checkered grooves of the pistol grip and snaked up and along the sigils engraved into the barrel. Zarya's flesh had charged my body with Phi, so much of it that I had to rein back how much charge the gun accepted. When it began to pulse in time with my heartbeat, I leveled the Wardbreaker at the grate, and barked the command word as I pulled the trigger. "*IAL!*"

The round left the barrel with a puff of sound, blowing into the steel grate with disproportionate force. The flow of phi in the design snapped like lightning, sparking and discharging down into the elevator shaft below. The ward consumed the steel as it warped, briefly sucking the all light of the room into it as it buckled and imploded.

"Come on. You can do better than that." I muttered as I kicked in the crumpled metal. It bounced off the walls of the ventilation shaft, clattering down on top of the elevator car. It was a little over six feet below. I navigated down the shaft with my flashlight, and dropped down feet first. I landed on top of the car. It jostled, bouncing a little under my weight, but held firm underneath me.

The trapdoor on the top of the car was padlocked closed, so I cut the bolt, then checked my watch. Fifteen minutes until the assault teams arrived. Resolute, I pulled the door open and slid in, the keycard already in my teeth, ready to go. My feet hadn't even completely touched the ground when the trapdoor slammed shut over my head, and the ward I hadn't seen or felt activated around me: walls, floor, and ceiling.

That was when I remembered that Scorpio, more than anything, ruled secrets and surprises.

"Oh shit," was all I got out before the elevator buckled in, metal groaning under the wave of powerful magic that swept in from all sides, and fell.

CHAPTER 44

The cables whipped loose somewhere over my head. There were no rails to slow the descent. The power cut as I slammed back up against the ceiling, the hollow steel cage plummeting in freefall. I had three seconds, maybe four before it slammed into the ground. The elevator bounced—I didn't. Gravity reversed direction and slapped me down before I'd even finished shouting '*CHET!*' with all the force I could muster. The barrier I conjured was all that saved my life, forming an air bag between me and the floor as it crumpled and buckled up into the cabin. Instead of being crushed by inertia, the magical shield threw me into one of the walls, upside down. I slid before I tumbled head-first to the ground with a mouth full of panic: ears banging, heart hammering, light flashing behind my eyes. I wasn't even on my feet when the doors rammed open and a grenade rolled in, spewing gas into the small room.

Even wearing the mask I'd looted from the Vigiles soldier, enough tear gas got in around the displaced seal that my eyes stung. I struggled to my feet, reached for a weapon, and found myself facing a circle of rifles and piercingly bright, scope-mounted flashlights.

"Drop it!"

"Down! On the ground!"

"Down!"

"Get down! *Get down*!"

Security poured in. Something yanked the Wardbreaker out of my hand, and I started swinging. I cracked one across the visor with the '*Tzain*' spell, shattering it and knocking him against a wall, kneed another between the legs with enough force that not even his cup could save him, and nearly brought a third down while I shouted telepathically to Zarya.

Ten or so guards swarmed and pinned me. I struggled, bit, spat, and cursed under their weight, shoving one away while another clamped a black glass collar around my neck. As soon as it touched my skin, my connection to Kutkha dulled and my subliminal awareness of Binah's location dropped entirely. Guards hauled me up by my elbows and cuffed my wrists. I was pulled out of the elevator after they were on, and roughly wrenched back and forth into the small ocean of guns waiting in the corridor beyond.

My escort half-dragged, half-marched me up a grimy stairwell, where we lost about half the troops, then pushed me out a door into a wide, clean-looking corridor that smelled like the bottom of a trash can. We cleared a checkpoint, where everything I was wearing except my underwear was cut off, and continued past it to a pair of heavy steel doors. They opened into a cavernous, cold, truck-delivery room milling with people in various states of organized alarm. Techs in lab scrubs surrounded a tanker truck like the one Glory had stolen. It sat beside a steel capsule-shaped hyperbaric chamber with a transparent glassy door. The chamber was overgrown with what looked like purplish vines studded with pieces of obsidian, alien tentacle-like things that originated from sucking fleshy holes in the sides of the tank, places where the steel had been cored out and replaced with Morphordian tissue.

Joshua Keen was signing off on a clipboard behind the tanker truck, Tomas an expressionless pillar behind him with his hands folded over his belt. It was Tomas who noticed us first, staring placidly as security brought me over to them and shoved me down to my knees, a barrel pressed against the back of my head.

"Ah, good. I was hoping we could rely on your profile," Keen said, handing the pen and clipboard over to the waiting tech. "Really, though, I expected better out of you, Sokolsky. You fell for a stick-and-box trap, you realize?"

My eyes narrowed as I watched the tech put a fist to their left breast and bow from the neck, then pull away. "I realize I've been busting your wards for years. You're a Phitometrist, you hypocritical piece of shit."

"I am. I am also a Knight Vigilant of the Holy Order of Saint Peter, and not a criminal warlock," Keen replied stiffly.

"That machine sure looks like something a holy order would field." I barked a short laugh. "All those pulsating black tentacles. Holy, *sure*."

Joshua rolled his eyes and looked over my shoulder at my escort. "Take him to the rubber room and double tap him twice, just to be certain. Charlie Team, fetch Otto and his thugs from the freight room. They should be almost done. We need to wrap up and get moving."

"You don't want to kill me." I cocked my chin as the soldiers saluted and pulled me up by my armpits.

"You could not possibly be more wrong." Keen wasn't looking at me any longer, instead watching the techs as they pulled hoses out from the base of the truck. Clusters of small tentacles yearned from the holes in the sides of the hyperbaric chamber, reaching for the black glass-capped ends. My skin crawled.

"You don't!" I called out as I was pulled away. "Because I killed Lee, and now I'm the only one who knows where Eden is."

The thin Agent turned on me. "Wait. Halt."

The soldiers stopped dead.

Keen caught up with us, a slow, wary stalk. "Come again?"

"Eden," I repeated. "You couldn't make Lee talk, you do-gooder piece of shit. We sprung this place, and when she thought she was safe, I got her to tell me where to find the Garden."

"And then you killed her," Keen finished flatly. "We found her body with the heart cut out."

The extent of the bullshit was almost funny. I shrugged. "Well, I had to eat *something*."

Keen suddenly looked very tired. He drew himself up like a statue, studying me down his nose. "What do you hope to gain with this gambit, Sokolsky? Clemency? You won't find mercy here."

"Insurance." I shrugged again, still hanging from the guards' hands. "What else?"

Keen's mouth thinned as he regarded me in silence for several seconds. "Fine. Have it your way. Under Rutherford's Law, you have been declared a non-person in perpetuity. Your citizenship is hereby revoked. Once we have extracted this information from you, which will at best take a couple of days, you will be subject to exorcism and summary execution. We will insure that your spiritual infection never graces the Earth again."

I stared back at him. "You let Otto Roth rape and murder a woman. You gunned down a mother of two in cold blood. The MahTree's Ruined because you took her from her rightful guardian. What the hell makes you think you have the right to judge me?"

Keen sighed and pinched the bridge of his nose. "Take him to the containment circle. If he moves a muscle, shoot him. I'll call Transport.

"Sir." The man on my left saluted, and off we went.

The containment circle was an example of Keen's best work—a six foot warded circle drawn in rendered Weeder Phi. The lines shimmered and crawled when I was thrown in, but didn't smear as I scrambled for the edge. I felt like

I'd run into a clear plexiglass barrier. It held mages the way that most magical circles held demons.

The doors at the end of the room swung out, admitting a number of people walking alongside a forklift. It was carrying a stack of four small, heavy battery cages, three-by-three-foot cubes barely large enough to fold a person inside. From here, I made out Jenner, Zane, Talya, and Ron inside. Jenner was small enough that she could breathe and move her head a little. Talya was weeping; Ron was purple, struggling for air. Zane, the largest, was packed in so tightly that he was quite literally suffocating. His dark skin was ashen, and he wasn't moving.

Where the fuck are you!? I tried to reach out to Zarya again, struggling to stay still, composed, calm. Otto, Dogboy, and Gator were strutting alongside the forklift, shit-eating grins on their faces, and a horrible instinct gnawed at me. What if someone in ANSWER had sabotaged the operation? What if the Vigiles had found them before they'd arrived, alerted by my presence? They had telepaths and seers, surely... had someone foreseen what we were doing, and interrupted it?

Jenner saw me across the room and blanched as the forklift swung around to a smooth stop near the hyperbaric chamber. I shook my head, eyeing the guards who still had their weapons trained on my face at opposite sides of the circle.

"Okay, Agent. Time's up!" Otto called to Keen as the processions met in front of the tanker truck. "Otto wants his money, and then we're getting the hell out."

"Of course. Tomas?" Keen motioned to Tomas, who nodded. He left at a quick walk. Keen beckoned to Otto to join him at a small field table set up at an angle to the chamber. "Come here, and we'll settle up."

The big Weeder was wary as he strolled over, Dogboy and Gator trailing him like bodyguards. "Tell you what. How about you keep ten K, and Otto takes the kitten girl?"

My eyes narrowed, and I looked over at the stack of cages. Talya was wide-eyed and trembling, bound naked inside her box. She had dried blood on her face, but no injuries. Not ones visible to the eye, anyway.

"Try it! I'll rip your fucking dick off!" She shouted.

Keen made a show of thinking about it. "Fifteen?"

"Ten. No piece of tail is worth fifteen." Otto squinted over at Tomas as he returned with a big silver carry-on suitcase.

"What? Can't handle me, Otto?" Jenner called out harshly from her cage. "Come on, boy. Take me outta here, and I'll give you the ride of your fuckin' life!"

I was so enraged while listening to this bullshit that I almost didn't notice the way that the collar had loosened around my neck until it was too late. It was drooping, sagging like cold lava dribbling into the ocean. My body was still flush with Zarya's blood, and while my heart pumped her Phi through my veins, there were few locks that could hold me. *Thank you, Zarya.*

The two guards had their heads turned. They were watching Keen and the trio of Nightbrothers with wary anticipation of trouble. Their guns were still pointing toward me, but the muzzles had dipped.

Moving carefully, I reached up and slowly pulled the collar free, set it down, and looked down to study the magic circle.

Tomas placed the suitcase on the table and opened it, revealing rows of neatly stacked Benjamins. Otto sniffed hard as he approached, pulling out a note and examining it against the lights above. "Huh. Brand new."

"Indeed." Keen had moved aside, putting himself closest to Dogboy. "Compliments of the Federal Reserve for service to the community."

"Right. Well, so long and thanks for the fish. Time to go, right?" Dogboy was eyeing the steel tube nervously.

"Last offer. Ten for the girl." Otto slammed the case closed and jerked it off the table. His thick hand barely fit through the suitcase's handle. "Otto'll take her off your hands."

"I wish we could oblige, but the raw material she provides is worth more than what you're offering. We need manpower more than anything, especially given what's going on outside." Keen pushed his glasses up his nose with a small, fleeting smile. "We will begin with the largest animal first. Gentlemen."

At the softly spoken trigger word, every guard in the room opened fire on Otto Roth.

CHAPTER 45

Otto dropped the briefcase, roaring as explosive rounds tore his chest and gut apart. By the time his knees hit the ground, Gator was dead, the shaman's magical shields shattered under multiple impacts. Keen lunged forward fearlessly, and pulled his sword out in a blindingly fast, sweeping arc. Dogboy had the best reflexes of the three of them, and he ducked the blade... but he didn't get back up. The vampire's already-pale face drained of all color, and he reached up to pluck at his head as the top third of his skull separated and fell to the floor beside him. There was little blood: just an orange goo, like decaying pumpkin flesh, that jiggled, then splattered as he collapsed to his face and went still.

"Filth, the lot of you." Joshua Keen spun the sword, flicking Feeder goop from the edge, then pulled a tissue from his jacket pocket and ran it along the blade. "Alright. Proceed."

Security converged around Otto, who was struggling to keep his internal organs inside as he forced himself to his feet. When they lay hands on him, he bellowed wordlessly and began to shift—but not in time. The giant centipede erupted from his skin just as he was shoved into the hyperbaric chamber, twisting and lunging at the door that slammed in its face. Six men held it shut while two more turned the vault lock. The centipede thrashed inside, squealing as the machine came to life.

A horrible, discordant feeling passed through my limbs, sucking the strength out of them: a magical pressure drop that was followed by a revolting alkaline smell. It gnawed at my sinuses like a burst abscess. The tubes leading to the chamber surged, vomiting liquid into the tank and engulfing Otto in fluid that burned whatever it touched, peeling the giant insect in fine, fine layers, like translucent glass ash. He screamed. Relentless, shrill, agonized wails pierced the steel capsule and filled the room. Otto lashed from side to side, desperately seeking escape and finding none as his soul was torn apart and dissolved into scintillating white liquid.

"... in salt and get him ready for transport." Keen's voice broke through the hellish noise, cold and calm. "Take the spook and prep him for the flight. The works: sedation, enema, saline, nutrients. The director will want him interrogated straight away. Tomas, which one of these creatures turned into the lion?"

"It was either the fat man or the girl."

"Put the male through next. Make sure we pack as much into that tanker as possible. You're in charge while I update Delta-1 on the new intake."

"Yes, Sir."

"You fucking *monsters!*" Jenner howled out through the bars of her cage. "What the fuck is *wrong* with you?!"

My vision cleared as Otto's anguished cries became weaker and less frequent, then they ended entirely as the digestion reached the point of no return. The creeper-vine tentacles that encircled the chamber had swollen with an unholy dark light, channeling and pumping energy into the tubes connected to the truck. Keen glided away from the chamber to make his call, and I resumed my frantic study of the ward.

This circle *did* have a power sink built into it—a reserve of Phi that was replenished by my presence inside of the design. It was impossible to defuse the ward from within the circle while it slowly leeched the Phi from me. Oddly, I didn't feel depleted by it. Zarya's Phi, possibly... or perhaps the MahTree's Rhizomes.

I felt back for the collar. While the guards watched Ron being pulled out of his cage, I carefully and quietly patted at the invisible barrier between me and the rest of the room, then experimentally slid the open collar outside of the edge of the circle. It penetrated the ward as if it weren't there, able to be moved back and forth over the edge of the circle.

Ron shifted as soon as he was free, and the Men in Black suddenly had a pony-sized African Lion on their hands. They were unfortunately well-prepared. Even as Ron reared and plunged, roaring, he was taken out with high-powered tasers that sizzled in the air as they snapped and cracked. It took six or seven of them all at once, but they put him down and dragged him to the chamber as Jenner and Talya screamed for them to stop.

Focus. I had to focus. There was only one chance to get this right. Now that I knew the collar could extend beyond the circle, I cautiously kindled a tiny sliver of compressed matter at the end of one of my fingers, watching Keen and the guards. Neither reacted: Keen was on the phone, and security was busy keeping an eye on their comrades as they shoved Ron into the digestion chamber.

The spike of matter also extended beyond the circle when pushed over the line, though it kept my finger trapped behind. I swallowed and sat back on my ass, hands on the floor. One of the guards, alerted by the movement, glanced down at me. He didn't seem to notice the missing collar from overhead.

The Vigiles slammed the chamber door shut, muffling Ron's roars as they became all-too-human screams of pain.

"Ron! RON, *NO!*" Talya was hoarse with terror and fury, her voice ripping through the air. "I'll kill you! I'll kill you *all*, you motherfuckers!"

Focus. I knew what was happening to Ron, and I couldn't stop it. I closed my eyes, letting my senses play out through the air, and called to the dust on the floor.

Fresh Kills was filthy, and so was this building. With the swamp, the city, and cubic miles of trash, everything had a fine film of dirt, exhaust, lead, rust, and grime. I had to work slowly, carefully, pulling in slithering streams of particle earth across the ground in such a way that no one noticed. The raw shouts of the women were drowned out by Ron's nightmarish cries as he died, his soul peeled away in layers like onion skin. Across the room, Keen stepped away from the phone.

"Do the girl next." Tomas spoke to the mass of eight MiB who had caught Ron.

The tanker hummed as it hungrily sucked Ron's Phitonic mass from the chamber. Talya was red with fury, rattling the bars of her cage as she wrestled and struggled inside. They ripped her out, kicking and spitting, and carried her toward the chamber door.

Focus. The timing had to be perfect.

"*I'll kill you all!*" Talya shrieked, kicking one man off, ignoring the second as he tasered her. She shrugged off the electricity with a snarl that deepened and grew in volume as the shift took hold of her. Other guards— HuMans and Men in Black—swarmed her as the gigantic American Lion erupted out of the thick of them, throwing a soldier across the room before the others could jump on her. Talya's shifted form was half again as big as Ron's. It was too late for him, but not for her, Jenner, and Zane.

"*AYSH!*" I yelled the command word, short and sharp, and slapped my hands on the ground. The jarring spike of pain through my palms manifested in reality: a pair of seven-foot shards of razor-sharp detritus erupted from the ground and impaled the guards outside my circle. In through the pelvis, out through the chest. They gurgled around mouths full of blood: the smaller man bled red, the other white.

The ward flared brightly as I stood, calling the white blood to my hand. It was weaker, thicker Phi than Zarya's, polluted and homogenized, but it was a substance that was still more vital than my own. It ran down the spear of matter and into the circle, which flared as it switched from me to the stronger source of energy, feeding on it greedily.

"Get that thing in the digester! Open fire!" Keen shouted over the top of the sudden ruckus, and drew his sword. Tomas began casting, even as Talya snarled and clamped her massive jaws down on the head of a HuMan soldier, tearing it from his shoulders.

I drew the energy and blood of the dual sacrifice back toward me. Instead of a Phitonic shield, I built a shield of matter around the edge of the circle. It cracked and splintered as bullets struck it. They blew through the Phitonic matrix, but were caught up in the physical mass of iron, lead, water, and dirt, blowing parts of it into glass spikes that extruded back toward me. That was when the endorphins hit, and with them came wisdom, the ability to see the air and shape it.

There was a massive roar that cut to a squeal as Talya was brought down. She lurched up to her paws, still under fire, and sunk down to her chest again as men encircled her with tasers and rifles. Keen rushed me, a blur of motion through the foul ice-like barricade I'd formed. I held it, held it... and then shouted a second word of command that shattered the wall into a million fine shards that hung in the air. I slashed my hands down, and the shards congealed into long whips of razor-sharp, dirty crystal bound by Phi the texture and color of craft glue.

Keen tried to dodge, but there were too many moving parts to avoid. He took a faceful of needles as he rolled to the side and came up on his feet, bleeding heavily. "Start the pumps! Start the goddamn pump!"

Behind him, the Men in Black shoved Talya, mortally wounded, into the digester. Instead of finishing off Keen, I swept the crystalline cords around, meshed them together into a single, flexible razor-edged whip, and smashed it over the hoses connecting the tanker to the digester. It shredded them, spraying gray fluid into the air and then across the ground. When it splashed ordinary humans, nothing happened. Whenever it touched a Man in Black, they collapsed like sand at the first wetting of their clothes. The ones closest to the mess didn't even have time to open their mouths before their empty uniforms and rifles fell. Others had a chance to back away a step or two before they were spattered. One lived long enough to claw at his faceplate and spin down to his knees before he turned to slime and slumped formlessly like the rest.

Heaving for breath, bathed in sweat, I hauled the Phi back toward my body. I spun a semi-circular defensive cocoon and dropped to the floor with my arms up over my head. Bullets struck the outside, chipping pieces of the shield away. There was a dull, crumpling rumble, and for a moment, I thought someone had pitched a grenade at me... but then the gunfire turned, I heard shouts of alarm, and then a klaxon.

The sound dropped me. I shook my hands, worked my jaws, moaned and heaved through the piercing, skull-drilling white noise, flailing at the inside of my cocoon and pushing away from it. Burned out on magic, I couldn't do anything except cover my ears and try to see past the blur of involuntary tears. The air raid siren burrowed in behind my eyes, blinding me. I saw the world in slices: ANSWER rolling in, pouring through both sets of doors ahead of gunfire at head height. People bleeding across the concrete, Tomas and Keen hiding behind the cover of the tanker. Talya, rapidly healing, burst free of her confinement and rampaged through the nearest pack of soldiers. She soaked off the automatic fire that hit her from all angles as she slapped a man's arm clean off his shoulder. The fluid was still gushing from the tanker truck. It oxidized and evaporated quickly. The residue formed crusts of eerily familiar grayish glass: Yen crystals. The liquid slopped through these crusts, forming channels that wound toward the forklift and the cages. Jenner and Zane were still trapped inside, unable to move and unable to shift.

Retching, I crept up to hands and knees and made like a lizard under the hail of gunfire overhead, pushing through the slight resistance still offered by the containment circle. I got to the cages before the Yen did, seized the bars between me and Jenner, and hauled her away from it across the floor.

"Jesus Christ, Rex!" Her sharp yellow voice was a flash of color against the blinding light of the klaxon. "Why are you... what the hell...?"

"No time to explain!" I yelled, already running back for Zane. I wasn't sure he was alive, but it wasn't his body at risk. Grunting, I braced my shoulder against the cage, dug my feet into the floor, and charged forward to push it out of the liquid crawling toward us. We got maybe three feet before a crushing blow hit me across the back of the head. I collapsed in a heap, my face against the wet ground. Sokolsky men are built like bricks, so I didn't pass out, but I was slow to sway back up—too slow to stop

Joshua Keen from thrusting his long sword through my back and out the front of my shoulder.

CHAPTER 46

I roared more from shock than pain, rolling to the side and pulling the sword out of his sweat-slick hands. He'd hit me in my right side, immobilizing that arm, but the left was free to come up. Keen blocked my punch, then collapsed, breathless, when I slammed a knee up between his legs and ground it in. The man's eyes bulged.

"Come on, princess! You want to fucking brawl!?" I shouted at him in Ukrainian. I grabbed him by the front of his shirt and pulled him close as he tried to push back. He was gangly, fast, hard with lean muscle and jacked up on magic, but still couldn't match my raw strength. I headbutted him, knocking his glasses off, and did it a second time hard enough that I saw stars. The Agent coughed blood onto my neck, snarling as he wrenched his shirt from my hand. He clubbed me across the face, two or three hits that brought a surge of fresh bile to my throat. He reached for the sword, and I lunged up and bit him on the arm just above his elbow, holding on, curling up, and driving my fist into his ribs until they finally cracked under my knuckles. The Agent collapsed on top of me, teeth bared, and went for my eyes with his fingers. My right arm still wasn't working: all I had were my jaws. Clawing at him, shaking my head from side to side, I managed to keep his nails out of my eyes and got a finger in my mouth. He screamed before I even bit down, jerking back, but I hung on like a pitbull.

"Let go! Let go of me!" Keen's voice was shrill, barely registering against the full-body sensory overload of the air-raid klaxon. I felt him groping for a weapon with his other hand, voice rising in pitch and volume as I ground the joint between my teeth until the cartilage splintered and crunched. Finger-crushing, unlike stabbing, hurts from the time it starts to the final wrench of the phalanx that dislocates the joint. I was vaguely aware of Keen hitting me, of the blows raining against my ribs and shoulder, but nothing registered until he jammed the fingers of his other hand into the wound in my shoulder. "Let go of me, you waste of space! I'm a Federal-"

"Fuck you!" I screamed, put my knees up against his abdomen, and shoved him off of me. Keen tried to catch himself on his bad hand, yelped in pain, somehow got to his feet, and finally pulled his pistol. He leveled it at my face, eyes hazy and wet with involuntary tears, and was about to pull the trigger when a spinning blur whirled past him and took off his right hand at the wrist. The Agent stared at the spurting mess of meat and bone in shock for all of a second before his eyes rolled back in his head. He swooned into a faint on the Yen-encrusted floor.

"Alexi!" It was Angkor. He ran to my side as I rolled to an elbow, wheezing, and spat. Something hard and white came out. *A tooth*, I thought numbly. *How hilarious.*

"Jenner. Zane. Let them out." I gasped, voice deep and thick. Angkor helped me up to my knees. "Go!"

"You're bleeding to death." Angkor caught my shoulder in both hands, and I swung weakly at the back of his knee on reflex as he bent his will to the wound. There was a rippling, hot pain, then a numb warmth that spread through my arm. It spasmed as the severed nerves started to heal, enough relief that I was able to stand on my own.

"Get them." I was weak, dizzy and sick, panting with the effort to breathe. "I have to find Binah."

Angkor didn't argue. He left me to get the Weeders out of their cages. I clumsily moved forward a step, then finally noticed the carnage wrought in the extraction room. There were bodies everywhere. Tomas was missing - fled, presumably. ANSWER fighters were mopping up. Led by Zarya, they were cleansing the Morphordian additions to the hyperbaric chamber, spraying them with backpacks and hoses, like the kind used to spray pesticide on weeds.

Keen was crawling across the floor, straining for his sword with the fingers he had left. I had a brief vision of stabbing him with it, over and over again, until arterial blood spurted and he stopped moving. He managed to clap his hand down over it as I stalked toward him, and looked at me with eyes red from tears and raw with hatred. "*Sacratus adytum!*"

I froze at the command word, a defensive word of power jerking my tongue. It never manifested. Keen disappeared in a flash of light. The afterimage lingered on the backs of my eyelids.

Binah's panic broke through my fugue, and I instinctively swung in the direction of the freight room door, pushing past someone—I didn't see who—on my way to reach her. Her meowing was a dark blue sawing sound. I barely needed vision to find her in the piles of empty crates and refuse in here. When she saw me, her cries grew in intensity and depth, a rolling *miiaww, miiaww, miaawww.*

"Binah, Binah. Calm." I came to a stop in front of her and unlocked her carrier cage with shaking hands. She clung to my skin with claws when I pulled her out of it, still meowing with frantic terror while I petted her, rubbed my cheek against her head, rocked her gently. "My kitten, my girl... it's alright."

She was still in good condition: physically, at least. Thirsty and hungry. I closed my eyes and buried my nose in her soft fur, embracing her small, lithe form with deep urgency. She helped with the sensory pain, somehow. Some part of me, deep down, was howling at the fresh memories of Ron's and Otto's screams, Keen's cold Final Solution-style attitude. The mere thought of something dissolving Kutkha made my stomach quake with a weird, paradoxically erotic sensation, disgust so profound that it was interwoven with a kind of fascinated lust.

Binah grasped my head with her small paws and began to frantically groom my nose, and that, out of everything, made me break down. The tears flowed as I stroked her, the conversation I'd had with Norgay playing through my head like a recording. He'd started with a warning.

"What I ask you to do would destroy anyone else. But with the Rhizomes, your courage, your abilities, and your background, you

are uniquely qualified to achieve what no one else has been able to do."

"What's that?"

"I want you to break into the Vigiles prison. And I want you to bring the place down."

"You think that's possible?"

"Yes. This is a very difficult thing to ask of someone, Alexi. It will be humiliating and degrading, hard, and the price for failure is very steep. But you face a choice between this temporary pain and the inevitability of the Engine. I ask you to take pain over the destruction of you, your world, your blood-brother. We MUST learn where this prison is, and stop them before it's too late. In return, we will help you hunt down Yaroshenko and Vassily. If you die, then I swear we will still take them out."

"I'll think about it," I had replied. *"But I don't know. I have no idea who you are or why I should trust anything you say. How do I know you're not setting me up to be dumped?"*

"Because deception is not in our best interest," Norgay had said. *"GOD is a massive multicellular being, Alexi. Individual parts of a complex whole are only useful when those parts are all functioning together. Spotting a Morphorde is easy when you think of it this way, because the NO is inherently pointless and purposeless. Why do Morphorde do what they do? We don't know, and neither do they. They have no true purpose, except very abstract things, like 'transcendence' or 'power' or 'hygiene' or 'destruction'. Not stewardship. Not growth, unless it is rampant, cancerous growth without end. They will never profess a commitment to digging the truth out of history or understand why we need to preserve oceans or save animals from extinction, or the conservation of precious, rare cenotes untouched since Mayan times. There is a theme underlying*

all of the practical goals of life and livingness. Do you know what it is?"

"Yes." I'd answered. *"Freedom."*

"Almost correct. The theme of all life is submission."

I'd frowned, not understanding. *"Submission is the opposite of freedom."*

"All beings are in service to something," Norgay replied. *"Every cell in your body submits to the greater whole. Every urge you have makes you a servant to it. You depend on the animals, microbes, and plants who have died for your continued life, even as they are of service to you. Altruism exists in nature for that reason. Freedom is merely the exercise of choice within the confines of life—life which would not exist without submission and interdependence. Why do you think the most common motivator of HuMan Morphorde is transcendence? Bodilessness? Nothingness?"*

I'd wanted to disagree, but hadn't been able to think of anything to say in reply.

"Morphorde hate choice, because for them, the answer is always 'no'. The act of working for the greater good is inevitably an act of submission that requires someone to say 'yes'. And that's another easy way to pick a Morphorde: they embody mastery and denial. To them, submission is degrading, and those who submit are less worthy than those who oppress. Torture and rape are their primary weapons for this reason. To us, submission is the backbone of everything we do. It is something you can only understand with time."

"How does that work out for a soldier? They can't submit to the enemy."

"But they do. What is courage, Alexi?"

"The willingness to do battle against the things that frighten you, no matter what."

"The soldier submits to his command, his command to the needs of the war. And through it all, the bravest are the ones who continue to say 'yes' – not just to the orders they receive, but to their own consciences and the needs of their comrades, and to the actions they must take on the field."

"So you want me to serve you, then?"

"I want you to understand that all submit to the inevitability of being part of the future of your Cell. GOD is suffering an infection that will become fatal if the NO-thing burrows its way into GOD's core, and we HuMans can choose to serve it, or resist being a part of its journey. I don't want a servant. I want someone smart enough to know when they're on the bottom rung of the ladder, they get to choose when to knock it down and kill everyone at the top in a single master stroke. Extract our last Keeper from this 'Delta Site' and pull the place down on their heads, and we will do everything in our power to aid you."

"Bat'ko!"

I turned to see Zarya at the head of a three-person team. She strode toward me from the doors, the visor of her helmet lifted to show her face. "*Bat'ko!* We have to go! The Army is here!"

Binah was purring now, kneading my neck with her claws to soothe herself. I breathed in the cat's familiar dust-and-sunlight smell, exhaling against her coat. "I'm sorry, girl. You're not going to see me for a while again, and there's nothing I can do about it."

"Come on, Alexi!"

I turned, and held the Siamese tightly in my arms as I broke into a jog. We met Zarya halfway, following her as she pivoted and ran for the door with us in tow.

ANSWER was rallying inside the digester room, forming rank. Jenner, Zane, and Talya milled around with them. Zane was pale and drawn, skin still ashy blue-brown. Talya was weeping, her arms wrapped around Zane's waist. Angkor was with Jenner, still in her tiger form.

"Angkor." I went to him and Jenner, Binah cradled in my arms. "Jenner. Talya, Zane. Thank goodness you're alright."

Talya looked up at me, her face a red, puffy mask of grief. "R-Rex. They killed him, Rex. T-They killed him!"

The tiger turned her nose toward the smashed digester and moaned.

I touched Angkor on the shoulder and went to Talya to kiss her cheek. She hugged me with hunched shoulders, frightened and in pain, and only let me go when Binah began to squirm. Zane came to a stop in front of us, solemn and glassy-eyed with dissociation.

I opened my mouth to speak: to tell them that Ron had probably betrayed them, that he'd been in on it, but the words faltered. In the end, they would all have been victims of Keen's purge. "I'm sorry we didn't make it in time."

"You made it. That's the point." Talya wrapped an arm around Zane's waist. He was still in shock. "Thank you. Angkor, we… we…"

"Don't worry about it." Angkor had drawn up beside us while Zarya got everyone else together. "We have to go. Doug's reporting that a military helicopter is preparing to land on us."

"Okay, time to move! Move out!" Zarya called to the assembled ranks. "We have to get out of here, ASAP!"

I bowed my head. "I have to stay."

"What?" Angkor's expression immediately shifted toward suspicion. "Alexi-"

I drew a deep breath, the precursor to all magic, and stood up straight. "Take Binah, find my things, and go," I said. "I have to stay here."

The tiger reared up on her haunches, smoothly morphing back into Jenner's much smaller, wiry human form. "Rex, don't be a fucking idiot."

"I have to, just this once." I held Binah out to Angkor, trying not to look at Jenner. She was nude. "Angkor... this cat means the world to me. If I know that you, Zarya, and she are alive, I'll stay alive. Protect her."

Angkor's eyes darkened, and his lips parted as if in surprise for a moment before he nodded. He took the purring cat from my arms. She looked back at me with innocent, predatory, loving eyes, her throat still vibrating. Binah somehow understood my intent... and was at peace with it.

"You took the Delta Site mission," he said, matter-of-factly.

"Protect her." I lay one hand on his arms, and one on Binah's head. "And tell Norgay I said yes."

"Rex? What's going on?" Talya's voice was trembling, but before she could say anything else, Zane rested a hand on her shoulder. She fretfully glanced at him, wide-eyed and stricken. "What do you mean-?"

"Leave it, Kitten." Jenner had her arms crossed, her face hard and resolute. "I got no idea what you're talking about, Rex, but I want you to know something. You showed real class back there. You always have. I love you like a brother. Whatever you're up to, we'll be waiting for you."

"We'll find you," Angkor said to me, his voice heating like a brand. "I *swear* we'll find you. And we won't let them have her, or you, or this world."

"*Bat'ko!*" Zarya called from across the room. "Angkor! Come on!"

My chest tightened in a way that had nothing to do with my aching ribs. Tongue-tied, I bowed my head to her and took a couple of steps closer to Angkor. When Binah was pressed between our chests, I kissed him chastely on the mouth. He breathed softly against my lips, almost a sigh.

An explosion rocked the ceiling overhead. I pushed Angkor and Binah away, and turned around. "Go."

"*Bat'ko!*"

"Leave it, Zarya!" Angkor called back to her. "It's a directive!"

I glimpsed Zarya's worried expression as they reached the door and hurried out. She was the last thing I saw before the roof caved in overhead.

Twenty or so soldiers in black fatigues dropped to the ground, scattering into teams. More burst out of the freight room, having entered through the truck delivery doors. The room was still charged with Phi, the air humming. I closed my eyes, felt for the course of magic, and meshed my two best spells together.

The debris and water pouring in rushed to the doorway where ANSWER had fled, plugging in the gaps, sealing edges and locks. I went to my knees and laced my hands behind my head while the magic burned through me, barricading the door with scrap metal, ice, and hardened dust. The remaining energy I had left with the shockwave, and the resistance I'd mustered against the siren wail collapsed entirely as the gift of Zarya's Phi drained from my body.

The soldiers rushed me, shouting for me to stop casting, lie down, stay still. I stayed where I was, unresisting as they surrounded me, and waited.

Joshua Keen and Tomas Black walked out from the freight room with an escort, their faces drawn into hard, grim lines. Keen was stony and jowly. Eyes sunken, face pale, still covered in blood, he was riding a high, some form of drug replacing the pain of his severed hand with numb vigor. His wrist was bandaged. Tomas looked... unwell. Pinched and hard, like a dry pastry left in the sun for too long.

"You." Keen was still weak, still hurting, but his voice was cold and clear. He pulled his pistol with the left hand, cocking the hammer. "You did this. This was your plan all along, wasn't it?"

"Surprise," I replied. "Remember that thing about the stick-and-box trap?"

His eyes narrowed to furious slits. "Who do you work for?"

Submit. "I work for myself, stumpy."

"You arrogant…" The Agent's eyes were mad with rage as he lined up the shot.

"But I do still know where the Shard is," I lied calmly. "And if you kill me here and your superiors rip out your memories during their review-"

"Shut up."

"-They'll see you putting yourself above your organization," I continued. "And the next thing you know, your brothers will be throwing you into the meat grinder or the crematorium or whatever it is your 'knighthood' uses to kill Phitometrists like us."

"No." Keen shook his head, pouring sweat. It ran down his face in streams, soaking his collar. "No, Sokolsky. I will *never* be like you."

I stared at him levelly, and a few of the soldiers flinched as I lifted my head. "No. You won't."

"You're a monster. And when they tear that demon that passes for your soul out of your arrogant, insolent ass, I'll be there." His nostrils were trembling, and so was his shooting arm. "I'll be there, and I'll pray for you, and for your friends, and when I find the Garden I'll go to my knees to beg God to forgive whatever is left of you. Because that's what godly men do. Even for sick fools like you."

"You ever wonder why your God is silent whenever you kneel down to pray?" I asked. "Because it's NO-thing."

Keen lowered the pistol from my face to my crotch. "One last chance before I blow your dick off to Kingdom Come. Where's the Garden?"

Angkor, Zarya, the Weeders, and Binah were moving further and further away, much faster than they had before. "I care more about Eden than my dick. I'm almost as much a virgin as you are."

Keen's finger trembled. He shot the ground between my knees.

"I'll be sure to make special care recommendations to the Director." His voice was shaky with pain and stress and impotent rage. "We will grind you to a fine powder, Sokolsky, and we *will* find the Garden, whether you give up the secret alive or dead. Theta One and Fourteen, prep him for transport with the vampire. Make sure you 'forget' to lubricate him for contraband inspection when we get there."

I couldn't help it: I began to laugh, a dry raven's caw. Vassily was a vampire, the Engine was coming, New York City was being overrun by a corrupted MahTree, and that was the best he could muster? Threatening me with a rectal exam?

Heavy hands cuffed me and yanked me up to my feet. I was still laughing the wheezy, exasperated, dark laughter of someone looking damnation in the face when the rifle butt came down on the back of my neck.

It knocked me out cold.

GET YOUR FREE COPY
OF BURN ARTIST

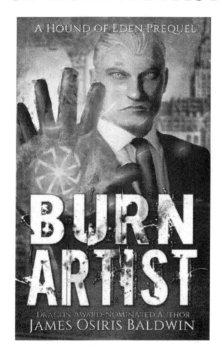

**GET YOUR FREE COPY OF BURN
ARTIST AT:**
HTTP://JAMESOSIRIS.COM/

More Books by James Osiris Baldwin

The Alexi Sokolsky Series

Available now from Amazon and Kindle Unlimited

Prequel: Burn Artist

http://jamesosiris.com/alexi-sokolsky-starter-library/

Book 1: Blood Hound

http://hyperurl.co/bloodhoundnovel

Book 2: Stained Glass

http://hyperurl.co/stainedglassnovel

Book 3: Zero Sum

http://hyperurl.co/zerosumnovel

**Find all my books at
http://www.jamesosiris.com**

Other Titles

Fix Your Damn Book! – A Self-Editing Guide for Authors

Paperback, Kindle & Hardcover. Read on Kindle Unlimited!

AFTERWORD & ACKNOWLEDGMENTS

If you enjoyed Zero Sum, please consider leaving a review on the book here:
http://hyperurl.co/zerosumnovel

2017 has been one continuous bout of shell-shock for me. When it doesn't seem like it can get any worse, it does. The fact that The Handmaid's Tale was produced as a (brilliant) T.V series this year is somewhat telling.

The terrifying thing about Morphorde is that they are quite real—not in the fantastic way depicted in my novels, but in the factual way that we saw in Charlottesville. In the words of Margaret Atwood, *Nolite te bastardes carborundorum.*

Zero Sum was a bitch to write: no lie. I struggled on this book from start to finish. Hopefully it was worth the grief. It would not have been possible without the loving support of my queer-ass family, House Decided, and the patient, sometimes viciously pointed support of my wife, Canth.

Canth is the creator of the Dermal Highway setting where Alexi's story takes place. You can see her amazing art (and commission her!) on her Facebook page:
http://www.facebook.com/gifthorseproductions.

You can also get in touch with me (outside of the mailing list) at: author@jamesosiris.com.

Find me on Facebook at:
www.facebook.com/groups/houndofeden.

Major Organizations in the Hound of Eden Series:

The Yaroshenko Organizatsiya

New York's largest Russian Mafiya organization, based in Brighton Beach and Red Hook.

The Manelli Family (Italian Mafia)

The largest Italian Mafia family in the NY/NJ/PA tri-state area. Most of them are in service to Munificence. They are enemies of the Yaroshenko Organizatsiya and are (mostly) allied with the Crusaders of the Deutsche Ordern.

The Laguetta Family (Italian Mafia)

The oldest Mafia family in New York. Based in Queens. Allies of the Yaroshenko Organizatsiya.

The Templum Voctus Sol

A mysterious Morphorde cult affiliated with a being known as 'Providence'. They seem to have some kind of relationship with the Church of the Voice of the Lord, an eccentric 'prosperity gospel' megachurch.

The Vigiles Magicarum

The FBI agency tasked with handling all supernatural or paranormal crimes in the USA. They were established in 1983 after the assassination of President Robert

Rutherford by a 'magical terrorist'. They work closely with the P-SAD (Paranormal Special Activities Division) and elements of the military.

While theoretically a secular, vetted branch of law enforcement, the Vigiles Magicarum was founded and is controlled by modern-day Crusaders who belong to The *Deutsche Orden (Venator Dei, Gottes Jäger)*, a continuation of the ancient fraternity of Teutonic Knights who show every sign of being Morphorde.

ANSWER

A mysterious pro-GOD militia that operates on different worlds. ANSWER is quite large, with a number of 'sections' and several largely-independent agencies. One of these agencies is CEIDR ('seeder'), who target worlds threatened by Greater Morphorde and Morphordian organizations and seek to prevent them achieving their goals.

For more information (and possible spoilers), visit and submit contributions to the Dermal Highway Wiki:
http://www.thedermalhighway.jameso siris.com/

ABOUT THE AUTHOR

Dragon Award-nominated author James Osiris Baldwin writes gritty LGBT-inclusive, dark fantasy and science fiction. He was the former Contributing Editor for the Australian Journal of Dementia Care and has also worked for Alzheimer's Australia.

He currently lives in Seattle with his lovely wife, a precocious cat, and far too many rats. His obsession with the Occult is matched only by his preoccupation with motorcycles.

Contact James by email: author@jamesosiris.com.

View more books at:
http://amazon.com/author/jamesosiris

Sign up to the New Releases Mailing List!
http://jamesosiris.com/alexi-sokolsky-starter-library/

Made in the USA
Lexington, KY
28 September 2017